F LILLEY UP #3
Lilley, R. K.
Grounded

12/13

S0-AFK-655

GROUNDED

By R.K. Lilley

Nevada Public Library
631 K Avenue
Nevada, IA 50201
515-382-2628

Copyright © 2013 R.K. Lilley

All rights reserved.

ISBN-13: 978-0615765679

ISBN-10: 061576567X

All rights reserved. This book may not be reproduced, scanned, or distributed in any printed or electronic form without permission. This is a work of fiction. Any resemblance of events to real life, or of characters to actual persons, is purely coincidental. The author acknowledges the trademarked status and trademark owners of various products referenced in this work of fiction.

This book is dedicated to all of the wonderful bloggers and readers who have gone out of their way to spread the word about these books. I'm eternally grateful. You have changed my life.

Nevada Public Library

CHAPTER ONE

Mr. Cavendish

We sped towards Manhattan in a luxurious town car. Stephan and Javier sat close together, clutching hands, their eyes fixed on me in concern. James held me close against him, his hands comforting as they stroked over me.

I'd found out just a few days ago that my father had remarried after my mother's death. On the tail of that revelation, I had found out that I had a half-brother who was just one year younger than I am. That meant that my father had been with this other woman for years before my mother had died. Before he had killed her.

I had no love for the woman, Sharon, who my father had married. In fact, I felt a cold distaste shiver through my body at just the thought of her.

I'd just discovered that she had been killed last night, and in the same method that my mother had been. I hadn't liked the woman, but since I had discovered her existence, I had felt the need to warn her about my father. I was positive that she must have known firsthand just how abusive and violent he was, but I had wanted to warn her just what he was capable of, if only to clear my conscience.

I had tried, several times, to get ahold of her, but I'd had no luck. Logical or not, I felt a crushing guilt at my failure. James seemed to sense my inner turmoil, and sought to comfort me with his touch.

He just held me for several minutes before breaking the heavy silence that had overtaken the four of us. "Would you guys like to have breakfast at a restaurant or at our apartment?" His tone was polite.

Stephan didn't hesitate. "Your apartment. I saw a spread on it in an interior design magazine a few weeks ago. I've been looking forward to getting a tour."

James nodded. "Good." He checked his watch. "Unfortunately, I only have about an hour before I need to get back to my office."

I stiffened, feeling unreasonably disappointed at the news, though I hadn't even thought he'd be there to meet us at the airport. He had mentioned several meetings today, but I still couldn't seem to help feeling let down that we wouldn't get more time together before he had to go back to work.

He seemed to feel the change in me and began to rub my back comfortingly. He spoke softly to me. "I should be able to cut my workday short, and make it back to the apartment by four, but I'd still love for you to come by my office for lunch. Say around eleven? I—"

"I'll be there," I told him quickly, wanting any time with him that I could get.

I felt needy for him, as though we'd been parted for weeks or months instead of days. I hadn't been this desperate ever before, even during the time I'd forced him to stay away for nearly a month. I thought I was more desperate now because I had allowed myself to begin to think that he and I might actually have a future together. The thought both excited me and made my gut twist with an acute anxiety.

He kissed the top of my head but didn't say anything more about it. We let Stephan and Javier chatter excitedly about their plans for the day, which included a jog in Central Park and a Broadway show, though they couldn't decide on what.

"Do you guys mind if I make us all early dinner reservations? I'll make it somewhere good, though that may be my own bias showing, since I'll most likely own the place." James smiled that self-deprecating smile of his that I always wanted to trace away with my fingertips.

Stephan and Javier agreed enthusiastically. I thought it was sweet of him to think of it, but I felt just a tiny bit disappointed. I wanted time alone with him, and even a few extra hours of waiting seemed torturous.

Clark drove us to the underground garage elevator without having to be told, giving me a very friendly smile as James helped me from the car. I smiled back. James's chauffeur/bodyguard was apparently pleased that we'd gotten back together. I thought it was nice that he seemed to approve of me.

Stephan was restless with excitement as the elevator climbed to the penthouse.

James gave us a rather rushed tour through the opulent space, making a point of showing off all of the spaces that now sported my paintings. I flushed every time he did that, still uncomfortable with compliments about my favorite hobby.

The whole place was modern and sleek with the Cavendish designer touch all over it. I'd seen it all before, and even I was impressed.

He led us down a long hallway with stark modern gray wood lining the floors, ending the tour at the intimidating dining room.

Stephan and Javier immediately moved to the window that lined nearly the entire wall of the room and looked out on the spectacular view of Central Park.

"Wow," Javier said quietly.

"Amazing," Stephan breathed.

I moved to the window beside Stephan, equally awed by the

now familiar view.

James wrapped himself around me from behind, leaning down to my ear. "I need to go. Your security will be waiting at the elevator at ten thirty to take you to my office. If you need to go anywhere before then, just call the security number saved into your phone."

A door opened from the kitchen, a smiling Marion peeking in. She got our breakfast orders and cheerfully bustled back into the kitchen.

"Walk me out?" James asked softly, mouth still right at my ear.

I shivered, nodding.

James said his goodbyes to Stephan and Javier, tugging me swiftly from the room.

He took a shortcut to the elevator. Or rather, I thought it was a shortcut, right up until he was yanking me into a small sitting area.

I barely got a glance at the vaguely familiar room before he was closing the door and crushing me against it, kissing me like his life depended on it. The kiss had none of his finesse, and not an ounce of his restraint. It was a rough, bruising kiss, and I reveled in it. I would have kissed him back, but it wasn't that kind of kiss. All that I could do was submit, my mouth softening for him—my whole body softening.

He pulled back abruptly.

I moaned a protest.

He wrapped one hand around my throat, squeezing just enough to make me gasp, the other hand going to my mouth. He pressed just one finger over my lips. "I have to go. But I need to have you. Promise me you'll come to my office at eleven."

I met his beautiful eyes, searching them. His face and voice were raw with need. And fear.

"I told you I'd be there," I said to him, not sure what he

needed from me, or how to take that awful look from his eyes.

"Promise me," he said softly, his voice close enough to a plea to make my chest hurt.

"I promise," I said softly.

He just nodded, his face painfully solemn. He tugged me after him, and I followed him to the elevator.

He pushed the button, pulling me into his chest as he waited for the car. It wasn't a coincidence that he pressed my cheek over his heart. Right over the place where he'd tattooed my name in crimson.

He didn't kiss me again. In fact, he barely looked at me. His professional mask was in place as the elevator closed on my last glimpse of him.

I walked back to the dining room on heavy feet.

We finished breakfast quickly, all of us ready for a nap.

Stephan and Javier were staying on the floor below my bedroom with James, lined up with that perfect view of Central Park. I walked them to their door, giving Stephan a perfunctory kiss goodnight before heading up to the room I shared with James. I could hear their amazed and excited exclamations even as I walked away, and I smiled fondly. That was the greatest benefit of wealth, I thought. To make others happy.

I made my way to our lonely bedroom.

I stood frozen in the doorway to our room for long moments, feeling so odd being there without James. It felt so empty and strange.

I did the minimum amount to get ready for bed, crawling into bed only after I had carefully set an alarm. I would only be getting a short nap, but it would be worth it to see James in a few hours.

I woke up groggy and disoriented but as the fog cleared from my brain and I realized whose bed I was in, and who I would be seeing in just one hour, the fog cleared completely, and I rushed into the shower, nervous and excited.

My phone beeped a text at me right as I was re-entering the bedroom, and I went to read it, still wrapped in a towel.

James: Wear a skirt.

It was an innocent enough request, from anyone but James perhaps, but from him, my breath caught in breathless anticipation. I hadn't known just what we would be able to do at his office, so I had been braced for just an innocent lunch, though of course I had been hoping for more. My mood soared as I got ready, excitement pulsing through me. He had plans for me; I just knew it.

I tried not to be intimidated by my new wardrobe as I browsed through it for a skirt. The labels were things I never could have afforded on my own though, so it was hard for me not to dwell on the fact that I was letting James spend a fortune on me. I had been counting my pennies for so long that I couldn't help but think it was all a bit of a waste. Half of his colossal closet was now filled with extravagant designer women's clothing. There was no way that he hadn't spent tens of thousands of dollars on it all.

I knew it was silly, but somehow the clothing intimidated me even more than all of the diamond jewelry that he seemed to need to lavish on me. Yes, it was silly, but the fact was that I knew enough about clothes to have a clue what *those* labels were worth, whereas my knowledge on the price of jewelry was beyond negligible.

The clothing was all paired together into outfits. I would have been more grateful for that convenience if I hadn't known that it had to be the work of Jackie. I wasn't exactly a fan.

I quickly picked out a comfortable looking azure blue, silk dress. I tried not to even look at the label, but it didn't work, since the Armani Collezioni tag practically jumped out at me.

I donned my bra and panties, pulled the decadently soft fabric over my head, and fell instantly in love.

It was beyond comfortable, and actually looked great to boot. It hugged my curves in the most flattering way, without being the slightest bit tight. And unlike most of the clothing I usually tried on, it was made for my height, the proportions just right, not too short in either my torso or legs. Apparently there was something to spending a fortune on clothing. Of course, most of the clothes I'd owned previously never cost more than twenty dollars, tops...

There was an entire section of the closet devoted entirely to shoes and I went there next. My mouth curved and my heart warmed as I saw what James had done there.

There were nothing but wedges and running shoes. Of all the things he'd purchased for me in this monstrosity of a closet, I thought that this was the sweetest. I'd made the barest mention to him once that the only shoes I liked were wedges and running shoes, and it was apparent that he had been listening.

All of the women's shoes were peeking out of boxes, and all of the boxes were marked with yellow tags sporting numbers in big red letters. My brow furrowed. The tags on all of the clothing had the same thing. I reached back with a sigh, carefully trying to rip off the tag at my back without causing damage to the lovely dress.

My brow furrowed as I saw the number 543 listed on the tag. I studied the rows of shoeboxes, my eyes eventually finding a matching number there. I sighed, my mouth twisting wryly, as I saw the system that had been set up. Jackie apparently didn't trust me to pair my shoes and clothing without help.

Part of me wanted to ignore her not so subtle suggestions and just wear whatever I felt like wearing, but she *was* a professional shopper, and I barely ever shopped.

I decided gamely to give her recommendation a try. *Why not?* If I hated the shoes she'd picked, I'd just wear something else.

I opened the box to find a pair of yellow, Prada patent-leather wedges with a peep toe and a smart little leather bow. I thought they were adorable.

I put them on and found that Jackie knew her stuff. As a bonus, they were comfortable and easy to walk in.

I went a little heavy with my eye makeup, going for a smoky eye, but I thought it worked. I was liberal with the black mascara, and went with my usual lip stain and soft pink gloss. I was pleased with the end result. I had taken longer than usual with my makeup, but it had still only taken ten minutes, which gave me a solid ten minutes for my hair, which only needed a quick blow-dry. I gave myself a quick once over, noting that the haircut had been a very good idea for me. Straight blonde bangs now framed my face, bringing out my eyes until they were an almost startling, pale aquamarine.

I was running right on time when I heard a knock on the bedroom door. I opened the door, thinking that it had to be Marion. I was less than thrilled to look down at Jackie. She smiled at me.

She eyed me up and down, smiling as though she hadn't already clearly expressed how much she disliked me. "Very nice. Armani fits you well. I'll make a note of it."

My face had schooled into a carefully blank expression at the sight of her. I just couldn't make myself smile back at her, but I *would* manage to remain civil. "I'm in a hurry, if you'll please excuse me..."

She held up a finger. "One thing. I set up your bag collection in the fitting room. James hates clutter and they take up a lot of room, so this seemed like the best option. Come right this way."

She strode off without waiting for my agreement.

I followed unenthusiastically, determined to see what she was talking about and get on my way in a timely fashion.

She led me to the guest bedroom I had used just a few days

ago to try on dresses. The large closet now had roughly half of it devoted solely to handbags.

I groaned.

Jackie shot me a look. It was very nearly hostile. “You don’t like bags?” she asked incredulously.

I grimaced. “I like some of them, but clutches are not happening for me. I can’t stand having to hold something all the time. I need something with a long strap.”

She made a noise of pure disgust, but didn’t waste any time selecting a bag for me. She thrust a large, cream-colored leather satchel-style bag in my direction.

“For the love of God, at least hook it on your arm. If I see you wearing it cross-body, I may just scream.”

I took the bag from her, gave her a very unfriendly look, and strode out of the room. I had to return to our bedroom briefly to put all of my things in the bag before rushing downstairs, now late.

CHAPTER TWO

Mr. Violent

I descended the stairs, rushing to the elevators. A security team awaited me at the elevators. A team…

I blinked at the three austere men in suits and the one woman who managed to be the most intimidating of the bunch.

Blake nodded at me, speaking first. "Ms. Karlsson, let me introduce you to the rest of your security detail." She pointed to the man closest to her. He was massive with muscles and obviously armed under his finely tailored suit. His dark hair was cut very short and his features were severe but appealing. "This is Williams."

"Ms. Karlsson," he said, nodding at me politely.

I nodded back, trying to file the name into my memory. I was apparently going to need to learn a lot of them, with this much security.

The elevator car arrived and Blake waved me inside. I walked in, trying not to feel intimidated as the four of them flanked me.

Blake cleared her throat. "We need to hurry. Mr. Cavendish won't be pleased if you're late." She quickly introduced the other two men.

One was shorter than the others, at least an inch shorter than me, if I wasn't wearing three inch heels. He was still intimidatingly swollen with muscles though, and his short blond hair made him look unquestionably ex-military. Blake introduced him as Henry.

The last one was my height almost exactly in my heels, with medium brown hair and smiling brown eyes. He was less severe than the others, and more attractive, but he still held himself in that disciplined way that had law-enforcement written all over it. Blake introduced him as Johnny.

I thought it was odd that some of them used their first names, and some their last names, but I didn't ask them about it. I had been conditioned from a very young age not to pry.

It was late June, and hot as hell in New York. I was thankful for my lightweight clothing, since the heat and humidity instantly attached themselves to me the second we stepped outside. My security flanked me closely as we moved from the elevator to a swank limo that was lined up directly with the lobby entrance.

I tried to act as though I wasn't uncomfortable with my extremely affluent settings and my ridiculous overabundance of security, but I felt very stiff as I moved from the elevator to the car.

My security team arranged themselves as though they had choreographed it, which I supposed they had. Blake and Johnny joined me in the cab of the vehicle, Henry taking shotgun, and Williams driving. The short ride to the Cavendish property was a strange affair. Blake maintained complete and utter silence, and Johnny seemed almost too friendly to fit in with the rest of the security guards I'd met so far.

"So, Bianca, how are you liking the move to New York?"

I blinked at him, nonplussed. I'd gotten so used to how the other bodyguards were professional to a fault that I hadn't been prepared for even idle chat. And the question…

"I haven't really moved here. I'm going back and forth from Vegas. But I do like New York. I've had a route here for years, with no plans to change it."

Johnny shot me a bewildered look. "You're keeping your job? You're staying a stewardess?"

I eyed him suspiciously. I wasn't one to pry, but Johnny apparently was. "Well, yes. It's my job. Why would I quit?"

"Um, maybe because Mr. Cavendish is spending four times what you make a week on security for every *single* one of your flights—"

"Enough," Blake interrupted him harshly. "You know better, Johnny. If you upset Ms. Karlsson, Mr. Cavendish *will* fire you. Hell, he'll fire all of us."

The car grew painfully awkward after that, as I had no idea how to respond to such an unexpected outburst from a stranger, and of course I wouldn't, since I didn't owe anyone any explanations about my life. *The nerve...*

I brooded all the way to our destination, staring out the window, my face a blank mask.

I had never been inside the Manhattan Cavendish Hotel, but I recognized the colossal building. The blue, modern reflective glass windows that lined the entire building made it stand out as a new and sparkling gem amongst skyscrapers.

My security detail moved into their well-choreographed formation as I stepped out of the car, escorting me into the lobby as though I were a threatened head of state. I felt ridiculous.

I had no idea where to go, but luckily I didn't need to. Blake led me unerringly through the sumptuous marble lobby.

We were nearly to a bank of well-guarded elevators when I heard a female voice call my name. Surprised, I turned to see who it was, and stiffened.

Jolene sauntered over to us, a lush smile on her lips. She was beyond scantily clad, wearing only the tiniest bike shorts I'd ever seen and a sports bra that was so minuscule I didn't imagine for a second that it could actually do its job. I couldn't guess what she was dressed for. I'd almost have thought working out except that she was wearing sexy black sandals and her hair was down, hanging in curling ringlets around her shoulders and back.

Johnny whistled appreciatively as she approached. He stood directly at my right but I didn't spare him a glance. "Hottest fucking chick I've ever seen," he muttered, not quite keeping it under his breath. Okay, I was not a Johnny fan; it was official.

Jolene tried to move close to me, but Blake got in her way before she was within three feet of me. She pouted a little, but it was obviously an affectation. "Bianca! How are you?"

I had always considered myself a controlled person. Things rarely came out of my mouth unless I meant for them to. I knew right away that this would be one of those rare times when my brain would not be doing the talking. "What are you doing here? And why are you dressed like that?" I asked her coldly.

She gave me a look that made me stiffen. It was pointed and knowing. She was up to trouble. "I just got finished working out. This place has a great gym. And I'm dressed like this because James loves to see my skin. He says I have the sexiest stomach on the planet." As she spoke, she ran a manicured hand from her throat to the low waist of those obscene shorts. She did have a lovely stomach, all well-toned hollows and dusky skin, her waist ridiculously tiny, especially compared to the oversized breasts that nearly spilled from her top. She exuded sex, and I hated her.

My breath caught at her implication. Was she saying that she was here to see James? That he was still seeing *her*? Was she flat-out lying, or telling some twisted version of the truth? Either way, I was sick to death of her, and I'd only met her twice...

"Are you saying that you're here to see James? That he *invited* you here? Just speak plainly, because I have absolutely no patience for these games," I told her in my blankest, coldest voice. That voice was an old defense mechanism for me.

She pursed her lips, running her tongue over her teeth. I wanted to smack her. I was shocked by the urge, but even my shock didn't seem to make my sudden rage abate.

"None of your business," she said petulantly, crossing her arms, which pushed her fake, ample breasts even higher. That bra was so useless that I could make out just the barest hint of the top of her nipples as she pushed them up.

I couldn't believe that James had spent so much time with this woman, even with her over the top sex appeal. To my mind, he was the epitome of class, with his charm and his manners and his impossible beauty, whereas she seemed to relish her own trashiness.

"It is certainly her business," a voice that made me want to melt spoke from behind me. A big, warm hand pressed into the nape of my neck, gently brushing aside my long hair to settle there possessively. I didn't look at James. I was too angry and upset and just plain hungry for the sight of him.

"Why are you still here, Jolene?" he asked coldly. "I told you to leave this morning, when you tried to barge, uninvited, into my office. Do I need to have you escorted from the property?"

A raw expression passed over her features so briefly that I thought I might have imagined it. Her beautiful face swiftly worked itself into a satisfied smile. She flipped her curly black hair behind her shoulders, thrusting her breasts into prominent display. As though they needed the help. "I'm here with Scott. He's staying in the penthouse, and I'm his guest. Are you going to ask him to leave, as well?"

James moved close against my back, wrapping his arms around my shoulders. I could tell by her eyes on those arms that Jolene did not appreciate the sight. "Perhaps I'll tell him what you've been up to. Just how tolerant do you think your husband will be if he knows that you've been up to your old tricks?"

She stiffened, looking just a touch alarmed, before schooling her face into a serene expression. “He won’t believe you. And even if he did, you’d never do that. You know how much it would hurt him.”

“It’s becoming very clear to me that the truth couldn’t possibly hurt Scott as much as you have, Jolene. I don’t have an ounce of patience left where you’re concerned. Keep that in mind.”

A movement caught the corner of my eye and I glanced behind Jolene, to where a figure was eating up the ground as a large man strode purposefully towards our group.

He was tall and lanky but still moved with the fit stride of an athlete. His coloring was similar to James’s, with light brown hair and very tan skin, though his had most likely come from the sun. As he got closer, I saw that his turbulent eyes were dark brown. At a glance he might have resembled James, but on closer inspection, his good looks were more rugged—less refined.

“I told you to stay away from my *wife*,” the man growled as soon as he was within earshot. I realized with a little jolt of surprise that the man looked very familiar. I couldn’t place where, but I had definitely seen his face somewhere. “Yet somehow, every time I turn my back for five minutes, here you are. You need to let her go, James.”

James stiffened against me, but his tone was surprisingly bland when he spoke. “You need to think about what you’re saying, my friend. She hasn’t been honest with you, and if it was up to me, I’d never set eyes on her again. Your *wife* has been stalking me and my girlfriend, and I have had enough of it. I’m in a serious, committed relationship, and I want nothing to do with her. I didn’t touch Jolene when I found out she was your wife three years ago, and I most certainly wouldn’t now. If I could go back in time and save you some pain, Scott, I would have never touched her at all, and I certainly never would have introduced her to you. She’s not who you think she is. She’s not worthy of the pedestal you've put her on."

Scott did not take his words the way that I knew James had intended him. I could tell by the sincerity in his voice that James had only been speaking the brutal truth.

Scott sneered. It made his face ugly. "Watch your mouth. You're talking about my wife." His raw gaze turned to me. "So he's in a *serious* committed relationship with you, huh? You should know that he doesn't know the meaning of those words. He'll toss you aside like all the rest. If you're lucky, he'll pass you off to a rich friend when he's done with you."

I was turning into James's chest even as he moved. I buried my face in his neck, gripping my arms around his ribs, holding on tight.

"Don't," I murmured into his neck. It stopped his movements. Scott had been trying to goad him, and I knew it had worked, but I *needed* James to control his temper—to control his fists. James wrapped stiff arms around me, as though unable to ignore my affectionate gesture, even in a rage.

"If you ever speak to her like that again, you will regret it," James said, his voice filled with an awful rage.

Scott snorted, and even from that noise I could tell that his temper was every bit as close to the surface as James's. "You're worried what I'll say to her? You fucked my *wife*, James, God only knows how many times, and you're worried that I'll what...hurt your latest fuck's feelings?"

James turned me gently, ushering me to the elevators directly behind us. He stroked his hand over my hair, and I could feel that it was trembling. "My love," he said, his voice hoarse, but still managing to be tender. "I need you to go upstairs. Please, wait for me. I'll be joining you momentarily." He pressed the button as he spoke, still clutching me close.

I wanted to say something, wanted to plead with him not to do anything rash, not to get himself into trouble, or worse, hurt, but I couldn't seem to make myself speak.

The elevator stopped, the doors opening, and I stepped inside without a word. Blake and Johnny filed in behind me, and I was relieved that at least two of the bodyguards remained with James.

The elevator doors closed and we began to go up. I had no idea what floor we were going to, or even how many floors there were. I glanced at the panel to see, but my eyes just glossed over and I lost my train of thought.

The elevator finally stopped and I followed Blake out. My mind distractedly noticed that my surroundings were rich and opulent, my heels clicking smartly on dark marble floors, but my mind was still stuck on what could be going on downstairs—what I'd been too much of a coward to stay and watch, or even stay and prevent.

A young, polished brunette greeted us from behind a massive desk. "Ms. Karlsson, Ms. Blake, Johnny," she murmured as we passed her. I wondered how she could have known me by sight. No doubt it was obvious by my armed escorts...

All of this was just a distracted, distant thought, as well, as Blake led me into a huge office that had windows lining more walls than not.

Blake did a thorough search of the office, checking every inch of the space and inside of the two doors that attached. Johnny stayed close to my side as she did so. I thought they were a little overzealous, but what did I know?

Blake finished her search, giving me a severe nod when she finished. "All clear, Ms. Karlsson. We'll be right outside if you need anything."

I heard the door click shut behind me. I dropped my purse somewhere on the floor as I made my way to the windows. I noted absently that the office decor didn't have the James touch. The mood of the office was all old-fashioned New York, with an antique desk and ancient hardwood flooring. The chair behind the desk was antique brown leather, as well as the couch. Even the rugs had an old money feel. It was so uncharacteristic for James that I stood pondering it for a long time, letting the strange decor distract me.

When that grew tiresome, I moved to the window, looking sightlessly at the spectacular view of Manhattan.

I had no idea how long I stood there like a statue before I heard the door open and then close behind me. The click of a lock being engaged was unnaturally loud in the quiet as death silence of the room.

"Turn around and look at me," James said after a long moment, his voice low and rough.

It was insane, it was unreasonable, it was self-destructive... and masochistic, but I grew wet at the sound of that violence-roughened voice.

I turned around.

CHAPTER THREE

Mr. Sadistic

I studied him for a long time, my legs trembling as I took him in. I leaned back against the window for support.

His suit jacket was missing, his tie askew. The sleeves of his white dress shirt were rolled up. Rather messily, too, at least for him. I saw one lone drop of blood on his collar. I studied his face, then his arms. His knuckles looked a little swollen, his fists clenched, but his face was untouched.

"He was a grown man who had insulted the most important person in my life. The most *precious* thing in my world. Twice. Wipe that fucking scared look off your face. I would *never* punch you, never attack you without restraint. But I will punish you." As he spoke, he began to unbutton his shirt, pulling it free of his beige slacks. His erection was outlined heavily against that pale fabric.

I licked numb lips. "For what?"

"For that look. For that lack of trust. For leaving me for days, whatever the fucking reason. And you were late."

He strode to me, shirtless and impossibly beautiful, his stark muscles working along his perfect golden skin with every step. I watched my name, etched in crimson on his chest, as he moved closer to me.

His heavy hand fell to my nape. He pushed me slowly to the desk with just that contact. He pressed me, firmly but gradually, until the front of my torso was flush against the top of his desk, my hipbones digging into the edge. His hands moved up under my dress with no hesitation, gripping my lacy thong and pulling it down my legs with one smooth motion. He touched one ankle. "Lift," he ordered curtly.

I lifted my foot. He repeated the process on the other leg.

His fingers moved against my back, unclasping my bra through the silk of my dress, as only someone experienced with that process could be. He worked it off me swiftly, leaving my dress intact.

He flipped the silky skirt of my dress up over my hips, leaving my ass and sex bare for his perusal. He stood silently at my back for a long time. I squirmed.

"Close your eyes," he ordered.

I obeyed.

I heard him stride away. A door to my left opened, then closed. I could hear my own breath panting out of me. I was in a state.

I heard him approach me again long minutes later. He wasn't trying to be quiet.

"Grip the edge of the desk," he ordered.

I gripped.

"Anything to say?" he asked me coldly.

I didn't know where to begin, didn't know what he wanted, but I had to try. "I'm sorry, Mr. Cavendish."

"What are you sorry for?"

"For all of it. For leaving you for days, whatever the reason. For being late. Please…"

He struck, harsh bristles striking against my backside. I wriggled. It smarted, but didn't precisely hurt. It was like being whipped with very thick hair. That was perhaps why he didn't hold back, striking again and again without pause. I shifted against the desk, moaning.

He pressed a hard hand to the small of my back, holding me immobile while he worked me over. He spread the whips over my butt and thighs liberally. This went on for endless moments while I writhed.

Abruptly, he stopped. I could hear his harsh breath.

"Do you like the horse-hair flogger?" he asked.

I made a little humming noise in my throat. "I do, Mr. Cavendish."

"That was what would be considered a warm-up, Bianca. Do you know what that means?"

I shook my head. "No, Mr. Cavendish."

He moved into me, pressing his heavy, trouser-clad erection flush into my sex and leaning down heavily against my back. He breathed his next words into my ear. "Open your eyes."

I did, getting only a sideways view of the desk that I was sprawled against, since James was on my back. He laid a heavy black and blue object there. I couldn't understand what I was seeing at first.

It looked almost like a bouquet of flowers, yet not...

Heavy, dyed leather was shaped beautifully into blue roses on the ends of thick black leather tails.

I licked my lips, suddenly more nervous and scared. There were a dozen of the ominous looking buds.

James brought the stiff leather handle of the torture device up to my cheek, and I watched those heavy flowers drag across the desk as the flogger moved. He traced my cheek.

"The horse-hair flogger was a warm-up," he repeated, "and what that means is that I have plans for you, Bianca, and the pain hasn't even begun."

I took unsteady breaths, then stiffened as I heard the unmistakable sound of a zipper.

"Do the roses scare you?" he asked softly, his voice almost taunting. He was gripping my thighs, pulling my legs apart from behind as he shifted me on the desk.

"Yes," I said breathlessly.

"I'll tell you what," he began, thrusting hard inside of me even as he spoke. I whimpered, shocked at the unexpected penetration. "If you can manage not to come while I take the edge off, I'll spare you the roses. For today." As he spoke, he was pulling out of me, dragging that perfect cock along every wonderful nerve inside of me.

He pulled completely out before plunging in again, a slow, heavy stroke that made my toes curl.

"To make it fair, I'll make it quick," he said, a cold smile in his voice. He pulled out and ground into me again, then began to pound in earnest.

It was painfully hard, his thick length beating into me, working me over from the inside out. Even his cock was dominant and sadistic today.

One of his hands gripped my inner thigh so hard that I knew I would bruise, the other hand on my back, pinning me firmly to the desk.

He fucked me as he rarely fucked me, to bring *himself* to a quick release.

When he came inside of me, a loud, raw noise escaped his throat, the sound muffled, as though he couldn't help it. That noise brought me over the edge. I came with a whimper even as he jerked inside of me, rubbing out the last of his own savage release.

He didn't linger, pulling out of me as I was still clenching around him. I felt warm liquid still spurting from his stiff length as he leaned against my ass.

He tugged me back until my feet were touching the ground. I had forgotten that I was even wearing heels until they touched the ground again unsteadily.

He tugged my dress higher, then pulled me up by the shoulders. "Arms up," he murmured when I was standing again.

I did.

He pulled my dress over my head. I turned my head to watch him as he draped it carefully over his office chair.

He studied me for a moment. "Step out of your shoes."

I wobbled out of them as steadily as I could manage.

James reached for me, hooking a finger into the hoop at my neck, his other hand gripping a handful of my hair. He tugged me across the room.

He brought me to one of the doors that led somewhere other than the reception area. I hadn't checked to see where it led, but James quickly showed me.

He pulled me into a small bedroom with a big window. I gasped when I saw the bed.

It took up nearly the entire space, large enough to fit into one of the colossal bedrooms in his homes. It had a latticed top, with a daunting collection of restraints already arrayed.

"Your work fuck-pad?" I asked him, not hiding the accusation in my voice. He'd been a slut, I got that, but I was sick of seeing the evidence of it literally everywhere we went.

"It's new. Before it was just a bed that I only slept in alone. If you want any more answers, you'll be getting them later. Get on the bed."

I scrambled onto the bed, moving to the center. I started to kneel.

"Stand up," he barked.

I obeyed.

He gripped my wrist in his hand, raising it high but pulled out from my body. He tugged one of the black restraints from the latticed top of the bed. I was surprised to realize that it was made of rubber. It was like a soft tube, comfortable and stretchy. He wrapped it around my wrist several times until it pulled very tight. He tied it, then twisted my hand around until I was gripping it. He repeated the motion on my other hand, my arms held wide apart when he'd finished. I thought it was ominous that he'd chosen to use something so comfortable to restrain me. It told me something about those roses, though...

He positioned my feet, making me comfortable. I was trembling as he moved away from the bed.

He'd tied me so that I faced the window squarely, with a lovely view of Manhattan, but all of his movements were behind me, keeping me in the dark as to his actions.

I felt him move onto the bed several minutes later. He stayed at my back.

He made me wait for so long that I began to relax slightly when he struck.

My back bowed with the blow to my thighs. It was by far the harshest punishment he'd ever dealt me. I knew it with only one blow. It felt like I was being pummeled by a dozen hard little fists. James paused for long moments after the first blow, and I trembled.

The next blow struck my ass and made my body rock back and forth with my rubber restraints.

I whimpered, my head falling forward.

He struck again, and not even pausing, struck yet again. Tears ran down my face, and I couldn't quite stifle a scream as he struck yet again.

It was the first time he'd ever tried something on me that was so profoundly painful that I wasn't sure if I could take it. I was the closest I'd ever come to safe-wording when he stopped.

I was sobbing when he gripped the front of my thighs from behind, pulling my legs up and back so that I was completely suspended.

He kept me like that as he moved between my legs from behind. He pounded into me brutally, as though this too was a punishment. He drove into me again and again with angry thrusts, our only two points of contact his hands on my thighs, and his cock inside of me. He had me on the edge in moments, and I came around him with a little sob, my inner walls clenching him again and again, milking him until he bottomed out in me, coming with a surprised little shout.

I didn't think I'd ever had a more powerful orgasm, and I sobbed with the pleasure and the pain of it as he finally pulled out of me, and lowered my feet back to the bed. He untied me quickly, pulling me down onto the bed with him. He pushed my face into his naked chest, murmuring soothing words as I cried all over the *Bianca* on his chest. He stroked his hands over my back, and kissed my hair, and none of it made me feel better.

He had worked me over harder than ever before, fucking me twice without a second of intimate eye contact, without a second of intimacy in general. And I had come so hard that I couldn't stop sobbing for the loss of control. For the first time since we had gotten together, I began to worry that the things we brought out in each other wasn't something I could live with. Or rather, the things he brought out in *me*.

I had always known I had a masochistic streak, though I'd kept it buried deeply, but I'd thought that being with James, doing the things we did, would help to sate those urges in me. For the first time I wondered, *what if it'd only made it worse?*

James seemed to sense my withdrawal. "I need to get back to work soon, but first..."

He flipped me onto my back, parting my legs and moving between them in one smooth motion. He pushed my legs far apart, then pushed them up high against me. I was watching his magnificent cock as he lined himself up at my core.

"Look at me," he snapped, sounding furious.

I looked at those beloved eyes and got lost, as though just the sight of them could make my troubled mind go blank.

He drove into me with one smooth thrust. "Get out of your own head, Bianca. I won't let you withdraw from me."

He began to move inside of me, thrusting steadily, his eyes holding me captive. He circled his hips, moving that long, thick cock along the walls of my sex. I moaned, then gasped. He had so many tricks to make me come and when he tried the move again, I clenched around him with my release.

His eyes were so tender and so intimate as he found his own release long moments later, his hand finding my cheek. I knew my eyes held that same raw vulnerability.

CHAPTER FOUR

Mr. Excessive

James tucked me in tenderly, kissing my forehead and telling me to get some sleep. I didn't argue. I doubted I could have walked out of there, let alone gotten back to his apartment still standing, without some sleep. I drifted off.

I awoke slowly, languorously, stretching my sore body against soft sheets, my eyes drifting open with an effort. The sight that met my eyes brought me fully awake.

The black and blue bouquet of wicked roses was arranged on the pillow as though it were a real arrangement. James wasn't in bed with me, of course—he was working, but the bouquet was apparently his replacement. I turned away from the brutal reminder of our earlier activities, sitting up.

I didn't know what had happened to my clothes, other than that they weren't in the room with me, and out there was an office. I found myself in the awkward position of having to wrap myself in a sheet to peek carefully into the office. I would be mortified if James had company.

Thankfully he was alone, sitting at his desk silently, a phone to his ear. He noticed me immediately. He waved me to him. I approached him slowly, clutching the huge, soft white sheet to me tightly.

He covered the mouthpiece on his phone carefully. "Morning, my love. Lose the sheet and sit here," he said, patting the spot on his desk directly in front of his chair.

Oh my.

He had more plans for me.

I felt self-conscious as I dropped the sheet, but I forgot the feeling almost instantly as I saw his hot gaze on my body.

"So what's the problem?" he said into his phone, his voice a little gruff.

I had to brush against him to move to the spot he had indicated. I knew it wasn't an accident. He gave my hip a brief kiss as I moved to arrange myself.

I perched myself on the edge of his desk, facing him.

He was fully clothed in a crisp, fresh suit. Of course he'd have ungodly expensive extra suits on hand, just in case. This one was a traditional dark gray suit, perfectly tailored in the modern style. His dress shirt was the same color but with a bright white collar, his tie a shocking crimson. He looked devastating, perfect, and sinister—all at once.

He was finely dressed down to his toes, and I had not a stitch on. I was soaking wet and he'd barely even touched me. The old-fashioned office setting wasn't helping the situation. There was something so inherently erotic about him mastering me from behind the desk where he reigned over his own powerful empire.

He used his free hand to push my thighs wider apart with a firm touch. He covered the mouthpiece of his phone again. "Lean back on your elbows," he ordered.

I complied.

"Handle it," he said curtly into the phone.

He rubbed my thigh almost idly, tracing the index finger of his free hand in a leisurely path to my sex.

I writhed.

He used a rather soft touch to sift through my folds. It drove me insane. I shifted against the desk until I could reach the sides of my breasts with my hands. I kneaded at my own flesh roughly.

James gave me a pointed look. That look said I was being very naughty, but he didn't stop me.

He jammed two fingers into me without warning and I cried out.

He covered his mouthpiece. "Quiet," he said chidingly, then got swiftly back to his phone call.

He dragged his fingers out, dragging along the most perfect nerves mercilessly.

I could barely process what he said into his phone as he plunged those expert fingers back into me. It was something along the line of, "that's what I pay you for," but no one could have paid me to care at that point.

He worked me with those thick fingers for long moments, still with the phone to his ear. I was on the edge of release when I felt him shift a little, leaning towards me.

"Send me the report. Yes. That will be all," he said.

Seconds later, he buried his face between my legs, his pretty mouth going directly for my clit and sucking as his hands stayed busy inside of me.

I didn't last ten seconds before he had me crying out in release, a hand burying itself in his silky hair. I clenched tightly around those skillful fingers.

He pulled them out slowly, standing. He sucked on his fingers and I writhed under his stare. His hands moved down to the waist of his pants. I watched with hungry eyes as he released his hard, heavy erection from its confines.

He bent down and kissed me, an open-mouthed, hot kiss where I tasted myself on his mouth. I sucked on his tongue.

He straightened abruptly, gripping one of my nearly limp legs, bringing my ankle up to his shoulder. He arranged my other leg on his other shoulder. He kissed the inside of my ankle, and drove into me.

His turquoise eyes were intense on mine as he moved inside of me. Those eyes were so tarnished. It made them impossibly more beautiful to me.

That angle, with my hips on the very edge of the desk, and my legs pushed so high, felt so deep and intense that he was pushing me over the edge and into another orgasm with a few hard strokes.

"Come," he ordered through gritted teeth.

I fell apart.

He didn't let up as my inner muscles spasmed around him, didn't even slow down. He leaned down hard, pushing my legs nearly flush with my torso. His eyes were close to angry on mine, our foreheads almost touching, as he rasped, "I'm going to make you come so many times that you forget all of the ways that you can find to doubt us."

And he did. He hammered away at me, pressing the hot spots on my body with consummate skill. I wasn't sure I could form a coherent thought when he finally allowed himself to empty inside of me. I certainly couldn't think well enough to count my own orgasms. He twisted his hips viciously right at the end, making me come again despite the fact that I was beyond sated.

I couldn't even lift an arm as he pulled out of me slowly.

"Go to sleep, Love. I'll tell the guys that we'll have a late dinner. You need to rest a bit." As he spoke, he was lowering my legs, and then shifting me into his arms. I was asleep before he could carry me back into the bedroom.

When I woke again, James was in the same position he'd been in the last time. He was at his desk, a phone to his ear. He swiveled his chair as I stepped tentatively into his office. He smiled wickedly as he studied me. It was his Dom smile. *Mercurial man.*

He covered the mouthpiece of his phone. "Drop the sheet

and come here," he ordered, his tone, oh so casual.

I obeyed, feeling surreal as the scene before my second nap seemed to be playing itself out again.

He covered his phone again. "Get on your knees and suck me off," he ordered casually.

I lowered myself, licking my lips as I watched him. It was as though he'd read my mind. When I'd seen him sitting there, sprawled out like an insolent king on his throne, this was exactly what I'd wanted to do to him.

I freed him from his slacks with greedy hands. I gripped both hands around that perfect cock, stroking.

He plunged his free hand in my hair tightly, pulling me to him. He shoved me between his legs, moving his hips to the very edge of his chair. He pushed into my mouth. I opened for him, sucking in his tip with a little moan. He thrust in deep, fucking my mouth so deep that I gagged.

He pulled out, then thrust in again.

I barely noticed when he loudly hung up his phone.

"Relax your throat muscles," he told me. "Take me deeper." I took a little more of him that time.

"Use your hands," he ordered, and I twisted my hands around his base as I sucked him in as deep as I could manage, bobbing my head furiously.

He gripped both hands in my hair, guiding me with hard tugs. He made the loveliest sound in his throat as he poured into me, jerking his hips. I loved it, making my own little sounds as I continued to suck even after he came. He had to tug me away rather firmly. He gave me the warmest look for my efforts.

"You love having your mouth fucked, don't you?" he murmured, stroking my lip.

I hummed in agreement. "I love all of it," I told him, my voice low.

We showered together in the office's well-appointed restroom. He washed me with tender hands and lingering caresses, as was his wont.

"Your office isn't what I expected," I said as he dried me thoroughly. "It doesn't have the James touch."

He kissed a hip as he dried my legs. "It was my father's office, as well. I could never bring myself to change any of it."

I stroked a hand through his wet hair. My sentimental James.

I shouldn't have been surprised that the bedroom had a closet, or that that closet had clothing for me. James seemed more interested in finding clothes for me than in dressing himself as he perused the large rack of women's clothing that took up exactly one half of the closet. He was mostly dry, though some of that golden skin was still deliciously damp. He had a towel slung low across his hips. It made it hard to focus on what I was supposed to be doing; to even remember that I was trying to do anything but watch him with hungry eyes.

James pulled a pale gray sheath dress with a boatneck off the rack. "This," he said.

I rolled my eyes at him. "And do I get to pick out *your* clothes?"

He waved a hand at his side of the closet, still rifling through my rack of clothes. "As you wish, Buttercup," he said, moving to a display of belts set against a large dresser at the back of the closet.

My breath caught at the phrase, and I glanced at him. He wasn't even looking at me…

I moved to his side of the closet, shaking it off.

I sifted through clothing so expensive it felt wrong to even touch it. "Do you need to wear a suit?" I asked, because I had so seldom seen him dress in anything else.

"It would be preferable, since we're dining at one of my properties, and I prefer to appear professional at my place of business. But if something else catches your eye, I'm certainly amenable."

I shot him an arch look. "Do you suppose beating a guy up

for insulting your girlfriend appears professional?"

He grinned at me, not the least repentant. It was a little infuriating. "I'm only human," he said.

I shook my head at him. He was impossible.

I picked out a beautiful pale gray suit. I quickly located a brilliant turquoise shirt and tie. I'd seen him wear the color before, and it was beyond stunning on him.

I turned to show him my selections to see him bending down to collect a pair of suede turquoise wedges. He held a thin turquoise belt in his hand to go with the sheath. I studied his choices, and then mine, and began to laugh.

I laughed so hard that I had to sit on the floor, my towel falling off me.

I giggled harder as a grinning James pounced, our clothing falling in heaps around us as he pinned me to the floor.

He brushed wet hair out of my face and smiled into my eyes.

"Did you see what I was picking out, or are we really this crazy?" I asked him, laughter still in my voice.

He stroked my cheek, giving me the sweetest smile. I didn't think there was a person on the planet that could be on the receiving end of that smile and not fall in love with it. With him.

"Of course I peeked," he told me. "I was prepared to change your whole outfit until we matched."

I giggled harder and he kissed my laughing lips. He didn't linger, pulling back quickly.

"You're insane," I told him, and stood up to dress.

He hugged me from behind, pressing hard against me, rubbing his smooth chest along my back. He spoke into my ear, "Insane for you, my love."

I stiffened, warmed by his words but instantly uncomfortable. What did he mean by that? Was it as serious as it sounded, or just his naturally affectionate nature showing itself? He had been saying outrageous things to me from the start, so I had tended not to take them seriously, but it was becoming clearer by the day that he was *very* serious—that he always had been. *Was he expecting me to respond in kind?* Because I wasn't ready for that—didn't even know how.

The awkward moment quickly passed. James simply kissed my neck softly, and let me go to dress.

He had his office bathroom stocked with toiletries and cosmetics for me. I found this both completely insane and totally convenient. He even had a hair dryer for me. I was ready in less than twenty minutes, James in under ten.

"Do you mind going to dinner with Frankie next time we're in Vegas?" James asked as I finished up. "Next week sometime."

"Not at all," I said quickly, still embarrassed at how jealous I'd been of the woman's easy affection with James at our first meeting. But she was apparently one of the few beautiful women on the planet that James *hadn't* slept with, and I felt too silly for assuming that they had some sort of a past together. I wouldn't mind a chance to let the woman get a better impression of me.

"And Lana called me. She wants to do lunch with you. She's in New York this week, and said she'd make herself flexible for you. I told her to contact you, since I wasn't sure of your plans while I'm working."

"Oh, that sounds nice," I said, and meant it. I'd liked the other woman instantly. She was refreshingly candid and easy to talk to. I didn't expect to make fast friends with many of the people in James's affluent circles, and so one such friend was a huge comfort.

"Also, Parker and Sophia want to have us over for dinner. I told them maybe in a few weeks. Parker's version of not scaring you off alarms me, to be honest."

I smiled, silently agreeing. Baby talk was so not the way to *not* scare me off.

James wrapped a possessive arm tightly around my waist as we left his office. Blake was waiting for us at the elevator. She nodded at James, her face set in its usual severe lines.

"Reassign Johnny," James told her shortly.

She was visibly nonplussed. "Sir, what did he do?" she asked, even as we filed into the elevator.

I turned my head to study his face. His jaw was clenched, but that told me nothing of what he was thinking.

"He wants Bianca. I saw him checking out her legs when he was supposed to be escorting her safely into the elevator. You don't need to fire him; he just needs to be moved. He doesn't get to guard her *body*."

I hadn't particularly liked Johnny, not at all, in fact, but he was being beyond ridiculous. "James—" I began.

"Don't," James interrupted, his tone bland. His words were not. "If you make a case for why you want him close to you, it won't help him, trust me."

I stiffened. Of all of the hair-brained, arbitrary, completely unreasonable things I'd ever heard, this had to top it. "I think *you* are being crazy. This has nothing to do with Johnny—"

"I don't like the way you say his name. It's much too familiar, considering how short a time you've known each oth—"

"Are you joking?" I burst out.

"I'll see to it as soon as I am able, sir," Blake said, not questioning his crazy actions. I didn't suppose he would tolerate it if she did. But *I* could certainly question them.

"James, I won't allow you to be a tyrant. Johnny did nothing wrong. You can't say he wants me because of how you interpreted a *look*."

"This isn't about my jealousy, Bianca. Or at least, not only about that. This is about your safety, and if he's too busy ogling your legs to do his job, he's of no use to me."

"And this is based off one look?" I asked him, my jaw setting.

"Yes. I have good instincts."

"I don't care. You're not reassigning him after one look. You told me that I had a say in who was hired or fired, or anything else, and I say that he is not being reassigned based on one look."

His jaw clenched hard, but I saw immediately that I had won. "Fine. You need more proof. I'll keep him around long enough to get it. Blake, keep me updated on his behavior when I'm not present."

"Yes, sir," she said with no expression. I wondered what she thought about his crazy antics, but I sure wasn't going to ask.

"Where are we going?" I asked him, trying to move on from the silly altercation, trying not to stay upset when he had at least conceded to my wishes.

"It's called Red. It's one of my restaurants. It's just next door. The guys are meeting us there for dinner."

I smiled when he called them 'the guys', because it sounded so familiar and so comfortable, as though Stephan and Javier had been his 'guys' forever.

The second we emerged from the elevator and into the massive hotel lobby, we were flanked by my security and Clark.

I shot James an arch look. "Don't you think this is all a bit excessive?" I asked him.

He squeezed my hip in his hand hard enough to bruise. "Until your father has been found and imprisoned, *nothing* is too excessive. I can afford it, so indulge me."

"Hmm," I said, not sure what to do about his overzealous measures. If I was honest, a part of me liked the protection, liked knowing that my father couldn't get to me even if he tried his best, but the rest of me knew that four people to guard one insignificant woman was completely ludicrous.

CHAPTER FIVE

Mr. Magnanimous

Red was as outrageously luxe as I had pictured it would be. James didn't seem to own a property that wasn't. Every inch of the place was, of course, red. Every shade of red was represented in splashy print on the walls, deep red hardwood floors, and red crystal chandeliers over every table and lounge area.

The first room of the establishment was a massive bar area with high ceilings and red marble topping every surface. The line that wrapped around the block to get into the place meant that it was obviously in high demand, but you wouldn't know it by the spacious bar. The patrons were well-dressed and well-behaved. The trendy mixing with the affluent in a tasteful atmosphere.

An earnest, black-haired hostess, that probably spent her days modeling, led us briskly through the bars and to one of the extravagant dining rooms. There were three that I could see.

Huge mixed floral arrangements topped every table. All of the flowers were red, of course.

"It's very red," I told James.

He just smiled.

The hostess led us to a table in the very center of the large room. No private dining room for us. James apparently wanted to be seen tonight.

Stephan and Javier were already waiting for us at the table. Stephan greeted me with a long hug, Javier a shorter one.

We sat at the beautifully arranged table, and I watched, impressed, as the security team began to position themselves around the room without a word.

"They're so choreographed," I said.

Stephan and Javier were both drinking red wine, and James and I had water.

"Bring us the evening's special," James told the waitress, who looked star-struck at the sight of him. "If that sounds okay to everyone?"

We all nodded. We were flight attendants, which left us in a strange middle ground where we were all strangely cultured, very well-traveled, but none of our travels had taken us to anywhere quite so intimidatingly expensive. I thought it made us all a little nervous.

We chatted comfortably as we waited for food. The guys all got along remarkably well, which was a relief to me. Aside from having me in common, Stephan and James always had so much to talk about. From sports, to cars, to friendly political debates that only gave me a slight headache, they talked like they were old friends. It warmed my heart.

Dinner came in waves of delicious courses that were small portions of richly seasoned foods, and I only knew what it was all even called because the waitress presented each dish with a flourish and an explanation. The main course, pan-roasted halibut with spring asparagus risotto, practically melted in my mouth.

"Very good," James told her when she'd served another course.

She practically glowed as she floated away, obviously affected by his praise.

"You shouldn't throw out that charm so carelessly. You'll make the whole world fall in love with you," I told him, smiling slightly.

He grabbed my hand, kissing my fingers. He studied me. "You think so, Love?"

I looked away, blushing, at a loss for words.

Dessert was even more delectable than dinner, with roasted banana gateau and frozen rum custard. The servings were tiny, but I was still stuffed by the time we finished the drawn-out meal.

We lingered for a long time even after dinner, enjoying the beautiful setting and the wonderful company. The guys were headed to a Broadway play after dinner. The thought made me grin. Broadway was *not* Stephan's thing, so it was sweet that he would go for Javier.

"Oh, I almost forgot," James said with a grin. "A men's health magazine asked me to do a last minute photo shoot and a short interview piece."

I just blinked at him for a moment. "A photo shoot?" I asked him. I shouldn't have been surprised. He was a supermodel among men. What magazine wouldn't want him on their cover?

"I saw your last spread. It was very good," Javier said.

James shrugged. "I do them every once in a while. They wanted me to do this shoot for a fall issue, but I insisted on doing the next one that comes out. I have a good relationship with the magazine."

I had a thought. "Are you just doing it to show off your tattoos?" I asked.

He grinned a wicked grin and the guys started laughing. It was so crazy, over-the-top romantic, and so James, wanting to show the evidence of his devotion to the world. I blushed scarlet.

"Will you come with me to the shoot? It's Wednesday afternoon, right after I finish at the office."

I gave my little shrug. "If you want me to be there, I'll go."

His eyes practically glowed at me from his grinning face. "Love, I want you everywhere I go. I'd put you in my pocket, if I could."

All of us laughed, but I don't think any of us thought for a second that he didn't mean it.

"Also, Stephan and Javier have some news for you," James said, looking at the other men.

I studied them, surprised to see that they looked nervous. I gave Stephan the look that he knew meant, 'spit it out.'

He chewed on his lip as he thought of what to say. "I had a meeting with James today, while you were sleeping," he began. That was news to me. I'd had no idea he'd been to the office. "He's magnanimously agreed to put up the starter capital for Javier and me to open up a bar in Vegas."

I didn't react, just studied all of the men, surprised at what had transpired without my knowledge.

James couldn't seem to help himself, ingratiating himself into every aspect of my life, but how could I be mad, when he did such wonderful things for my best friend? The answer was simple. I couldn't.

I looked at James. "Thank you," I told him sincerely.

He shrugged. "It's an investment. Stephan presented me with an idea that I think will be successful. It's as simple as that. No need to thank me."

I gave him a wry look, but that was all.

We finished up, walking out with the guys. I hugged Stephan goodbye and told them to have a good night. James had gotten them their own car and driver for the evening, and they were in heaven, loving the VIP treatment.

Our car was awkwardly silent on the short drive back to the apartment, since Blake and Johnny had joined us in the back. James linked his fingers with mine, but that was all.

"Are you going to explain to me about what happened this

morning? Jolene is married? And you were *friends* with her husband?" I asked, my voice pitched low. I was trying to be reasonable, trying to get through the day without any more drama, but I needed some things made clear for me.

He sighed. It was a resigned sigh, and his face was troubled as he looked at me. "Yes, of course I'll explain. Thank you for asking, and not just reacting. Let's go up to bed. I'll tell you whatever you want to know there."

I studied him rather suspiciously. "You can't just tie me up whenever we need to have a talk that you think I won't like."

He gave me a smug look. It was infuriating. "As a matter of fact, I can. But that's not my plan right now. I would just prefer to talk in the bedroom."

We were in the closet, undressing for bed, before he spoke again. "Scott met Jolene when she was my sub. He was instantly taken with her. When I ended our arrangement, Scott asked me if I minded if he asked her out. I didn't mind, but I told him that it may not be the best idea, for his sake. That was all I said and all I knew. Unbeknownst to me, they married less than two weeks later."

He managed to undress first, and moved close to watch me finish.

"A few months after that Jolene called me, asked me to meet her for dinner. I didn't see a problem with that—didn't even know whether or not she and Scott had gone out, and I was between subs, so I simply saw it as a chance to blow off steam."

I made my face go carefully blank as I looked at him. The blowing off steam comment made me feel...delicate, for reasons that I didn't want to investigate.

"We were...together that night, and again a few days later. She expressed interest in resuming our previous arrangement. I tried to tell her gently that I wasn't interested, and that I thought that she should move on. That's when she told me that she'd married Scott. She threw it out as proof that she'd already moved on, thinking it would actually encourage me to reconsider."

"Needless to say, it didn't do that. I told her I wouldn't see her, wouldn't touch her, if she was married. I never wanted to be an adulterer; the idea is abhorrent to me, especially when I was cuckolding a friend of mine."

I pulled a sheer slip over my head.

"I stopped seeing her, stopped taking her calls, for at least a year," he continued. "I was between subs again when she finally managed to pin me down. She was divorced by then, which I knew, though I didn't know exactly what had happened at the time. Later I would learn that she had filed because I'd refused to see her when she was married. I never should have touched her after we ended our original arrangement. I see that clearly now. My friendship with Scott is irreparable now, unfortunately I figured it out too late. He is completely enamored with her, so much so that he is incapable of seeing reason. I used to be baffled by it—by him losing his head so completely over a woman." He gave me a self-deprecating smile. "I'm not baffled by it anymore. Now the only thing that baffles me is his *taste* in women."

I had to stifle the urge to tell him that they seemed to *share* a taste in women. I told myself firmly that it wouldn't be a constructive thing to say. There was a lot about his past that I would need to overlook if we were going to have any hope of staying together. And as long as it really was the past, I thought I could learn to deal, though his explanation troubled me on a number of levels.

I was silent for a long time while I examined my own thoughts, and finished getting ready for bed.

James didn't appreciate me keeping my own council. "Tell me what you're thinking," he burst out finally. "Are you upset?"

I went into the bathroom, washing my face and brushing my

teeth. James dogged my footsteps the entire time, trouble in those brilliant eyes that never left my face.

I was climbing onto the bed when I finally answered. "I guess I'm just a little surprised with you, that after all of that, you were still seeing her just a day before I met you. I'm not upset, just—is it so hard for you to stay away from her?"

I was glancing at him only as I finished speaking, but I clearly saw him flinch.

"It's not like you're thinking. I don't know if you'll think it's better or worse, but I didn't continue to see her for all that time because I couldn't stay away. It's sort of the opposite. We had preferences in common, but I never even *liked* her. I've known from the start that she was mercenary. Perhaps not the extent of it until she went after Scott, but I realized at least enough to know, that I could never care for her. I saw her because I needed an outlet for the things I do, and at my worst, I thought that we deserved each other. I didn't even contact her that often, only when I was between subs and in a particularly dark mood. Most of the time she wasn't even allowed to talk—"

I held up a hand, having heard more than enough. "I don't think I can bear to hear those kinds of details. One last question, and then I'll drop it. Why does Scott still call her his wife?"

He grimaced. "Scott never got over her. He never saw her as she is. He just sees the package, and the fact that she's insatiabl—"

I held up that hand again. "Please."

He brushed my hair from my face. I saw his tan throat work as he swallowed hard, leaning over me. "I'm sorry. I don't mean to be insensitive. It's hard to explain these things without touching on sensitive things."

"As long as I don't have to hear any more about *her* sensitive things," I said wryly.

He grinned. "You know I'm only interested in *your* sensitive things."

I wrinkled my nose at him.

"Too soon to joke about it?" he asked.

I nodded.

He sighed. "Anyway, word is that they remarried a few weeks ago. Poor bastard. She's going to wring him out to dry. Nothing I can do about it, though I did try to warn him. And I didn't lose control, Bianca, not like you're thinking. He took a swing at me, he missed, and I didn't. They were escorted off the premises. They won't be allowed back on. Anything else you need to know?"

I shook my head. A part of me could have questioned him all night. Everything about him interested me, from his past to his present, and the masochist in me wanted to know every little detail. I knew what I needed to know, though, and that would have to be enough.

He did his kinky doctor routine, examining every inch of me, and then massaging my body slowly and carefully. I was well-sated from the afternoon's vigorous activities, but I still wanted him again by the time he finished.

He studied my back for a very long time, but said nothing, just softly kissing the marks he had left there with the black and blue roses.

I felt like I'd slept the day away, but somehow I felt myself drifting off even as he tended to me. He didn't try to stop me.

I was in that house again. I sat up as though pulled by a string. My father was shouting somewhere in the house, an indecipherable string of Swedish that my ears picked up but that my brain couldn't translate. Knowing it was a bad idea, I got out of bed.

I glanced down at my cold bare feet, and they were bigger, more grown up, not at all like I remembered. Something was wrong, even more wrong than normal. Still, I padded silently down that long hallway.

The kitchen was where it was supposed to be, but everything else was wrong. A thick red pool was soaking the light blue carpet of the hallway, visible before I'd even made it to the kitchen. I glanced down at my hands. They were already covered in blood. *Wrong, wrong, wrong.*

Still, I approached that kitchen, unable to stay away.

My mother's body lay on the floor, and it was all I could see for long moments as I stood in the doorway. Her head was gone—just so many pieces on the floor, and in my hair, and on my nightgown. I recognized her only by the hunks of long golden hair scattered around her body. I knelt at her side, clutching one of her delicate hands. It was the only part of her still unmarred by gore.

The moment I touched her, more of the room came into focus.

Hers wasn't the only body on the ground. Another woman lay scant feet away, and I saw by her garish red hair that it was Sharon. I stared at her, confused and horrified, as my mind refused to see the other horror in the room. Only my father's yelling made me finally look over, and only because his words changed, a heavily accented sentence in English getting my attention.

"Look, sotnos, look."

I looked. I stood, a scream building in my throat. My father stood facing me, but it wasn't him I looked at—wasn't him I saw. A large figure stood in front of him, his back facing me. Perfect golden brown hair just brushed the white collar of a crisp dress shirt, a strong back showing tensed muscles that were painfully familiar.

"James," I said brokenly, my voice barely more than a

whisper.

He didn't turn, didn't so much as twitch at my presence.

I stepped closer, unable to look away. "James," I said again, drawing even with the horrifying tableau in front of me. My heart stopped in my chest as all of the pieces of the picture snapped into place with a terrifying clarity.

My father stood almost propped against that still as death James, a gun already shoved inside his mouth, pushed far into his throat.

James's eyes were open, but they were glassy, as though the trigger had already been pulled. His arms were limp at his sides. I grabbed an arm, but the feel of his slack muscles made me recoil.

"Watch, sotnos, watch," my father said coldly. I began to sob as my father pulled the trigger, unable to stop him—unable to look away.

James crumpled in a heap to the floor, the back of his head disappearing in a gory splash of red.

I sat up with a scream, my eyes wide in the dark.

I began to move, needing action, though I couldn't see where I was, or where I was going. I was sobbing brokenly when strong, hard arms wrapped around me from behind, lifting and turning me gently into a heart-achingly familiar chest. I gasped and clutched at James even as he lifted me.

I shut my eyes as James carried me into the bathroom, turning on the blindingly bright lights. He didn't let me go as he got into the bath, still clutching me tightly with one strong arm. I gripped him with both arms, clinging as tightly as I could. I wouldn't even let go when he tried to strip off my nightgown.

"No," I protested, gripping him.

"Okay, shh, that's fine, Love, I won't let go."

He sank to the bottom of the tub, keeping me tightly against him, rubbing a soothing hand against my back and keeping me close, murmuring soothing words as I slowly calmed. Eventually he pulled back far enough to lift off my nightgown and then worked slowly out of his boxers. He pulled me flush against him when he'd finished, until we were flesh to flesh.

He washed me, scrubbing me gently but thoroughly, as though he knew about my bloody dream, and knew exactly what I needed.

He didn't ask me about the nightmare—didn't ask me for anything at all, but instead gave comfort, anticipating my needs better than I could have communicated, if I'd been able to communicate.

Eventually I spoke, spilling every detail of the dream in a quiet, agonized whisper.

He stroked my back as I spoke, staying silent while I told him about the nightmare. He only spoke when I'd finished and fell silent. "It was just a dream, Bianca. I'm here, and I'm fine. Your father wouldn't be able to get to me if he tried. And we will take every precaution to make sure he can *never* get to you. We'll be fine, Love. Everything is going to be okay."

I felt better after I got it all out and of course after James reassured me with so much conviction in his voice. We dried off and fell asleep. I clutched him even as I drifted off.

I awoke when I felt James leaving the bed. I sat up when the bathroom door closed, the shower turning on a moment later. I had nearly drifted off again when he re-emerged. I made myself get up.

I watched him get dressed from the closet entrance, barely managing not to drool even in my sleep-dazed state.

James shot me a warm look. "Go back to bed, Love. I have to go into work, but that doesn't mean you have to wake up at this ungodly hour," he said, shrugging into a crisp white dress shirt.

I gave a little shrug. I'd slept enough.

He finished dressing swiftly, moving to me with a purpose. He kissed me, a slow, hot kiss, but pulled back without doing more. His golden hair trailed into his face as he bent down to me. It wasn't even dry yet, but it still looked model perfect. I ran a strand between my fingers.

James pulled back reluctantly. "All of the paintings that you're working on have been moved into your studio here. And I believe that Lana is going to try to rope you into lunch today, though if she doesn't, I'd love to get the privilege."

My brows furrowed. I'd gotten a brief tour of my brand new window-lined studio, but I hadn't seen my current projects there.

"All of them?" I asked, thinking of the nude I'd started painting of him, the one I'd buried in a chest in the guest bedroom of my small home.

He grinned wickedly. "*All* of them. I need to go. If you aren't going back to bed, then walk me out." As he spoke, he hooked a finger into the collar at my neck.

He kissed me at the elevator. "We'll dine in tonight, then I'm taking you to the fourth floor," he told me as the door closed.

I missed him the second he was gone. I had it so bad.

I couldn't go back to that empty bed, so I painted.

I had to smile when I saw that he'd been quite literal about moving all of the paintings I was working on into my studio. Even the nude of him had somehow been found in my house and shipped here. The man had no boundaries whatsoever.

I worked on the portrait of a fourteen-year-old James that I had begun working on the week before. I worked for hours, becoming utterly absorbed in that image of him, that picture of an outrageously beautiful child with the sorrow of loss and the weight of the world on his shoulders.

I had made good progress on the painting, but still wore just the barest slip, when I heard a brisk knock on the door of my studio.

I cringed. I hadn't thought that through. I'd started at maybe five a.m., forgetting there was even anyone else in the monstrosity of an apartment.

I set down my brush and opened the door, keeping my body hidden.

I was surprised to find Blake at the door, holding my phone, though I shouldn't have been. I had just naturally assumed it would be either Marion or Stephan at the door, and I'd been hoping for Stephan. If anyone had to see me in a see-through nightie besides James, of course I'd pick Stephan.

"Ms. Karlsson. Mr. Cavendish would like a word. Please try to keep your phone on you, for security purposes," she said, her face set in those painfully severe lines.

I just nodded and shut the door in her face. I wasn't trying to be rude, but it was hard not to be, when I was a grown woman and she seemed to feel the need to tell me what to do.

I didn't even have a chance to dial James before he was calling me.

"Hello, Mr. Cavendish," I said into the phone.

"You're painting," he said in the warmest voice.

"Mmmhmm. How could you tell?"

"Just by the sound of your voice. It's sort of dreamy and soft. I wish I were there. I love to watch you paint. I love to watch those dreams in your eyes."

I shivered, adoring those romantic words and the low raspy cadence of his voice. "I wish you were here, too, though if you were, I'd be working on the nude."

"I'll pose tonight, if you like."

"I like."

"Mostly I called because I'm between meetings and I wanted to hear the sound of your voice, but also Lana is trying to get ahold of you. She is a ruthlessly persistent woman, and she made me agree to ask you to call her. She's been trying, but you obviously forgot that you have a phone. Again."

"I did," I agreed. I could hardly deny it.

I heard him sigh heavily. "I need to go, but please keep your phone on you."

"Okay," I said. I could tell by his tone that he needed to rush, so I kept it short. "I'll see you tonight," I told him softly.

"Yes, you will. Goodbye, Love."

CHAPTER SIX

Mr. Romantic

I was looking through my contact list, hoping that someone had added Lana's number, when my phone began to ring in my hand. It was a strange New York area code, so I thought it must be her.

I answered right away. "Hello," I said with a smile. I was looking forward to our lunch date.

A definitely male, definitely unfamiliar voice answered back. "Bianca Karlsson?"

I didn't answer right away, confused and leery of someone unfamiliar having my number. *Was it a tabloid? Was it part of the Cavendish army of security guards?*

"This is she," I said finally, keeping my voice cool and polite.

The man cleared his throat on the other end. He was nervous. I was almost certain of it. *Who was this?*

"I'm sorry to bother you...I'm Sven. Sven Karlsson."

My heart felt like it froze in my chest when I heard my father's name. My ears just sort of filled with white noise, and for a long time I just stood there, silently stunned.

"I'm your, um, half-brother. Sven Jr., I guess."

I still couldn't find any words to speak. I needed to sit down, but couldn't make myself turn to look for a chair.

Finally he spoke again, "Sorry to bother you. I probably shouldn't have called." His voice sounded so forlorn that I suddenly found I could speak again.

"No, no, don't be sorry. I just heard about your mother. I'm so sorry for your loss. I didn't even know that you both existed until a few days ago."

"Oh," he said. "Well, I know this is strange, but I'd heard that you spend a lot of time in Manhattan. I live here, and I was wondering if we could just meet up for coffee sometime. I don't have any family, and to be honest, I've wanted to meet you for a long time."

He had stunned me into silence again. This was the last thing I'd expected when I heard I had a half-brother. The thought of someone who was related to me by blood that would actually want to meet me was just so…foreign. I couldn't say I loved the idea, but how could I refuse?

"Okay," I agreed finally. "I'm not sure when I'll be able to, though."

"That's fine. You can just get back to me on that. Whenever and wherever you're comfortable with."

He seemed so…nice. When I'd thought of my father's son, I'd just automatically thought of my father, but this man did not sound like *that*.

"Okay," I said with more certainty. I wanted this, wanted to see this man who was a strange missing piece of my broken family. "I'll do that. Perhaps in a week or two, on a Friday around lunchtime?"

"Sounds great. Just let me know. I can take a few hours whenever I need to, so last minute plans are fine with me, as well."

We said our awkward goodbyes, and I finally sprawled out on the studio's white divan, trying to wrap my numb mind around the strange turn of events.

I was just starting to sit up, trying to do something other than just sit and think, when my phone rang in my hand.

It was another strange New York number, and I just answered, really hoping it was Lana this time.

"Ha! I found you," Lana said without preamble. "Come meet me at the Cavendish property, at the Light Café. James said he'd loan you to me for lunch, but only if we ate at his hotel. Have you noticed that your boyfriend's kind of bossy?"

I laughed. "I have noticed that," I said, my mood instantly lifting. Lunch with a fun girlfriend was just what I needed.

We decided to meet at noon, ending the conversation quickly.

I showered quickly and dressed in a smart little gray pleated skirt paired with a high-necked light blue sleeveless silk blouse. Orange patent leather wedge sandals completed the ensemble. I used Jackie's suggestion for the shoes, and again wasn't sorry, though I never would have paired them together on my own.

I had noticed that the vanity now sported an entire section just for my jewelry. I'd been wary to even look at it, but knowing that I would probably be seeing James, since we were going to his hotel, and that not much would please him more, I peeked at what were obviously new additions to my jewelry collection.

I wore my collar, so I only looked at the earring selection. I noticed a small white box immediately, since it looked different from the rest. It was older, with more dated packaging, and a note on the top. I plucked that note up, feeling brave.

Bianca, my love,

These were my mother's. Please take them. It will break my heart if you reject them.

James

My hand shook and my eyes filled with tears. With love and

with guilt, because I *would* have rejected them, especially knowing that they were his mother's, if it weren't for that terribly romantic note. I opened the box with trembling hands.

Inside sat large, princess cut, diamond studs surrounded by small sapphire baguettes. Or rather, that's what I guessed the gemstones were.

I didn't let myself think about it—didn't let myself doubt. I just put the lovely things on, knowing that they were so much more than ungodly expensive earrings.

I brushed my drying hair behind my shoulders. They sparkled even through my hair, but I decided to clip one side back to showcase them more clearly.

I took more time than usual with my makeup, knowing that Lana would look model perfect, and that I'd be seeing James.

I knocked on Stephan and Javier's door when I was ready to go.

Stephan answered the door, wearing only his boxers and looking gorgeous. We smiled at each other. He pulled me into his chest in a warm hug, kissing the top of my head. I hugged him tightly back, burrowing into his chest. He smelled like family...and Javier, but I took that as a good sign.

"I'm going to lunch with Lana, this really nice lady, and a close friend of James's that I met last week. You guys have a late night?" Clearly they had, since Javier was face down on the bed, out cold.

Stephan chuckled. "You could say that. We went a little nuts with the car and driver."

Javier made a very sexual sound from the bed, moving against the covers in a suggestive way.

I blushed.

Stephan laughed. "He's dreaming about me. Have fun, Bee. Love you."

"Love you, too," I said, beating a hasty retreat. The guys obviously needed their privacy.

Lana was already waiting inside of the Light Café in the Cavendish hotel when I got there. She was seated in one of the well-spaced center tables, next to a huge, but strangely quiet, stone fountain. It was a huge dining room, with the top and three sides lined with windows, letting in an almost blinding amount of light. I had to put my shades back on as I entered the café.

The decor was all gray stone and red detailing, as though little pieces of Red, which was next door, had bled into the restaurant.

She stood and gave me a warm hug when I approached the table. She wore an ivory pencil skirt, with a white men's dress shirt. It would have been very business-like attire, if not for her swimsuit model figure and her peep-toe crimson stilettos. Her jewelry was simple and gold, with hoops at her ears, and a plain band at her neck and wrist. All of the wealthy women I'd been introduced to of late seemed to wear less extravagant jewelry than I did. It was an alarming thought.

Out of the corner of my eye, I saw my security positioning themselves around the room.

We sat.

"James is incorrigible. I swear he called the paparazzi on me! They were outside photographing me when I arrived. I usually don't get paparazzi, unless of course I'm hanging out with James. I'm just too boring. But now they're going to print a piece about how even the Middleton heiress prefers the Cavendish hotel, damn him."

I laughed, because she was damning him with a genuinely fond smile on her face.

We both ordered plain tea and water. Lana smiled at me. "We really *could* be sisters. So tell me, how is it going with James? You know he's hopelessly in love with you, right?"

I blushed and swallowed. "He's wonderful, but so overwhelming. I'm not the type to rush into anything, even if it's something small, but he just doesn't get it. I love being with him, but it's been a roller-coaster."

"That's why you needed time apart. I get it," she said, her voice rich with understanding and sympathy. "He was so sad that month, so...bereft. I'd never seen him like that before. I'm glad he got you back. He needs you, Bianca. Everyone should get to experience a love like that. That kind of love makes us better people."

Her words made me think of the man she'd referred to briefly the first time we'd met. I still remembered the name, since it had held such meaning to her just at its utterance.

The waitress returned just then to bring our drinks and take our orders. I got a turkey melt on wheat bread with sweet potato fries. I thought it was strange fair for such a posh café to have on the menu, but it sounded good to me.

"Tell me about Akira Kalua," I said, because she'd promised me she would.

She gave me a mock glare. "I knew you wouldn't forget about that." She sighed heavily. "I've been in love with him since I was ten. Unfortunately, he was *twenty* when I was ten. That was fine. I was content to wait. I bided my time, enjoying his company, taking up as much of his time as I could manage. He taught me to surf. His family as good as adopted me when my parents left Maui. He made me laugh. God, did he make me laugh. My happiest memories are of playing jokes on him. I would torment him, but he never got mad, never lost his patience. He was so wonderful to me, and I thought he was the most beautiful creature on the planet."

She looked down at her hands, and I knew that the story was about to take a turn for the worse. "When I was eighteen I seduced him. I was completely ruthless about it. I told him that if he didn't take my virginity, and make it good for me, that I'd give it up to some drunk frat boy, and probably hate sex for life after that, *and* probably get an STD."

I stifled a laugh, because it was such an outrageous thing to do.

She didn't take offense. "Oh, yeah, I guilted him into it. There's no other way to look at it. After that, I had to leave. I thought that sex would change everything for us, and it did. It *ruined* everything. I was in deeper than ever after that, and he saw me as a kid sister. He was still in love with his ex-girlfriend. He got back together with her the day after we were together. I overheard what he told her about me. He said I was a family friend with an inconvenient infatuation. He wasn't wrong, but it still broke my heart. I left that day. God, I miss that rock."

I studied her. I had a hard time believing that he'd only had sex with her out of pity. "He must have wanted you if he took you up on your offer. I'm no expert, but I don't think men have sex with women they don't want. And men *always* want women who look like you."

She shrugged. "None of it matters now. It's all in the past. I like being alone. Romantic entanglements just don't interest me. I'm content with work. I keep busy."

"You're still in love with him," I said, certain I was right.

She shrugged. "I can't help it, other than to try to think about it as seldom as possible. Last I heard, he was engaged to his high school sweetheart."

"You need to go back to Maui. You still think of it as home. Even if it's just to get closure, you should go visit. How many years has it been since you left?"

"Eight." She shrugged again. "Maybe I will, sometime. I *do* miss it. Your turn. Tell me about you and James."

I glanced around, making sure we had privacy. I leaned towards her. "He's into BDSM. Well, *we* are into it, actually."

She smiled wryly, not looking in the least surprised.

"You knew?"

"Not firsthand, but Jules tried to tell me about that once, when she thought he and I were dating. She was trying to scare me off. Have you noticed that all of the really pretty men always have a *thing*? Women are just too easy for them, I think, so they always seem to develop...quirks, yanno?"

I laughed, because I loved her take on it, and the fact that it didn't faze her a bit. "No, I don't know. I only know James, and he and I share...quirks."

She shrugged. "I have a thing for giant Hawaiian men who look like ripped pro-wrestlers, and are covered in tattoos."

"Men? So this is a pattern for you?" I asked, genuinely curious.

She wrinkled her nose, those violet eyes sparkling. "Just Akira."

She looked at something behind my shoulder. "Oh, lord, here comes Jackie." She caught my expression. "You don't like her?"

I gave my little shrug. "Not so far."

Lana waved an elegant hand towards the woman. "It's a fact that she's more than half-crazy. Did you know that she actually thinks that *shopping* is a legitimate job? But she's very funny when you get to know her. She's just rough around the edges, that's all."

I would have taken nice over funny any day, but I held my tongue.

Jackie approached us with her no-nonsense little walk, wearing smartly tailored, cuffed shorts, and an almost severely modest collared shirt. The whole ensemble was pea-green, a color that worked with her complexion, but that I didn't think would work for many. Her cute legs, and her nude stilettos with red soles, kept the outfit from being too conservative.

Jackie was looking at my lap as though I had something disgusting growing there.

I looked down at the cream bag she had picked out the day

before.

"Twice in a row with the same bag, Bianca? You have a closet full of bags! Are you trying to embarrass me?"

Lana tutted at her rather affectionately. "Looks like you're doing that all on your own, Jackie. Chill out. It's a bag. A lovely bag. Go away if you aren't here to be nice."

Jackie looked surprised but not at all offended. "You aren't going to invite me to join you for lunch?"

Lana shook her head. "Nope. What are you up to?"

Jackie shrugged. "I come here all the time. It's a good place to be seen. I wanted to discuss some things with Bianca."

"Nope. Are you stalking her?"

"Noooo. I just need a minute."

"Then make an appointment," Lana said with a sweet smile.

"What do you want, Jackie?" I asked, trying to make my tone bland rather than hostile.

She reached into her own monstrosity of a bag. It was pea-green leather with a big red stripe down the side. She pulled out a small piece of paper, brandishing it like a weapon. "I have a list of functions that you need to attend. Mostly luncheons."

I sighed, waving at one of the empty chairs at our table. "Sit down and tell me what you're talking about, Jackie."

She sat and started in, as if she had rehearsed the whole spiel. "As the significant other of a powerful and influential man in this town, you have some new obligations. You'll be expected to attend lunches and brunches, and tea parties, nearly every day of the week."

I felt my face stiffening the more she spoke.

"Being with James is a full-time job. I'm willing to show you the ropes, since you can't possibly understand what all of this entails—"

"I have a job," I interrupted her. "I'm not looking for another one. I have no wish to go to functions with a bunch of strange women every day."

She let out a very put-upon sigh. "I was afraid you'd say that. You can't possibly comprehend the kind of responsibilities that James and I have had to own since our childhoods—"

I laughed in her face, my extremely rare temper rearing its very ugly head, the words she'd chosen setting me off. "Responsibility? *You* are going to lecture *me* about responsibility? I have had to care for myself since I was a child. You probably still live off your parents' wealth," I guessed. I saw by her expression that I was right. "Don't you dare speak a word to me about responsibility!"

I instantly regretted losing my cool, but I didn't take anything I'd said back. It was nothing but the truth, if an indelicate one.

"I didn't mean to upset you again," she said carefully. "I know you don't like me. And I know you think I don't like you, but that's a nonissue to me. I'm trying to help you."

I raised a hand. "Don't. Don't try to help me. Don't try to tell me what I need to do with my time."

She sighed that put-upon sigh of hers. "Fine, I'll go, but let me know if you reconsider."

I looked at Lana after she'd left. "What's with her?"

Lana shook her head. "She's an odd one, so I can't say for sure, but I'm guessing it's half self-promotion, since she could claim to dress you for all of the functions she's plotting. The other half would be that she actually thinks she's trying to help you, in her own misguided way. My advice would be to challenge her. Her personality demands it. Give her some arbitrary conditions to being your dresser." She snapped her fingers as though an idea had struck her. "I know. Tell her you only want to wear clothes from up-and-coming fashion designers. Insist that you won't wear anything else. That will drive her crazy, but she's perverse enough that she'll enjoy it."

I wrinkled my nose at her. "I'll try it, though I don't understand it."

She just shrugged. "Jackie takes time to understand, but I

guarantee she'll grow on you."

Grounded

CHAPTER SEVEN

Mr. Muse

We chatted and ate and chatted some more. We had been talking and laughing for hours when Lana looked at her phone and groaned.

"I need to get to a meeting. Thanks for doing this," Lana said, beginning to gather up her things.

"Thanks for inviting me. It's nice to discover that James has some female friends that aren't complete psychopaths."

She threw back her head and laughed. She was a sight, with her blonde mermaid hair and her twinkling eyes.

We were just standing up from the table when I spotted James striding through the door of the now crowded café. People stopped in their tracks to watch him, myself included.

He only had eyes for me as he approached.

He wrapped an arm around my waist, gripping tightly, before he turned a dazzling smile on Lana. "We'll walk you out," he said.

We walked her out, flanked by our security, of which Lana had said not one word, and said our goodbyes. I was surprised when James led me to the car, and then followed me into the large SUV. It was only two p.m. I hadn't imagined he'd get off work so early.

"Are you done for the day?" I asked him as he crowded me into the middle seat.

He buckled me in like the control freak he is, before answering. "I am." He grinned. It was the most charming, incorrigible smile, the smile of a kid ditching school and getting away with it because no one could tell him no.

I traced his lips with one finger. "That's good news," I said softly.

"I pawned some meetings off on my VP. Meetings that were above his pay grade, so I may need to give him a raise. I want to watch you paint. I needed to see those dreams in your eyes firsthand."

He fingered one of my earrings, his eyes as tender as I'd ever seen them. "Thank you for that," he whispered, a catch in his voice.

I melted.

We went straight to the apartment. We found Stephan and Javier in one of the larger entertainment areas, playing video games and eating sandwiches. They were still wearing pajamas.

I laughed when I saw them.

Stephan grinned back at me.

Javier didn't even look up. He was too busy trying to hunt down and kill Stephan's character in the game. He wasn't successful.

Stephan shot Javier's character in the head within seconds, barely even glancing at the screen. He was the worst to play against. He never lost.

Javier cursed. "I almost had you!"

"Headshot," Stephan pointed out.

James tugged at my hand, drawing my gaze to him. He grinned at me, a twinkle in his eye. "Well, we *have* to play a match or two. I'm playing hooky from work. Gaming is practically a requirement."

"I'm on Stephan's team," I said quickly. If I was going to play, it may as well be to win.

James pointed at me. "You're going to pay for that."

And I did. We ended up playing for hours, and I got *camped*. James killed me, again and again, with no remorse. He apparently took it personal when I picked someone else's team. *Good to know*.

Marion brought us food while we played, since we were at it for so long.

We won some matches, and lost some, but it was more of a contest between James and Stephan. Javier and I were hopelessly outmatched.

I elbowed James as he shot my army guy in the head yet again.

"This game is so sexist," I complained. "I can't believe that there isn't even an option for me to play as a girl."

"Do you think that if you were playing as a busty blonde it would distract me?" James asked, amused.

"It couldn't hurt."

He tossed his controller on the ground. I gave a little embarrassing shriek as he tossed me over his shoulder. "We're done, guys. Buttercup wants to distract me. Consider me distracted."

The guys called out goodnights as James carried me away, even though it couldn't have been even six p.m. It seemed that they understood that if we went to our bedroom, we wouldn't be coming back out.

I was surprised when James didn't take me to our bedroom, instead heading to the studio.

"Will you pose for the nude?" I asked breathlessly, as he jostled me on his shoulder.

"Yes. With a condition."

"What condition?"

"I want you naked, as well, while you paint."

It didn't seem fair to argue with that stipulation, but I still sort of wanted to.

My breath whooshed from my lungs in a rush as James suddenly dumped me onto the cushy divan that took up a corner of the studio near the window. He didn't pounce on me, as I'd half assumed, and wished, that he would. Instead, he began to strip.

"Take off your clothes and paint me, Love," he said with a heart-stopping smile.

I set up my supplies first, setting everything up just so. The sun was slowly setting, and the best of the day's light had passed, so I turned on the bright overhead lights to illuminate the most beautiful man in the world lounging on a divan, naked and at my service.

I started to paint, forgetting that I was supposed to be nude, as well.

James had no qualms about reminding me. "Take the clothes off. All of them. Now."

I stripped slowly and a little awkwardly. It was no strip tease. I didn't think I had that in me. I didn't doubt that I had something wild inside of me, but it just wasn't *that*.

I wore nothing but my collar and my earrings as I began to paint. Surprisingly, I was able to jump right into the project, not nearly as distracted by my own nudity as I'd thought I would be. That was probably because I was utterly captivated by the man that had inspired the painting.

James watched me paint, as he'd said he needed to. It was hard to feel self-conscious, even nude, when someone was looking at you as though you were the most beautiful and fascinating creature on the planet.

I had painted most of his face and torso before I got distracted by the subject at hand. When I'd painted his chest, I'd wanted to touch his chest, to kiss it, and bury my face there. I'd felt a similar urge when I'd been working on the curve of his neck, and his abdomen, hell, even his hair. But when I started to work on that sexy little V shaped pelvic muscle, I got sidetracked in a hurry.

I felt myself licking my lips a lot, as I studied that area of his body. Felt it, but couldn't seem to stop it.

As though it had snapped me out of the dreamy trance I seemed to go into when I lost myself in a painting, I suddenly felt the air against my bare skin, like the temperature had just risen ten degrees in the room. My skin felt hot, my breasts so heavy, my nipples hardening until they quivered. I knew with a certainty that I wasn't going to make any more progress on the nude that night.

I set down my palette, reaching for another one. They were a luxury I'd never indulged in before. Generally, I mixed paints on whatever piece of plastic I found that was the right shape and size. James had a dozen for me here, in their own designated drawer.

I began to rifle through a selection of acrylic paints that were sorted by color. I found one named Turquoise, but it wasn't quite right, so I mixed in just a touch of emerald on the palette.

"What are you doing? You mix mediums like that on paintings? I didn't notice that on any of your work," James asked, sounding surprised.

My cheeks flushed in pleasure. That he knew so much about my little hobby, that he studied what I did, it still surprised me, but more and more, it was only a good surprise. My natural instinct to doubt everything he said and did was turning into something else now. He didn't lie. Not about anything. It was freeing for me somehow as I realized that. If he didn't lie, I didn't have to question every little thing he did and said. It was a liberating realization.

I grabbed a larger sable brush, dipping it lightly into the paint of my new palette as I returned to my easel. I stood as though I were going to paint on the paper, then brought the brush slowly to my own chest. I traced the large globe of my right breast with a light touch.

James sucked in a breath, sitting up to watch me. His cock had calmed down to semi-hard, for once, but it quickly stood at attention, inflating like a particularly wonderful toy.

I traced the brush down the middle of my abdomen, nearly reaching my sex before tracing to the side to paint one hip.

"Come here," James said gruffly.

I had been intending to tease him a bit, but my body began to move instantly at his words, walking to him slowly, dragging the paintbrush to my other hip with a leisurely stroke.

He licked his lips. "Keep going," he said, making no move to touch me even after I'd moved close.

I painted up my torso again, tracing my ribs one by one slowly, first one side and then the other. I dipped into my palette, picking up a generous amount of the turquoise. I painted the bones of my collar, being very careful not to graze my locked choker. I painted my other breast, moving the brush in wide circles over its roundness until I reached the rock hard nipple in the center.

James made a little, "hmm," of approval in his throat, so I lingered there, painting small circles while he watched my brush move with rapt attention. I gave the opposite breast the same slow treatment.

James leaned back on his elbows. He patted a spot near his hip. "Put your foot right here. I want you to paint your thighs for me."

I propped my foot at his hip, and he sucked in a gasp. "Fuck, I can see how wet you are from here."

I painted down my body, down my hip and to my thighs. I painted the very upper edges of my thighs carefully, stopping just shy of my mound. I painted back and forth, back and forth, from the top of my inner thigh to my knee and back again, teasing him with the movement.

"Are you sore?" he asked, his voice thick.

"Sore how? From the roses?" I asked, painting an idle pattern down my shin, then back up my calf.

"I know you're sore from the roses. I saw the marks on you. I'm talking about inside. Are you too sore for rough fucking?"

"Hmmm. Only one way to find out," I told him.

I moved over him, straddling his thighs, skimming over his quivering erection, finally settling myself against his taut stomach. I traced the brush over one perfect cheek. He tilted his face up to give me better access. I'd thought I'd done the color of his eyes justice, but as I saw the paint set against that tarnished color, I saw that I hadn't even come close. His had little gold flecks around the iris, and his eyes were paler, a paleness that pierced, as though being lighter somehow gave them more substance.

"You have the most beautiful eyes in the world, James."

He hummed in pleasure. He soaked up every little compliment I gave him like a sponge, which always surprised me, since I couldn't imagine that he didn't hear things like that every day.

I painted a thin line down his nose, then along his perfect jawline. I dragged the brush down his neck to his collarbone. I lingered there, enjoying just looking at him. I could never get enough of the sight of his skin, and no matter how much I got, I still felt deprived.

I painted little circles all over his right pectoral muscle, loving the hard and supple play of muscle under his skin.

I leaned forward to kiss the red *Bianca* over his heart before I painted there. As I bent forward, I felt his cock between my ass cheeks and I arched against the hard length, making solid contact. I circled my hips, rubbing my wet sex against his stomach, my butt against his twitching erection.

"When are you going to take me here?" I asked him, grinding back against him. "You said you would take every inch of me."

He grabbed my hips, stilling me to do his own grinding. The tip of him dragged along my lower back as his length moved against my butt.

"Do you want that?" he asked. "I'll hurt you more than I'm willing to if I just ram in with no prep. I plan to make you come so many times that every muscle in your body is relaxed before we try that."

I rubbed against him. "Hmmm. That sounds nice."

He let out a choked laugh. "It won't be nice. It will be a lot of things, but not that."

I moved my brush along his torso. He was so much more fun to paint than I was, with so many more angles, defined lines, and hard ridges. I loved the spot just below his chest, where a deep line defined the spot between his muscle and his ribs. And his abs. *God, his abs.*

My hips made little involuntary circles against him as I moved the brush lower and lower, over the rock hard ridges of his abdomen. I had to move my own body to work lower, and I groaned as I passed over his cock again on my way down. I rose high to rub my wet sex there. I groaned but kept moving to straddle his thighs. I shivered with pleasure when I saw his wet tip.

I painted his hips, and that perfect edible V, stroking my brush just shy of his jutting cock. When I began to paint slow circles on his thighs, brushing up against his scrotum, he snapped.

Hard hands gripped my hips, drawing me abruptly over his member. He let go. "Take me inside you," he rasped.

I worked him into me slowly, enjoying the stretch as I pushed every perfect inch of him deep. A powerful shiver wracked my body when I was finally seated to the hilt.

James took the palette and brush from me, and after dipping the brush, began to paint me with leisurely strokes. The paint on my skin was already beginning to dry, and the wet paint he spread over me dragged deliciously over the first coat.

"Ride me," he ordered.

My body began to move into a posting trot naturally. The exaggerated movements were perfect with his long, thick cock.

"How do your wrists feel?" he asked, moving the brush along a taut nipple.

"Good," I said, my voice low and thick.

He snagged one of the wrists in question, studying it and then bringing it to his lips. "Good."

He bucked against me suddenly, jostling me just enough to make me clench deliciously around him.

He groaned and gripped my hips, unseating me completely and sprawling me onto my back.

He stood above me, leaning down to hook a finger into the ring at my collar. He pulled me up slowly, carefully, until I stood beside him. He gripped my hair, pulling my head back. We watched each other for long moments. I honestly couldn't tell which was driving him tonight, the Dom or my tender lover, there was such a mix of feelings in his eyes.

He broke eye contact to drag me to the window, one hand pulling my hair, the other my collar. He pressed me hard against the window, crushing my breasts against the cold glass. I gasped and shivered.

He pressed my palms to the glass, spread out wide from my body.

"Don't move an inch," he told me, moving away.

I saw him move to a spot on the wall beside the large window, then heard the whir and clank of something grinding metal. That sound made me think of the contraption he had used on me on the fouth floor, when he'd held me suspended to flog, and then fuck. I loved that sound.

I shifted a little, wanting so badly to look around, to see what had made that noise. As it continued and got louder, I realized it was directly above me. It took every ounce of self-control I possessed not to look up.

I felt James move behind me again and then he was lifting my arms. I felt firm padding against one wrist right before the solid click of a handcuff held it captive. He pushed some sort of bar into my palm. “Grip,” he ordered. I gripped the bar tightly. He repeated the process on my other wrist, moving back to that spot on the wall just at the edge of my vision.

I gave a little yelp as the chains began to clank again, drawing me up until I was right on the balls of my feet. I had no leverage in this position, no control whatsoever. My eyes closed as I felt James at my back again. He pushed me hard against the glass. “I’m going to fuck you against the glass, but you don’t get to come until you’re looking into my eyes.”

I whimpered, because I didn’t want to wait, because I was already on that fine edge, ready to come, and because I wouldn’t, not without his permission.

He gripped my hips, tilting them back so that my breasts pressed harder into the glass. My cheekbone stung where it dug into the window, but I just didn’t care.

He drove into me, stopping only halfway inside of me, and I moaned a protest. He worked the rest of the way in slowly, agonizingly, working my hips with his hands to control every inch of me that he penetrated.

He put his mouth to my ear when he hit the end of me, grinding hard. “Now remember, you don’t get to come until I’ve turned you around.”

I had some evil thoughts about the sadistic bastard as he began to pound against me, his hips slapping against my ass with the heavy movements. I could have come, wanted to come, within the first few thrusts, but he didn’t relent, dragging himself out then driving back in with fast thrusts. I cried out against the glass as he moved behind me, against me, inside me.

He didn’t stop, didn’t let up, thrusting relentlessly. I thought my body would betray me and ignore his command, my release building so powerfully that I didn't know how to stop it.

He wrenched out of me, turning me on the chain with surprising ease. It must have been what the thing was designed for.

He gripped my hair in one hand, tilting my head back to look at his eyes straight on. His other hand moved to my ass. He pushed himself inside of me with the smoothest motion. He thrust once, twice, three times, and I was going over the edge.

"Come," he grunted, but I was already lost. I knew my eyes showed my need for him, that vulnerable, raw thing that had become my feelings for him. His eyes were so tender, so loving as they absorbed the look in mine. It was a perfect and terrifying moment of absolute clarity. I'd never go back from this. I would be as lost as Lana if this ended, pining hopelessly for this man, if it all went up in flames.

The thought should have made me want to withdraw from him. My sense of self-preservation had been perfectly healthy before I'd met James, and I wondered now if it had deserted me completely, but as I came back down from my own little slice of heaven, I found it hard to summon up the energy to care.

CHAPTER EIGHT

Mr. Damaged

He unfastened me swiftly, cradling me against him. He laid me on the couch, crawling on top of me. He smiled down into my eyes, his dark golden hair framing his face. He looked like an angel.

"We're going to need a new divan in here. This one is covered in paint," he said softly, but not like he minded.

I shook my head, running a hand along his cheek and into his hair. "No. This room is going to see a lot more painting sessions. I say we leave it."

He smiled, a joyful smile, the most carefree expression I'd ever seen on his perfect face. "I love the sound of that. Have I told you today how happy you make me? I can never go back from this, Bianca. It would break me to let you go. You know that, right?" *Had he read my mind?*

I felt a tear slide down my cheek, then another. What was it about being in love that had turned me into a baby? I didn't know, but I couldn't seem to stop it, whatever it was, no more than I could stop the being in love part. I had fought it every step of the way, but that hadn't helped, not even a little. I had it bad. So bad.

"I wouldn't know how to go back from this, James," I said in a whisper. It was perhaps the closest thing to making a long-term commitment that I'd ever given to him, paltry as it was. But he knew what I'd given him, and he accepted it with such a loving promise in his eyes that I couldn't be sorry for it.

"If you could pick one place in the world that you want to visit, any city, any country, any continent, where would it be?"

I studied him, my brows drawing together as I tried to follow his strange thought process. I didn't even have to think to have my answer, though. "Japan. Especially Tokyo."

He looked a little puzzled. "That was a quick but unexpected answer. Why Japan?"

I gave my little shrug, though it wasn't quite the same with him pinning me to the bed. "It just fascinates me. It always has. And it *is* the home of manga and anime."

He grinned. "Of course. Okay, Japan, especially Tokyo. Got it."

I jabbed a finger into his chest. "Why? What are you planning?"

"Nothing yet, but in a few weeks, maybe a month, I want us to get away for a week or two."

That sounded divine, but... "James, I can't take any more time off work. I used it all up with my...injuries."

He gave me an imploring look.

I caved in a heartbeat.

"You just need to find someone to pick up your shifts, right?" he asked. "You can drop as many as you want, if you find someone else to work them. Stephan explained it to me. Leave it to me. I'll handle everything. Just say you'll go."

I should have said no. I should have told him that yes, I could drop the shifts, but it was really hard to find people to pick them up at straight time, when they could be working overtime for similar shifts, not to mention that if I dropped those shifts, I wouldn't be making any money for those days. I meant to tell him all of that, but instead I looked into his eyes and *just caved.*

"Yes. I can't think of anything I'd love more."

He squeezed me so tightly that I yelped. "Thank you."

He picked me up again, cradling me as he left the studio and carried me to our bedroom. It was on the same floor and close, thank God, because we were both buck naked and covered in blue paint.

He took us directly to the bath, stepping into the deep tub with me as it filled with water.

He washed me slowly but thoroughly, scrubbing the paint where it was caked onto my skin. The bath quickly turned blue. We laughed as it just got darker and darker.

James had to work on us both for a while.

"Want me to help?" I asked, so relaxed that I wasn't sure I could work up the energy to be that helpful.

"No, Love. I want you to relax. When we're done in here, I'm going to take you to the fourth floor and give you a very thorough massage."

"Mmm," I said, closing my eyes. I felt his fingers move between my legs, and I opened them wider. He began to stroke me, humming against my throat as his clever fingers got to work. He pleasured me with his hands while he sucked on just the perfect spot on my neck. It was an almost leisurely orgasm, at least compared to what he usually gave me.

When he continued to thrust his fingers into me even after I'd come, I wiggled. "I want you inside me, James."

He bit my neck, hard. "You'll know when I'm ready to give you my cock because *you'll have it inside of you*," he said, thrusting the cock in question hard against my butt. "In the meantime, open your legs wider."

He worked at me with two fingers thrusting inside, dragging his other hand down my body to rub my clit just so.

"Come," he said into my neck, and I fell again.

We ended up showering after the bath. I had been a little overzealous with the paint apparently, because the bathtub ended up looking like it had been attacked by a paint-gun.

James dried me but left us both nude, pulling me to the elevator by the collar.

I had a thought, fingering his mother's earrings still in my ears, wet hair trailing around them. "Oh, James. I forgot I was wearing your mother's earrings. I didn't mean to get them wet."

He shot me a very doting smile over his shoulder. "They aren't my mother's. They're yours now, and a little water won't hurt them."

He went directly to the elevator, pushing the button. He grinned down at me. "Just pleasure tonight, Love. You need some time to heal from the roses. The fourth floor isn't only about the pain."

"I know," I said softly.

It had always been about more than pain, every bit of it.

He pulled me into the car as it opened, pushing me hard into the wall, pinning me there. "Have you ever been fucked in an elevator?" he asked with a smile.

I laughed. "You know I haven't."

I had thought that he was joking, but of course he wasn't, and he slid a leg between my thighs, pushing them open, and lifting me up. He had me wrapping my legs around his hips and was sliding into me in a flash. He pinned my arms above my head with his hands and began to thrust. I gripped him tightly with my thighs, whimpering as he pulled out of me, dragging along those perfect nerves and drove in again, driving me relentlessly towards another orgasm. He pounded at me, those mesmerizing eyes of his watching me with desperation, and an ardor that made it seem impossible that he'd already taken me less than an hour ago.

"Fucking come," he gritted, his words hard, his tone hard, but his eyes so unbelievably soft on mine.

I obeyed, losing all control at his command. "James," I cried.

He kissed me, not letting me down, not pulling out of me. He let my wrists free to wrap his arms around my back.

He began to walk, but didn't let up kissing me, didn't pull himself out of me. He padded down that ominous gray hallway and into our playground.

He was bending forward at his waist, and abruptly let me fall back.

I gasped. I didn't fall far, my back making contact with a firmly cushioned table. He thrust into me twice roughly before letting himself come with a low groan. "Mine," he said.

I only then realized that I was lying on a massage table as he dragged his thick length out of me, turned me over onto my stomach, and shifted me until my face was over the table's opening.

Within swift moments, he was pouring warm liquid into the center of my back, rubbing the oil firmly into my skin. He massaged up to my neck, rubbing on that sensitive area for long minutes, working over to my shoulders, taking his time, rubbing until each of my muscles had been loosened thoroughly by his strong hands.

He worked down one arm, paying special attention all the way down to each of my fingertips. He worked back up and over, paying equal attention to my other half.

"Your hands are magic," I said to him, my eyes shut in pleasure.

He didn't respond, working on my back, kneading and rubbing that tissue into relaxed submission. He spent extra time on my lower back, working with teasing slowness into my ass. He made a delicious little noise in his throat as he kneaded my butt. I felt a kiss there a scant moment before I felt a finger at that entrance. I gasped and tensed as he pushed a well-lubricated finger into me.

"Shhh, Bianca, relax. Relax." He pulled that sneaky finger out of me, leaving me for too long before coming back. He began the massage where he'd left off, kneading at my butt and upper thighs.

He covered every inch of my back with strong kneading strokes, all the way down to my toes, before he flipped me onto my back. He began the same treatment at the front of my shoulders, taking his time, relaxing every part of me as he worked down. When he reached my sex, he plunged a finger into me. I was wet, of course, and he worked that flesh with sure strokes, using his other hand to part my legs wide, drawing my knees up into my chest. I gasped and tensed as he used his other hand to breach my other entrance again, working a lone finger in slowly, not stopping the smooth strokes at my sex with his other hand.

"You see why you need to be relaxed?" he asked me, leaning close as those wicked hands worked together to bring my overwhelmed body so much pleasure.

I did see; the other penetration more alarmingly intense than I would have guessed. It wasn't even about pain, but more about the oddness of it, the strange fullness in a place where perhaps it shouldn't be, whereas having him fill my sex only ever just felt *right*. Still, I didn't want him to stop, didn't want him to let up. The strangeness gave the act an almost forbidden quality that the perverse part of me relished, as it did all of the taboo things James was attracted to.

Both fingers moved inside of me, working together, and he had me gasping out another orgasm with consummate skill. Before I'd even come down from that blissful trip he was shoving another finger into each entrance, one cleft getting hard thrusts, the other a gentler, easier touch, just working inside and making delicious little circles.

"Relax and push out, yes, like that," James said, jamming the fingers inside of my sex harder and rougher until I came again.

He pulled one set of fingers out, using that hand to shift me back onto my stomach and dragging my hips until my legs hung off the edge of the table. He moved his hips against me from behind, bringing a hand to the front of my neck and applying a light pressure.

"Don't move," he said. I heard him walk away, knew he left the room, heard a door down that daunting hallway open and close, then open again. Short minutes later he was at my back, moving close behind me, parting my legs to get close.

I felt something warm and hard and vibrating brush my clit and I knew it wasn't a part of James.

"James," I protested, as he worked my clit with that too intense pressure.

"Shhh," he said, moving the vibrator from my clit, teasingly over my cleft. He dipped it in once, and then again, holding it inside of me while he worked another well-lubricated, softer object into my other entrance. I knew it wasn't him because it was smaller, and though it was firm, it wasn't hard enough.

"James," I said again, my voice more urgent this time.

He worked the toy into me slowly, the vibrator in my sex still embedded deeply. "Relax.

"It's too—"

"Yes, you want my cock, I know. Relax for this and I'll give you what you want." He growled, and I tried to obey him, tried to relax around those two strange pressures.

I felt like I was just growing accustomed when he pulled it out and replaced it almost immediately with his cock. It was so slick, but also so much bigger than the other. But it was James, and I found that my body submitted much more quickly with that knowledge. He worked in slowly.

He dragged the vibrator out of one entrance even as he pushed himself into the other. I heard a 'thunk' as he dropped it to the floor, bringing his now free hand to the front of me, circling my clit.

He began to thrust when he was nearly in, small thrusts that went a little deeper with each movement, but never pulled all the way out. I whimpered. The feelings were strange, but still not precisely painful, more of a stretching that felt like it went too far.

"James," I cried as his fingers worked and his thrusts got bigger and faster.

"Say it, Bianca," he said into my back, then bit hard enough to leave marks. I thought that the bite was to distract from the fact that he was pounding into me now, and that it did hurt. But pain had never been a deterrent to my own pleasure, and I came, a hard release that left me limp.

"I'm yours, James," I gasped. "Yours."

He emptied himself inside of me, lingering long enough to kiss my back and soothe me before pulling slowly out of me.

He picked me up, cradling me. He carried me down the gray hallway. He slipped into one of those dark, mysterious rooms, and as he turned on the light, I saw that the room closest to the playground was just a large bathroom with an insanely large white tub.

"Since our other tub is blue at the moment, I guess we'll be using this one," he said, a smile in his voice.

I giggled, a little delirious from what felt like a hundred orgasms.

He carried me into the tub, arranged me until I was straddling him, my cheek pillowed against his delicious chest, and started the water.

He stroked my hair and I sighed in pleasure as the hot water slowly covered us. I didn't think I'd ever felt so relaxed, so deliriously content to just lie down and enjoy the moment. I had been restless since I could remember, always having the instincts of a runaway, always anxious that the next moment would bring something bad, and it felt so good to just let that anxious part of me go, and savor something so wonderful.

I was lost in my own thoughts, practically purring against him, when I looked up.

His face was a carefully blank mask.

I stroked his cheek with a hand. "What's wrong, James?" I asked.

He closed his eyes, leaning into my touch. He didn't answer for a long time, but I knew he wasn't ignoring me. I knew as well as anyone that the really rough stuff always took time to form into words.

"That thing we just did—that act, takes my head into a dark place," he said finally, his words so quiet that I had to strain to hear him.

Of the two of us, he was by far better at showing his feelings, but I could tell that it was a struggle for him to share that with me.

I rubbed my hand soothingly over the spot where my name was etched so beautifully. "Will you tell me about it?"

He swallowed hard. "We won't be doing that often, if ever. I don't want to disappoint you. I needed to do it once, needed to claim you like that, but it doesn't take me to a good place. It's like the roses for you, I think, taking me too deeply into the thing that made me like this."

I understood so well just what he meant. We were so alike in the really important ways. I cupped his face in my hands. "I won't be disappointed. I liked what you did, I enjoyed it, but I certainly don't *need* that. You fulfill so many needs that I didn't even understand about myself, and that was *not* one of them. Thank you for showing me, for initiating me into so many things that I find wonderful. Don't ever think that you could disappoint me by telling me your preferences—by telling me no."

He was silent again, and I couldn't tell if my words had reassured him, or if I had even reached him at all. His eyes were faraway and a little glazed over as he stared up at the ceiling.

"Spencer did that to me," he said finally, his voice raw but his eyes still blankly looking up. "It made me feel so helpless, so... worthless. I don't know how to explain it. I know you weren't unwilling, but I just remember how I felt after he would do that, and some part of me feels like I've done something awful to you, something *terrible*, something like what he did to me."

"I knew it would make me feel that way, if not during, then at least after, and I still did it, still managed to enjoy it. I feel... *loathing*, for my weakness, for my need, wondering if it made you feel even an inkling of what I did. It makes me wonder if everything I do to you is a sort of rape—if I'm taking advantage of that beautiful submission that you give to me."

I started to speak, to try to reassure him, but he cut me off. "I know you'll tell me that's not true, and some part of me even knows it, but I still feel it. Like I said, that act just puts me in a dark place."

I cupped his face softly. "I understand. The roses *were* like that for me. They reminded me more of my father than anything you've done, and they terrified me. I felt more pain and more fear on the violent end of those than anything else we've done, but the pleasure was just as great...more so. It made me think of those dark things even as it made me come. I couldn't control my pleasure any more than I could control my fear. *That* terrifies me."

I had to take a few deep breaths before continuing, still finding it hard to be generous with my emotions, and my words, even though *he* had been nothing *but* generous.

"We don't have to face those dark thoughts alone anymore, James. I can't say I've been through what you've been through, but I do understand your self-loathing about a thing you can't control. You admit you've been a slut with your body, but I think you're more well adjusted than I am when it comes to sex. You have a preference, but you can still function without that preference. I have a *fetish*. I wasn't even interested in a man until I found you, until I found *this*. That terrifies me too, how broken I am. But I also know I'm lucky, *so lucky*, to have found someone so perfect for me, so safe, to help give me the things I need without taking my self-respect, and without putting me in danger. You're a gift to someone like me, James. Don't ever forget that."

He pushed my face hard into his damp chest, my chin just skimming the water, but not before I saw the tears in his eyes. "Thank you, Bianca," he said, his voice shaky.

I closed my eyes, my tears sliding slowly down my cheeks and onto his chest.

"Thank *you*, James," I said, my voice thick.

Nevada Public Library

CHAPTER NINE

Mr. Wonderful

I was waking up slowly, alone in a giant bed, when I heard the door of the bedroom open. I opened my eyes to a grinning Stephan.

He climbed onto the bed beside me, perching his chin on his palm as he looked down at me.

I reached a hand up, stroking his wavy blond hair. "Mornin'," I said, my voice still rough from sleep.

"Morning, Buttercup. Javier is out cold, James has left for work, and we are having breakfast in your new, giant-ass bed. Marion is bringing it up when it's ready."

I smiled. "That's sweet. What a nice way to wake up."

"Don't you want to know what's for breakfast?"

I gave him my little shrug. "I don't really care. The company is so good, the food is kind of secondary."

We shared a look.

"It always was," he said. "Remember when the food used to be nonexistent?"

I laughed and nodded, thinking about what a wonder it was that something that was once such a painful struggle could become just a memory—a memory that gave me nothing but relief that we were past it.

"Remember when we lived in that ditch by that grocery store for a month?"

I smiled, again surprised to feel nothing but comforted in the knowledge that that distant time was past. "I do. I remember that we thought we were lucky then, because we didn't starve there, and no one bothered us, and you didn't even have to fight, for a while."

"Are you going to keep your house now that you're living with James?" he asked, his voice just curious, though I couldn't imagine that it was an idle question.

"Of course I am. I'll still be staying there, too."

"Don't keep the house just for me, Bianca. Don't do it just because of our old plans. You won't be homeless again, even if things don't work out with James. You don't need to keep that place to have a sense of security. Life won't be like that again. We can't live our lives always thinking that it will—always bracing for it. And commitment for you won't be what it was for your mother, because James isn't your father. You can't keep comparing them, and you can't keep treating a good thing like a potential disaster. That's no kind of life. "

I listened without comment, taking the lecture in the way he intended it. It was a Stephan pep talk, and I didn't take offense. "I'm working on it, Steph, I really am. I'm facing it and dealing with it, and I'm not running away."

"So things are good with you two? You're still planning to live with him?"

I laughed. "Why? Do you think I changed my mind already?"

He shrugged. "I don't know. I guess I was afraid that you got all wrapped up in him, and that, in the light of day, you'd panic about what you'd agreed to and change your mind."

"Well, I haven't, not yet anyway. That's got to be a good sign, right?"

He just nodded, smiling.

Marion arrived with breakfast and we ate blueberry waffles in bed and laughed and caught up on every little detail of each other's lives. We usually didn't need to update each other, since we were so used to being constant companions, but this was nice, too. He told me how crazy he was about Javier, and I told him how crazy James and I were in general. It was a good talk, and I realized that even if I didn't see Stephan every *single* day, he could still be my rock. I hoped he could draw even a fraction of the comfort from me that I did from him.

"Javier and I are meeting up with one of the crews tonight, if you guys want to join us. I know you have that photo shoot, but I thought I'd tell you."

I nodded. "Thanks. I'm not sure what the plan is, but I'll tell James. Do I know the crew?"

He grimaced. "Vance and company. Not sure it's the best idea, but I'm trying to play nice."

I grimaced right back. Vance was an ex of Javier's, and neither he nor the rest of the crew were huge Stephan fans. I had always personally thought that was because Vance was still hung up on Javier. "That's nice of you. Hopefully they try to play nice, too."

"Javier swears they'll be well-behaved."

I nodded, hoping it worked out that way, though ex situations never tended to be so simple. What looked good on paper got real messy when emotions factored in. I had come to learn that fact all too well lately.

I told him about my brother and he was a little shocked that I was going to meet with him. I shrugged when he asked me why. "He sounded...nice. Nothing like my father. What could it hurt to meet for coffee sometime?"

"I think it's a good idea, but I think you should be cautious. Can I go with you?"

I waved him off. "It will be a strange, awkward meeting. I'll take security, though, so you don't need to worry about me."

He nodded, but he still looked a little worried.

We were both laughing hard as Stephan told me a story from the night before. They had been so excited to get their own driver that they'd gone from club to club, not staying more than twenty minutes at any of them before moving on, enjoying the car and driver even more than the clubbing. My phone rang from the bedside table.

I answered with a laugh still on my lips.

It was James. "Ah now, there's a sound that I love to hear. How are you this morning, my love?"

"Mmm, good. How are you?"

"Better now. It's been a...rough morning. What are you doing?"

I glanced around at my rather strange surroundings. "I'm having breakfast in our ridiculously huge bed with Stephan," I told him bluntly. No reason to prevaricate.

There was a long pause on the other end of the line. Stephan had fallen silent, giving me wide eyes. I noticed for the first time that he wore only boxers and a smile, and I wore nothing but a sheet. It occurred to me, rather belatedly, that our breakfast in bed could look bad to an outside observer.

"I have to say, if you had said any other name in that sentence, I'd be on the verge of murder."

I laughed. I heard the nervous tenor of it. I felt strangely tense to hear his reaction.

"Tell Stephan I said good morning," he said, his voice neutral.

I told him.

Stephan smiled. "Morning, James," he called loud enough to be heard on the other end.

"Give him the phone," James said into my ear.

I handed Stephan the phone.

I watched him warily but relaxed completely when Stephan began to laugh almost the instant that he put the phone to his ear.

"My pleasure, James," he said, still laughing. He handed me

the phone.

I held it to my ear.

"I have to go, but we have the photo shoot at three this afternoon," he said. "Do you mind coming by my office before we go? Say, two thirty?"

"I'll be there," I told him. "What did you say to Stephan?" I asked. I couldn't help it. Their exchange had just been too quick and strange.

"I told him that next I'm buying him a house next door to mine for making you laugh like that. There's nothing I wouldn't do to hear that joy in your voice, even if I'm not the one to put it there."

My chest hurt a little. I struggled to find the words to respond. He was so terribly romantic, in a heart-wrenching kind of way. "You do put it there, James. I'm not good with the words, but just knowing you makes me feel privileged."

He made a happy little hum of a noise into my ear. "There you go, making my day again."

Words caught in my throat. I didn't even know how to respond.

"I'll see you at two thirty. Take care, Bianca," he said softly, sounding just a touch sad.

"I'll be there," I told him.

He hung up.

Stephan gave me a pointed look. "If you don't know that he's completely in love with you, it's only because you have commitment issues, and you are flat-out lying to yourself."

I knew he had a point. Pretending that he didn't return my feelings in some way was only my way of buying time. *Time for what?* I didn't know. It was swiftly getting to the point that I didn't even want to resist him. Perhaps it was just me trying to slow down Mr. Cavendish's runaway train of a personality. One thing I knew for sure, though. I would do a lot to keep him in my life now. For better or worse, he was becoming essential to me.

"You worry that the S&M stuff makes you a victim of your childhood, but it doesn't, Bee," Stephan said.

I swallowed and he caught my hand, pulling me close, making me look at his eyes, showing me how serious he was. "But if you run from what you feel for James, if you would rather *lose him* than open up enough to tell him how you feel, it just may. I get that you have doubts, but I just want you to look at those doubts and tell me if they have *anything* to do with James, with the person that you know he is, and the way he feels about you."

If it had been anyone else in the world holding me and lecturing me and speaking to me this way, I would have run, or withdrawn, or lashed out, but Stephan saying these things in such a serious tone, knowing that it might make me mad, knowing that I wouldn't like what he was saying, but feeling the need to say it anyway, had a completely different effect on me. With Stephan, I just listened and tried to find the true answer.

"You're right," I told him finally. The way I felt wasn't going away, and not looking at it directly was just another way I'd been a coward. "You're absolutely right about all of it. I do need to tell him. He's been wonderful to me, and I owe him the truth. It's just the next step that scares me...and also, just how short a time I've known him. I feel like real love should take time, or at least, more time than this. I've been trying to make my head rule my actions, when my heart has so obviously taken over, but I feel how I feel, and I know it's not going away."

"Quit over-thinking it. Just tell him how you feel. It doesn't have to be so complicated."

I nodded. "You're right. I've been doing that from the start, and he's only tried to be close to me, to show me how he feels for me. I owe him my own emotional honesty."

He stroked my hair, smiling at me in that way he had, like I was the most wonderful thing in the world—like I was family. I hoped my eyes communicated the same thing, because my heart felt it. "Yes. That's all. I'm done with the lecture. I just thought you needed a little poke in the right direction. I don't want to see you throw away something that makes you so... incandescent with love."

I blushed down to my toes, because he was right, and because I'd done a dismal job of hiding it. James did that to me. He was so wonderful that I just couldn't help it. *And didn't something so wonderful deserve a little leap of faith?* Did I really need time to reaffirm something that I felt on such a profound level? My heart already knew the answer.

I clutched Stephan's hand. "I love you. I have no idea what I would do without you."

He nodded, smiling, his eyes so soft. "I love you. There is nothing I wouldn't do for you, but I *can't* hold you back. We don't have to be neighbors to be best friends, just like we didn't have to live together. This move will be no different than that. We're growing up, Bianca, but we will *never* grow apart. I know you too well, and I know that's part of what is holding you back, so just get that fear out of your head. You're stuck with me *forever*."

CHAPTER TEN

Mr. Supermodel

It took me an unusually long time to get ready. I tried on a good number of outfits, making Stephan give me his opinion about everything, and changing my mind several times. It was a strange role reversal for us. Something about going to my supermodel boyfriend's photo shoot made me want to look my best, apparently.

I finally settled on a little yellow Betsy Johnson dress. It was a little fussy for me, with a flared skirt, fitted bodice, and a bit of cleavage, but when I put it on I just felt sexy and cute, and I needed an extra boost of confidence for the intimidating shoot. Shiny red heels completed the ensemble, and I secretly loved Jackie's flair for outrageous color pairings.

I spent extra time on my hair, blow-drying and then smoothing it out, and even took my usual sparse makeup routine up a notch, with a dusky pink lip, a deep violet shadow on my lids, and a darker color lining my eyes.

I did a little twirl for Stephan when I was done, and he gave me an approving smile.

"Most beautiful woman in the world," he said, and I knew he meant it, because in his eyes, I really was.

I was actually running early as he walked me out. We said

goodbye at the elevator.

Blake was already waiting for me there, looking as severe as ever.

"Be sure to notify security when you want to leave the apartment, Ms. Karlsson," Blake said chidingly.

I had forgotten. I realized that she must have just been waiting at the elevator, trying to anticipate my actions.

"Sorry," I mumbled, feeling like a child whenever I dealt with her, which didn't endear her to me at all. But I saw where I had erred this time. "I'll call next time I'm leaving, so no one has to wait around for no reason."

She just nodded like she didn't believe me, and then fell awkwardly silent.

My security detail hadn't changed, rather it had been reconfigured so that Johnny was the furthest from me at all times. I found this both ridiculous and a bit of a relief, since he'd hardly endeared himself to me on our short acquaintance.

We took a limo, Williams and Johnny sitting up front, and Blake and Henry taking seats with me in the spacious cabin of the car. We arrived at the hotel early, waiting at the curb, no one saying a word. I watched the building carefully for James.

When I spotted his beautiful suit-clad figure emerging briskly from the front entrance of the hotel, my heart did a mean little flip in my chest.

People stopped and stared even in the short time it took him to pass quickly from the building to the car. He was just so arresting, so impossibly stunning. It had to be a shock just to see a vision like that on the street. He certainly had my attention.

He was in the cab beside me in a flash and his eyes were so soft when they fell on me that I felt like I was melting as I looked at him. His face had changed so drastically at just the sight of me that I felt like my heart had warmed in my chest.

He gripped a hand into my hair, leaning close to me,

obviously conscious of the fact that we weren't alone. He kissed my cheek. "God, did I miss you, Love. Is thirty too young to retire from working? I'd love to just make love to you full-time, instead." He spoke softly, and by the last sentence, his voice was only a whisper into my ear.

I smiled at him, gripping a hand over his in my hair, pulling that hand to my face, and kissing his palm softly. "You're thirty?" I asked him, surprised. I'd just always assumed he was younger. I would have sworn I'd heard that he was in his twenties. And he didn't look thirty to me, though it wasn't as though he acted young. He did carry the heavy weight of countless responsibilities with unconscious ease on those elegant shoulders.

He nodded, those soft, tarnished eyes smiling at me. "Just had a birthday a few weeks ago. You thought I was younger?"

I nodded, unable to deny it. But I was suddenly distracted by what he'd said, and what it meant. "I missed your birthday?" I asked, feeling just awful with guilt.

He bit his lip, and for some reason it made me want to cry. He seemed worlds more vulnerable suddenly. "Yes. That was a rough couple of days, though you did text me on my birthday, and that helped."

I was horrified as a tear slipped down my cheek, but I couldn't seem to help it. "I didn't know," I whispered, leaning close. "I feel terrible. How can I make it up to you?"

He traced that tear down my face with a sad smile on his. "Don't miss another one. Not *ever.* That would more than make up for it."

I shook my head. "I wouldn't know what to get you—what you would want, but I have to do something for you."

He grinned suddenly, his pretty mouth wicked but his eyes still so tender. "There's a picture I want you to paint for me. That would be a wonderful gift. But that won't cancel out the other thing I mentioned. You don't get to miss any more of my birthdays."

I nodded, agreeing with him, even knowing that it was insane.

His brows shot up in genuine surprise. "Just like that, you agree? You understand that I'm asking for a long-term commitment from you when I say that?"

I nodded again, and his eyes went wild for the barest second before they became shuttered and he buried his face in my neck. I understood his actions perfectly. I wouldn't want anyone to see me in such a raw moment, either.

"You mean it?" he whispered.

I was a little shocked at *his* shock. I had already agreed to live with him, after all. I wanted right then to tell him that I loved him, to reassure him, to express myself with more freedom, but the four other people in the car made me hold my tongue about the deepest of what I wanted to say.

"I do mean it, James. I want so much for this to last—for us to stay together. I'm desperate for it." My voice was the barest whisper as I spoke into his ear.

He clutched me to him tightly, his mouth at my ear. "I'm desperate for it too. I'm willing to fight for it, Bianca, willing to fight for us, because it *will* be a fight sometimes. The life I lead can be overwhelming, and the press can be relentless. Can you swear that no matter what they throw at us, you'll stay at my side?"

I tensed at his words, suddenly apprehensive that he was referring to some undefined threat in the future, something worse than anything we'd been through before. I didn't know if it was my imagination—if I was just so used to expecting the worst, or if I could read a strange thread of fear in his voice, but I was suddenly filled with my own fear.

"I promise to try," I told him finally.

"Thank you," he murmured softly.

He pulled away, looking resolutely out the window, clutching my hand, and I could tell by his demeanor that he was trying to regain his composure. I got it. I did my own window staring as I tried to regain my own customary calm façade.

We reached our destination quickly, disembarking from the car slowly, the security stepping out first, and then flanking us. The whole process still felt surreal to me, but as James gripped a warm hand on my nape, I thought that I could grow used to anything, with him at my side.

The entire photo shoot episode felt strange to me. I knew from the second we walked in the door that I was out of place. I had dressed the part of the billionaire's girlfriend, but it just wasn't me, and I felt a little uncomfortable in my own skin as they swept James off to prep for the photo, and I was expected to just stand around and wait.

Everyone was polite enough, asking me if I needed anything, finding me the best spot to sit and watch the shoot, but it all just made me more self-conscious. I was quickly hiding behind my calmest, blankest expression, and I was all nerves on the inside.

The security wasn't helping, of course, looking severe and intimidating as they positioned themselves around me and stared down the room. I finally resorted to playing on my phone. I saw a missed text from Stephan and clicked on it immediately.

Stephan: I think meeting up with these guys was a bad idea. They are openly hostile and I'm not sure why.

Bianca: Vance is hung up on Javier, I think. I've always gotten that vibe. Is there anything I can do to help? Want me to come there for moral support?

I felt my face heat up in agitation at even the thought of

someone being mean to Stephan. He was a very strong man—a very strong person, but I still couldn't bear the thought.

Stephan: Nah, it's not that serious, B. I'll prolly just duck out ahead of schedule. I would like to hang out when u r done there, so give me a holler.

Bianca: Of course. You name the time and place, and I'll be there. Always.

Stephan: Your swank pad, as soon as you're done watching your supermodel get photographed.

Bianca: You got it. Love you.

Stephan: Love you, B.

I felt a strong urge to ignore what he said and just go and find him and make sure he was okay, but I stifled it. Stephan was usually very good at telling me just what he needed from me, and if he said that it wasn't that serious—that he just wanted to hang out when he was done, then that was what he wanted, and that's what I would do.

I was still stewing about it when James emerged from the changing area. My jaw went a little slack and my mind went completely blank.

He was wearing pale gray slacks and a bright white tie. And that was all. His chest and even his feet were bare, his skin dark and golden against the pale fabric of the tie. His chest was oiled and the sight of it literally made my mouth water. His pants were ridiculously low-slung for dress slacks, which meant they were from wardrobe, and not his. I couldn't imagine him wearing a suit to work that didn't fit just perfectly, and those pants looked in danger of falling off, and showing his most delectable parts to the room.

I swallowed hard as he strode to me, watching that V above his waistband move distractingly with stark muscles.

He drew close.

"Hello, Mr. Beautiful," I said, my voice very soft. It just sort of slipped out.

"You shouldn't look at me like that right now, Bianca," he said with a fond smile. "Not unless you want a lot of magazine subscribers to get a really clear picture of my hard-on."

I nodded. He had a very good point, but I still couldn't stop looking at him. His chest had the finest sheen of oil on it.

I touched it with a finger.

He grabbed my hand. "Now, now," he said, but there was still a smile in his voice.

I made myself look at his face. Of course, that view was just as distracting. Someone had tied his hair back from his face. His hair looked darker like that, all of the highlights hidden away.

I clenched my fists to keep from touching him. I was finding it so difficult to keep my hands to myself lately. It was a strange new development for me, when I'd almost always found touching and being touched to be anathema.

I cleared my throat. "You look…" *Delectable. Edible. Mouth-watering.* "Very nice."

"Thank you." He cleared his throat. "Hopefully I can get this finished quickly."

He strode away before I could respond, moving towards where they were setting up the shoot.

I observed the whole process very much as an outsider looking in. An obsessed, infatuated, outsider looking in. But going by the similar, glassy-eyed female stares I noted wherever I glanced, I wasn't the only one.

One lucky woman got the task of showing him where to stand and what to do. I didn't miss the fact that she used every excuse to touch him. *Could I blame her?* Yes. But I found that I wasn't even the slightest bit jealous. How could I be when James tried to withdraw from every touch? He was professional but very cool with the woman.

The woman was almost too thin, but still indisputably attractive, with dark hair and eyes, and Hollywood lips. She could have been anywhere from thirty to forty-five. It didn't matter on her. Youth or the lack thereof was not where her beauty lay. Still, I didn't feel even a stirring of insecurity as she put her hands on him. Instead, I almost pitied the awkward position he found himself in. He shot me occasional, uncomfortable glances as she handled him, as though he were more afraid of upsetting me than he was concerned about doing the shoot. It made me flush a little every time he did it, though those were the only looks he was sparing me.

The woman backed away from him finally, and the shoot began. When she began to call out orders to the crew, I realized that she must be the director. By the way she'd been acting, I'd assumed she was some sort of star-struck assistant. I supposed I knew better than anyone how Mr. Beautiful could turn even the most stoic woman into a love-struck fool.

Every move that he made suddenly became extra fascinating, and it had always been pretty damned fascinating to me. He didn't smile, just moved his face by infinitesimal degrees, this way and that way, catching every perfect angle for the various shots.

His hands started at his hips but moved up to lace behind his head, drawing his abs taut and making his arms bulge in the most appealing way. It might have just been me, but his tie seemed to be pointing suggestively down, and I couldn't help but notice how the pose stretched the *Bianca* on his chest, displaying it like a prize. It made me smile. He *was* insane, but that was becoming just another thing that I adored about him. It was also becoming apparent that I only had a passing relationship with sanity myself.

They took shot after shot as he shifted around at the director's command. She called a halt maybe ten minutes in.

"Annie, get me some suspenders!" she barked.

A small blonde woman scurried back into wardrobe.

The two women were swiftly attaching suspenders to his low-slung slacks, which seemed wholly unnecessary, and very unprofessional to me, but what did I know? They resumed the shot quickly.

James had to pull one suspender to the side to show off his red ink, but no one stopped him.

I could see why they'd added the suspenders, though I'd thought it was a strange thing to do. It was sexy. Like insane sex on horseback sexy. Something about the business attire set against his tan oiled chest was obscene, bordering on mind-blowing orgasm just looking at him, sexy.

They took endless pictures of his every shift in posture and expression. Eventually they made him turn, taking shot after shot of his ripped back. He shrugged out of one errant suspender to show off the tattoo on his back.

I shifted closer to study it, still feeling a little shell-shocked every time I caught a glimpse of my face on his back. I knew from hearing several friends talk about it that tattoos scabbed over at first, sometimes marring the ink for weeks, but I could see no sign of that yet on this one. It seemed perfect, still looking like a painting on his back.

I still thought the tattoo was insane, though I was beginning to understand why he'd done it.

He was committed to me, for whatever crazy reason, and I was so closed off that he hadn't been able to just come out and say it, and have me believe him. I was too damaged, too skeptical of everything good in life. This had been his bat-shit crazy way of trying to prove it to me. He was so like Stephan in that way, so willing to throw all pride aside for the sake of loving me. I knew in my soul that there was nothing Stephan wouldn't do for me, and I was beginning to see that James had that same startling quality. What had I done to deserve such devoted men in my life? I couldn't fathom it. It all just seemed to be good to be true.

CHAPTER ELEVEN

Mr. Gorgeous

After an exhaustive amount of posing, James was led off to change into another outfit for the shoot. I couldn't imagine why. I'd seen the shoot. There was no way they hadn't gotten a good string of pictures out of it.

The director approached me as James disappeared into the dressing area. She smiled at me. It was a polished, professional kind of smile. I wondered if she'd been a model before she'd directed photo shoots.

She waved a hand at her own chest. "So I take it you're this Bianca?" she asked, and I realized she was referencing the tattoo she'd just been staring at for an hour.

I nodded, not really sure how to respond.

She held out a hand. "I'm Beatrice Stoker. I'm the director."

I shook her hand, and she squeezed hard, like it was some kind of a test. I gave her a half-hearted response, not interested in whatever way she thought she was testing me with such a strange action.

"Bianca," I told her, even though she obviously knew that.

"You are one lucky lady, Bianca," she said. Something a little too familiar about her tone raised my hackles just a bit.

I gave her very solid eye contact. "I'm very well aware of that.

Trust me when I say that you can't even imagine how lucky."

She blinked, but didn't seem at all put off by my awkward statement. I didn't know what made me want to goad her, but more and more, I seemed to be having a hard time holding my tongue.

"Well, good for you," she finally said. "About that, with Mr. Cavendish's new tattoos being devoted to you and all, I had an idea for the shoot, if you don't object."

"Object to what?" I asked suspiciously.

She smiled that polished smile. "If you wouldn't mind going through the hassle of hair, makeup, and wardrobe, I'd love to have you involved in some of the shots. More as an accessory to James than as a focal point, if you get my meaning."

I didn't. "You want me to be *in* the photo?" I asked, baffled. It was something I'd never expected.

"Well, he's showing off tattoos that are obviously in your honor, so I thought it would be nice to squeeze you into a few shots. Nothing much. I'd just like to have you maybe hug him from behind, something very innocent and low-key. He's been shirtless on our covers several times, sans tats. I thought it might be nice to show the reader what's inspired his new passion for ink."

I grimaced, uncomfortable with the idea. "You'd have to ask James. This is his thing."

She nodded and strode off with a purpose, and I felt a little like I'd just thrown him to the wolves.

Sure enough, James strode out of the dressing room scant moments later, moving to me in swift strides, his brow furrowed. He was in a new mouthwatering getup with pale beige slacks, a bare golden chest, and the softest looking beige scarf I'd ever seen in my life wrapped around his neck until it formed a sort of X-rated cowl.

"What do you think of this idea?" he asked me quietly.

I shrugged, not sure *what* to think, and having a hard time focusing on anything but what I wanted him to do to me with that scarf.

"My first inclination was to say fuck no, I don't want you exposed like that, but my need to shelter you from the world is obviously a moot point. They've gotten a look at you, so I think we should let them look at you on our terms, if that makes sense. So I guess what I'm saying is that, yes, I would like you to be involved with the shoot, if you're comfortable with that."

He sounded almost defensive as he mapped out his reasonings to me. It was so unusual for him to be defensive that I was a little taken aback. He looked so worked up in fact, that I decided to just put him out of his misery.

"Fine, I'll do it," I said quietly. It was a fact that there were already too many horrible pictures of me out there to even keep track of, so what would one not so horrible picture hurt?

He seemed stunned, and not altogether pleased, which I found rather perverse of him, but he just nodded.

After that, it felt like a whirlwind of activity as I had my hair, makeup, and nails done.

The dressing room was a total fiasco. There was just no other way to look at it. The wardrobe people, used to working with professionals, and hardly used to dealing with unreasonably jealous boyfriends, tried to go about business as usual.

Someone started to lift my skirt up and I just sort of yelped, surprised. I turned to look at the girl behind me. She was giving me an impatient look, just doing her job. And then there was James...

"Don't touch her," he told the poor girl, his tone bordering on mean. I hadn't appreciated her familiarity, but I felt a strong stirring of pity at the crushed look on her face. He addressed the room at large. "Everyone out. She does not need an audience. Only one *female* dresser gets to stay."

That one lucky female dresser looked like she'd just drawn

the short straw as she rifled through clothes. She was the little blonde assistant that had been helping with the shoot. She pulled out a pair of jeans and gave me a dubious look. "I don't suppose you'd agree to go topless? Everything would be covered, of course—"

"Out of the question," James said. He sounded real putout about it, too.

She sighed, no more happy than he was about the whole situation. "Maybe I should just let *you* choose her wardrobe. Only her hands and maybe the top of her head will be showing, so it doesn't really matter, and you're obviously going to have an opinion about it."

I thought she'd been sarcastic when she told him to choose, but he took her at her word, rifling through the racks of clothes with a purpose.

James didn't waste any time choosing, at least. I rolled my eyes but had to smile as I saw what he'd chosen.

The stylist actually seemed pleased with his choices. "Ohh, that's a nice idea. That would be a good way to have her compliment the shot."

"She doesn't need help dressing, but she does need privacy," James said bluntly.

The stylist shot him an unfriendly look, but left in a hurry.

I studied James, half-expecting him to pounce on me. It was a natural assumption. We were alone now, and when we were alone...

He didn't though, just started acting like he was dressing me. I didn't need help dressing, but I knew that wasn't the point. He wanted to do this, needed to do this. If I tried to analyze him, as I seemed to do with everything, I thought he did this because he loved to feel like he was taking care of me. He, being as much of a relationship novice as myself, thought that this was what couples did, something that made them closer. I was pretty positive that not many couples did do it, but odd as it was, it did make me feel closer to him, and more cherished.

He dressed me in beige slacks and a soft, knit, beige tank top that was nearly a match to his scarf. I fingered that scarf when it got within my reach.

He gave me a hot look. "I'm keeping the scarf. I have plans."

"Of course you do," I murmured back.

His eyes narrowed on me. "That look in your eyes is going to get you in trouble."

I just stared at him, letting that 'look' do its worst.

He grinned. "Lucky for us both, you like to get into trouble."

I felt my insides clench in a very good way, sure that meant he was going to do something, like now, but he just finished dressing me and stepped back.

"Wear the same red heels," he said. I stepped into them, and he tugged me back out into the studio.

The shoot was both less and more awkward than I'd anticipated. On my end, posing was a breeze. All I had to do was stand behind him, arms wrapped around his middle, hands on his chest and abs. I tried not to let those hands wander, or caress, but it was a struggle. My face wasn't really even visible, just the top of my head and my eyes peeking over his shoulder when I wasn't laying my cheek against his lovely back. Posing was easy. Not getting wildly turned on was the hard part. I managed that part better than James, though that was only because *his* part was harder to control in general.

The director cleared her throat just a few shots in. "Um, so, is there anything you can do about that, Mr. Cavendish? This is not an X-rated publication..."

James, shameless bastard that he was, seemed completely unfazed. "You'll just need to shoot me waist up. You were the one who wanted my girlfriend in the shot, putting her hands on me. What did you think was going to happen?"

"If we could shoot just waist up, that might *not* be a problem, but it seems to be a...bigger problem than that."

I felt him shrug against my cheek and I just lost it. I started giggling and I couldn't stop for a solid five minutes.

James turned around until our fronts were pressed together. He was smiling at me, laughter in his eyes. "I can't think of a sound that I love to hear more than that one."

It went better after I got that long giggling fit out of my system. James seemed to get a better handle on things as well, and they shot his back and front while I leaned against him. They stopped briefly to fix his hair, letting it hang loose, then tying it back again. The whole thing seemed kind of silly and frivolous to me, but what did I know about photo shoots? And I couldn't say that I didn't enjoy myself. Just the opposite; once I shook the nerves off, I had a really good time.

They did one more wardrobe change for James, and I was left out of that one. I didn't mind.

They put him in nothing but low-slung athletic shorts and some running shoes. They didn't give him socks, which seemed pretty impractical, but he did have sexy ankles, so I got why they'd done it.

They braided the longer pieces of his hair back, which I thought was weird, but it worked on him. He looked gorgeous, as usual.

They went through the standard poses that he'd been doing, then moved on to some action shots. These I watched with renewed fascination. They had him jump impressively high, do some push-ups, and then pull-ups. I had to contain a little smirk when they made him do curls.

He used more expression for these shots, even grinning into the camera for some of them. He hardly needed direction, going about the whole process like I imagined a professional model would.

Someone brought me a turkey sandwich, and I thanked them. I ate the entire thing, not taking my eyes off James for a second.

They took a few breaks to do what I thought was some very unnecessary oiling down. He tried to brush off the two women swarming him, shooting me a very uncomfortable look. I thought I read the look perfectly. He was worried I'd be upset at all of the hands trying to touch him, and he wanted it to stop.

They finally relented, but still insisted on doing his back. His jaw was clenched, and he looked positively agitated by the time they finished. I watched with no expression on my face, though I only felt the slightest twinge of annoyance. If I had been inclined to get upset about all of the touching, his reaction would have quickly cured me. He was far more upset about it than I was.

He approached me to chat during one of the short breaks, and one of the many assistants approached us, a sheepish look on her face. I saw that she was holding a rolled up magazine.

She unrolled it and held it out to him when she got close, a black permanent marker in her other hand. "Sorry to bug you, but would you mind signing this?" she asked.

James took the magazine without hesitation, signing the cover. I froze when I saw it. It was a picture him and Jules. I knew by their clothes that it was from the night I'd run from his apartment. He saw my expression as he handed the magazine back to the girl.

"Thanks so much," she muttered, quickly moving away. She knew not to press her luck, I thought.

"You look upset," James said quietly, studying me.

I gave him my little shrug, not wanting to talk about, but also not knowing if I could keep my mouth shut about it.

"That night," I said finally, when he just kept watching me. "I know you said it wasn't a date, but it hurt that you still went with her to that gala, after all that had happened.

His eyes widened. "No," he said softly. "I didn't. I wouldn't. I went to that gala for thirty minutes, because I felt obligated to, for my mother's sake. But I was miserable, *and I went alone.*

Those pictures were typical Jules, crashing my obligatory press photos. The only time I even spoke to her was to tell her to leave me the hell alone. I swear it, Bianca. Once I saw how you felt, I wouldn't have done that."

I felt weak with relief. I hadn't even known I was that bothered by it.

While I was humiliating myself, though, I had to clear it all up. "That collar she wore that night... Did you give it to her?"

He shook his head. "I've never given her a piece of jewelry."

"She noticed my collar, and she implied that her own choker was something similar..."

He flushed. His hand made a cutting motion through the air. "She's preoccupied with my personal life, and she's a *liar*. I'm sorry you were bothered by this, but she was manipulating you. I didn't give her that."

I just nodded to show him that I'd heard him. They were already waving him back for the shoot.

"Are you okay? Do you have any other questions?"

I shook my head, meeting his gaze to show him I was fine. Reluctantly, he went back to finish up.

When all was said and done, the entire photo shoot took nearly four hours. I was surprised to notice what time it was when I checked my phone.

James was in the back changing as I saw that I'd missed several texts from Stephan.

Stephan: B, will you call me when you can?

Stephan: I'm heading back to the apartment. Please let me know when you're free. I don't want to be alone right now.

A little shiver of dread ran down my spine, and I felt instantly guilty for forgetting about my phone yet again. I tried to call him five times in a row, my heart pounding into overdrive when he didn't answer.

His text about not wanting to be alone had really gotten to me. He shouldn't have to be alone, not ever, not while I still breathed, because that was just how it worked with us, but he was obviously alone and hurting, and I needed to get to him.

I tried texting him, though I knew it was pointless if he wasn't even answering his phone.

Bianca: Just saw your messages. Coming back to the apartment as fast as I can get there. Please tell me u r okay.

James was striding towards me when I looked up from my phone. He must have seen something on my face because his changed from smiling to alarmed between one step and the next.

"What is it?" he asked me quietly when he drew close.

"It's Stephan. I need to get back to the apartment. He's upset about something and he needs me."

He nodded, shooting a quick glance to a spot behind me. He took my elbow and began to lead me out of the studio without further ado.

"Wait, Mr. Cavendish," the director was saying. "We just need to conduct the interview portion. It won't take more than thirty minutes."

He didn't even slow down. "Email the questions to me. We have some urgent business to attend to," he said brusquely.

She didn't protest. I doubted many would when he used such

a Mr. Cavendish tone.

He wasted no time getting us into the car and traveling swiftly back to the apartment.

"Thank you," I told him, my voice pitched very low, always conscious of the other people in the car. "I can't bear the thought of him being alone and upset."

He nodded and stroked a hand over my hair. "I know. We'll be home in just a few minutes. Do you have any idea what happened?"

I gave my little shrug. "He and Javier were going out with some other flight attendants tonight. It was a crew that was friends with Javier, but not with Stephan. Something must have happened with them. He mentioned earlier that they were being openly hostile. I should have gone to him then. I feel terrible."

"Did he ask you to come then?"

"No, but—"

"Did he ask you to come now?" he asked.

"Yes, but that was almost an hour ago—"

"Quit beating yourself up. You know Stephan wouldn't. We're going to him now, and everything will be fine."

CHAPTER TWELVE

Mr. Understanding

I rushed into the apartment the second the elevator opened, moving towards the room the guys had been staying in. James was a silent presence—keeping pace at my back.

I only knew I was heading in the right direction by the raised voice echoing down the long hallway. I broke into a run.

Javier was yelling, his voice harsh and angry. It was so uncharacteristic for him that I stopped in the open doorway to their room.

"We *will* talk about it now," Javier was saying in an awful voice. He was standing directly in front of Stephan, close enough to shout into his face. His tone and his demeanor instantly sparked my rare temper, but *he* wasn't what made me lose it.

Stephan stood with his arms crossed in front of him, looking at the floor, his posture defeated. He had withdrawn from the confrontation, gone into that dark place in his mind where his family abused him and deserted him without looking back. I knew it at a glance. Something horrible had happened between the two men, something so bad that Stephan had checked out, and everything that Javier was doing was just making him go further into that dark place. *That* was what made me lose it.

I was moving to Stephan before my brain fully processed what was even going on, as though my body knew what to do before my brain did. I moved between the two men, and into Stephan, burying my face in his chest, my arms wrapping tight around his ribs.

He gasped as though he'd been holding his breath, hugging me back. Those were his only reactions. His face and posture didn't change other than that. I knew it was a bad sign.

I turned my face just enough to glare at Javier. "You need to give him some space. Now."

Javier pointed at me, growing visibly more furious. "*This* is the problem with you two. How the *fuck* is anyone supposed to get close to either of you, to have any kind of a relationship with you, when you only care about each other, only *trust* each other?!"

Javier had a rare but memorable temper. He was a clear-headed, sweet guy ninety-nine percent of the time. He was sweet, gentle, and amiable, if a touch cool for my taste. But that other one percent was an emotional typhoon. I knew from their past breakup that when he got like this he said awful things, threw out ultimatums, and burned bridges. I got it. I understood that dysfunction all too well, but it had wounded Stephan once again, and I had a real serious problem with that.

I pointed right back at him. "I said, give him space."

His upper lip quivered. He gripped both hands into his hair as though he wanted to pull it all out. I couldn't tell if it was anger or pain that moved him, but I frankly didn't care at that moment. Priority one was Stephan, always.

"He doesn't need space! He needs to talk to me, instead of running to you every time he's upset!"

I started to move towards Javier, to do what, I wasn't quite sure. Push him from the room? Get in his face? I honestly couldn't say, but it didn't matter. Stephan stopped me, clutching me close.

"Leave her out of it, Javier," Stephan said, his voice toneless and quiet. I hated that tone, because I knew it hid a deep pain.

"No, *you* leave her out of it—" Javier shouted back.

"Go, Javier. I have nothing to say to you right now, and I've heard what you have to say. Now leave us alone," Stephan said, still in that alarmingly dead tone.

Javier visibly deflated. He turned and walked away.

Distractedly, I noted that James followed him out, closing the door softly behind them.

Stephan pulled me to a low couch, hugging me to him. I clutched him just as tightly as he did me. If he needed comfort, I needed just as badly to give it to him. He was hurting, and I hurt with him. We had never been able to maintain any level of detachment from each other's suffering, and we didn't now.

I stroked my hands through his soft wavy hair over and over, not speaking, just comforting and waiting. If he needed to tell me, he would tell me. I wouldn't pry.

We hugged like that for a long time, my face buried in his neck, his in my hair, before he spoke in a whisper into my ear. "I told him that I loved him yesterday," he said finally.

I tried not to tense, tried to stay comforting, relaxing, waiting for him to go on, but I didn't imagine he'd have good news after that. The I love you obviously hadn't been met with a positive response.

"He told me that he needed more time to know his feelings, that I was moving too fast. He said he wasn't sure he could trust me yet, with our history and all. I tried not to be hurt by that, even though it felt like a rejection."

He didn't speak for a while. I stroked his hair, rubbed his back.

"I shook it off pretty good, I thought. I could give him time. We have time, yanno? Maybe I was rushing. But then we went out tonight. To Melvin's bar. Not my idea, but I didn't figure there'd be a problem. And there wasn't. At least not on

Melvin's end. Melvin was completely civil, friendly even. Javier took exception to the friendly. He asked me if I'd gone out with Melvin. I said yeah, briefly. He went into a jealous tantrum. I went to the bathroom. When I came back out, I found Javier pinned to the wall, being kissed by Vance. He wasn't exactly putting up a fight. I left. Javier followed me here."

"*He* was mad at *me*. He had the nerve to turn it around on me, said I was overreacting. *I hate this.* I just can't take this kind of stuff, the jealousy and the disloyalty. I'd rather be alone than deal with all of that."

"I can't make him love me," he continued, an awful quaver in his voice. My tear ducts responded accordingly, producing a dreaded tear like a button had been pushed. "I've been down that road. Before I met you, that was all I knew. I did everything I could think of to make my family love me, but in the end, they said that I was toxic, and un-savable, and they thought that I was scum. I won't do that again, won't be that pathetic kid who can't make someone love them, not even for Javier."

"Oh, Stephan," I whispered, crying like a baby now, because he was crying, and because there was no distance between his pain and my heart. "You are the most beautiful person I've ever met. There is nothing ugly inside of you, nothing bad. If he can't love you, if he doesn't already, it can only be because he's not worthy of your love. You don't need to try to make anyone love you ever again. You're the most lovable person I know."

"I'm not, Bee. My own family threw me away. There has to be something wrong with me. They didn't throw the other kids away. It was only me, and I tried my hardest—" he was crying too hard to finish. I was right there with him. We held each other and cried like babies. The tears seemed to be flowing more freely these days. The stoic, hard-eyed street kids we'd once been would have been ashamed.

"I love you so much," I said quietly into his ear when the tears had passed. "I wouldn't have survived without you. You saved me in so many ways. You still do, every day. I'm not sure I'd even be capable of loving another person if you hadn't come along when you did. I was so numb inside, so resigned to just watching my life play out in one horrible episode after another, until one of those episodes finally ended me for good."

He whimpered, squeezing me so tightly that I had to pause for a moment.

"You saved me from so many horrible things," I continued. "You kept me from having to make so many of the hard choices that a girl would have to make living out on the street. You were a teenage boy, but you provided for me better, and loved me better, than some parents do for their own children."

"Oh, Bee," he whispered.

"We met in the gutter," I continued, "but even there, you shone like a light in the dark for me. You were the *only* good thing in my life, but you were *so good* that I knew it had all evened out. All of the bad was balanced because I got you out of it. Even jaded and abused and dead inside, I saw that clearly. If Javier can't see it, trust me, *he's not worthy of your love."*

He kissed my forehead.

We didn't talk about this stuff often, so once I started it was hard to stop. "I never met your family," I continued, "but I can tell you that you were the *best* of them, not the worst. They did throw you away," I said, and he made the faintest whimper of a noise. It killed me to hear that, to know that it still hurt him so badly, still affected him that much. "They did throw you away, but that says *nothing* about you, and *everything* about them. You would never throw someone away, never turn on someone that needed you."

I had said my piece, and so fell silent. He hugged me to him for a long time, burrowing his face into my hair.

"I love you, Buttercup. You're my rock. Best thing that ever happened to me," he whispered.

I closed my eyes, feeling unworthy of those words, but relishing them all the same.

I didn't realize I had drifted off until quiet voices woke me up. Stephan's chest was my pillow. He spoke in a low voice to someone behind me as he stroked my hair.

"You have to understand how proud she is, if you're going to keep her with you. It's a resilient kind of pride. She had exactly one pair of pants and three tops in our junior year of high school, but no one ever would have suspected that it was because she was homeless, just because of the way she held herself. And that was just a taste of it, just a tiny piece of the superficial part of it. It goes so much deeper than that. It's the kind of pride that would keep a person from ever saying how they feel, at the risk of being rejected. Do you understand?"

I heard a deep hum of noise behind me and knew that it was James.

Oh Stephan, I thought.

He was matchmaking, trying to bring two stubborn souls closer; two people who he was afraid were incapable of doing it themselves.

I felt a weight settle onto the couch beside us, a hand resting on my hip with a soft touch.

"I understand," James said quietly.

I couldn't begin to read his tone.

"Are you okay, Stephan?" he asked.

I felt Stephan nod. "I'm better. I vented, got it all out, and it actually helped."

"Are you up to talking to Javier tonight? I set him up in another room, but he's asked to speak to you at your earliest convenience. He swears he's done yelling—swears he'll be civil."

I felt Stephan nod again. "Yeah. I'm ready to talk. Are you going to wake her?"

"I'll carry her to our room."

I felt Stephan kiss my head and then James was shifting me into his arms. I let him take a few steps before I rubbed my cheek against his chest. "I can walk," I told him, my voice sleepy.

"And I can carry you," he said, just gripping me more tightly.

And he did, carrying me upstairs and laying me on our bed. I let him strip me down to nothing without a word, just watching him. I couldn't begin to read his mood. Was he upset? The evening couldn't have gone how he'd been planning.

He shrugged out of his own clothes, lying on the bed beside me. I was flat on my back, and he perched himself at my side, one hand propping his head up, the other moving to my belly with a light touch.

It was a peaceful kind of standoff. We lay and watched and waited for the other to speak. I thought I was well suited to the contest.

James broke first.

"I listened to you and Stephan talking," he said finally.

I was hardly surprised, so I didn't react. "Why?" was all I asked.

"I led Javier to the furthest room down the hall from Stephan, and when I stepped out into the hall, I heard you sobbing. I couldn't stay away. I couldn't hear you crying like that and just let it go. You have to know that about me by now."

I did know that. I just nodded for him to go on.

"I just sat outside the door and listened. I tried to give you space, but that was the best I could do. Let me start by saying that I'm grateful for Stephan. I feel like I owe him a debt, a debt that I can never repay, for taking care of you, for keeping you safe, body *and* soul, before we met. He's a part of you. I see that. But Javier was right, in a way."

I opened my mouth to speak.

He just covered it with his hand. "Let me finish. He was right in that, every time you get upset about something, you can't only turn to each other. You *can* depend on other people. Letting someone other Stephan past your guard won't diminish what you have with him, or what you are to each other. Your love for each other is a beautiful thing, but it shouldn't be such a selfish thing. You've turned that love into a wall that keeps everyone else out, and that's unfortunate, because you have so much more to give than that."

"As we're finding out together, relationships can be rocky. This thing that we have can be hard. But if you turn away from me, if you run to Stephan every time it gets hard, where will that leave us? Where will that leave Javier and Stephan? You need to make room in your heart for more than Stephan."

I didn't respond, didn't know what to say, because he was so right and so wrong. Stephan and I did depend on each other to the exclusion of the rest of the world. It had served us so well for so long that it was hard to make myself want to break the habit. Impossible, really. But he was wrong about the rest of it. I had so clearly let more than just Stephan into my heart.

He lowered his head very slowly to my chest, placing one light kiss right over my heart. He looked up at me through the dark golden strands of his hair, keeping his head lowered. "You need to make room here for *me*," he said quietly, placing another soft kiss there.

I gripped his hair in my fists, searching desperately for the words to say to him.

He pulled himself gently out of my grasp. "That's all I wanted to say."

I couldn't speak past the lump in my throat.

CHAPTER THIRTEEN

Stephan

STEPHAN

I took a long shower and slipped into some black running shorts, not bothering with a shirt. I thought about going for a nice, mind-clearing run. I could be in Central Park in minutes. I loved running there. It was dark out, and I knew that it wasn't the safest thing to do, but hell, I'd almost welcome some trouble. I'd have enjoyed a good fight just then, even knowing that I'd hate myself after the violence. Even when the violence was self-defense, I hated myself for it.

I was standing in the doorway to the closet, my running shoes clutched in my hand, when Javier walked into the bedroom.

I had been planning to go to him, knew that we had to talk, but I'd been putting it off. A conversation that would most likely end in a break-up was not something I had any wish to rush into.

He stared at me, something raw and fierce moving behind his dark eyes. I could tell he'd been crying, but it didn't take away from his lovely features.

"I know that you're going to break up with me," he said quietly, his voice shaky. "I know you well enough to see that you're just working up the nerve. I only ask one thing before you do it."

I looked down at my feet, my still wet hair trailing into my face. "What is it?" I asked.

"I just want you to sit down and hear me out. And look at me while I do it. If you care about me, you'll give me at least that much before you write me off."

I moved to the low couch across the room. I sat and finally looked at him steadily. "Go ahead," I told him calmly.

He moved to me. His chin had a proud tilt to it, as it always did. Bianca thought he was a little cold, but I'd never seen him that way. In fact, he reminded me a lot of Bianca, so composed, so controlled, so hidden away to the casual observer. But nothing between Javier and I had ever been casual, so I hadn't bought it for a second. He was reserved, yes, but never cold.

He knelt at my feet.

"Can I touch you?" he asked. His eyes on mine were more open, and more raw than I'd ever seen them.

It was hard to tell him no when he was looking at me like that, but I refused to be that self-destructive, so I shook my head at him. "No."

His lip quivered, and it almost broke my resolve. It was an effort not to look away.

He was on his knees and he moved as close to me as he could possibly be without actually touching me. He was wearing a very fitted black shirt, and his taut stomach was just a breath away from my knees. I tried not to let that distract me.

"I know what you think," Javier said. "You think I like drama. You think I got jealous of that bartender and tried to make *you* jealous. I can admit that I have been that guy before. I've been in that kind of high drama relationship before, but I am not like that anymore. That's what I had with Vance, in fact."

My jaw clenched hard, but I let him continue without a word, just staring at him.

"That drama-seeking bullshit is the sort of thing you do when you *aren't* in love, when you don't really care where your relationship is going, and that is not what we have, Stephan. We're the real deal. I wouldn't do that to you, *not ever.* I admit that I was jealous of Melvin, and that I was being a child about it, but I would not retaliate by cheating on you. I wouldn't throw this away for *anything.*"

His chin lowered as he spoke, but he never looked away from me. He gazed up at me with those lovely dark eyes through the thickest set of lashes I'd ever seen.

I wanted to buy his words, would have loved nothing more, but again I refused to be self-destructive. I'd worked too hard to value myself to stop now.

"You can't put a spin on what I saw, Javier. Vance was all over you, and you weren't so much as twitching. You weren't even *trying* to pull away." I tried not to raise my voice, but it was a struggle.

He put a hand on my knee, as though it was involuntary—as though he couldn't help the touching.

I pushed it off. "Don't," I said, my voice low and mean.

I tried not to be affected as a lone tear trailed down his cheek.

"To explain what you saw I have to explain a little of what Vance and I were like together." He swallowed hard, and I watched his throat work. I made myself look back into his eyes.

"We were toxic," he said. "We were that drama couple. It was just about the only thing we had going for us. He was obsessed with me, and I was immature enough to think that was enough to make a relationship work. He stroked my ego, and I made him crazy, and he *liked* being crazy. He wanted a reaction from me, always. Whether that reaction was good or bad, he didn't really care. He would say or do something horrible to me, and I would react, and he loved it. It got to the point where we could have been the same person, as far as the relationship was concerned. We did hurtful things, we said hurtful things, and we didn't even love each other. That's the emptiest feeling, to know that you would hurt someone else just to *feel something*. I'm not proud of it, but I have been that person. I am *not* that person now."

He put that hand back on my knee, and I didn't push it away, even thinking that I should. He moved closer, bumping his hips between my knees until they parted enough to let him move closer. I could see his other hand trembling as he put it on my chest.

I kept my hands to myself, but I let him touch me.

"Vance is still that person. He's still obsessed with me, obsessed with what we had, even though it ended more than three years ago. He pulls stunts, wanting nothing more than a reaction from me. I learned a long time ago that the best thing to do was not to give him one. Not to give him anything at all. Not even so much as a twitch..."

He moved closer slowly, giving me every opportunity to tell him no. He moved until he could nuzzle his face into my chest. My breathing grew ragged.

"He kissed me to get a reaction. He wanted me to fight him, slap him, chew him out, anything at all. So I gave him *nothing* at all. I waited passively for him to finish, for him to realize that I don't care enough anymore to give him that reaction."

I gripped a hand into that thick black hair. I pulled his face back until he was looking directly into my eyes again. "Are you saying that he assaulted you? That he's done it before? He put his hands on you, knowing that you didn't want him to touch you?"

Those dark mysterious eyes opened wide, their depths turning a little panicked. He moved close against me, running soothing hands over my shoulders.

"Yes," he finally answered.

I grew stiff as a board, my mind going a bit hazy and red with temper.

"Don't do anything rash, Stephan," he pleaded. "He's not worth it."

A picture of Vance came into my head, a very clear picture of me pounding his face in. I would destroy him in a physical altercation. It wasn't even a question. He was a little short, a little thin, with a handsome face that I'd have no problems messing up.

"Why do you still hang out with him? Why did we meet up with him tonight, if he's like that?"

"I'm good friends with all of his friends. I'm close with everyone on that crew, and he swore he wouldn't push me around anymore. And with you there, I didn't think he'd even be able to. I didn't imagine he'd try something the second you left my sight. And I figured if he did, you'd defend me. I'm not a fighter."

My eyes widened in horror. "Are you saying that he assaulted you, I saw it, and then I walked away? Is that what happened back there?"

I tried to stand but he clung to me tightly. "It's not a big deal," he said very softly. "Just don't break up with me because of a misunderstanding. Please. I'm begging you, Stephan."

"You don't think it's a big deal that someone pushes you around in front of me, and I just walk away?"

He rubbed his cheek across my chest, and I swallowed hard. "Vance doesn't bother me. This was his last chance to be civil, and he blew it. I'll stay far, far away from him. The only thing that he could do to hurt me now is cost me you. I love you. I know I said I needed time, but that was a *big fat lie*. I fell in love with you more than a year ago, and those feelings never went away, not for me. I was just trying to protect my heart when I told you that I needed more time to fall for you. I've been here all along."

I wasn't one to analyze a good thing to death. I studied his earnest face and let myself fall all over again. I believed him, and loved him, and that was enough for me.

I ran my hands through his pitch-black hair, gripping it into my fists to pull his face close. I kissed him hard and he melted against me. He pushed his chest against mine, rubbing.

I pulled back. "No more drama. I can't stand this stuff. And if I see Vance again, I'm kicking his ass. You can warn him, if you want, but that's what's going to happen."

He just nodded, giving me a little smile. That smile was trouble. The good kind. I kept my hands gripped in his velvety hair as he began to kiss my chest. My head fell back as he moved that wicked mouth lower with a purpose. The things Javier could do with his mouth boggled my mind. He had a rare and exquisite talent. He tugged my shorts off, and I let him work his magic.

A good blowjob often involved as much hands as mouth, but not with Javier. He sucked me so hard and so deep that I forgot where I even was: coming so fast that I would have been embarrassing myself if it had been anything but fellatio. He kept me deep in his throat as I came, stroking his hands over any part of me they could reach.

I pulled him up to my mouth for a long kiss. I stood, leading him to the bed with a firm grip in his hair. I pinned him onto his stomach, lying on his back. I kissed his neck and felt him tremble.

I wasn't done with him, far from it, but I just held him for a long time, letting his anticipation build and giving him comfort. Javier loved to be held, and I loved to hold him. I nuzzled my face into his neck, grinding my lower half into from behind.

"Did you tell Bianca what happened with Vance?" he finally asked.

I was a little surprised that that was what he'd been thinking about just then, but I answered. "Yes. I tell her everything."

He made a little sound of distress. "She'll hate me now.

Even if you tell her the full story, she'll never trust me now, and if she hates me, we don't have a chance. I know how it is. She's the most important person in your life, and if she's working against us, we're as good as done."

I sighed. "You don't understand Bianca at all. She would never do that. She'd never work against us. That would be too much like working against me, and she doesn't have that in her. She is on my side without reserve, and she respects my judgement. If I tell her that I'm with you, that will just be it. She has my back, no exceptions. We've been partners through too much bad stuff for it to work any other way."

"I hope you're right...," he said.

I bit the tendon between his neck and shoulder hard enough to make him moan. "What were you saying?" I asked him with a smile.

"I forget," he breathed.

I got to work peeling off his clothes from behind. My smile grew wicked. "That's what I thought..."

CHAPTER FOURTEEN

Mr. Perfect

BIANCA

James rose, striding to the closet. He came back out in a pair of boxers. "Don't move," he told me. "I need to get something from the entryway real fast."

I didn't say anything, and he looked at me. He pointed, the twist to his mouth almost playful now. "I mean it. Don't move." With that, he strode out.

"Crazy bastard," I muttered loud enough for him to hear, but I didn't move. I heard him laugh as he walked down the hallway.

I let out my own laugh when he strode back into the room. He had the soft beige scarf from the photo shoot wrapped around his neck. He grinned a wicked kind of grin. I felt myself grow wet just from that look.

He was out of his boxers and back on the bed in a flash of naked golden skin. I couldn't look away.

He straddled me, unwrapping the long scarf from his neck slowly, teasingly. It took forever the thing was so long.

I watched him, captivated. I felt like I was getting an X-rated strip tease from a glorious God. "You're the most beautiful thing on the planet, James," I told him.

At the bottom of my vision I saw his erection twitch, and he closed his eyes for a long moment. There was no denying that he was susceptible to flattery, but that wasn't why I'd said it. I'd said it because I couldn't look directly at the sun and not remark that it was blinding and brilliant.

Once the scarf was free, he covered my eyes with it, wrapping it twice around my head. He raised my arms above my head, stretching them taut, his hard length rubbing along my torso as he did so. His cock pushed hard into my sternum as he wrapped the scarf around my arms. I gasped.

He wrapped that soft length from my wrists to my elbows. It was a firm hold but not tight. When that was secure, he wrapped it over my collarbone, lining it even with my underarms. He barely jostled me as he wrapped it around me twice there before moving down to my breasts and then ribs. He wrapped it around and around with smooth sure motions, somehow managing to get it under my body while barely moving me. He wound it around my waist next, bringing it back up to wrap around both my eyes and arms, binding them together.

He had me well and truly caught when he pulled back, straddling my hips.

He said one word before he set to work on my body with his mouth. "Struggle."

I tested my restraints rather hesitantly at first, not imagining that the scarf would pose any real challenge. It was so soft, so stretchy, but the man knew what he was doing. Always.

I gasped as he licked a path down my navel to my inner thighs. He sucked at a tender spot while I worked against the scarf, making no progress, just moving the wicked thing against my body deliciously while he did even more delicious things down below. He worked that clever mouth from my groin to that sensitive spot behind my knee and back again. I struggled hard, because it felt good, because I couldn't believe that the ridiculous scarf could hold me so securely, and because I wanted my hands free to push that teasing mouth where I needed it to be.

I only succeeded in trapping myself more securely, and James took his sweet time moving that tongue just where I craved it.

I stopped struggling when he finally buried his face between my legs, thrusting his tongue inside of me before licking up to my clit.

He lifted his head as I stilled. "Keep struggling," he told me.

I couldn't see a thing, but I could hear the wicked smile in his voice.

He plunged two hard fingers inside of me, once, twice, and I came on a dime. He was kissing up my body, nudging aside the material where it covered a nipple. He sucked hard on my nipple as he plunged inside of me. I gasped and struggled harder against the soft bindings.

He was dragging his cock out of me, hitting every perfect nerve, when he uncovered my eyes. The rest he left imprisoned as he dug his elbows into the mattress on the sides of my breasts and drove into me again and again. His eyes showed me that the tender-lover was driving for this ride, though the warm smile in his voice as he tormented me had given me fair warning.

"Say it, Bianca," he said, his voice more tender than demanding. Still, I knew it was an order.

"I'm yours, James," I told him softly.

His eyelids fluttered briefly as he started to come inside of me. He bottomed out in me with the sexiest little moan, and I came.

"Cashmere fucking," he told me with a smile as we caught our breath.

I laughed. "So that's what that was called. Good to know."

He unwrapped me from the long scarf slowly, rubbing it along my body as he did so. I rubbed against him, always craving his touch, even as my eyes drifted closed and I fell into a hard sleep.

I had the dream again and woke up scrambling out of bed in the dark, disoriented and scared. Hard familiar arms caught me almost immediately, lifting me from behind, and carrying me into the bathroom. I had to shut my eyes tight as light flooded the room.

We were already naked so he just stepped into the tub, never letting me go as he turned on the water and leaned back against the edge of the huge tub. I turned into him, wrapping my arms around his neck, clinging as hard as I could. Soothing arms stroked my back, washing and comforting, soft whispers telling me everything would be fine.

"I can't stand it. I know it's a dream, but it feels so real," I whispered. I didn't break down, didn't cry this time, though the dream had shaken me as badly as before. More so.

"Shhh, Love. Just breathe. The memories will fade. Nightmare memories always do."

He said it like someone well acquainted with nightmares. I wasn't surprised.

I lifted my head to look at him. He stroked my hair, meeting my eyes squarely. He could communicate so much to me with just those exquisite, tarnished eyes of his.

I swallowed hard. Residual fear from the dream still haunted me. The thought of losing him made me desperate and empty and filled me with despair darker than anything I'd ever known, and I was hardly a stranger to dark thoughts.

I pulled back enough to move up his body, straddling his hips in the rising water. I traced a finger over that smooth brow, the hollow in his cheek, that perfectly straight nose, those pretty lips, and then across that hard jaw.

I cupped his face in my hands, watching him steadily. He

pressed his own hands over mine, giving me such a loving look that I melted.

"The thought of losing you makes me desperate," I said, shifting our faces closer. My eyes were steady on his when I took the leap. "I love you, James," I said, my voice just a whisper. "So much."

His eyes closed for just an instant, and he took a deep breath. When he opened them again there was such a raw relief there that it made me shake.

"Thank you," he said roughly. "I've been waiting for that, and wanting that, for so long."

He stroked his hands over my hair, watching me, his eyes going to that soft loving place that I'd come to crave and depend on so quickly.

He was silent for so long, just watching me and touching me, that I lost our silent standoff.

"Do you…love me?" I asked him, my chest hurting.

"That's a silly question," he said, stroking my cheek. "An unnecessary question. I've never made a secret of my feelings, Bianca. I know you're a skeptic, but you must have realized that I fell for you right away."

I leaned my cheek into his hand. "Why haven't you ever said the words, then?"

He bit his lip.

I watched that vulnerable action with rapt attention.

"I wanted you to say it first. Not for pride, and not for my ego, but for my heart. I haven't said those words to anyone since my parents died, and I didn't want the first time to be met with a rejection. I was afraid you would get spooked and run again. I preferred to give you time rather than break my own heart. Can you understand that?"

I nodded, feeling crushed under the weight of my own skepticism. I hated what my baggage had done to him, what it might do in the future, all of the pain it had caused him, because there was no cure-all for my issues. One big one was rearing its ugly head even as I had the thought.

"But why?" I asked him, my voice much smaller than I liked it to be. "That's what I don't understand.

His brows shot up, and he gave me a genuinely baffled look. "Why?"

"Why do you love me?"

His eyes got so soft, changed in an instant from confused and into that impossibly tender look that got me every time. "You want me to break it down for you?" he asked succinctly.

I nodded.

He traced a finger across my brow. "I can do that. I'd enjoy that actually. You're my favorite subject, Love. I'll start with your eyes. I fell in love with those first. One look was like a punch to the gut. You have these ageless eyes on such a young face. I just knew that you had seen bad things, lived bad things, and from the start, I knew that you could understand pain. Understand loneliness and despair. Understand feeling hopeless and helpless and alone. I fell in love with your eyes first because I looked into their depths and saw the other half of my soul."

That got to me, and my eyes filled with those humiliating tears that I couldn't seem to avoid lately.

He traced a tear down my face, giving me his fondest smile. "I freely admit that was enough to catch me, and you're going to tell me I'm crazy, but I've been around the block too many times to count, and I was experienced enough to know, right from that first meeting, that I was falling for you. I didn't understand it until after our first time together, wouldn't have given it that name, but that doesn't change the fact that I was lost from then on. But let's get back to my favorite subject."

He reached across the tub, turning the water off. He plunged that hand back into my hair to cup the back of my head.

"Next, I fell for that hard-won composure of yours, that steely self-control. When I got you to smile at me, or even to acknowledge my presence, it felt like an accomplishment. I've never needed the chase, never wanted it, really, but I relished it with you, even knowing that it was trouble for me, that *you* were trouble."

"Next, hmm, let's see, that's harder to pin down, because that was a lot of things at once. I'll lump it all together and say that I fell for your reaction to me next. Your submission. I've never felt anything like this kind of chemistry before. The way you trembled at my touch, that innocent response that you couldn't hide, and that I couldn't doubt. And then we made love. After that, I couldn't call what I felt for you anything but love, not to myself, even knowing that you didn't feel the same, at least not like I did—not yet."

There was such an adoring sort of understanding in his eyes that I felt something raw heal inside of me. Yes, my natural skepticism had hurt him, but at least he seemed to get why I was this way. He seemed to get *me*.

He wasn't done.

"And then there were your paintings. Those dreams in your eyes. The world *cannot* have been a beautiful place for you, but it becomes so beautiful through those paintings of yours. You put your soul into those paintings, and nothing in this world is more beautiful to me than that soul of yours."

I had always been uncomfortable with praise, any kind of praise, and his outpouring was in a league of its own, as far as compliments that moved me went. I felt so overwhelmed that it was hard to keep looking directly at him, deep into those tarnished turquoise depths, but I managed it through sheer force of will, my whole body trembling with the effort.

He continued relentlessly. "And then there's the fact that you're stunningly beautiful, and you couldn't care less about it. Your beauty *devastates* me, Bianca, yet you put less value on that beauty than any woman I've ever met. Even if you realized just how stunning you are, which I know you don't, it wouldn't matter to you, wouldn't make any difference at all, and I find that so charming about you."

"Sometimes I feel like I've made a muddle of it all," he continued. "Like all I do is screw up, but I swear to you that I'm trying my best. I'm only terrible at this relationship thing because I've never done it before, but I promise I'll keep working until I get it right. I'm nothing if not determined."

The thought floored me. I spoke without thinking. "Now that's a depressing thought, James, because if you're terrible at this, there isn't even a word to describe how much I *suck* at it."

He threw back his head and laughed, and my mouth moved into a smile automatically. He brought his laughing lips close to mine. "Not true, Love. You're doing perfect, as far as I'm concerned."

His mouth was a whisper away from mine when I spoke. "You haven't made a muddle of it, James. You couldn't be terrible at anything, even if you tried. I think you're perfect."

He kissed me, a kiss that started out soft but as always our unquenchable hunger for each other quickly took it further. He was gripping my hair and plundering my mouth within hot, drugging moments. I rubbed my wet chest against his.

We made love slowly, leisurely, lovingly. I lay my cheek against his wet chest when we finished, kissing my crimson name on his pounding heart.

He stroked my hair for long minutes, still buried inside of me. He seemed in no hurry to pull out.

"I love you, Bianca," he said very quietly. "There isn't a thing about you that I don't adore. Even the things that have made it hard for you to let me in hold a special place in my heart. I never thought I'd meet a woman that I couldn't doubt, a person that I could so easily give my trust to, but I know your soul, and it is so pure and clear to me that I feel like I can see right into it."

I didn't know how he could say that. I felt so cynical

sometimes. But I soaked up his words, loving the way they made me feel. I didn't have to agree with the words to be touched by them.

"I love you," I told him simply.

We were silent for long minutes, communicating only through stroking touches and soft kisses. Eventually, reluctantly, he pulled slowly out of me, pulling me flush against him right away.

"Can I tell you about my parents?" he asked finally.

"Of course," I said quickly, surprised that he thought he had to ask. "I would love to hear about them. I love to learn about you."

"You would have liked my mother. She was so passionate, so opinionated, but also kind. She didn't come from my father's world, but she didn't put up with any of the nonsense that the high society set tried to throw her way. She hated luncheons and teas, hell, she hated all of the insufferable social functions that weren't directly helping a charity, and the term 'socialite' made her see red."

His words brought me a staggering sense of relief. If he had expected me to do what Jackie suggested and devote my life to a pointless string of unenjoyable social functions just for the sake of keeping up appearances, I would have been troubled, because that just wasn't for me.

"She kept a few close friends very close, and devoted her time to her family and to her charities. She was so beautiful."

He paused, stroking my cheek.

"My father was a reserved man, but he was loving. I do remember that. He worked a lot, but when he didn't, he devoted his time to my mother and me. He worshipped the ground she walked on." He stroked my hair when he said it, his eyes loving.

"They had a good marriage. I was young, but even I could see how devoted they were to each other. They would share these looks... Even as I child I knew that they had something special."

"As I got older, long after they'd passed, I didn't imagine I could ever find something similar for myself, that I could ever *feel* something like what they had. I honestly didn't think I was capable of it...Until I met you, I didn't know I had those kinds of feelings inside of me. Now I see clearly that with the right person, it's so simple. Those feelings aren't something one can force, and they aren't something I could deny once I felt them. It still just floors me that I felt them so fast and so deep with you."

"My father liked to claim that he fell in love with my mother at first sight. Even back then, I thought he was just waxing poetic, but I believe him now. I did exactly the same thing."

I looked up at him. "You're insane," I told him. The idea of love at first sight was just so far-fetched, especially since it was me he was talking about. "But undeniably, terribly romantic," I allowed.

He just smiled. "I know. But I'm honest, and that's just how it was for me."

I rubbed my cheek against his chest, feeling like this was all a dream. He was just too perfect to be real.

CHAPTER FIFTEEN

Mr. Dubious

We slept in late the next morning. I was pleasantly surprised that James had taken the morning off so we could spend the morning together before I had to fly out. I would only be gone for the day, arriving back in New York early in the morning the next day, but it still felt like such a treat to get more time with him.

We lingered in bed, which was hardly surprising, since I woke up as he was pushing himself inside of me. He must have been at it for a while because I was wet enough that my body accepted him easily. He held my legs so far apart that the stretch bordered on painful, and pounded into me mercilessly, his eyes snapping at me all the while.

"Say it, Bianca," he said roughly.

I wasn't actually sure which 'it' he meant, after our confessions from the night before, so I went with my instincts. He was fucking me like he wanted to own me, so I said what came to mind. "I'm yours, Mr. Cavendish. Only yours."

I found out that my instincts were right on as he came inside of me, shouting my name roughly.

I was right there with him, watching him with fascination and love as my body clenched deliciously around him in a perfect orgasm.

He was tender afterwards, but it was a possessive sort of tender. We showered, and he took over completely, washing my body and hair, as was his custom. I was beyond questioning it. Letting him care for me like that fulfilled a need in both of us, and now I only cherished it, as he cherished me.

He dressed me, placing soft kisses all over my body right before he covered each spot with clothes. I ran hungry hands through his wet hair as he tended to me. He dressed me in a dark T-shirt and boxers, because I would have to get dressed again in work clothes in just a few hours.

We went downstairs for breakfast. It would have been tempting to have breakfast in bed that morning, but I was dying to see Stephan. I needed to make sure he was okay, so we headed to the dining room to eat. James didn't even ask me. He seemed to always understand how Stephan and I worked. I didn't know if he was just that observant, or if Stephan had explained it to him in even more detail than what I'd imparted. The how didn't matter, though, because it was only his understanding that was crucial.

I felt my whole body get a little limp with relief when I heard laughter coming from the dining room as we approached. I recognized Javier's laugh first, and the one that joined it was one that was more familiar to me than my own laugh. And more welcome.

I smiled at the sound, my step quickening to reach them. James was a silent presence at my back.

Stephan stood when he saw me, grinning ear to ear.

He was across the room and enfolding me into his arms in a flash. I burrowed into that familiar chest.

"Are you okay?" I asked him.

He squeezed me. "I'm great."

"I take it you guys worked it out," I said wryly.

"We did." No hesitation.

I nodded against him and after a moment, he let me go to get back to his breakfast.

I didn't need to know any more than that. He'd made up his mind, and I could only hope that Javier, who was giving me very cautious glances, wouldn't hurt him again.

James pulled my chair out for me, acting the gentleman. "Egg white omelet okay with you?" he asked me, heading into the kitchen.

I nodded, wondering what about me had attracted what seemed to be the last two gentlemen left on the planet.

I noticed that Stephan and Javier were eating crepes covered in syrup, whipped cream, and chocolate chips. I was surprised that James even kept the ingredients for that in his house.

James returned quickly, carrying a very English tea service. He served us all tea, acting the epitome of the well-mannered English host. I told him so.

He smiled. "I get it from my father. English from head to toe. Every cup of English tea that I drink makes me think of him."

I thought that was a sweet thing for him to share and I gave him a sweet smile.

He winked at me.

I was startled at the response it caused in me. It was a pretty innocent gesture, considering the things he said and did to me on a daily basis, but it still had me turned on in a heartbeat. The man was hot.

We were almost through with our breakfast when I noticed James checking his phone, his expression growing carefully blank from one second to the next.

"Excuse me," he said curtly.

He rose from the table and strode from the room.

I hadn't realized how polite he usually was about taking calls during our time together simply because he didn't do it. Which made me even more curious about what had gotten his attention, and what had put that look on his face. I was on instant alert.

A rare streak of uncontrollable curiosity had me following him within seconds. I wanted to see what had troubled him so badly with just a few words.

I caught him with his back to me in one of the sitting rooms. The door wasn't completely closed, but he was speaking very quietly into the phone.

"Then offer them more. I mean it when I say I don't have a limit to what I will pay to keep this from getting out." He paused. "I don't give a *fuck* if it's a smart business decision, Roger. This isn't about business. This is about keeping my life intact, the way I need for it to be, and I don't give a fuck if it takes my fortune to accomplish that. Do you understand?" Another long pause. "I am not a fourteen-year-old that you are managing, Roger. I don't need time to think. I need you to do what I'm asking you to. *Take care of this.*"

Fear froze me in my tracks, and I stood in the doorway, listening. His tone was so panicked, so desperate. I did not want to know what had put that fear in him.

I didn't move from the doorway as he ended the call and turned. I had been eavesdropping on him, and I'd just as soon have him know it. Perhaps he would tell me what had happened, and it wouldn't be as bad as the dread coursing through me was telling me it was.

He flinched when he saw me standing there, and that was *so* not good for my peace of mind. We suffered through a very long, awkward silence while he rubbed his temples and I watched him.

"Everything okay?" I finally asked him.

He grimaced. "It will be," he said. That was all.

"Who is Roger?" I asked. Being with James seemed to have added nosy quite firmly to my list of character flaws.

"An old family friend. A sort of mentor to me. And my lawyer."

I thought that sounded ominous, but he didn't elaborate, and I didn't ask him to. If he didn't want to share, I couldn't make him.

He moved to me finally. He ran a hand over my hair, grabbing it firmly at my nape. He used it like a handle to tilt my face up to him. There was trouble in his eyes. "Did you mean what you said last night?"

I studied him, beyond confused. "About what?"

His jaw clenched and he watched me for a long time. "About loving me. I know you were tired and scared from the nightm—"

I couldn't take it. I interrupted him rudely. "Of course I did! I wouldn't say something like that just because I was tired."

"Say it again," he ordered roughly.

"I love you. Of course I do. You shouldn't doubt me. I wouldn't say it unless I meant it."

"How conditional is that love? How much are you willing to withstand just to stay with me?"

I was starting to get angry. "I don't like the *question*. Love in a monogamous relationship has to have some conditions, James. If you were unfaithful—"

"I'm not talking about that. I'd never do that. Does your love have other conditions?"

I glared at him, but I shook my head, finding the answer way too quickly. "I don't think that it does, James. But again, I don't like the question. Do you want to tell me why you're asking it?"

He was gripping my hair to the point of pain now. "I'm asking it because every time I think that we're on our way to building a future together, something from the past gets in the way, and I need to know that won't happen to us again."

I thought he was being deliberately vague, but I let it go. I was in no mood to open Pandora's Box. "The past can only hurt us if we let it, if it really *is* the past that we're talking about."

He studied me, then kissed me roughly. He brought his mouth to my ear. "I want to tie you to my bed. Now. I want to keep you there."

My brain short-circuited for an instant, going to that sublime place that only James could take me to. "I need to leave for the airport soon."

"I know. That's why I want to do it. So you *can't leave*."

I tried to meet his eyes to give him an exasperated look, but he was kissing me, invading my mouth until I forgot why what he'd said was so outrageous.

He pulled back only when he'd left me breathless and wanting.

"Have you given any thought to your painting career?" he demanded. "When would you like to start planning your first showing?"

I had, in fact, been thinking about it. It was a persistent sort of distraction in my brain. Especially when I considered that James currently paid much more to have me followed and protected on flights than I was actually *earning* on those flights. It seemed so wasteful and senseless.

"I have," I admitted.

His jaw clenched when I didn't elaborate. "And what are your thoughts?"

I gave him my little shrug. "I'm mulling it over."

He gave me a rather pained smile. "Well, you let me know when you're done *mulling*," he bit out. "I would love to know your thoughts on the matter."

He was obviously upset, but he dropped it after that.

We made our way upstairs. I put on my uniform while he put on his ungodly expensive suit. He was ready first, taking another mysterious phone call. He strode from the room, phone to his ear, while I put on a bit of makeup.

He was quiet and a little distant on the drive to the airport. He kept me close, a hand in my hair and the other on my knee. The distance was all in his eyes and his expression, which had been very carefully blank since that second phone call.

He only came to life briefly when we reached the airport and it was time to say goodbye. He let the guys file out before crushing his mouth against mine, his kiss was hungry and desperate.

We were both breathless and agitated when he pulled back.

"Are you okay?" I asked him.

He nodded, but that trouble hadn't left his eyes.

"Bye," I told him.

He got out first to hand me out. "I love you, Bianca," he said.

I nodded. "I love you too, James," I said steadily. I didn't even feel the need to panic or withdraw at the words. They already came easily to my lips. I had it so bad.

Stephan, Javier and I were lucky to get a row of seats together for the flight, since we were flying space available. We all tried to sleep since we'd be working well into the next morning, but I didn't think any of us got more than a one-hour nap on the four and a half hour flight.

I woke up from my nap as the plane began to descend for landing, the feeling familiar enough to act like an alarm on my body. My head was pillowed against Stephan's shoulder. I rubbed my cheek against that supple muscle before pulling back to look at him. His arms were crossed over his chest, making his muscles bulge attractively. He was smiling and awake. He looked as happy as I'd ever seen him. It was a good sight for my heart, especially after all of the drama from the night before.

I saw that Javier was still passed out; his head pillowed onto Stephan's other shoulder.

"Morning, Buttercup," Stephan said softly.

"Just sitting here smiling while we sleep on you?" I asked him with a smile.

He just flashed a dimple at me, nodding. "Sandwiched by my two favorite people in the world. What's not to smile about?"

I had to laugh. "So what happened last night?" I asked him. I didn't want to ruin the mood, but I needed to know. That had been a lot of drama to be squashed so easily.

"Javier said he loves me," he said with a very soft smile.

I was relieved and confused all at once. "What about before that?"

He grimaced and told me briefly about Vance and the way he'd bullied Javier.

I gripped his hand when he finished. I wasn't sure what to think about all of it. Javier did have a reputation for loving drama, but on the other hand, I'd met Vance, and that one lived and breathed the stuff. I did know one thing, though. Stephan believed Javier with a certainty, and he would feel horrible for not defending the other man—instead walking away when he was being harassed.

"If that was what really happened, you couldn't have known."

He gave me a stern look. "You don't believe that's what happened?"

I gave him my little shrug. "You know I'm more cynical than you. I don't know what to believe, but of course, I have my doubts. That doesn't matter, though. If you're together, I support that, because it's what you want."

He gave me a sad smile. "You shouldn't be so cynical. I have no doubts about Javier, Bianca."

I nodded, watching him carefully. "I know. And like I said, that's enough for me."

"When are you going to learn that I'm not the only trustworthy person in the world?"

I didn't have an answer for that. At least, not one that he wanted to hear. Nothing but time and consistency would make me trust Javier with Stephan's heart, and the drama of the night before had done nothing but set that time further back, whatever his story was.

"You don't think he's good enough for me," he said, clear reproof in his voice.

I had to smile at that. "I don't think *anyone* is good enough for you, myself included."

He just shook his head.

We'd been over this, and neither of us ever budged.

"I told James that I love him," I told him quietly.

I heard the familiar sound of the wheels coming down from the plane. I was surprised that Javier was still sleeping peacefully.

Stephan beamed at me. "That's wonderful. Your therapist would be proud."

I laughed, hardly offended, since he only spoke the truth.

"Aren't you going to ask me what *he* said?" I asked him.

He shook his head without hesitation. "He's been head over heels from the start, Buttercup. I had no doubts. That man worships the ground you walk on."

CHAPTER SIXTEEN

Mr. Callous

We had almost no downtime once we got to Las Vegas. Javier and Stephan said a quick and circumspect goodbye, though I could practically see the heat snapping between them.

We shuttled to our airline's headquarters, checked in, and prepped for our flight, though that entire process was hardly uneventful.

All of the other crews that we greeted were abuzz with the recent announcement that our airline had filed for Chapter eleven bankruptcy. We were still in business for the moment, but speculation as to what that meant for us was running rampant.

I was mostly in shock about the whole thing. Stephan and I shared a very long look that meant we would talk about it later. The shuttle we took back to the airport was so loud with everyone voicing opinions and fears that we couldn't have heard each other over the noise if we'd tried.

I texted James.

Bianca: Did you hear the news about the airline?

James: Yes. Can you talk on the phone right now?

Bianca: It's too loud on the bus. I'll call you from the plane.

I had a few brief minutes to call him once we got on the plane, between prep time and boarding.

He was very much Mr. Cavendish when he answered the phone. "Hello, Bianca."

"Hello, Mr. Cavendish," I said, because I knew who I was talking to. "What do you think of all this bankruptcy stuff? I don't know what any of it means. It sounds really bad, but people are saying that we could still stay in business."

I heard his audible sigh over the line. It didn't bode well. "If you want my candid professional opinion on the matter, what it means is that the airline will stay in business for around a year before its fleet of aircrafts will be grounded for good. Your CEO has exhausted literally every avenue of funding at his disposal, gone to every connection, large and small, that he has. He refuses to give up control of the airline, and he's never run one successfully, though he has tried several times. He approached me about funding, which is actually why I was on the flight where I met you, but I had to decline based solely on the fact that it would have been a disastrous business decision for me. He was not willing to make any leadership concessions, and I wasn't willing to throw a hundred mil away on a man with a clear history of failure."

"In the near future," he continued relentlessly. "Say the next days and weeks, you will most likely be given an option for a voluntary furlough, and if that fails to yield enough willing candidates, an involuntary one. The airline will be cutting costs and staffing. Any routes that aren't profitable will be aborted within the next month. Any other questions?"

I felt deflated by his revelations, though I didn't doubt for a second that he knew what he was talking about. "Did you know all along that this was going to happen?"

"Yes," he said with no hesitation. "It was all only a countdown. The airline has been hemorrhaging money from the start. This is the era of discount fares, and your airline was a start-up luxury carrier. Everyone in the industry is just surprised that it lasted this long. Have you given any more thought to your painting career? Just say the word, and I'll have my people prepare your showing."

I thought that was rather callous of him. Of the two of us, I'd thought I had the monopoly on being insensitive.

"I have not," I told him, my voice stiff. "I haven't had time to process any of this."

There was a long pause on the other end. "Well, I will leave you to it then. I need to go. I'll see you in the morning."

"Goodbye, Mr. Cavendish," I said coldly, wondering at his mood. When I had called him, I hadn't expected to talk to this callous man.

"Goodbye, Bianca."

I hung up, feeling a little stung at his cold manner. *Was my hesitation about showing my paintings really bothering him this much? Or was it something else?* Whatever was going on with Roger, perhaps?

I knew speculating was pointless, so I got to work. It bothered me persistently, though. Not knowing the cause for his distant demeanor left my mind free to run wild with possibilities and paranoid fears, each one more alarming than the last.

I tried my hardest to distract myself for the duration of the flight. It was at least full, my bodyguards in each cabin included, of course. Even full, though, I was left with nothing to do by halfway into the flight.

Damien and Murphy had been uncharacteristically quiet for the pre-board procedures and the flight. I knew they must be upset about the bad news. If they started at another airline, they likely wouldn't get to work together for years. Damien would probably be demoted to the first officer position, making it impossible for them to work the same flights. Even after he made captain again, it would take time for them to get enough seniority to get regular routes, let alone routes together. I was sad for them. They made such a fun team.

I visited with them in the flight deck for a while. They still joked nonstop and went to great efforts to charm me, but I sensed an undercurrent of tension in the two men.

This was what upset me most about the collapse of the airline. It wasn't so much my future that I feared for. I liked my job, and I was grateful for the opportunities it had given me, but I was a survivor. Even without James, I would find another way to get by. But the people who had put all of their hopes into the airline for four and a half years, the ones who would be most affected by it, that's what got me. Businessmen played with their monopoly money while the rest of us rolled with the punches. It made me angry. Of course, there was nothing to do for any of it, so it was a futile kind of anger.

I had a long talk with Stephan on the flight about the expected voluntary furlough. I had made a quick but tough decision about it. I broached the subject with trepidation, but as usual, Stephan only responded with his unconditional support.

He just cupped my shoulders in his big gentle hands, giving me his best smile. "I think that makes *perfect* sense, Bianca. You were dreading telling me, weren't you?"

I nodded.

He kissed my forehead. "You should know better," he scolded softly.

He was right. *God, I loved him. How did I get so lucky?*

I was tired and exhausted by the time we got to New York, my mind running me ragged with all of the imminent changes in my life. Just when I made one huge change, didn't it just figure that it would *all* have to start changing?

I wasn't sure what the plan was when we walked as a crew out to the pickup spot. James, or rather, Cold Mr. Cavendish, hadn't said. I figured if he sent a car, I'd take it, if not, I'd go to the hotel with the crew.

He had sent a car. In fact, he'd sent himself, I realized as he met me at the door, taking my bag and my arm without a word. His face was a beautiful mask, his eyes a little blank.

James nodded stiffly at Stephan. Stephan had to stay with the crew for the hotel check-in, so he kissed me on the forehead and said goodbye.

I didn't get a chance to say goodbye to anyone else since James was leading me away as soon as he had Stephan's assumed blessing.

He handed my bags off to Clark, handing me into the car swiftly. My security detail filed into the car mere moments after James and I were settled. They'd been my silent shadow for the duration of my commute and workday.

"Bodyguards are unnecessary when I'm working, James," I told him, my voice pitched low to keep the conversation private. "I'm quite safe at work."

He looked at me. It was the first direct look he'd given me since he'd met me at the door. His face was as unreadable as I'd ever seen it. "I find it very necessary," he said shortly.

He looked out the window.

I hated his mood, hated his distance, but it still made me want to cling to him. I knew how unhealthy that urge was, and I tried my best to squelch it. Still, I found my hand seeking his knee, rubbing it comfortingly.

It did not have the intended effect. His hand covered mine

instantly, pushing it hard into his leg. I couldn't have pulled it away if I'd tried.

"You in the mood to be pinned to the seat and fucked with an audience, Love?" he said, his voice soft with danger.

I tried to snatch my hand away, but he held it fast. I didn't answer the ridiculous question, and he didn't say another word, looking out the window, a storm in his eyes.

"Are you going to tell me what's going on with you?" I finally asked him quietly.

He squeezed my hand, his jaw working. "Bear with me, Bianca. I am going through some rather trying legal issues, and letting you leave me every week tests every last *ounce* of my self-control."

I was silent for a long time, debating if I should tell him about my decision. It seemed rather like rewarding his bad behavior just then, but I had already made up my mind. It just made sense, as much as I hadn't wanted it to.

The voluntary furlough for flight attendants had already been announced. I'd received the email as we were taxiing into JFK. I had the seniority to keep working even if there weren't enough people to sign up for the voluntary furlough and it became involuntary, but I saw that as such a selfish thing. I didn't need the job, not as much as so many others did. Perhaps there had only ever been this solution, and the bankruptcy was just forcing my hand more quickly. I suspected that might be the case, but it didn't really matter anymore.

"I'll be taking the voluntary furlough," I told him.

I saw his hand shake with a fine tremor. He didn't look at me. I understood that he didn't appreciate that we weren't alone just then.

"Thank you," he said very quietly, in an unsteady voice.

"I'm doing it because I feel ridiculous having more money spent to protect me at work than what I'm actually making. And because there are people that need the job more than I do," I told him, my tone hard. This was *not* because of his tantrum. "And I would like to begin planning the gallery showing."

He nodded, head still turned away. "Of course. Thank you. I'll set up a meeting for you with Danika when we're in Vegas. She manages both my L.A. and Las Vegas galleries. She went to bat against my New York team to get your work in her gallery. She's quite a fan."

I had a hard time believing that. The idea of having fans was too far-fetched of a concept for me to grasp easily.

We arrived at our place via the underground garage, and James walked me into the apartment and up to our room.

He watched me from the doorway of the closet as I got undressed for my nap.

"I can't linger. I really do need to get back to the hotel, since I'll be heading back to Las Vegas with you tomorrow."

I just nodded, half undressed, my back to him. I felt him watching me for long minutes before he left.

I got ready for bed and lay down to sleep, but it eluded me for a long time. The way James was acting filled me with tension and anxiety. I tried to tell myself that he was just a moody and unpredictable man. That was one of the first things I'd learned about him. But I just knew, deep down in my gut, that it was something bad, something that he felt threatened him, or perhaps threatened us. He had told Roger to offer his entire fortune to protect from the mysterious threat, and I knew that he wouldn't use those words lightly.

My phone woke me, and even as I answered it, I knew I'd overslept. I had that groggy feeling that I only got when I took too long of a nap.

"Buttercup, you coming out with us tonight?" Stephan asked.

I blinked awake. "Who is us? And where are you going?"

"The crew is going to Red with the other two crews that are here on a layover. They are driving into the city from the airport hotels. A few extra people are coming into town, as well. I talked Javier, Jessa, Marnie, and Judith into flying in for the night. Our morning flight has like thirty open seats, so they'll have no problem flying home with us. It's turned into a kind of bankruptcy party. I talked to James. He said that people could crash at your place, *and* at his hotel. He's even setting up a VIP section at Red for us. He was supposed to tell you about it, but I guess you were sleeping."

I had to smile a little at Stephan turning a bankruptcy into a party, *but hell, why not?*

"We all have to get up so early in the morning," I told him. It wouldn't do at all to have a bunch of no-shows in the morning.

"It's fine. It's not like we do this often. Everyone just really needs to blow off steam."

I well understood. I felt the same urge. "What time do I need to be there?"

He laughed. "In an hour. Get a move on, Buttercup!"

I did, showering, blow-drying my hair, and getting my makeup on in record time. There was a food tray set just inside my bedroom door when I came out of the bathroom.

I ate the turkey burger on wheat quickly, impressed with Marion's efficiency. It was good, stacked with fresh vegetables, a spicy guacamole sauce giving it flavor. Either I was getting used to the fanatically healthy menu, or Marion was especially talented at making healthy taste good.

I cleared my plate in minutes, rushing to get ready.

I wore red. It seemed appropriate for the venue, and I loved the little dress. It draped over one shoulder, leaving the other bare, and the way it hung flattered my figure. It set off my collar just right, and I found the diamond cuffs on my jewelry vanity, which went perfectly. I wore diamond hoops in my ears as well, which may have been overkill, but why not? I had a whole team of bodyguards to keep me from getting robbed.

Jackie's system pointed me in the direction of some nude

heels with a red sole. These ones came with a note.

This dress needs stilettos. Please, I am begging you to change your mind on the wedge stance.
Jackie

The note made me laugh. I was almost beginning to enjoy tormenting that strange woman. I knew some fashionistas, but she took it to a whole new level. The idea that she had chosen every outfit, shoe, and bag so carefully, and then apparently left notes on some of them, just cracked me up.

I took the little yellow note to the bag closet and grabbed the tiny nude clutch with the matching number. At least it had a long strap.

I sent out a few texts before I went downstairs. The first one went to James.

Bianca: I'm going to Red for Stephan's party. Will I see you there?

He responded quickly but shortly.

James: You will.

Cryptic man.

The second text went to the security contact on my phone. I wasn't sure what the protocol was, but I'd prefer to keep them informed of my actions, as opposed to having them just wait for me at all hours.

Bianca: I'm going out. Heading downstairs now.

The response came back in under a minute.

Security: Roger that.

I thought that was an odd text response, but I just went downstairs.

Blake was waiting for me, wearing a black suit and looking as severe as always. I nodded at her.

She nodded back. "The others are waiting for us downstairs, Ms. Karlsson."

We got into the elevator.

"You know you don't have to call me that," I told her. It was worth at least one try.

She looked startled. "Of course, Mrs. Cavendish."

I slapped a hand to my forehead. Literally. "Don't call me *that*. Call me Bianca."

"That's against my orders, Mrs. Cavendish."

Hand to the forehead. Again. "Okay. Call me Ms. Karlsson, then, please."

"Of course, Ms. Karlsson."

I wouldn't be trying that again. I had most definitely learned my lesson.

I was flanked by the rest of my security the second we stepped into the lobby of the swank building. I had the surreal realization as we walked through that lobby that all of the rich people were watching *me*, as though *I* was a person of note. I supposed having a team of bodyguards would do that for anyone.

Johnny walked slightly in front of me and to my left. He shot me a rather familiar glance over his shoulder, very obviously eying up my legs.

I blinked slowly, a little shocked that James wasn't just being crazy possessive about the Johnny issue. That had definitely been a look, and he couldn't be guarding me that well if he was that distracted.

"Looking *hot*, Ms. Karlsson," he said under his breath, reaffirming my opinion.

And the point goes to Crazy Cavendish, I thought.

CHAPTER SEVENTEEN

Mr. Controlling

Blake and Williams rode in the passenger cab of the limo with me, Johnny and Henry up front. It was a very short drive. I got the VIP treatment from the car to the club, being ushered in without a soul even trying to make eye contact with me. I even got a little perfunctory bow from the bouncer. Being the owner's girlfriend had some bizarre little perks.

I was led to a VIP section that was already packed with familiar faces. The party was well under way. A loud shout went out from the crowd when they spotted me.

I had to smile. "You guys been at it for that long already?" I asked as Marnie and Judith rushed me, nearly spilling their red martinis in the process. I got side hugs on account of their drinks.

Jessa was right on their heels.

We all laughed as we realized that we were all wearing different shades of red.

"I heard the name of the place, and it just seemed like a good idea," Jessa said, laughing. She swept a hand down her red halter dress as she spoke. She had a spectacular figure, with long legs, a small waist, and high breasts.

Judith was wearing a red mini skirt with a white off the

shoulder top, Marnie a black skirt with a red ruffled blouse. They had planned it, of course, and wore matching red heels.

"This place is luxe. Can't believe we got VIP here without having to blow anybody!" Marnie shouted over the noise. She came off a little louder than I think she intended, because she got several looks from the various crews for that one.

One of those looks was from Jessa. "Really, Marnie? Do you always have to go there?" she asked, laughing.

Marnie shrugged, her cute nose wrinkling. "I never said I was a classy chick. Far from it. Judith is the classy one in our duo."

Judith raised her brows. "Now how damn sad is that?"

I felt a hard chest press against my back, but I didn't stiffen or draw away. I knew the height and feel of that chest just perfectly. It used to sleep against my back when we'd huddled together for comfort, safety, and warmth.

Stephan wrapped his arms around me, kissing the top of my head. "Glad you came, Bee. It's never the same without you."

I smiled, turning my head to look at him. "I feel the same, Steph."

As though reading my mind, he bent so I could kiss his cheek.

"Where's Javier?" I asked as he pulled back, looking around for the other man.

"Bathroom," he said, moving away. He had to do some mingling, I knew. That was just how he operated.

"I heard about the drama with Vance last night," Jessa said after he walked away. "Rumor is he and Javier were making out in a bathroom..."

I grimaced. "I'm not surprised that's the rumor. Javier's side is different. He says that Vance pushed him against the wall and started kissing him. According to Javier, Vance just pushes him around like that to try to get a reaction, and Javier didn't push him away because he's learned that the best way to deal with Vance is not to react."

Jessa nodded, pursing her lips. "I've seen Vance do that. He's still crazy stupid in love with Javier. He's been pushing him around like that for years. Vance needs to move on." She shot a strangely malevolent look Damien's way. "Kind of like a certain stubborn pilot I know..."

I shot a look at Damien myself. Jessa definitely had a point there.

"I believe Javier," Judith said loudly. "I've seen how Vance treats him. He does crazy shit just hoping to make Javier snap."

"I've seen it, too. He wouldn't stop touching him at a party last year, even though Javier was clearly telling him to back off. Finally Javier slapped him across the face, and I'd swear that made Vance happy, from the look on his face when it happened."

I felt a wave of relief at their reaffirmation. I really did want to believe Javier's side of it. Wanting and believing were just two different things, unfortunately. Still, their words gave me hope that Javier wasn't just playing the drama game with Stephan, which was my biggest fear.

"I wouldn't mind getting slapped by Javier. He's fucking *hot*," Marnie said.

That surprised a laugh out of all of us. Of course she went there.

Damien approached our group, Murphy in tow. He looked a little weary as he eyed up our laughing group. "Why do my ears always burn when I see you all laughing like that?" he asked.

Marnie held up her hands, as though showing a good ten-inch measurement. "Don't worry, babe, it's all flattering."

Damien rubbed his temples, looking pained.

Murphy nodded, rubbing his chin and looking impressed. "I knew it!" he said.

I couldn't help it that made me laugh harder.

"Yeah, he has a big dick, but him running away after the sex kind of cancels that one out for me, personally," Jessa said wryly.

I was shocked. I hadn't known that Jessa and Damien had hooked up. Jessa *never* did the casual hook-up thing. Or so I'd thought.

Marnie held up her hands, making a rather large circle with her fingers, clearly illustrating girth. "This right here is what makes up for the running away part."

Murphy cursed loudly. "I fucking knew it!"

Marnie broke down in adorable giggles, clutching her stomach. Judith was right there with her. They high-fived.

I felt a little sorry for Damien, since he looked like he was in real pain, but I still couldn't stop laughing.

Stephan walked up to us, shaking his head and smiling. "Poor Damien. What did he ever do to deserve such relentless teasing?"

Marnie answered, of course. "He fucked too many of us, and he was too good at it, that's what."

"Speak for yourself," Jessa said. "There was nothing too good about my experience. Size isn't everything."

"Ooouuch," Murphy said, drawing out the sound. "Buuurrn."

Jessa shrugged. "Not a burn. Just stating facts."

"Brutal," Murphy said.

I felt a light tap on my shoulder and turned to find Javier just behind me. He looked a little nervous as he bent to my ear.

"Can we go somewhere and talk?" he asked.

I studied him, wondering what was going on now, but I just nodded. "Sure. Where to?"

I followed him to an empty section along the bar that attached to our VIP section. The bartender approached us instantly.

"I'm fine," I told him.

"I'll take another of your house specials," Javier said.

I studied him. He looked a little glassy-eyed. I didn't think I'd ever seen Javier drunk before, but I suspected that I might be seeing it now.

I sat in one of the cushioned stools at the bar.

He didn't sit, but moved close to me, leaning in to talk in a low voice. "I know you're worried about Stephan being with me. You think I'm not good enough for him. You think I'm trouble."

I opened my mouth to protest, even though most of what he said was somewhat true, but he continued in a rush. "I get it. I'm not trying to argue with you. I just wanted to clear some things up."

I nodded at him to go on.

"You don't have to worry about me hurting him, Bianca. If anyone is going to get hurt here, it will be me. I haven't even gone out with a guy since he dumped me. And that was, what, over a year and a half ago? I *pined* for him, Bianca. I know he's too good for me. I know he's too good for anyone. Every guy I know has a crush on him. He's damn near perfect. And I am bat-shit crazy in love with him. I thank God every day that he stays with me. I wouldn't mess this up for anything."

I felt a relief at his words that threatened to floor me. But there were still some things that he needed to clear up...

"What about the Vance nonsense? If he's been so awful to you, why on earth would you still be hanging out with him?"

He winced. "He wrote me a very long, drawn-out letter, talked about squashing our beef and moving on. For once, he sounded really sincere about it, and he and I were friends before we were a couple. He was a good friend, just a horrible boyfriend, and a worse ex. His letter had me thinking that we could go back to being casual friends. I wanted that, because so many of the guys on his crew are friends of mine, and I'd like for it to be less awkward every time he and I are in the same room. It's been so long since we were together. I just don't understand why he hasn't gotten over it. Thinking that he finally had was just something I wanted to believe, I guess. It won't ever happen again. I'm so done with him."

I nodded. That seemed for the best. I only hoped he meant it.

It was like he read my mind. "I know you won't trust me right away. That's just not how you work. But I hope that you will eventually. I intend to prove myself. This is it for me, Bianca. Stephan is the real deal, and if he wants me, I'm sticking around."

He moved into me, wrapping his arms around me tightly. It should have been awkward, since I was sitting and he was standing, but somehow we fit just right. I hugged him back.

"I hope so, Javier. You know, the first time you guys went out he came home with this dreamy look on his face. He was so happy. I know you think I haven't been a fan of yours, but I became a fan that night. There's nothing I'd love more than for Stephan to be with someone that makes him that happy. And you shouldn't downplay his feelings for you. He pined for you too, Javier. I know a lot of guys have a crush on him, but you're the only one he sees. Trust me on that. And I'll be eternally grateful to you for helping him to see that he doesn't need to hide who he is anymore, or who he's with."

He squeezed me tighter. I hugged him back.

Javier laughed. "Look at Stephan," he said. "Us hugging has made his day."

I pulled back to look.

Stephan was across the lounge, standing next to Jessa, grinning at us like he'd just been granted a wish.

Javier toasted him with the dark red martini that the bartender had left for him on the bar while we'd been talking.

"That looks tasty," I told him, pointing at his drink.

His brows lifted. "Want me to order you one?"

I shook my head. "Alcohol doesn't really agree with me. I don't seem to have a spot between dead sober and crazy drunk."

He held the glass out to me. "Just taste it. It's a black

raspberry martini. It's Red's signature cocktail. It's my new favorite drink."

I took the glass from him, sniffing it. It smelled good. "What's in it?" I asked, taking a very tiny sip, and, tasting it, a slightly bigger one.

"Chambord, raspberry vodka, and blood orange juice."

"It tastes awesome. What's Chambord?"

"Raspberry liqueur. To die for, right? Best tasting drink ever."

I nodded. "So good."

I felt a hard body press against me from behind, and I stiffened. I handed Javier his drink.

"How many of those have you had?" James purred in my ear. He dug a hand into my hair, gripping a tight handful of it into a fist. His other arm snaked around my waist from behind, gripping a hip in his hand.

His tone was silky smooth, but I still heard the menace in it.

"None," I told him calmly. "Javier just let me have a taste of his."

"Are you going to drink tonight?" he demanded.

I hadn't been planning on it, but his tone and his attitude almost had me changing my mind.

"I hadn't been planning on it," I said finally.

"That's good," he said, smooth as silk. "You know I don't care for alcohol. And I won't fuck you mindless when you've been drinking."

My eyes shot to Javier. James hadn't bothered to lower his voice, but the other man hadn't seemed to notice.

James turned me in his arms, his hold unbreakable. He tilted my chin up until I had a clear look at his tarnished eyes. "Tell me something," he began in that silky tone. "Is it romantic or psychotic when I say that I'll never let you leave me?"

I studied him. I just couldn't tell if there was even a hint of humor to his words when he was in this mood. "I suppose that would depend on whether I'm trying to leave you or not. If I never tried, it's romantic, and if I ever did, and you didn't let me, definitely psychotic. Why are you trying to scare me, James?" My voice was steady and calm. I would cope with this. I would not run just because he was acting so strange.

His smile was a bitter twist to his pretty mouth. I didn't like it a bit. It spoke of secrets and fears. "I'm not trying to scare you, Love. I mean to keep you. I'm just trying to gauge how badly you want to be kept."

"I want you to tell me what's going on. Is it something to do with that conversation you had with Roger?"

His brows shot up. "So happy you asked about Roger. I just finished having a meeting with him, and he's dying to meet you, so he'll be here shortly. You'll like him. Very nice man."

I traced a finger down the smooth plane of his cheek. I rubbed at a spot there where it dimpled when he smiled. "So you refuse to tell me? Is that how it's going to be with us?" I asked him.

The mask he'd been maintaining slipped for an instant, giving me a glimpse into raw, desperate eyes.

"No, Bianca. I want us to share everything. I mean that. Will you just give me time?"

"Will you stop acting like the world is about to fall down around us?"

"Yes, of course. If I know that you're devoted to me, and devoted to us staying together, it will help immensely."

"I've told you how I feel. But you can't make me depend on you so quickly, so desperately, and then close yourself off. I can't take that, James. It raises all of my defenses—sets off all of my alarms, when you act scared and secretive.

He nodded. "Yes. I'm sorry. I've been on edge with a crucial negotiation. It is a lose-lose type of scenario. I'll try not to take it home with me anymore. Ah, here comes Roger."

Roger was an attractive man, with slate gray hair and a face that looked like it had been lined and weathered with smiles rather than frowns. He was a fit man, maybe in his early fifties. His smile was big and sincere as he approached us.

"Leave it to James to drag me clubbing in my fifties," he said by way of greeting.

I smiled at him. He held out a hand, and I pulled back far enough from James to shake it.

"I'm Roger, an old friend of the family. And you're Bianca. I've heard so much about you. I begin to see why my young friend has turned over a new leaf." His tone was rich and warm with sincerity.

A waiter approached our group, looking nervous and anxious. James leveled a hard stare at him that made the waiter's anxiety understandable.

"Mr. Cavendish, sir. Jeff, the manager, needs a moment of your time."

James watched the other man, his cold stare the epitome of intimidation. "Really? He *needs* my presence right now? Does he think that I'm here for business?"

"No, sir. He knows you are here, uh, socially. He said it was very important."

James smiled a sharp smile that was all perfect white teeth. It was scary. "Tell him I'll be with him momentarily."

He nodded at Roger, kissing my cheek roughly. He looked agitated, his jaw clenched. "If you'll both excuse me, I'll be back in a moment. This had better be good."

CHAPTER EIGHTEEN

Mr. Curious

We watched him stride away.

Roger spoke when he was a good distance away. "Pardon my bluntness, Bianca, but are you at all aware of James's past?"

I turned to look at him, meeting his eyes very steadily. "What are you referring to exactly?"

He sighed, looking uncomfortable. "He was given into the care of a cousin of his shortly after his parents died. I fought this decision—fought it hard, but I was overturned by his family. I had no legal ability to protect him. I only have my suspicions about his guardian, and it really isn't my place to be telling you this, but in order to understand some of what James has done, I think you should know—"

"I know all about Spencer, if that's what you're getting at. Why are you telling me this?"

He studied me. "He told you about Spencer?"

I nodded.

He looked startled. "It's probably a very good sign that he shared something like that with you. The reason I bring it up, though, is that after he left Spencer's care, he became a different kid for a long time. He was wild and unruly. I barely knew him anymore. Whatever happened with his guardian, it affected him in a very negative way. I don't know if you know this, but he used to be quite...promiscuous."

I felt my eyes harden as I looked at him. "I'm well aware of that. Trust me when I say that it's been brought to my attention *many* times."

"So you know how he used to be? Up until he met you, he was..."

"He was a slut. Yes, I know. What's your point?" I felt rude even as I said the words, but God was I sick of this subject.

"Well...I got the impression from James that he would be quite distraught if some things about his past were brought to light. I was led to believe that he feared that you would leave him if you knew about his former indiscretions, and that was why he was so upset about certain things being revealed. Do you know about his...unorthodox preferences?"

I sighed, thoroughly confused and sooo done with the conversation. "Yes. I'm very aware," I said, trying not to blush as I kept his steady gaze. Something about the man was just so dignified. I couldn't believe that I was as good as discussing my BDSM lifestyle with him.

His thick, dark eyebrows shot up. "Well, that's a relief, though it doesn't exactly clear anything up for *me*. Again, pardon my bluntness, but perhaps you should let James know that his past won't scare you off."

"Why? What is the point to all this? What's been going on with James?"

He shot a glance behind me and looked particularly uncomfortable. "I am not at liberty to say," he said absently.

"Now you sound like a lawyer," I told him.

As I spoke, a firm hand descended to my nape.

"That was quick," Roger told James, who was pressing himself tightly against my back.

"It was nothing," James stated dismissively. "What have you

two been chatting about? Why does he sound like a lawyer, Love?"

I turned to look at him.

He shifted with me, not relinquishing the hand on my nape.

"What was the emergency?" I asked with an arched brow.

His upper lipped curled. "There wasn't one. There was only a part-time manager in need of a demotion. Tell me what you were talking about?"

"That's a nosy question. Did you really demote someone for wasting five minutes of your time?"

He moved until he was standing close against me, pressing himself against my side. Even knowing that he was doing it to distract me, I was far from unaffected by his nearness.

"I demoted him, and put him on probation pending termination, because he is managing one of the most profitable clubs in Manhattan, and he can't handle a simple wine shortage. Him wasting five minutes of my time only illuminated the facts for me. Your turn. What were you two talking about?"

Roger cleared his throat. "Nothing important, James. I really do need to get going. I'll call you if I learn anything new."

Roger shook our hands, bowing his head politely before turning away.

"I'll walk you out, Roger," James said to his back.

Roger waved him off. "No, that's fine. Get some time with Bianca. It's obvious that you don't get enough of that. Have a good night."

"Are you going to tell me what you two talked about?" James asked me as Roger strode out of sight.

I shook my head. "Why are you so curious?"

He moved into me, pressing his front against mine. He bent as though to kiss me. "I'm curious about everything you do, Bianca. What do I need to do to get you to tell me what he said to you?"

I just shook my head at him again.

He let out a little growl in his throat, kissing me. It was an overwhelming, possessive kind of kiss. We were in public, in one of *his* clubs, but he didn't hold back. He sucked at my mouth, his hands moving to my butt to pull me hard against the proof of his desire. He rubbed against me like a cat.

I purred. My hand curled into the lapels of his suit jacket, gripping desperately.

He snaked one hand up into my hair, gripping it then pulling it sharply enough to elicit one involuntary little moan. He pulled back just far enough to breathe against my mouth. "You're in the mood to get fucked against a wall tonight, aren't you?"

He was kissing me again before I could respond, the hand on my ass moving to the back of my thigh, hitching it up so that he could grind right into me.

He stopped abruptly, pulling back but not away.

My hips twisted against him before I registered that we weren't alone. *Oh yeah*. We'd never been alone. We were in a club.

He pulled back, grabbed my hand, and began to pull me.

"We'll be right back," he called out to Stephan. "We're just going to go have a chat."

I didn't look at Stephan, didn't hear him respond. I was lost in a sensual haze, just putting one foot in front of the other, following him blindly. James had said something about fucking me against a wall. *Yes*. That sounded perfect.

He led me out of the VIP lounge, down a long red hallway, and then another. He pulled me into a large office. There was a man behind the desk, typing on a computer. He looked startled at our entrance.

"Give us privacy," James told him, his voice sharp.

The man beat a hasty retreat.

James shut and locked the door behind him. Handy that, a lock.

He started loosening his tie. When it was untied, he hooked

a finger into the hoop at my neck. He pushed my back to the wall. Or rather, the door.

He reached above my head and I looked up. There was a coat hanger above me, hooked over the top of the tall door. James was tying his tie to it with swift, sure motions. He pulled my arms up and together, wrapping the tie around them, tying more swift knots around my wrists. This took longer, and I watched those skillful hands with rapt attention.

"This is going to get loud, Bianca. I'm going to fuck you so hard that you scream my name. And you are going to scream so loudly that *nobody* will doubt just why you're screaming. Would you like to tell me what you and Roger were talking about before I'm inside of you? Or will this be a mid-fuck confession?"

I just shook my head again.

He smiled a very troublesome smile. Mr. Cavendish was about to take the reins.

He worked on his own clothing first, pulling his shirt out of his pants, then unbuttoning and spreading his slacks open. He pulled that delicious cock out slowly, tauntingly. He stroked himself while he watched me.

He pulled the strapless side of my dress down, saw that I was wearing a strapless bra, and yanked that down too. He bent slightly and began to suck hard at my nipple while he slid his hands up my skirt and slipped my panties off.

He straightened very slowly when he finished, leaning into me, pushing my leg up, and thrusting into me hard with that same motion. I watched him and I saw his cold smile when he elicited a sharp little gasp out of me.

He pounded into me so hard and fast that it did wrench a little scream out of me. A scream that formed into a very long version of the word James. I was on that fine edge when he yanked out, his eyes intense and angry on mine.

"Tell me what you and Roger talked about, Bianca," he

ordered.

It took me long moments to gain any semblance of coherency. When I did, a spark of anger shot through me.

"You can't use sex to control me, James. You shouldn't play with my heart like that."

He laughed. It was sinister. "Oh Love, it's not your heart I'm playing with. And I'll play with your body whenever I damn well please."

He moved back against me and then he was driving roughly into me again. "Don't even think about letting yourself come," he murmured to me in an almost offhanded way. He jackhammered into me, so hard and so fast, again and again, for long moments before wrenching out of me again. I made a noise that sounded suspiciously like a scream of distress when he pulled out.

He touched my bottom lip softly with an index finger. "Tell me, Bianca. Tell me what you talked about with Roger."

"You're being a bastard," I told him after a while. He just smiled that sinister smile and stroked my lips with his finger. "A sadistic bastard."

He laughed. "Yes. I am that. Just tell me what you talked about, Bianca. Before this gets out of hand."

We had a long, silent standoff before I caved. I did it because I'd realized that it wasn't really that important, and because I didn't want to see how far he would go to prove a point just then.

"We talked about *you*, James. About your past, about your promiscuity, your...preferences. I think he just wanted to know what I knew. He seemed to think that you'd kept me in the dark about it all. I got the sense that he was afraid that something about your past was about to be leaked, and that it was something that would drive me away. Why did he think that, James? What's going on?"

He cursed fluently. "Goddamn Roger. It's nothing, Bianca.

It's being taken care of. Someone was threatening to be... indiscreet about some of my exploits. I'm handling it. I've been agitated because I've been trying to distance myself from my past, to clean up my image, if you will, for your sake, for the sake of our future, and this leak would have the opposite effect. But as I said, I'm handling it. Thank you for answering my question."

He moved against me again.

I spoke just as he was lining himself up at my entrance. "It's not like I had a choice," I muttered sullenly.

He thrust into me, bottoming out in one hard motion.

I cried his name brokenly.

"How about I make it up to you with a handful of orgasms?"

I didn't answer. He already had me incoherent as he made good on his offer.

He pounded into me relentlessly, one hand pulling my hair, the other rubbing my clit. He brought me over, again, and then again. He was merciless. I was completely wrung out by the time he let himself come with a rough groan, grinding deep inside of me, the hand in my hair moving to my chin. He gripped it hard as he watched me.

He gave me one swift kiss before pulling out of me.

He left me where I was, leaning against the door for support, my arms still tied, while he moved to the desk.

He cleaned us both as well as he could with just tissues. He kissed me deeply but softly, a romantic kind of kiss, while he untied my wrists. He pulled me against him, supporting me while I regained my balance, massaging the feeling back into my wrists slowly and thoroughly.

"I love you, Bianca," he said when he finally pulled back.

"I love you, too, James, but that doesn't give you a free pass."

"No, it doesn't. Being your Dom does that, Love. I've compromised far more for you than I've ever done for anyone or anything in my life. Controlling you sexually is something I won't be bending on, but I'm pretty sure you already knew that."

CHAPTER NINETEEN

Mr. Amenable

James was in a remarkably better mood as we returned to our group. We stayed for hours, laughing and joking with my friends. He was even friendly with Damien, though the man couldn't get within six feet of me without James grabbing handfuls of me to prove a point. Though, if I was fair, he rarely kept his hands off me when we were together, Damien or no.

Damien, for his part, was giving James even less of a reason to be jealous than usual. He was distracted and quiet. He spent most of the night shooting Jessa baffled looks. I found that strangely encouraging. Maybe there was something there. It could have been that he just took it personal that she hadn't enjoyed their one-night stand, but I was hoping it was more than that. I caught a little snippet of their conversation as the night was winding down, when Damien had managed to corner Jessa just behind where we'd been standing and chatting with Murphy.

"Hey. Are we good?" Damien asked her, his voice worried.

"We're fine," Jessa replied in a flat voice, sounding anything but fine.

"I feel like a jerk. I didn't know you felt that way. Frankly, I thought you'd forgotten about the whole thing, since you never mention it."

"Don't worry about it, Damien. One unhappy customer out of a thousand should hardly mess up your average."

He cursed, and I couldn't help it, I glanced over at them.

Damien's back was to me, but Jessa was facing me, and I saw her face clearly as she rolled her eyes.

"I didn't know it was bad for you. It wasn't bad for me. In fact, it was pretty amazing. I'd like to...make it up to you, if you'd let me. You could show me what you didn't like—help me work on my technique."

Jessa snorted loudly.

Apparently, I wasn't the only one shamelessly eavesdropping. Murphy started swaying and singing, *"Player's gonna play..."*

"Here's the thing, Damien. It was a hell of a lot more than your technique that wasn't working out for me. The pining for a chick that's never going to look at you twice thing was the biggest turn off, and the fact that you didn't bother to clue me in about your little hang-up before we hopped in the sack. I never do the casual sex thing, and the way you turned into a stranger the second we were done reminded me very clearly why. Sex is not just a bodily function for me. I require some semblance of intimacy with the act, and you wouldn't know intimacy if it punched you in the face.

"I hear you've been celibate for the last few months," Jessa continued mercilessly. "Waiting for a chick *that is never going to want you.* You're not an idiot, you know she's not going to leave her drop-dead gorgeous, so fucking hot that they look like they want to fuck each other in public, billionaire boyfriend for you. It's just another crazy-ass way for you to avoid real feelings. The only way you could be good in bed for me would if you became a complete person, not just some *shell of a man* that doesn't have a middle ground between putting women on a pedestal and degrading them with meaningless sex."

Murphy clutched his chest, falling to his knees. "I felt that right here, my friend!" he called out to Damien, not even bothering to hide the fact that we'd all been shamelessly listening to the entire exchange.

"How about we have this little chat in private," Damien said, his tone hard. We all watched silently while he grabbed Jessa by the arm and led her resolutely away.

She went easily enough, just muttering one loud, "Neanderthal," as they walked away.

I looked at James, who'd been silent throughout the exchange. "Maybe those two will work things out and start dating," I said hopefully.

James studied me. "Do you want that?"

I sent him a baffled look. "Of course I do. Damien needs to move on, and Jessa would be good for anybody. She's one of the most open and honest people I've ever met. Talking to her is like chatting with a really good therapist."

"Nah," Murphy said, getting back up. "Damien's pretty clear about what he likes from women. He likes to be ignored, not yelled at. She's not his type at all."

I gave my little shrug. "Maybe he needs to find a new type."

Murphy grinned. "Now wouldn't that be awesome."

Damien and Jessa never returned to the club, at least not before James and I left, and I took that as a very good sign.

We made our rounds, saying goodbye to everyone at around eleven. James was rather quiet but sweet on the short trip back to the apartment. He nuzzled into my neck, placing soft, sweet kisses there. It wasn't his usual style, but I still melted.

He made love to me again before I sank into a deep and dreamless sleep.

I was pleasantly surprised the next morning when I realized that he was traveling to Vegas with me that day. I'd known that he was planning to spend part of his week there with me, but we hadn't discussed when he was flying out.

We got dressed together, holding hands quietly while we

made our way down to the waiting car.

"I discussed it with Stephan last night. You don't have to take the airport shuttle with the crew. It's at your lead's discretion, and he gave us the green light, so you can ride with me."

I just nodded.

The flight went well. The whole day did, in fact. There was a brief moment of tension when James found out that, though I was taking the furlough, I would still be working my regular schedule for at least two more weeks. He didn't like that. I hadn't thought he would, but I wouldn't budge.

"This company gave me an invaluable opportunity that changed my life. That means a lot to me. They've asked us to stay on our schedules for two more weeks, and I won't bail early and mess up staffing in the meantime. I won't budge on this, James."

My little speech was impassioned enough that he let it go pretty quickly, for him. Even if he couldn't understand why I would have a feeling of loyalty towards a company that was on its way out, he at least respected it. That warmed me. He didn't always understand me, but I could have no doubts that he tried to.

The next few days went like that. Every possible bump in the road gave us little resistance. He didn't complain when I had to work for most of Sunday, just kissed me a lingering goodbye with a murmured, "I love you."

Things were good between us. Good was putting it mildly. We were amazing together. Things became so easy but that heat between us didn't cool for a moment. It became very clear to me just how perfect it could be between us if we just let it. It all felt so perfect, in fact, that I began to get a little paranoid, always waiting for that other shoe to drop.

I told myself that life didn't just have to be a series of tragedies. Maybe I could just have this wonderful thing, no conditions. Perhaps life would be blissfully smooth sailing from here on out. I wanted to believe it, but a sick tension never quite left my gut, and my nightmares were more persistent than ever.

We stayed at his Vegas home that week, agreeing to stay at my little place on the next Vegas rotation.

On Monday, we went out to dinner with the tattoo artist, Frankie. I was nervous. I knew I'd made a bad impression the first time we'd met, and I wanted to rectify that, but I didn't know the woman, so I wasn't sure how.

We met her at a trendy restaurant in the Cavendish Hotel & Casino. I dressed Vegas casual, in a pretty, white blouse, beige short-shorts, and pumpkin orange heels. You could never show too much skin in Vegas, and the heels made the outfit just dressy enough that I could fit in anywhere.

Frankie was warm and friendly, hugging us both and giving me a genuine smile right off the bat. I felt my tension ease. She was going to make it easy on me.

Frankie was wearing a tight gray T-shirt that was torn so short at the bottom that I got a good look at some of her under-boob. Her cutoff jean shorts weren't much more decent. Her ink-covered skin was well displayed in all its glory.

She caught me looking and smiled. "My reality show is shooting. The producers love to see the ink. I swear they talk me into less and less clothing every season. Next season they might just get me to walk around naked.

I smiled back at her. She had a very nice smile. Her makeup was dark, her lips nearly black. Her look was harsh but managed not to detract from her pretty face. With that endearing smile she was actually kind of adorable. With her corkscrew black curls, she kind of looked like a grown-up goth Shirley Temple.

We hit it off with no problems. Frankie wasn't at all what I'd been worried she'd be. I began to see why she and James got along so well. She laid the charm on thick; add that to her undeniable charisma, and I saw easily why she had her own reality show. I didn't like reality shows. I never saw the appeal to watching people that I didn't like or respect make fools of themselves, but I would have bet that I'd like Frankie's show.

"What would I have to do to get you on my table, Bianca?" Frankie asked with a charming smile after we'd been chatting for a solid hour.

James made a disapproving noise, and I glanced at him. He was shooting an annoyed look in the other woman's direction. "Don't hit on my girl, Frankie."

She raised her hands in a show of innocence, laughing. She was clearly unaffected by his jealousy. "I wouldn't, James. You've got it all wrong. I just think she'd look lovely with some ink on that perfect skin of hers."

James looked far from appeased by that. "Knock it off, Frankie."

She waved him off. "Oh, chill out, James. I'm really not. I have a girlfriend now, and I've never been happier. Just let me have some fun."

I saw his eyes move to somewhere behind Frankie. My gaze followed his. A huge man strode towards us. He was several tables away, but I could tell from that purposeful stride and his intent stare that he was headed our way.

He looked...sinister. And sexy. He had pitch-black hair that hung straight to his massive shoulders. He was so big that I would have pegged him for a football player, or some kind of professional athlete, if it weren't for the way he dressed. He wore a white T-shirt with what looked like some band's logo on the front of it. It was so tight that I could see every ridge in his six-pack, and every bit of the extensive tattoos that covered his chest. His jeans looked like he'd been in a war-zone, they were so torn up. His arms were covered in full sleeve tattoos. I thought that he must work in Frankie's tattoo parlor, since he was so inked up.

As he drew closer, I saw that his hard jaw had a five o'clock shadow that looked like it never went away. He had even features, with thick brows over thickly lashed eyes, a straight, rounded nose, and a mouth made for sin. He was a handsome devil.

He grinned as he drew close to us, flashing twin dimples that were pure trouble.

James cursed. "What the hell is he doing here?" he asked Frankie. He sounded very putout.

Frankie turned to see who he was talking about, but had the opposite reaction when she saw who approached. She grinned.

"Tristan is getting a new tat today. Of course, my producer just had to catch it for the show. They love it when celebrities come into the shop. Your episode is airing in two weeks, by the way."

Of course he'd made an exhibition out of the tattoos, I thought, as my mind connected the dots.

I didn't have time to address the issue, however, before Tristan was on us. His eyes were all on me as he reached our table. They were golden and twinkling, disarming really. I smiled back tentatively, clued into a strange tension from James.

Tristan sat at the only empty chair at the table, sliding it until he was sitting almost too close to me. His eyes were warm on me.

"The infamous Bianca. I have to say, I've been looking forward to meeting you. James and I go way back. I'm Tristan."

He held out his hand to shake and I did automatically. James sucked in a gasp when Tristan raised my hand to his mouth, and he was wrenching my hand out of the other man's grasp before I could react.

"Watch yourself, Tristan," James said through gritted teeth.

Tristan just grinned that sinister grin with those troublesome dimples. "Relax, Cavendish, I know she's yours. I was just saying hi."

"Yeah, well, if you say 'hi' again I'm going to break your nose."

"I'd love to see you try, but I'd really hate to make you ruin your manicure."

I turned to James, giving him a stern look, and completely ignoring the other man. I rubbed his chest until he looked at me. I didn't say a word, just watched him, willing him to calm, to keep from escalating a small confrontation into something out of hand.

After a long moment he relaxed a fraction, pulling me until I was plastered against his side.

It was a while before I looked back at Tristan. He was a strange one, I thought, as he studied us intently, his brow furrowed. "Someone told me you'd fallen over the deep end, but I just didn't believe it. I stand corrected. You've got it bad, my friend."

"What are you getting a tattoo of?" I asked Tristan, trying to find a neutral topic for the hostile men. I looked at him as I asked the question.

"I'm getting a small five to commemorate five years clean and sober," he said without hesitation, as though he'd practiced it.

I blinked. "Congratulations," I told him, meaning it. Addiction was a horrible, powerful thing. I'd seen people ruined by it.

"Thank you. I did some bad things when I was using, things I can't make up for, but having five years of sobriety under my belt still feels pretty damn good."

Frankie smacked herself in the forehead. It was an attention getter. We all looked at her. "You can say that without adding a disclaimer about all of your sins," she chided him. "You have every right to be proud of yourself."

He shrugged, frowning harshly. He was a tough looking guy, but somehow that frown made him look vulnerable rather than mean. "I don't see it that way. Even with all of the touchy-feely rehab bullshit, I still know that it was me doing all those things, not the alcohol or the drugs, and there are some things a person can't just forgive themselves for, especially when the one I hurt the most can't forgive me, either."

Frankie cursed, pointing at him. I could tell just from the last two minutes that these two had a tough love kind of relationship, but a close one. "I'm calling your therapist just because you said that. You're supposed to be past that by now, and the fact that you aren't says you need to start seeing her more."

Tristan ignored her, turning to address me. He had that kind of intense regard that it was difficult not to return. He reminded me of a certain billionaire I knew...

He waved a hand between James and me. It was a strangely elegant gesture for such a huge man. "I used to have what you guys have. I found a sub once that suited me so perfectly..."

I felt a little shocked at his words, referring to our lifestyle so casually and including himself in that life with a few words. I remembered that James had described Frankie as a Domme as well. I wondered if they had their own club... Did they meet up once a week for coffee? The whole thing seemed surreal.

"All of this other shit I do is just a cheap imitation of that," he continued. "She was so exquisite."

"What happened?" I asked him.

He bit his lush bottom lip. I thought that everything the man did came off sinful. "What else?" he asked bitterly. "I fucked it up. I pushed her so hard that I drove her away. If I'm honest, I pushed her away on purpose. Things were getting too intimate, and I couldn't have that. I was the same as every other addict. Being self-destructive used to be a way of life for me."

He looked at James. "How's Danika? She been doing alright?"

James sighed, and I studied him as he answered. "She's good, as far as I can tell. She's great at her job. I'm actually putting her in charge of all of my galleries, not just the west coast ones. Beth in New York will have a fit being under her, but I've decided that I need to work less and live more, so my best managers are being promoted in a hurry. You should call her, Tristan. I know you worry about her, so just call her, see for yourself how she's doing."

Tristan let out a frustrated breath. "You think I haven't tried calling her? I keep tabs on her. That's it. I need to know she's okay, but the woman will have nothing to do with me."

"Have you tried calling her lately?"

"You know Danika. She won't change her mind."

"If you contacted her with something other than a casual fuck on your mind, and used that annoying persistence of yours, I wouldn't be surprised if she gave you another shot," James said, his tone idle.

Tristan's eyes sharpened on him with that laser focus that reminded me so much of James. "Why do you think that? Has she said something to you?"

James shrugged and grimaced, the arm around my shoulder jostling me with the movement. "She's just...I don't know, missing something. She's too reserved, too controlled, too damned disinterested about every part of her life except for work. And she works too much. I know from personal experience that if you make good money and still get the urge to spend the majority of your life working, it's because something important is missing there."

Tristan looked very raw as he studied the other man, his golden eyes holding a familiar sort of tarnish that spoke of pain, but that I found beautiful. "Is she seeing anyone?" he asked finally, the words sounding like they'd been torn out of him against his will.

James sighed. "I'm not sure. She was a few months back. I'm not sure how serious it was, or if he's still around. She doesn't go out of her way to mention her personal life, and I'm not asking. I just saw him stop by the gallery when I was visiting on business."

"They're meeting with her tomorrow. Bianca is having a gallery showing in L.A.," Frankie spoke up suddenly. "They haven't set a date for it yet, but I know I'll be attending. You should come as my date, Tristan."

He gave her a wry smile. "Your little Latin fireball of a sub would scratch my eyes out for that."

"So we'll make it a threesome. She won't mind that. She might like it a little bit too much, in fact."

Frankie addressed me, pointing at Tristan. "He's my straight detector. If I'm lucky enough to turn one gay, he flips her straight again. Bastard."

That surprised a loud laugh out of me.

Tristan shrugged and flashed a dimple at her. "Just here to help."

CHAPTER TWENTY

Mr. Playful

We lingered over dinner with the strange pair. Tristan ordered food even though we'd all already finished eating. He made himself right at home without asking, joking and talking to Frankie and me. I liked him. A lot. I liked them both. They were fun.

James was quiet and a little tense at my back, but he made no move to leave.

When we did finally leave after hours of talking, Frankie gave me a big hug. Tristan tried to, as well, but James was there to block him, not even trying to be subtle about it.

Tristan was unfazed. He grinned that wicked grin at me, inclining his head. "It was a pleasure to meet you, Bianca. You are an absolute delight. I'll be seeing you."

James didn't speak until we were in the back of his limo driving home. "You liked him," he said, his tone bland, but I didn't believe that tone for a second.

"I liked them both," I said, rubbing his arm. "Your friends are very nice. It's nice to see that you have some more good ones. They're starting to outnumber all of the evil bitches I keep meeting that you felt the need to sleep with."

He completely ignored the last part of my statement, still

focused on Tristan.

"He's a Dom, as I'm sure you picked up. Purely BD without the SM. You were attracted to him."

Uh oh. "Well, I'm *in love* with you. I like him, just like I said. As a friend. He's an attractive man, I can't deny that, but that's it, James. You can't think that every Dom I meet is going to have some impossible pull on me, just because you did."

And it was actually that easy. A few reassurances and he relaxed back into his smiling, amenable persona. I thought that boded well for us. The little things were already resolving themselves with ease.

We met Danika at the tourist gallery of the Cavendish Hotel & Casino the next morning. Danika managed both the L.A. and Vegas galleries, which was especially impressive since she looked to still be in her early to mid-twenties.

With all of the talk the night before, my mind started trying to pair Danika and the physically imposing Tristan up the moment I saw her, and it was almost disconcerting to picture the two of them together. He was so massive and muscular that he could have been an MMA fighter. She, on the other hand, was the epitome of delicate grace.

She was maybe five foot seven, with smooth, straight, pitch-black hair that fell to her mid-back. She was thin, but she definitely had curves in all of the right places. She had a pale complexion, but her heritage was very obviously mixed. Part of the mix was Asian, but the rest was anybody's guess. At least part Caucasian, by her clear gray eyes.

Tristan had been right. No one could deny that she was exquisite.

She was dressed for business in a pencil skirt and a tidy dress shirt with the sleeves rolled up. She wore flats, I realized as she stepped out from behind the podium as we approached. I would have pegged her as a stiletto girl just because she was so painfully poised. I saw in an instant why she didn't, though.

She had just the slightest hitch to her step as she approached us with a lovely smile. Some old injury, I guessed. It was the most graceful limp I'd ever seen, as though she'd just absorbed the injury and made it a part of her, neither emphasizing or hiding it. That seemingly effortless gait told me a lot about the woman. She looked delicate, but there was steel in her.

"So nice to finally meet you, Bianca. I've been privileged to get the distinguished honor of being your first big fan. More will come, though, I can assure you."

"Hey, now," James said, shaking her hand with a smile. "Don't discount my adoration of her work. Remember who discovered her."

She inclined her head. "Touché, James. Please, follow me. We have a lot to discuss."

We sat at a large conference room at the back of the swank gallery. Danika pulled out a huge leather binder, and I only realized that it was a portfolio of my work when she flipped it open.

"Let me start by saying that art is my life, and I simply *adore* your work. It is, however, a rather eclectic mix of paintings. This can be handled in a number of ways. My personal preference would be to divide all of the different themes by rooms, since we have so many paintings to work with, and we will be utilizing every room in the L.A space for the showing."

I nodded. "That sounds good."

She looked a little nonplussed, as though she'd been expecting an argument. "Well, that was easy. If all of the issues are that easy to resolve, we can schedule a showing for next week!"

The entire meeting went similarly. Danika had very helpful suggestions about all of the things I needed to green light for the showing, and I was more than happy to defer to her expertise on something that I was a complete novice at.

She was swift and professional, covering details that I hadn't even considered, until she was satisfied that she had the showing thoroughly mapped out.

James stayed reasonably silent throughout the meeting, which I appreciated. If he had taken over, as he did with so many things, it wouldn't have felt like it was mine. But working with Danika, seeing every step in the process without his interference, it began to feel real, like I had a career here, instead of a hobby that was being funded by my rich boyfriend.

We went to lunch with Danika after we finished. Sandra, the assistant manager of the Vegas gallery who worked directly under Danika, joined us.

She was a small, brown-haired woman with brown eyes and a rather austere demeanor. If I had to guess, I'd have said she was in her late thirties.

I'd completely forgotten about Danika's limp until she was moving away from the table to use the restroom. Sandra murmured something about needing to check on the gallery, scurrying off.

"What happened to Danika's foot?" I asked James.

"It's her knee, I believe. And I don't know. She never talks about it, but I've gotten the distinct impression that it was somehow Tristan's fault."

I frowned. That sounded beyond ominous.

We wrapped up a productive and pleasant morning with Danika, setting up a date the following week, when she swore she'd be well into the thick of planning the showing. I was excited and elated when we parted. The crazy dream that was my painting career felt like it was shaping into something real and substantial.

James gave the staff at his house the afternoon off, and we spent hours swimming in his ridiculous pool. The thing was obnoxious, with fake mountains and fountains, and four different pools, and yes, a grotto underneath one of the falls.

"I didn't realize we were staying at the Playboy mansion," I teased him.

He grimaced. "This is actually a part of the house that I did *not* design. It's a long story, but I delegated this part of the design to my casino team, and since they knew I'd have to have some promotional parties here, this is what they did. I was not too happy when I saw it, but it *has* served its purpose. If I'm out of town and the casino needs to throw a pool party for some bigwigs, they do it here."

I wrinkled my nose at him. I knew the Vegas scene well enough, even if it wasn't really my scene. "I hope everything's been disinfected."

He tapped my nose. "Yes, of course. You know it drives me crazy when you do that with your nose. It makes you look so damn cute."

I tapped his nose. "Don't call me cute," I told him.

His nostrils flared, rather sexily, I thought.

I was lying on a cushioned lounger in a white bikini I wouldn't be caught dead wearing in public while he rubbed sunblock all over my body. He was not efficient about the process, rubbing more of the parts inside of the tiny bikini than out of it, and grinning the entire time.

"You don't have to work at all today?" I asked him. He'd worked the day before, but made no mention of going in that day.

"I'm taking a day off. I want to fuck you in broad daylight. I want to spread you out and strip you bare under the sun."

That made me squirm in my seat. I'd had my hopes when he was dismissing his staff, but now it was certain. We weren't just out here to swim.

"You're going to get me sunburned in some painful places," I predicted.

He held up the bottle of sunblock he was using. "I've got it covered. Come on now, you know me better."

He was thorough, but slow as molasses as he covered me in

the stuff. He even spent extra time on my feet, rubbing and kneading until I moaned in pleasure. He was good with his hands in every way imaginable.

The second leisurely rubbed on coat of sunblock was completely unnecessary, of course, but he did it all the same. Only James could turn sun protection into foreplay. I was writhing before he made it back up to my inner thighs.

His sunblock coated fingers teased around my sex, fingering my tiny string bikini bottoms, but he pulled them back with a wicked little smile. "For external use only, Love. I guess you'll have to settle for my tongue."

He pulled the strings on both of my hips loose with his teeth. I buried my hands in his hair as he buried his face between my legs.

It wasn't his usual oral technique, avoiding my clit at first to thrust his tongue as deep inside of me as it would go. It felt drugging—it felt good, but when he finally moved up to my clit and sucked with a vengeance I came hard, gasping his name.

He moved up my body in a flash, untying my top, and moving my leg across his torso, positioning it diagonally with my ankle on his shoulder, turning me on my side, and straddling my other leg. He poised himself at my entrance for a brief moment.

"Fucking me sideways," I told him breathlessly.

He grinned and thrust in hard. "Every which way, until we're sated or dead, Love."

He pulled out slowly, dragging himself along every perfect nerve, playing me like an instrument, then pounded in again. His size, and the unrelenting position, made each thrust border on painful. He repeated the torture, again and again, and I came with a ragged cry torn out of me.

He didn't stop, just pounded faster. He bottomed out and came inside of me with a rough shout. I loved it, absolutely relished the moments when he lost it like that.

He pushed my legs apart, shifted me onto my back, and

moved into me, kissing me languorously. He pulled out of me slowly, drawing it out, until I wanted him again as though we hadn't just made love.

Once he'd separated his body from mine, he moved flush against me again.

"Wrap your arms and legs around me," he ordered against my ear.

I did, my body obeying but my mind still in that soft dreamy place that only he could take me. He picked me up, rising slowly.

It was only as I was flying through the air that I realized his intent. I hit the water with a surprised little yelp. I was glaring as I surfaced.

He just grinned, diving in after me.

We played in the pool for a long time. Like children, I thought, only we were skinny dipping in broad daylight. I loved every second of it. I thought that playful James might just be my favorite.

He pulled me against him, kissing me hotly, and then thrust me away. "Run," he told me with a wicked grin.

I made it just to the edge of the pool and one step out before he caught me, yanking me back into the water and against him, his front flush against my back. He bit my neck and rubbed against me. His rock hard erection poked hard into my backside.

"You're insatiable," I told him, my voice breathless.

"Yes," he breathed into my ear. "I am. Now run."

I made it out of the pool, across the concrete, and into the grass that time. It was only as he was tackling me onto my stomach that I realized it was exactly what he'd wanted, exactly what he'd planned. He was entering me from behind rather roughly within seconds.

He fucked me in the grass, on hands and knees, pumping into me with a purpose.

"Say it, Bianca," he ordered into my ear, his voice so low and gruff.

I came apart, but not enough to keep from saying it. "I'm yours, James. Only yours."

He continued the jarring rhythm while my body squeezed him convulsively, as shivers of pleasure wracked my body. He kept going until every little shocking wave had passed. He moaned low in his throat when he let himself go.

My hands and knees were raw and grass stained when James carried me back to the pool. I couldn't imagine that his were in much better shape.

He tossed me back in the pool. Even knowing it was coming, I let out a little shriek before I hit the water. When I resurfaced, James was striding towards the house, a towel slung low across his hips.

"Where are you going?" I called out.

"To check in with the other man in your life," he called back.

I thought that was the sweetest thing in the world. And so very James. Nothing could soften me more than him understanding my bond with Stephan, and understand it, he did. He always knew which strings to pull. Manipulative, perceptive, wonderful man.

When he returned, he moved straight to the lounging sofa where we'd discarded all of our clothing. He pulled on his low-slung gray swim trunks and grabbed my bikini, moving back to the pool with a purpose.

He cornered me in the pool.

I kissed him. "Thank you for being so understanding about Stephan. That means everything to me."

"I have nothing but love for that man. If I have to share you with someone, I'm glad that it's him. And I will do anything it takes to stay on his good side. I know that a happy Stephan is a happy Bianca." He gave me one hard kiss and began to slip me back into the tiny series of strings that he called a bikini.

"The guys wanted to hang out," he continued. "So I told them to come over. Not sure how he did it, but Stephan turned the whole thing into an impromptu pool party. I don't even know who's coming. I may have met my match. That man is cunning."

That made me smile real big. Talk about the pot calling the kettle black…

"I need to go put on a cover-up or something," I told him. "If we're having a party, I'd rather not be showing this much skin."

He eyed me up, running a tongue over his teeth in a luscious display. "Yeah, I agree. I'd rather not share this much of your skin with company. Especially since I don't even know who's coming. I can't even tell you the havoc that will wreak with security. A last minute party with no guest list." He shook his head, then smiled suddenly. "I guess that's why I pay them so well. Now let's go get you a cover-up."

Stephan and Javier arrived first, not even thirty minutes later. They were both already in their swimsuits, shirtless and smiling.

I eyed the three hot, half-naked men around me. "What did I ever do to get so lucky?" I asked.

Stephan flashed a dimple at me, and that dimple was always mischievous. He picked me up, running through the house with a happy shout. He never had been able to behave himself around water.

Unlike James, Stephan jumped in still holding me, rather than throwing me. I had a sudden but clear epiphany about the two major men in my life, and just how alike they were in so many strange ways, both so relentlessly, affectionately physical, and emotionally open for me, if on different levels.

Stephan didn't let me go even when were both in the water, just cradling me to him and smiling.

"Who did you invite to this?" I asked him suspiciously. I could just tell by the look on his face that he was in an ornery mood. His huge grin at the question only confirmed it.

"Wrong question, Buttercup."

I pulled his hair lightly. "What's the right question, then?" I asked. I knew this game.

"Who *didn't* I invite?"

I heard a bark of a laugh behind me, and craned my head around to see James striding back to the house. "If it's going to be that sort of a party, I'll at least have it catered," he muttered as he walked. "And I don't suppose a house full of pilots and flight attendants won't want an open bar."

I had to laugh. He'd assessed the situation accurately. If Stephan had sent out a blanket invite to everyone he knew, we were a few minutes away from having a house full of pilots and flight attendants, and they would be *drinking*.

The first few people to arrive were complete strangers to me, and it felt beyond awkward meeting new people wearing a tiny bikini, and a tiny, sopping wet cover-up, but I tried to play it off.

I shot Stephan a glare. "Do you even know who they are?"

He shrugged. "I think they're pilots. Murphy's friends? They look vaguely familiar.

James dove into the pool, his form perfect. He swam straight to me, staying underwater until he reached me. He grabbed me around the waist and dragged me from where I was huddled with Stephan. He cornered me against the side of the pool. "Stephan gets to play host tonight, since this was his idea, and I planned to spend my entire day touching you, so I'm damn well going to do it."

I had no problem with that. I just smiled at him.

CHAPTER TWENTY-ONE

Mr. Scandalous

Of course a party at a swank mansion with an open bar attracted a lot of people, and within an hour the place was packed. I recognized maybe a third of the people that swarmed into the pools.

Our usual group ended up hanging out with us, taking one of the large pools to ourselves.

Marnie and Judith were there. I'd figured they would be. If they were in town, you couldn't drag them away from a good party. Marnie, however, wouldn't get in the water, which was unusual for her. I asked her why.

She waved her martini glass in the air. "You see this?"

I nodded, smiling. I knew there'd be a punch line.

"This is not a martini. This is a Midol-tini, cause I'm on the rag, folks, and it is a *heavy flow day*!"

"OOOhhhh," Murphy cried. "TMI, Marnie TMI! I picture things!"

"Well picture that whole pool turning red if I take one step in."

Every man within ten feet groaned in disgust. Except for Mr. Beautiful, who didn't seem to have a squeamish bone in his body. *He* just laughed.

"Women are *disgusting*!" Murphy told her. "And what does it say about me that I'm kind of turned on right now?"

"You want a shot at this?" Marnie taunted him, waving a hand at her cute little body. "Liz told me you were good in bed, but I'll warn you right now, if you don't make me come, I'm spreading the word."

Murphy slapped his forehead. "How am I supposed to perform under that kind of pressure?"

She pointed at him. "If you can't perform under pressure, that's a deal-breaker. If this makes you nervous, what will you do when I bust out my strap-on? The pressure hasn't even begun. Take it or leave it, Cap'n!"

Murphy's eyes widened comically. "Will you call me that while we're going at it? *That* might help my performance."

She gave him a smart little salute. "Ay Ay, Cap'n!"

She shouted the words, but could still barely be heard over the sounds of all of us laughing. The funniest part was, I had no idea if they were actually joking.

Murphy turned to Damien, holding out his hand as if to shake. "We'll finally be Eskimo brothers, mate! I've been looking forward to this day!"

Damien just shook his head, looking pained. He was particularly quiet tonight, chatting up Jessa in the corner of the pool. "So wrong," he muttered.

Murphy threw his arms up in the air. "Is that too crass? How about fish-sticks? Can we cross fish-sticks now?"

"What does that even mean?" I asked James, figuring it was a guy thing.

He grimaced. "It's a really crude way of saying that they hooked up with the same woman."

Judith held up two fingers to Murphy, bouncing over to him in the pool. "Fish-sticks!"

They began to have a long mock sword fight with their fingers.

"Your friends are a riot," James told me. "But I can't imagine they weren't a shock to a virgin."

I gave him a look. "I was a virgin, but I've seen plenty, James. I was on the streets as a young teen. I was past the ability to be shocked before I was sixteen. I think that Judith and Marnie were more shocked at my virginity than they've ever managed to shock me."

He laughed. "I can well imagine."

"They tried to relieve me of the 'condition' for months. I had to really chew them out to get them to stop."

His face darkened. "I'm glad they didn't succeed. The idea makes me feel violent."

I rolled my eyes. "They didn't even come close to succeeding. They were trying to hook me up with guys that *they* had hooked up with."

"Murphy is earning his red-wings tonight!" Marnie shouted loudly.

I looked at James, who had me crowded against the side of the pool. "What does *that* mean?" I asked him, knowing it was something kinky, and that he was the expert on kink.

He grinned, moving close against me. "When you go down on a girl on her period for the first time, that's called earning your red-wings. I'm going to earn my red-wings with you."

I felt like I blushed from head to toe. I had to look away. I didn't know how, but he could still manage to shock me.

He gripped my chin and turned me back to look at him.

"So you've never done that before?" I asked him.

He shook his head.

"And people actually do that?"

He shrugged. "I'm going to."

I wrinkled my nose at him. "You are so kinky in the strangest ways. I just kind of assumed that people just stopped doing... stuff...during that time of the month."

He laughed. "Look at you. You can't even say it. I won't be going a week without sex just because you have your period, I can tell you that much. And I won't be going a week without going down on you either. So yes, I'll be earning my red-wings soon."

I flushed hotly. The idea was so embarrassing, but the fact that nothing about me was a turn-off for him, was still always kind of a turn-on for me.

He grinned, gripping my chin in a hand, and leaning in close. "Words can't even express how much I love to put that scandalized look in your eyes."

"Why doesn't that surprise me?" I whispered back, still blushing.

"God you guys are good at eye-fucking each other!" Marnie shouted at us, just making me flush harder. "Get a room!"

"I might not be in the mood when I'm on my period," I told him, ignoring Marnie. "I can get tired and grumpy."

He laughed, unfazed. "Oh, trust me, I'll get you in the mood."

Knowing him, I could hardly doubt it.

"I need to go to the bathroom, you kinky bastard," I told him.

He made an embarrassing show of getting me out of the pool, drying me and putting my cover-up on. My friends cheered him on, and I flushed. He even tried to walk me to the bathroom.

I gave him a level stare. "James, I can go to the bathroom by myself."

He looked none-too-happy about it, but he handed me a key from the pocket of his swim trunks. "Use the one in our bedroom. It's locked."

I just nodded and walked off, keeping the towel wrapped tightly around my chest.

After I finished and came back down to the main floor, I was particularly surprised to find one partygoer that I did recognize, but that I certainly hadn't expected to come.

"Hi Melissa," I told her.

Melissa was drinking a martini and looked to be flirting with a bartender in one of the makeshift bars that had been set up around the house.

She sent me a pretty disgusted look for someone partying at my boyfriend's house.

"Bianca," she said with a sneer.

I'm not sure if it was her venom, or if it was the nerve of her bad attitude at this particular location, but that sneer just seemed to snap the class right out of me.

I grabbed her arm, pretty much dragging her into the nearest room. It was some sort of entertainment room, with a giant TV mounted on the wall, theatre seating, and a long sofa set up at the back of the room. I'd only seen the room once before and briefly, when I'd finally gotten the full tour of the house.

A couple was making out on the sofa. I ordered them out like I owned the place. They seemed to think I did, because they listened and obeyed without a protest. I shut the door behind them and turned to Melissa.

"Ok, let's hear it," I told her in my coldest voice. "*What* is your problem? Do you dislike me, or is your personality just this horrible in general?" Normally being this rude to someone literally made my skin crawl, but I didn't seem to be having any problem with it just then.

She folded her arms over her chest and glared at me, the look more pouty than convincing. "It's you. You are just the type of woman that I absolutely *despise*."

I raised my brows at her. I wasn't surprised that she didn't like me—that was hardly a shocker, she hadn't been keeping it a secret, but I rarely found myself described as a type. Unless maybe it was the distant, reserved type. And that type rarely inspired this kind of animosity. I didn't have to ask her what she meant; she was more than happy to elaborate.

"You act like a prissy bitch, you look down on the girls that want a sugar daddy, but you are *just like us*! You are playing the same game I am; you're just less honest about it. That is what I hate! And you landed the biggest rich guy of all! You don't deserve it. You don't deserve any of this! I was *born* rich. Born in to this life, born *deserving* this life, but then my daddy lost everything, and now I have to throw fucking peanuts to make ends meet, blowing sixty-year old men just to get the bags I used to get for giving my daddy a kiss on the cheek. And you, with your supposed virtue, land the ultimate rich guy on your first try. You give honest girls like me a bad name."

I laughed. I couldn't keep it in. I laughed right in her face. "So *that's* your deal," I told her, my tone scathing. I just couldn't believe that she was even more worthless than what I'd pegged her for. "You're a spoiled little brat that never grew up. Your daddy gave you everything, and look what you became. A whore for bags?"

She actually had the nerve to try to slap me. I saw it coming and caught her wrist mid-air.

"I am *nothing* like you," I continued as though she hadn't just taken a swing at me. "The fact that James has money worked against him with me, not for him, and I couldn't give a flying fuck about handbags. You need a little dose of the real world, little girl, and I hope you get it."

The door burst open, and James strode in, his eyes wild, four security guards behind him. He didn't even look at Melissa as he had her escorted her out.

I did, meeting her glare for glare as she stormed off.

Finally, I met his eyes. I knew what I'd find there. Enough concern and fury to make me tense.

"That's *fucking* it. You aren't going to the bathroom without security ever again."

I rolled my eyes. "Please. It was Melissa. She's hostile, but hardly a threat to me."

"She threw a fucking drink at your head!"

He was really working himself into a rage, I realized.

I moved to him, burying my face in his chest. He wrapped me in his arms. It was an automatic response, enraged or not. I thought that said a lot.

"I'm perfectly fine. We had an enlightening conversation, actually."

"Oh?" he asked, his hands running over my back possessively.

"Yeah. I found out what her deal is."

"I'd love to hear it."

"She's a spoiled brat," I said simply.

"Huh."

"And a whore for designer bags."

That got a real laugh out of him. "She must really like handbags," he said, a smile in his voice.

"I would hope so, since she claims she blew a sixty-year old just to get one." I don't know why it struck me funny when I said it, it really was just sad and pathetic, but I couldn't make the statement without laughing.

It must have been contagious because James started laughing just as hard as I was.

Stephan found us still laughing when he burst in the door, breathless. He pointed at James. "That was mean. You had me scared to death that she'd disappeared, and here you are, laughing and joking, and not bothering to call the search off."

"My bad," James said, still laughing. It must have been that tension relieving type of laughter, because I couldn't stop mine either.

"What's so funny?" Stephan asked, his face breaking into a smile at our delirious laughter. He was always quick to shake things off.

"Melissa blew a sixty-year old for a handbag," I gasped out. I knew it was bitchy to repeat what she'd said, but it was Stephan, and I just didn't care anymore about being a bitch where she was concerned.

His brows shot up, his grin widening. "That's hardly surprising, but I may turn you saying that into my ringtone."

"Why?" I asked him.

"Because I can't imagine a time of day where I would hear you saying something like that and not smile. So, did you two finally have it out?"

I nodded, still trying to hold in my helpless laughter. "She thought I was a gold-digger like her, just being sneaky about it. It insulted her oh-so refined sensibilities. I called her a spoiled little brat and a handbag whore."

That made Stephan laugh as hard as James and I. "Oh God," Stephan gasped. "I love that you said that to her. She had it coming."

We rejoined the party, and I felt more relaxed after the strange little confrontation. I hadn't imagined that having it out with Melissa would actually turn out to be a tension reliever for me. Maybe I needed to do that more often.

We didn't tell our other friends about Melissa's little confession. That would have felt like petty, mean gossip, even if it were the truth. Melissa's character spoke for itself. I didn't need to be its messenger.

CHAPTER TWENTY-TWO

Mr. Distant

James came home from working on Wednesday strangely tense and quiet. He was intense as he made love to me that night, his eyes full of...something. I couldn't identify it, but it worried me. And going to bed without him ever clearing it up worried me even more.

My worry didn't let up the next morning when I woke to find him turned away from me. He was nude, a whisper of a sheet playing low on one dusky hip. Even concerned, I had to admire that sleek play of muscle along his naked side. I never got to see this side of him. I stroked his hip with a hand.

He flinched away, still sound asleep.

My first instinct was to back off, to give him space. I could well understand the need for space. But I was beginning to understand him well enough to know that space wasn't what *he* wanted, or even what he needed.

I pressed my body against his back, rubbing my hand over that sexy golden hip. I nuzzled into his neck.

He stiffened, then relaxed against my touch. "Bianca," he moaned. I had to check again to see if he was sleeping. He was.

"Bianca," he said again in a rough whisper. "Stay, Bianca,

stay. Please."

I stroked his hip and kissed his neck. "I'm not going anywhere, Love," I told him reassuringly.

That seemed to help. He relaxed against me and I hugged his back and burrowed into him. It was an hour before he had to wake up, so I drifted off again, still clutching him.

When I awoke again two hours later, James was long gone.

I worked that night, flying to JFK for our usual layover, James occupying his customary seat in 2D. He'd come to the airport directly from his casino, so we didn't even get to see each other before the flight.

He seemed fine, just a little quiet and reserved.

It was a full flight, and he was asleep before I'd finished my service. I stewed about it, worried about him and his mood swings.

"The crew is going shopping tomorrow," Stephan was telling me. "Canal Street." Canal Street was the designer knock-off capital of the U.S. Every crew we'd ever worked with made at least one trip a month there. "You up for it?"

We were eating our crew meals in the galley. I shook my head, chewing and swallowing my food before I answered. "No thanks."

I had other plans tomorrow, plans that made me nervous and gave me a whole other reason to stew.

He didn't ask me about what I did plan, and I was relieved. I wouldn't have had the heart to lie to him, even knowing that he wouldn't like what I'd decided to do. In fact, he'd dislike it so much that I thought he might even try to interfere. Him not asking made the whole thing much easier for me.

James made it easier on me, as well, when we got to New York. He had the driver drop him off directly at his hotel, rather than going home for a nap.

"There are a lot of things I need to attend to today. I have to get to work right away," he explained.

"Do you want me to come have lunch with you?" I asked him. "I'm flexible. Just name the time."

He just shook his head, his face unreadable. "Not today," he said. That was all.

It was when he just gave me a brief kiss on the forehead, not even looking at me before he got out of the car, that I knew for certain that something was wrong. This wasn't just a mood.

I tried to take a nap back at our place, but it was no good. I was upset and nervous and out of sorts. Best to just get it over with. Perhaps it could even distract me, for a time, from dwelling on James.

I scrolled through my phone, looking for the contact Jr. I had tried to put his first name into my phone when I'd saved the number, but I just hadn't been able to do it. Even knowing it wasn't my father, I'd been horrified to have that name in my contact list.

Bianca: Would today be a good day for you to meet up?

His response was almost immediate, which I found encouraging.

JR: Yes! Anytime. I have a two hour lunch that I can take whenever I want. Just tell me when and where.

I started to text him back then decided to call him. Hearing his kind voice again would bolster my confidence.

He answered on the third ring.

"Hi!" Sven said. "How are you, Bianca?" His voice was as warm as I remembered.

"I'm good. I was wondering if you wanted to meet for coffee

sooner rather than later. Like now."

He didn't miss a beat. "That's perfect. Where at?"

I named off a place that I could walk to, one of the major chain coffee joints, so the place would be very public and likely crowded.

He agreed without hesitation.

"I work no more than five minutes away from there," he told me.

I found some conservative, cuffed navy shorts, with a blue and white striped boatneck shirt. I didn't want to dress up to meet my half-brother, but I didn't want to look like a slob either. I completely ignored Jackie's shoe suggestions, finding a pair of plain navy sandals with no heel to speak of.

I left my phone in the bedroom, and my purse. I only had my debit card with me when I boarded the elevator. That was a nerve-wracking endeavor, since I could hear Blake and Marion talking in another room as I waited impatiently for the elevator to arrive.

I didn't want security with me for what was already bound to be an awkward meeting, and I didn't think I was in any real danger, going out to a very public place, in broad daylight, for a brief meeting. If I could just slip away unnoticed, I could be there and back before anyone even realized that I wasn't asleep in bed.

I had another brief moment of panic as I passed through the lobby. Johnny was there, presumably to guard me. He was leaning over the lobby desk, chatting up a receptionist, and didn't even twitch as I walked briskly out the front door.

The doorman nodded to me, and I nodded back.

"Have a pleasant day, Ms. Karlsson," he said as I strode away.

Well, he had recognized me, but perhaps it didn't matter. James had posted security. Maybe the building's staff wouldn't be notifying anyone about my activities. Either way, I was planning to be too quick to garner attention.

Still, I took a sharp turn, walking fast, just in case. I would go the roundabout way to my destination, losing any potential tails. As far as I could tell, I was successful.

It was only as I approached the entrance to the café that I realized that I had no idea who to look for. It seemed like such a ridiculous thing to overlook. Why had I thought that I would just know what he looked like? Because we shared a tainted bloodline?

I was regretting not bringing my phone as I walked through the door. It turned out that I didn't need to sweat it. I knew Sven at a glance, as he did me.

I froze at the sight of him.

He would have been devastatingly handsome, if he didn't look so much like our father.

He had pale, beige blond hair, pin straight and clean cut. His eyes were ice blue, but not cold, not like those same eyes were on that other face. His features were even and attractive, with a Nordic cast to them. He had a perfect, clear complexion.

I don't know how long I stood there, just taking him in, struck profoundly by the recognition.

He had already secured us a table, and he stood as I approached.

He was tall. Taller than Stephan, taller than James, possibly as tall as our father, though more slender than all three of them.

He was the spitting image of the monster that haunted my nightmares, and he was giving me an open, friendly smile.

"Bianca," he said by way of greeting.

We sat at the same time, just staring at each other, taking it all in.

"Sven," I said finally.

We went back to staring.

"We could be twins," he said.

That made me blink, but as I processed his words, I realized that he wasn't wrong. It was just a conclusion that my mind hadn't wanted to make on its own.

"We look like *him*," I told him.

He nodded, pursing his lips. "Yes."

And we did. I'd always had a hope tucked away in some distant part of my brain that I somehow resembled my mother. She'd shared my coloring, at least. Though so had my father...

All of those hopes were dashed as I stared at my half-brother, who looked so much like me and my father that I couldn't deny it anymore.

Sven seemed to read my thoughts, which was beyond disconcerting. "We may take after him in looks, but at least we didn't inherit his crazy, violent, homicidal tendencies."

Oddly, that made me smile. "You don't know me that well," I told him.

He smiled.

It was my smile, not my father's. It was a kind but sad sort of smile, and Jr.'s was less reserved than my own. "Bianca, you and I would know at a glance. We're too familiar with monsters not to recognize them on sight."

His words made me realize several things at once.

The first was that I *would* recognize a monster on sight, and perhaps I spent too much time jumping at shadows, and doubting people that didn't deserve my doubt.

The second was that Sven must have endured so many of the things that I had, living in a house with my father.

"He was gone most of the time," Sven said. "And he rarely came after me. That was so hard for me, to watch him do that to my mother, and be spared. It made me feel so worthless. It still does. I don't think I'll ever be able let go of that shame."

As he spoke, I registered that looks might be the biggest thing we had in common. He was the open book to my closed one.

"I had to leave her," he continued. "I was out of there the second I turned eighteen, but she wouldn't leave. No matter what he did to her, she wouldn't leave him. It made me sick, and it broke my heart, but I saved myself and left. I haven't spoken to either one of them since. And now she's gone. Anyone could have seen it coming a mile away, but I'm still in shock."

His voice was so open and raw by the end of it that I felt the need to comfort him. I watched my hand cover his, feeling surreal.

He seemed to appreciate the gesture, smiling at me, though that smile died a quick death.

"Did he hit *you*?" he asked, and I stiffened.

"He did. Often. He treated my mother and I much the same when he was dealing out the blows."

Sven winced. "That's horrible. I thought he spared me because I was a kid."

"He thought that women were worthless. He always made that very clear when he was in one of his rages. I believe that his mother was the one that cut him off from his family's money when he married my mother, and so he blamed them both for his misfortune."

"I'm so sorry."

I gave a little shrug. The idea of someone pitying me where my father was concerned made me uncomfortable. I was the least of his victims…

"Sven, I have something to tell you," I said, wanting to get it off my chest.

He just nodded at me to go on.

"Our father killed my mother. That was why I ran away. I didn't know about you, and I didn't know about your mother, or I would have tried to warn you both. Your mother contacted me shortly before she died. She left before I could tell her, and then I couldn't get ahold of her. I wanted to warn her about just what he was capable of. I wasn't successful, and I feel responsible."

This time his hand covered mine. "You shouldn't. Even if my

mother had known about yours, she would've stayed. I doubt anything could have made her leave, so don't put that on yourself. All of this falls squarely on *his* shoulders. All that we can hope for is that they'll find the bastard, and lock him up for good."

CHAPTER TWENTY-THREE

Mr. Uncivilized

I stayed much longer than I'd planned to. I hadn't expected us to have so much to say to each other. I'd thought it would be awkward, and brief, and likely pointless. I had not expected this feeling of kinship. We instantly had some kind of a bond that I didn't understand, but I knew without a doubt that we would be seeing more of each other.

I had been so deprived of all blood ties for so long that it was a revelation to me that this tie could actually mean something. Sven and I had certain things in common that no one else did, and that no one else could. There was something here worth cultivating. I hadn't seen that coming.

"So what do you do here in New York?" I asked him. We had been working backwards towards small talk, starting with the really heavy stuff.

He smiled a self-deprecating smile. "Stockbroker. I do okay at it, though I acknowledge that my occupation means I got at least some of the family gambling gene. In my defense, though, New York gambling is a lot less destructive than Vegas gambling. I guess we all say that until we lose big. And you're a flight attendant. I confess, I've read everything about you that I could get my hands on. I'm curious by nature."

That made me visibly flinch.

He held up his hands in a sign of peace. "I know most of it's garbage, but the long lost sibling thing always got to me. I have so little family that it's always felt like something was missing. I just wanted to see you—to see pictures of you, and get an idea how you were doing. Though I have to admit, some of those pictures made me blush."

I blushed just thinking of it. The first picture that popped into my mind was me in that see-through slip on the cover of a magazine. I had little hope that he hadn't seen that one.

"How did you get my number?" I asked.

"My mother sent it to me. She said that she happened to run into one of your co-workers and talked them into giving it to her. I have no idea who or how."

"I might need to get a new number soon. A few media sources have gotten ahold of it. I'll let you know when it changes."

He inclined his head. "I appreciate it."

"And I won't be a flight attendant for much longer. My company filed for bankruptcy."

"I heard about that. Sorry to hear it."

I shrugged. "I'm taking a voluntary furlough. I'm going to try to turn painting into a career."

"Wow! That's amazing! I'd love to see your work."

I flushed. "I'm having a gallery showing in L.A. soon. I'll make sure you get an invitation, though of course, I'll understand if you can't make it. It *is* across the country."

He waved that off. "I'll be there. Just tell me when. That is such an accomplishment. I hear it's near to impossible to get a showing."

I flushed harder. "To be honest, my boyfriend played a big part there, but I'm still going to give it a shot."

"James Cavendish," he said.

I nodded.

"Well, let me know. I'm looking forward to seeing your work." He sounded sincere.

"I will. It's still being planned, but I'll keep you posted."

"I have a girlfriend," he volunteered. "She's very nice. It's serious. Hopefully you can meet her sometime."

I nodded. "That sounds nice. Maybe we can all have dinner sometime."

He nodded. "I'd like that. She works odd hours—a lot of them, but I'm sure we can work something out."

"What does she do?" I asked.

"She's a model. I went to one of her shoots. It's a strange sort of job, but she loves it."

I smiled, reminded of my recent and similar experience. "I was just at a photo shoot for James. They are bizarre. I swear they had a team just for rubbing him down with oil."

He laughed. "Yeah, it is a strange business."

He looked at his phone suddenly, the first time he'd done so since we'd gotten there.

"That's weird," he muttered.

"What is it?" I asked.

"It's from a co-worker of mine, asking where I am. Says my boss is looking for me, but I'm on my own time, so that's out of line." He began texting back.

"Did you tell him?" I asked, getting a sick feeling in my gut.

He nodded. "It's not his business, but I still don't want to get on his bad side. It's just bizarre for him to be looking for me on my own time. This isn't like him at all."

I'd left my phone at home, but no one should have even known I was gone. *So why was I suddenly tense and worried?*

I glanced around nervously. "I could be way off, but that might have something to do with my boyfriend. He's extremely overprotective of me, since the attack." I knew I was kidding myself with that statement. He'd likely be that way no matter what, with or without the attack as an excuse. It was his nature.

"What attack?" Sven asked, and I remembered that he didn't know. The attack must not have made the headlines as what it actually was. They'd probably turned my being shipped off in an ambulance and hospitalized for a week into an overdose story, or God only knew what. I hadn't wanted to check.

"It was our dad, over a month ago. He came to my house and attacked me. That was when I went to the police about what he'd done to my mother. The police and a team of private investigators have been looking for him ever since."

"Even after all this time, he was still coming after you?"

I explained some of the events leading up to the attack, as far as I understood it, anyway.

"He saw me in the headlines. He saw that I was dating someone wealthy, and he thought that that would make me more likely to turn him in. The crazy part is, he was right, at least about some of it. I *was* getting ready to turn him in, though money had nothing to do with it."

Sven glanced around, looking a little nervous. "I'm surprised that he didn't make you take security here with you, with the attack and all."

I sighed. "I actually didn't tell him I was coming. As far as he knows, I'm still asleep in bed."

"Do you live together?" he asked.

I nodded.

His eyes widened. "Yeah, I'm going to guess that he had something to do with my boss acting strange, then. Maybe I should walk you home before all hell breaks loose."

I waved my half-empty cup of coffee. We'd spent a half hour talking before I'd finally grabbed a cup. "Sounds good. Let me just finish my coffee and we'll go."

I had nearly completed that goal when Sven's expression froze. My back was to the entrance of the café, and he was facing it, so I knew right away who had just walked through the door.

"Looks like you weren't way off about your boyfriend," he said, his eyes staying glued to the door of the coffee house.

I took deep breaths, getting very nervous suddenly. I knew I should just get up and walk to the door. That would be the best thing I could do, as far as defusing the situation went. I told my body to do just that, but I was frozen in place, my body just waiting to see what James would do.

I didn't turn to look at him, but I would've sworn I felt his presence behind me—his eyes on me. I felt his stillness as he just stood in that doorway, and then I felt him move, walking slowly across the crowded room. I knew it with a certainty when he was standing directly at my back.

Sven seemed just as frozen, staring at the other man with wide eyes. It was a good minute before he tried to speak. "H—" was all he got out.

"Not now, Sven Karlsson," James said quietly. His tone was more menacing than I'd ever heard it. "You and I will talk later, but now is not a good time."

A hand descended to cup the nape of my neck, oh so gently. That hand left me almost instantly, as though James had recoiled. That did nothing good for my peace of mind. My heart felt like it was trying to pound right out of my chest.

"Stand up, Bianca," Mr. Cavendish said quietly. His voice was no less menacing for me. The Dom was driving him at that moment, no hint of his other side present.

I stood up, my body obeying that dangerous tone without hesitation.

James gripped my arm very lightly, that spot just above my elbow, and led me from the café without another word.

I saw that our security was there in force as we passed them. My usual detail was there, sans Johnny, and Clark was at the car. He nodded politely, his face blank, as he opened the door for us.

James handed me into the car. I scooted across the seat but

he didn't crowd me, staying as far away from me as possible on the long seat.

Clark started driving the second the doors closed, leaving the rest of the bodyguards at the café.

I turned my head to watch them as we drove away. Apparently, they'd be walking back.

I took a deep breath. "James—"

He held up a hand. "Not. Right. Now."

That shut me up. And if his words hadn't, the look he shot me before he turned away again would have.

His face was a stoic mask, but his eyes...they were uncivilized.

When we reached the underground garage entrance into the apartment, he handed me out of the car without a word, his touch light and brief.

He only took my arm again once we reached our apartment, pulling me out of the elevator and directly to the stairs.

We hadn't taken the first step up the stairs when a commotion from the direction of the kitchen caught my attention.

Stephan spilled around the corner, looking frantic. "Bee! Thank God! James had just about sent a search party out!"

He moved towards us and James held up a hand.

"Not now," James told him, sparing him a single glance.

That look must have held something that alarmed Stephan, because he strode to us, looking resolute.

"I think you need to take a breather, James. You aren't in any state to—"

"Don't you dare," James said in a dangerous voice, moving to meet the other man, dropping my arm in the process.

The two men were nose to nose, the very air in the room turning hostile between one breath and the next.

"You will *not* come between us. It is not your place to step in here, Stephan. I let that happen once, but I will be *damned* if it happens again. No one stands between me and Bianca, and that includes you."

"That's not up to you. I'll be here for Bianca whenever she needs me." Stephan looked at me, having to crane his neck to do so. "You okay, Bee?"

I nodded, hoping that would be enough to defuse the situation. It wasn't.

"Walk away, Stephan."

Stephan shook his head. "No. I can't do that. I don't feel comfortable with this. You look like you're ready to kill somebody, James. I've never seen you like this, and I'm not leaving my girl alone with you until you've calmed down."

"Your girl?" James growled, gripping the other man's shirt in his fists.

I saw that things were going to quickly get out of hand. I laid a hand on Mr. Cavendish's back. It wasn't comforting that a tremor ran through him at my touch.

"James. Take me upstairs. Please."

It did the trick, thank God. James released the other man, taking a step back.

I looked at Stephan. "We're okay, Stephan. He's upset, but he has impeccable self-control. You never have to worry about me with James, and he and I have some issues that we need to work out on our own."

Stephan studied me carefully, trying to figure me out, but he took my words in and finally just nodded. "I'm here for you if you need me. Always."

I nodded. "I know it."

James hooked a finger into my collar, gripped the back of my neck lightly and began to lead me upstairs without a word. He was in a state, and every obstacle between us and privacy was just antagonizing it.

He shut and locked the bedroom door behind us with a sharp and very definitive click.

I watched him loosening his tie as he strode directly to the elevator. He pressed the button and it opened instantly.

"Get in," he said brusquely.

I slipped out of my shoes and walked inside. He followed me in, and we descended to the fourth floor.

CHAPTER TWENTY-FOUR

Mr. Reticent

He hooked a finger into my collar when the car opened, leading me down that long hallway. He stopped short of the playground, instead opening a door just before it on the right.

Even feeling nervous and anxious, I was beyond curious to see what was in there. It didn't bode well though, that he was only taking me there now that he was in *this* mood.

It was a rather small and nondescript room, holding nothing but one twin bed.

"Get on the bed," he said in that worrisome voice. "On your stomach."

I did it, turning my head to look up at him as he approached my prone figure.

"Don't look at me," he said.

I turned my head away quickly, feeling stung.

"Arms above your head," he ordered.

I complied.

He secured my hands and feet together and to the small bed. I tugged experimentally, and saw that he'd left me quite a bit of slack.

I tensed when I felt him pulling at my clothes. A loud tearing sound told me that he was cutting them off. I was bare when he was done.

"James," I began again. Maybe now that I was restrained he would feel calmer.

"Don't. I don't trust myself right now," he said in a gruff voice.

He adjusted my head, wedging a soft pillow there. "Go to sleep. You were up all night, and I need to go get myself in hand. We'll talk later."

Before I could respond he was turning out the light, shutting the door and a loud lock was clicking into place.

I couldn't believe it. After all of that rage, he'd just left me. He knew that this was the punishment I hated the most, with the suspense and the unanswered questions, and he'd left me in the dark. In a cell. The *bastard*.

I had some dark thoughts about him for quite a while in that pitch-black room before I was able to relax my mind enough to let sleep take me. He hadn't left me so much as a light under the locked door. I was shut in tight.

I awoke as the door opened and a stream of light from the hallway fell across me. I turned my face away. The overhead light switched on. My restraints were already loose, but Mr. Cavendish added some slack to the rope, pulling me up by the shoulders until I was sitting up.

I squinted at him, my eyes still adjusting to the sudden light. He was shirtless and sweaty, his hair tied back. He held a plate of food on his lap.

He untied my hands, put the plate in my lap, and turned away. I watched his stiff back for a while, wondering what to say.

I ate. Because I was hungry, and because I was hoping that if I ate that James would start talking when I was done.

I ate maybe half of the seasoned chicken, brown rice, and spinach before I handed it back to him.

He took it without a word, stood up, and left.

He had turned off the light then shut and locked the door

before I realized his intent.

"James!" I shouted.

He didn't respond.

I was so frustrated that I screamed.

I was so furious and anxious that it took me even longer to relax into sleep that time. Eventually my body just gave into the relentless darkness.

When I woke again it was still dark, but there was the faintest line of light showing through the side of the door. It was ajar.

I sat up, testing my wrists and ankles. I was free. I moved slowly to the door, pushing it open.

I had to squint against the bright hallway light. I blinked away the darkness for long moments while I took in the hallway.

James sat in a chair that was set against the wall, wearing nothing but his boxers. He was slumped forward, his head in his hands, his elbows on his knees. It was such a defeated posture for him.

I approached him slowly, tentatively. I couldn't tell if he was napping.

"James," I said quietly.

"Call me Mr. Cavendish," he said in a low voice. He didn't move.

I'd been so angry with him, furious really, but it drained from me more quickly than I would have thought possible as I took him in.

He was like a wounded animal just then, and I only wanted to make it better.

I knelt in front of him. I touched his head, and he sat up, giving me a very mean look.

I shifted closer, moving between his legs.

He gripped my throat. "Why?" he asked quietly.

I swallowed, wetting my lips.

He watched the action with rapt attention.

"Why did I go see Sven without security?" I asked, for clarity.

"Yes. That."

"I was nervous about meeting him. I had a hard time even going. I knew it would be perfectly safe, since we'd be in a crowded public place in broad daylight. I saw no threat, and I wanted to have a normal meeting. My security team makes *me* nervous. I can't even imagine what an outsider looking in would think of the whole mess. I just wanted some semblance of a normal first meeting with him. That's all. I'm sorry I worried you."

"*Worried* me? Is that what you call it? I have that team guarding you, Bianca, because it's the only way that I can bear for you to leave my *sight*. There is a man out there, a man who has killed at least two women, and he wants to kill *you*. He is unhinged, and completely unpredictable. The only thing we can predict is his grudge against you. Do you know what that does to me? You are more precious to me than my own life, by far. It's not even a question. I would do *anything* for you. All I ask is that you let me protect you from a *known* threat. How could you be so careless, Bianca? So insensitive?"

I opened my mouth to respond and he covered it with his other hand, his lip curling into a snarl.

"Your father has been missing for weeks. We can only place his whereabouts at one place almost a week ago, and that is because a *body* marked the spot. He could be literally anywhere. And all he would have to do to see that you were in New York would be to look online. The paparazzi have mapped your weekly route with neon lights. I understand that you wanted to meet your half-brother. I wasn't trying to keep you from it. *All I asked was that you take your bodyguards with you.* Your father and brother could have been working together. Your brother could have been luring you there. They could have taken you before anyone could have stopped them."

I tried to protest even through his hand, but his eyes stopped me.

"Don't. Just because it didn't happen doesn't mean that you were safe. You weren't safe. A man with a gun wants you dead. It would only take one fucking bullet."

His eyes were terrible with anguish, and I knew that the fear was getting to him. He was doing everything he could, and I was still in danger. He felt like he was failing me, and it was eating him up inside.

He uncovered my mouth.

I spoke quietly. "I'm sorry. I thought I'd be there and back before you knew. I didn't mean to do that to you. I swear I won't ditch my security again. At least, not until my father is found."

He shut his eyes and nodded. "When I couldn't get ahold of you, and Blake told me she'd found your phone by our bed, I thought you'd left me."

My brow furrowed. "Why would you think I'd left you? I don't understand."

The hand at my neck moved and gripped into my hair. "No. No answers until you've been punished."

I licked my lips nervously. "That cell back there wasn't a punishment?"

He shook his head. "That was a nap. And a chance for me to work off some aggression at the gym. No more questions."

His other hand began to tug off his boxer briefs, and I tried to look down at what he was doing, but the hand in my hair held me fast.

He pushed my head down to his bared erection. He pushed himself into my mouth, and I sucked at him, thinking that this part was no punishment at all.

He guided my head up and down no more than four times before he was coming deep in my throat. I nearly gagged, I was so surprised. It was unusual for him to come so fast. His control over his own release constantly amazed me, though I supposed that it shouldn't have, since he was so good at controlling mine.

He pulled me off him mid-cum, pulling me up to my feet while I could see his cock still twitching with his orgasm. I murmured a protest.

He slapped my ass, hard, then hooked his finger into my collar. He began to pull me, but not to the playground. He headed in the opposite direction, back to that cell. I had to swallow a protest. I didn't want to be left in there again, but I knew that it was all in his hands now.

"Kneel on the ground," he told me as he let go of my collar.

I obeyed, watching him. He moved to the small bed. He had it retracting into the wall with one touch of his finger. I hadn't known it was that kind of bed.

One touch to the wall and he had something large descending from the ceiling. I watched with wide eyes as a large X lowered in front of me. It was the same height as James, which gave me a good idea what it was for.

"This is what's called a St. Andrew's cross," he told me quietly. That was all.

He pulled me up with a finger in my collar and a fist in my hair. He pressed my front hard into that ominous X. He strapped my wrists and ankles to it nice and quick, before pressing his body hard to my back. I felt his erection against my butt and tried to arch into it. He slapped my ass hard before moving away.

I laid my head against my arm, tilted forward as I waited and listened for what he would do next.

I started as something hard but smooth stroked against my other cheek. I turned my head to see a thick black oval paddle that was patterned with holes. He pulled it away before I could get a better look.

He struck swiftly and repeatedly along my butt and thighs. I was still sore from the roses, which added to the pain, but he was relentless, not holding back a bit. He worked me over hard.

I had nothing to hold onto, nothing to grip on the cross, so my hands curled and uncurled as the blows struck me.

My legs were spread wide, and a few rough blows to my sensitive inner thighs had me gasping with the pain. He had been the reticent Dom since he'd picked me up from the café, but the force of his blows were telling me plenty, communicating so much that he hadn't. He was furious and hurt and scared, and that pent-up, frustrated emotion was all for me.

My flesh was on fire when he finished. There was no pause between the last blow and him thrusting into me roughly from behind.

"That wasn't your punishment, Bianca," he rasped into my ear. "Do you want to know what your real punishment is?"

I nodded, unable to speak as he thrust into me again and again. I was on that fine edge when he pulled out of me abruptly.

"You don't get to come until tonight, Love. Not for hours. I'm going to work you over, fuck you thoroughly, and you don't get an orgasm. That's an order. And if by chance you disobey that order, you won't get to come for a *week*."

I wanted to scream in frustration, but instead I gasped as he thrust back into me, pounding inside of me, again and again.

"Don't," he said, knowing that I was so close.

He hit the end of me, coming with that rough little groan that I loved. I hated it right then, sobbing in frustration.

"Please," I begged as he pulled out of me.

"Not until tonight," he said firmly.

He left me there for long minutes before coming back to unfasten me. I didn't move after I was loose, instead I just lay against that X and waited.

He sighed and swept me up into a cradle hold.

He carried me to the playground, laying me onto a firmly cushioned surface. At the first touch of my back to the table, I began to look around. There were two such tables in this room that I knew of for sure. I saw from where I was positioned just what he had in mind, but not before he had my wrists and ankles strapped tightly to the corners of the table.

He watched me intently while he slipped on tight latex gloves. "Any objections?" he asked, a touch of a taunt in the question, almost like he was daring me.

I set my jaw hard, just watching him, daring *him* to do his worst.

He gave me a tight smile and got to work.

He washed and dried the area around my nipples with a clinical thoroughness. He pulled tiny metal forceps from the open drawer built into the table.

He didn't hesitate, using it to grip my left nipple firmly. At the end of the metal instrument was a small hoop that fit around my hard nipple perfectly. He held it captive while he leaned in close and marked it carefully on each side.

I had to tell myself to breathe as I watched him. I was painfully tense, not knowing what to expect. I'd never had anything pierced but my ears before.

He carefully studied the marks he'd made, my nipple still held firmly with those mean little forceps. He put the pen away, pulling out a sadistic looking needle with the same hand.

My eyes were glued to that thick needle as he pushed the sharp, hollowed-out tip of it into my skin. I took one very deep breath and held it.

He pushed it into my skin, and through, with a quick, almost smooth motion. It was painful but fast, the sight and feel of it a shock to my system.

He laced a tiny silver hoop into the needle, pulling it through, and then slipping the bigger needle out.

I watched my chest rise and fall as I started breathing again.

He pressed a cloth very gently to the newly pierced area before striding away.

He came back less than a minute later with two small, cold gel packs in his hands. One he set in the open drawer, the other against my pierced nipple.

"Are you up for the other?" he asked, watching me carefully. Even in this dangerous mood, I still saw concern.

I took a deep breath and nodded.

He changed his gloves before he gave my right breast the same treatment, quickly and with consummate skill. He tended to both breasts, carefully cleaning and icing them. The aftercare took much longer than the actual piercing had.

When he was done, he took off his gloves and unfastened me, picking me up and carrying me directly to the bed.

He laid me on my back, his hand moving between my legs to push one finger into me.

I glared at him.

He laughed. It was a cold laugh. My tender-lover was still very much missing, even with those little glimpses of concern I'd seen from him as he'd tended to me.

"Now, now, Love. Looking at me like that can get you punished, as well. Don't think that it can't get worse than a sore ass, some pierced nipples, and one day without an orgasm."

Very deliberately, I shut my eyes and turned my head away, defiant of what I knew he wanted from me. I was pissed.

He just laughed that merciless laugh. "Okay, have it your way. I was going to leave you alone, but this is certainly more fun for me."

He pushed me flat onto my back, and tied me spread-eagle to the bed. I kept my eyes shut tight.

He crawled between my legs and gripped my chin, very careful to avoid brushing against my tender breasts.

"Look at me. Now," he growled.

I hesitated, but finally looked at him. I swallowed hard then moaned loudly as he lined himself up at my entrance, ramming in to the hilt.

"Don't fucking come," he told me, jamming himself into me once, twice, three times. He came with that delicious groan of his, just shy of making me lose my mind.

"Very good, Love," he murmured as he pulled out of me, his thick length still twitching.

He unfastened my feet, but only one of my wrists. This he left tied, but with a lot of slack. He curled naked against my back, burying his face into my neck. I arranged myself carefully, shifting to avoid brushing my breasts against my arms or the bed.

"Are you afraid I'll try to run away? Is that why I'm still tied?" I asked him, since he'd never done this before. Something was seriously off.

"Yes," he said succinctly. "No more questions right now."

I tried to roll away, but he held me fast. He pressed hard against me. His cock was semi-hard against the back of my thigh. "Relax. All you have to do now is fall asleep. When you wake up again, your punishment will be over."

That was much easier said than done. I was agitated, confused and mad as hell, and the fact that James was soon sleeping heavily and peacefully against my back was no help at all.

CHAPTER TWENTY-FIVE

Mr. Manipulative

STEPHAN

I'd been woken up after only a thirty minute nap, but I still knew I wasn't going to be able to go back to sleep. And I couldn't leave her here alone, though I knew not to try to interfere again.

So I stayed. I ate and played video games, texted Javier a lot, and worried. I didn't like to be a worrier, but where Bianca was concerned, I just couldn't help it. If she was okay, I was okay, and if she wasn't...

I remembered the first time I'd seen her. She'd been wearing baggy jeans, and a hoody that covered most of her hair, but she hadn't been able to disguise the fact that she was breathtakingly beautiful, with clean features and a perfect complexion.

We'd been at a homeless shelter, but neither of us had lingered. At our age, if you stayed around people that wanted to help you for too long, it was inevitable that they would try to help you find your parents. It was always a good-natured intention, but almost insulting in its way. As though we'd have been living on the streets if we had any other acceptable choice... But even that was unfair, I knew. Some of the lost kids weren't really lost. Sometimes they were mad, or trying to worry their parents, or even just trying to prove a point that they didn't need anybody.

I knew at a glance that she wasn't one of those. Yes, she had a proud tilt to her delicate chin, but she was no spoiled brat. She was like *me*. She had nowhere to go. She was truly lost.

I had followed her, keeping my distance, instinctively wanting to make sure she was safe. If she was like me, perhaps we could help each other. She looked about my age. Maybe we could keep each other company. The thought gave me a pathetic amount of hope.

I stayed far away, just observing, but it wasn't long before I saw the old man stalking her.

I knew where she was headed. There was a warehouse not far away. It was a popular spot for squatters. None but the homeless were interested in the place. I trailed them there.

It was getting dark out, and so I didn't recognize the large man that stepped into my path. I squinted warily at the one who had stopped my progress, trying to make him out in the dark.

"Old Sam has a fight for you," the man said, and I vaguely placed who he was. I was almost positive his name was Mike.

"Now isn't a good time," I told him, shouldering my way around him. I wasn't comfortable leaving her alone near that old man for even a minute, not in the darkness, where no one would care what was happening.

I began to walk briskly towards the warehouse, my eyes shifting around frantically, trying to make out all of the shadowed shapes.

"You'll be sorry if you get on his bad side!" Mike shouted at my back.

I completely ignored him.

I was almost to the broken side entrance when I heard a faint noise down the alleyway. It had been a muffled grunt, a feminine one, and that was enough to have me tearing down the alley with no hesitation.

I saw the old pervert first, since he was on her back. He already had his pants down around his ankles, and was working at the front of her pants with one hand. The other was over her mouth.

He cursed, drawing the hand at her mouth away to punch the back of her head at the same time that she screamed.

I pounced with a furious roar. My vision went red for a long time, and I couldn't form a coherent thought again until I felt a soft touch on my shoulder.

"You can stop. He won't be bothering me now," she said, her voice soft and gentle.

I stopped beating his head against the ground, letting go to study my bloody hands.

She tugged on my shirt, trying to get me to stand. "Come on. I know a place where you can clean up. You shouldn't have to have his filthy blood on your hands."

She took my arm and began, in that gentle way of hers, to lead me behind the building. Her every touch was like a question. She was sure of her actions, but I didn't think she was capable of being bossy.

I looked at her, so afraid of what I'd see in her eyes.

She met my look, and hers was full of gratitude and understanding, and not an ounce of fear. "Thank you *so much*. I didn't know that there really were nice men in the world. I thought that was a myth, but you saved me."

That did it. I was lost.

"I'm Bianca," she said with a sad smile, her eyes a little lost, as she cleaned me up.

"I'm Stephan," I told her numbly. It had been so long since anyone had cared for me, or touched me in any way, that I felt almost in shock at her actions.

"You're like me," she said quietly, still working gently to wash the blood from my hands and wrists. She didn't look up.

I had to clear my throat to speak. "What do you mean?"

She glanced up then, meeting my eyes squarely. I saw the strength in her from those eyes, and her quiet resolve. "You can never go back home."

My jaw clenched, and I nodded slowly.

She never showed a hint of fear for me, and the longer I knew her, the more I realized that, considering her past, she'd had every right to.

We never asked if we'd be staying together, we just never separated.

"You don't ever have to worry about me...trying what that old man tried. I'm gay, so it's not an issue," I told her the first night we slept huddled close together, sharing one thin blanket.

It wasn't only to assuage her fears that I told her. If my preferences were going to make her recoil from me in disgust, I wanted to know it sooner rather than later.

She just wiggled closer. "I wasn't worried, Stephan. It didn't even occur to me that you would try to harm me. You're a good guy—a hero. I've never been more certain of anything in my life. I feel so safe with you. Safer than I've *ever* felt."

Her words gave me a warm feeling in my chest, and above her head, my eyes filled with foreign tears. For the first time in years, I felt a fierce joy in my heart. Maybe I'd found a person who could love me. Maybe I'd found a family.

I was beyond relieved when James reappeared about two hours after they'd gone upstairs, though I would have been more so if Bianca had been with him. He wore only a pair of black athletic shorts, and he was covered in sweat. His hair was tied back and his eyes were scary. He carried a small laptop in his hand.

I swallowed hard. I wanted to see Bianca, needed to know that the scary thing in his eyes wasn't more than she could take, but I knew she trusted me not to interfere, and I valued that trust.

"We need to talk," he told me.

I nodded. I would take any information I could get.

He sat beside me and opened his laptop. He set it on my lap. A video was playing on the screen. I watched it for maybe a minute before I had to turn away, blushing profusely. I handed it back to him with a grimace. "Jesus! Why would you show me that, James?"

"So Bianca hasn't mentioned it to you?"

I was livid in a heartbeat, ready to punch him. "You showed that to her?"

"No! Of course not."

My eyes widened in realization. "That's online?"

He nodded, looking miserable and furious all at once. "I don't know how. I'm looking into it. But I need to know if she knows about it yet. And I need your opinion. Will she leave me if she sees it?"

I rubbed my temples. "It's old, I assume. Long before you met her."

"*Of course*. I didn't even know it existed until a few weeks ago."

"It will be upsetting. And she's so skittish. I just have no idea what she'll do, James. She's so different with you. When she left you the first time, I was almost certain that she'd never give you another chance. All the rules changed for her when you came into the picture. I just can't predict what she'll do with you. But don't let her see that video. That certainly won't help. Knowing and seeing are two different things."

"How can I stop her? You know her. She'll want to see it for herself. I just know it. This is killing me, Stephan. What can I do?"

I shook my head. "So this is what has you so upset? It's not that she went out without security?"

I watched his fists clench and felt mine copying the motion.

"It's both. Do you know what she fucking did? She went all by herself to meet her brother. *Sven Karlsson*. He even has the same fucking name, and she went alone to see him."

I felt my gut clench. "What happened? Is he like her dad?"

He shook his head. "I don't know. I don't think so. I'll find out. Don't worry about him, Stephan. I'll make sure he's well vetted before he breathes the same air as her again. I swear it."

I nodded. I knew he would. And I saw that I'd been wrong to doubt him. Even in this dangerous mood, he was still only thinking of Bianca. He'd been like that from the start, which was why it had been so easy for me to share her with him. There was just something so steady about him. He'd swept into our lives with such a benevolent sort of authority. The messed-up, wounded kid that still lived inside of me longed for his approval, and he was generous with it, too. He thought I was amazing—he told me so often, and he found me worthy to help him take care of Bianca, who I knew he adored more than life; it took one to know one. He filled a role of both friend and mentor for me that I hadn't realized I'd been missing, which made it even harder for me to fight with him. But when it came to me and Bianca, he had to know that her side was *my* side. There could never be a question of *that*. "I'm sorry I tried to interfere, James. It's just so hard for me—"

"It's fine," he cut in impatiently. "We have something else to discuss."

I nodded for him to go on, relieved that he didn't seem to be holding a grudge.

"I know your first inclination is going to be to tell me no, but remember that this is for Bianca. I want her out of that house. *He* knows where it is, she was *attacked* there, and every time she's there without me, it drives me absolutely out of my fucking mind crazy. She won't leave that place until you do. I know it. I need you to sell your house."

I blinked at him, totally thrown for a loop.

"There's a property next to mine that I think will suit you well, and you would still be neighbors. She needs that. You *know* she does. I'm buying you that house. And you need to help me convince her to sell hers. She'll resist the idea, but this is important. She needs to get out of there. My property is much safer." He seemed to sense my uneasiness. "I'll give you time to think about it, but you'll see that I'm right. I know you're uncomfortable with my buying you a house, but it is literally *nothing* to me to do this, so if you can't do it for yourself, do it for Bianca."

I knew he was a manipulative man. Generous, but manipulative. I honestly didn't think he could even help himself; he was so used to getting things his way. Even knowing that, though, I considered the idea.

Playing by his rules means staying close to her forever. As I realized that, it wasn't even a question for me.

CHAPTER TWENTY-SIX

Mr. Desperate

BIANCA

I woke up as James pushed himself into me. I was so wet that it made for a smooth as silk entry. I shuddered and gasped in pleasure before the sleep had fully left my body. This was, without a doubt, my favorite way to wake up.

"Morning, my love," James rasped, his face just over mine, but his chest held carefully off my breasts.

I studied his eyes, my free hand moving to grip into his silky smooth hair. I wanted to catch a glimpse of my tender-lover in those intense eyes, and I was relieved to see it there in the warmth of those turquoise depths. He'd left me so cold before. I needed reassurances and answers now. I needed warmth. But first, I needed this...

He rocked into me with deliciously long strokes. His hands pushed my legs far apart until there was a near painful stretch added into his perfect thrusts. I gasped as he dragged out then buried himself to the hilt, again and again.

I clenched around him in the most delectable wake-up orgasm, but he just kept going, driving into me without pause, working me towards another pinnacle as I was still coming down from that high. I cried his name as I came again.

I cupped his cheek and watched with covetous eyes as he pounded out his own release long moments later.

Our eyes stayed locked as he hovered over me, staying buried deep while he watched me. It was one of our silent standoffs, and I broke first.

"Are you going to tell me what has you so worried that I'll leave you? So worried that you kept me tied to the bed while we slept?"

His jaw clenched and his eyes flinched but he nodded. "A... video of me was released this morning. It's all over the internet. There's no way to control it. I've known of the video for about a week, and I've been trying my best to keep it from leaking, but I failed. Whoever was behind this didn't care about making money."

I swallowed, a sick little ball of dread forming in my gut. "A sex tape," I guessed.

He broke eye contact, staring down at our joined bodies. "Yes. I'm sorry. Just when I've been trying to clean up my image, to clean up my life, this *would* happen. I'm disgusted with myself, if it makes you feel any better."

It didn't. "When was this video made?" I asked him.

He pulled himself out of me and I gasped at the raw sensation. His hair trailed into his beautiful face as he looked back up at me. "About three years ago, I think, or possibly closer to four. It was taken without my knowledge, I'm embarrassed to admit. It was a setup. One of the few times I wasn't at one of my own properties. I'm so sorry. My past just won't seem to go away. Please tell me this isn't your breaking point."

I studied him, wondering how his mind worked. "Of course I'm not happy about it, but I would hardly leave you over it, James."

I couldn't speak for a long minute because he crushed the breath out of me. I gasped at the raw sensation it caused in my tender nipples.

He pulled back when he heard the gasp, muttering an apology. He moved back over me, more carefully this time. "Thank you," he murmured into my ear.

"I know about your past," I continued, when he let me. "You've been forthcoming with me about your promiscuity. But you should have told me a week ago, when you first heard about this. You've been moody and strange and I don't like to be kept in the dark. You should know better. If we're going to make this thing work, you can't keep things like this from me. One of the things that makes me trust you is your honesty. I *need* that honesty, James. Do you understand?"

He nodded, his face buried in my hair. "I was just so terrified that you would run again."

I tugged hard on a lock of his hair. "What will keep me from running is you being upfront with me."

"Yes, okay. I understand."

I took a deep breath, hating this next part, but not enough not to ask. "Who is it?"

He tensed against me. "Jolene."

I nodded. Somehow I had known, though that didn't make me happy about it. "So she made the video, and leaked it. Obviously."

He shook his head. "I can't rule that out completely. And yes, she obviously set the thing up. But I just can't see her leaking it, not with the kind of money I was offering to keep it under wraps. And this will ruin whatever she has with Scott. She's too mercenary to do this just for spite, and with nothing to gain."

I took his word for that, since he obviously knew her better than I did.

He brushed my hair back from my face, and the light picked up those scars on his wrists. I caught his hand, bringing it to my lips. I kissed the inside of his wrist softly.

"Are you ever going to tell me what these are from?"

His eyes picked up a certain vulnerable glint that I was coming to recognize. It was going to be bad, though I had always assumed that the scars on his wrists were deep wounds.

"Spencer used sharp handcuffs. They cut me. It was one of the first things I noticed. These cuts on my wrists started appearing first. I hid them, because that's a conspicuous and embarrassing place to have a cut, especially being fourteen, and feeling self-conscious of every little thing to begin with."

"I can't say if he used that kind of cuff to make me hold still, or if he just wanted to make me bleed. If he was trying to keep me from struggling, it didn't work. If I could have cut my own hands off to get away from him, I swear I would have. I certainly tried."

He let me trace those tiny scars, then kiss every inch of them, very carefully. Tears ran silently down my cheeks. I couldn't hear what he was saying and not be affected by it.

He traced my tears with a soft finger. "It was about that time that I got real promiscuous. I didn't go a day without hooking up indiscriminately. I wasn't analyzing it back then, but I suppose I was trying to regain some control, since I'd lost so much of it. And it didn't help that I was one giant hormone at the time. It all just sort of escalated, and by the time I was an adult, it didn't get better. I preferred the most casual of hookups, so I almost always went out of my way to find women who were hot, but who I knew I wouldn't feel bad leaving, which I guess would explain Jules and Jolene, though I didn't stick exclusively to raging bitches."

I had to hold back a comment about that one. He was talking now, and I wanted him to get it all out. The last thing I wanted to do was stop the flow of information.

"It was never straight vanilla for me, but the really kinky stuff developed over time. I knew that I liked things a little more off-color than the norm, and I was always pushing it a step further. At about the age when a normal kid was getting excited to drive his first car, I was running a worldwide hotel chain, obsessively learning to tie knots, and fucking every female in sight. I got better when I started going to therapy. I became more focused, more controlled, but that took time. Getting into the BDSM scene when I was eighteen helped a lot, too. There were rules there, and people that were willing to sort of mentor me about how to do it right, and I got the proper training."

That was a bit of a shock to me, though perhaps it shouldn't have been. I wasn't experienced with the scene, but his control was so perfect that I should have assumed that he'd had some sort of training.

"That was when I met Frankie. She's three years older than I am, and she knew her stuff. They don't accept you into that scene until you're eighteen, for obvious reasons, so the three years she had on me were three years of experience with BDSM. I hit on her at first, tried to turn her into a sub, and ya know, straight, but she laughed in my face. Even after that, though, she went out of her way to mentor me—to teach me the rules. In that community you aren't even allowed to approach a woman until you're properly vetted. To this day she's one of my closest friends."

"I was still indiscriminately promiscuous for years, but the BDSM was so much more satisfying for me, and eventually I went all in, but even my contracted subs were strictly a sexual thing. There's an entrance to the fourth floor aside from my elevator, and most weren't even allowed into my home outside of that floor. You can't imagine what an anomaly you were for me, Bianca. Intimacy was unbearable to me before I set eyes on you. You've changed so many things for me, and I never dreamed that could be such a wonderful feeling. I feel like I've been brought to life, like I'm a real person now, instead of a pretender."

I knew all too well how that felt. I doubted many people could have understood as perfectly as I did just what he meant by that.

"Yes," I whispered, watching those exquisitely tarnished eyes. "I feel that way too. I know exactly what you mean."

He gave me a desperate kind of look. "I know you do. I've told you from the start that we were made for each other, and I truly believe that. Things are going to be extra rough for a while, because of this video, and particularly with the press. I'm *begging* you, Bianca, please stick it out with me. Don't withdraw, don't take a break. Not even a little one."

It stung a little that he didn't trust me, but I knew that was my fault. My eyes and voice were steady. "I won't, James. I'm staying. I love you."

His face went a little slack, as though the words were still a shock to him. "Thank you. I love you, too. More than life, Bianca."

I didn't like that last part. It sounded too self-sacrificing, bringing to mind my dark nightmares of late.

CHAPTER TWENTY-SEVEN

Mr. Porn Star

We decided to work out, since we'd slept most of the day, and I was flying out early the next morning. The idea was to work off the excess energy that too long of a nap had given me.

I didn't mind working out, but I took it easy, mostly sticking to a stationary bike and watching James as he worked over every piece of equipment in his large gym. He was a shirtless sight to behold as he strained himself. My jaw went completely slack as he did mouthwatering pull-ups, his shorts riding low. I thought I may have found a new reason to love hitting the gym.

He grinned at me as he moved to the free weights. "Keep looking at me like that if you want to get fucked on a stationary bike, Love."

I didn't have a problem with that, so I kept looking.

He watched me back in the room's mirror-lined walls. I ran my eyes over his body. Even his calves were sexy, I thought. So long and lean, but with that hard play of muscle under the surface.

He set down his weights. "That's it. Come here."

I walked over to him without hesitation.

He led me to a spot in front of the mirror. He began to peel off my clothes without another word. I let him, watching our reflections as he bent over me. I loved the look on his face as he tended to me. It was so tender, and almost peaceful, as he took care of me.

When I was naked, he lifted my arms above my head. We were next to a piece of equipment and there was a bar above my head. It was adjustable, and he shifted it until I could reach it. “Grip it,” he told me.

I reached up to grip it. The movement pulled harshly at my tender breasts, but I didn’t say a word, because then he might stop…

He pressed into my back, watching me in the mirror. His hands ran over the front of my body as we watched our reflections. He cupped just the undersides of my breasts very carefully, but quickly released them. One hand moved down to cup my hip, and the other snaked down, along my ribs, past my naval, and into my sex. He fingered me, but stopped abruptly. He held his wet fingers up.

“You’re always wet for me. Always. I fucking love that,” he said roughly.

His shorts hit the floor, and he positioned himself against me from behind. He parted me with hard hands on the fronts of my thighs, pulling me back against him. I watched his knees bend then straighten as his cock disappeared inside of me.

“Oh God,” I gasped as he rammed into me.

I watched as he pulled out. It was a long, drawn-out process, my view superb on his massive arousal between my legs from behind.

“How’s your grip?” he asked, driving back into me.

I had to swallow to answer, my eyes still glued to his magnificent cock.

“Good,” I managed.

“Good. Look at me, Bianca. I’m going to fuck you really hard. I need you to tell me if your grip is slipping.”

I nodded, meeting his eyes.

He bit his lip and started hammering into me in earnest. I whimpered, loving the mixture of pleasure and pain as he fucked me so hard that it hurt. I craved this the most, I thought.

My grip started to slip at the end, and I told him breathlessly.

He barely paused. "Let go," he told me, his hands moving to my hips. He pushed me close to the mirror, until my breasts were nearly touching the glass. He groaned at the sight.

"Hands on the mirror," he told me, and I did. His hips slapped against me with the force of his thrusts.

My eyes stayed open, but went a bit fuzzy as I fell to pieces, clenching around him. "James," I cried as I came.

He shuddered and groaned and buried himself to the hilt, his cock twitching inside of me as he came.

"So perfect," he told me simply, kissing my shoulder.

My legs felt shaky as he pulled out of me, but his weren't, and he swung me up into his arms.

"Shower time," he told me with a smile.

"Um, shouldn't we get dressed?" I asked.

The gym was on the second floor, and we'd have to walk down the hall, walk up the stairs, then walk down another hall, buck naked, just to get to our room.

His shoulder moved in a shrug. "I'll walk fast," he said.

I laughed.

Sure enough, Stephan spotted us as James was carrying me up the stairs.

"Um, hey," he called from the first floor. "I take it you guys worked it out?"

We both laughed.

"Everything is perfect," James told him, still walking up the stairs. I was sure that Stephan was getting a spectacular view of his ass.

"Clothes just get in the way, huh?" Stephan called back, laughing now.

"Yep," James said. "Goodnight."

"Goodnight," Stephan said.

"Goodnight," I said between helpless giggles.

We showered and there was food outside our door when we emerged. James fed me each bite, batting my hands away when I tried to grab the fork. It was some sort of vegetable soufflé. It was delicious, and I was starving, so I ate a huge portion before I waved him off.

He polished it off, putting the tray back outside the door.

He came back to the bed, pulling me against him. "Are you tired enough to sleep?" he asked.

I shook my head. "I slept too much today."

His fingers snaked between my legs, fingering me. "Wanna fuck until we both pass out cold?" he asked with a grin.

I laughed. "You're insatiable, and I'm sore."

He pulled his fingers away, giving me a regretful look. He sighed. "Fine. We'll find some clothes and go watch TV.

We wound up watching movies with Stephan for most of the night. The guys insisted that we watch Princess Bride again. James leaned into me at one point and whispered, "As you wish, Buttercup," into my ear.

I shot him a look. I suddenly recalled that he'd said that to me before, a few times in fact, and what it meant in the context of the movie, but we'd only been seeing each other for a few days the first time that had happened…

"You're insane," I told him quietly.

He nodded, smiling. "Completely off my rocker," he agreed.

He was on my flight to Vegas the next morning, doing his rich man stalker thing. He was even more attentive than usual on the flight that morning, rarely taking his eyes off me, as though afraid I would just disappear. As seemed to be his habit, his most distant mood was being followed by his most attentive.

Still, I was busy from wheels up to wheels down, with barely a moment to spare for him, aside from the expected service. We had a decent tailwind speeding up our flight time, so the trip was nice and quick.

We were staying at my place. I carpooled with Stephan. A car full of security tailed us closely. James was meeting us at the house.

He was waiting in my driveway, and looked to be yelling at a paparazzo when we pulled up.

"Shit," Stephan cursed. "Wish I had your garage door opener. We'll go directly into mine, and you can just jump the back fence into your yard. You shouldn't have to deal with that mess."

I sighed. "My security will have a conniption if I go anywhere before it's been searched, even your garage."

"Oh yeah," he said. "They've even been giving me the royal treatment. Did you know that I have a bodyguard when I go out now, too?"

I hadn't. I just stared at him, dumbfounded. I'd been so oblivious lately. But I felt an instant wave of relief, and got the warmest feeling in my chest. I loved that crazy man. So much.

He parked in his driveway, and we gave the security plenty of time to flank the car before we got out. Stephan and I shared a look before we got out of the car. The look said, 'This is crazy.'

James was at least done yelling at the photographer as we approached the house. He saw me and strode to us. Clark was blocking the paparazzo with consummate skill. So well, in fact, that I couldn't even see the man.

James took my arm, his face tense in annoyance. He nodded at Paterson to go ahead into my house. A bodyguard that I didn't recognize was already going into Stephan's house.

We waited just outside while Paterson searched the first room.

"Bianca! How does it feel to be living with a porn star? When are you planning to release your own video?" the paparazzo shouted loudly to our backs.

I turned into James before the man had even finished yelling.

He'd gone tense, and I knew what he wanted to do. I threw my arms around his neck. He hugged me around the ribs, but his head was turned in the direction of the obnoxious man.

"Let's go inside. Somebody get the door open!" I said loudly.

"Do you like to be spanked too, Bianca? I'll spank you anytime you want!" the foolish man shouted.

My hug turned into a death grip. James would have to take me with him if he went after the man. I sent a wild look at our security, who all seemed useless to me at that moment.

"If James hits that guy, I'm firing you all!" I shouted at them. "Get us inside, or get that man out of here!"

Finally, mercifully, we got into the house. James ended up carrying me inside, since I wouldn't let go of him.

I didn't realize that Stephan wasn't with us until I let go of James. I glanced around.

James was still seething, but he sounded calmer than he looked when he spoke. "You stopped *me*, but there's only one of you, and I wasn't the only one getting riled up."

I was out the door again before James saw my intent. He caught me just outside, his arms wrapping around my shoulders. There was no need, though.

Stephan and Clark were striding towards us, grinning.

"What happened?" I asked Stephan. There was no sign of the photographer.

Stephan shrugged. "I went to give Clark a hand with that prick, but he had it handled."

We all looked at Clark.

He shrugged. "I just explained some things to him, and he left. Some other paparazzi might come here, but *that* guy won't be back."

"What did you say to him?" I asked, beyond curious. Those photographers were hard to shake.

Clark laughed. He had a great laugh. "I just explained to him that what I would do to him if he *didn't* leave would affect him for the rest of his life, whereas *I* would only serve five to ten for it. And I explained that the millions of dollars that would be waiting for me on the other side of that five to ten, combined with the mood he'd put me in, would make doing the thing more than worthwhile for me. He just sort of went poof after that." He gestured with his hands as he spoke.

We laughed, and the tension that the horrible man had created vanished just like that. I hadn't realized that Clark was so funny. He was normally so straight-faced, but he was smiling freely now. Maybe Stephan and I were growing on him.

The house was cleared, and we made it to my room without any further incident.

"I'm surprised that you were able to come to Vegas again so quickly," I said to James as we were undressing in my closet. "Are things going smoothly in New York?"

"Things are going fine. I would have come even if they weren't, though."

I glanced back at him.

He gave me a sad smile. "I can't sleep without you anymore, Love. And letting you stay here in this house, where that man attacked you, well, I just can't do it again."

"There's an entire team guarding the place."

He shrugged. "I told myself that, and I even went a weekend letting you stay here without me, but I know my own limits, and I just can't do it again, not after he killed that woman."

"Maybe we should just stay at your place, at least until he's caught. I wonder if we could talk Stephan into staying there with us. I would feel—"

He pushed me back against the wall of the closet, tangling us both in clothes. He kissed me. "Thank you. I'll handle Stephan. We can nap here, and go to my place tonight, after you have a meeting with Danika. She needs your approval for some things, and she's in town for the day."

We took a three-hour nap, waking up at our leisure. Between

the shower sex, and James going down on me in the closet as I tried to pick out clothes, it was well over an hour after we woke up before we were ready to go to the casino for business.

I wore a navy and black, color-block pencil skirt. I paired it with a loose fitting royal blue silk blouse with three-quarter sleeves. I didn't know what Jackie would think of the outfit, but she hadn't paired my clothes in this closet, and I liked the ensemble.

After I'd done a quick job on my hair and makeup, I stepped into white heels, and watched as James finished getting ready. I was done first for once, and it was a show worth watching.

He was buttoning up his slacks as I perched on the bed, my eyes glued to his hands. He arched a brow at me as he shrugged into a white dress shirt.

"Enjoying the show?" he asked as he buttoned the shirt.

I nodded.

He grinned. "I feel like I should be dancing for you. You have an unmistakable glint in your eyes, Bianca. I'm not a piece of meat, you know."

I just smiled back, watching his every move.

He tucked his shirt into his slacks, shrugging into a dark gray vest that matched his slacks. He looped a yellow tie around his neck, his clever fingers making short work of it, before he buttoned the severely tailored vest.

"I love your hands," I told him.

"We're running late," he murmured.

I let my eyes show him just how much I didn't care.

It was another half an hour before we walked out the front door.

James walked me to the gallery before going to his office to do some paperwork. He greeted Danika with a smile.

"Just come to my office when you finish," James told me. "Blake or Danika can show you where it is." He gave me an affectionate kiss on the forehead before taking his leave.

Danika watched him go. She smiled at me. "He's so different with you. It's a lovely thing to see."

I smiled back.

Danika wore a very modern take on a woman's suit, with pleated, slate gray shorts, and a baggy white men's shirt that was belted at the waist. She looked delicate and lovely. I thought she was the most elegant woman I'd ever met. Her hair was parted down the middle, and as she bent down to show me some detail of her plans, it trailed into her face like a silky black curtain. I wondered again what had happened between her and Tristan, but I shook myself out of the pointless musings. We had lots of work to do, and I could hardly ask.

We worked well together. Danika was never pushy, but she did finally get me to settle on a date for the showing. We scheduled it for the first Friday after my furlough began. James would be ecstatic. I was nervous—so nervous that I felt a little nauseous just thinking about it.

"Do you have any other big plans for after you take your leave?"

I smiled, remembering our plans. That was something I could get very excited about. "James and I are going to Japan."

She raised her elegant brows in surprise. "Well, that's exciting. My mother was half-Japanese. I didn't know her well, but I've always had a fascination with Japanese culture."

I smiled. "I have no blood-ties there, but I've always been interested in the culture, as well. We're going there because James said pick a spot on a map of the world, and I knew just where I wanted to go."

She smiled back, tilting her head. "Well, have fun. I bet the locals will get a kick out of you two."

I laughed. "Yeah, right? I don't suppose we'll blend in."

She pursed her lips. "Do you ever? I don't see too many supermodel couples strolling around together."

I wrinkled my nose at her. "James is the supermodel."

Her lovely brow wrinkled in consternation. "So it's like that, huh? You're going to need to work on your self-esteem, girl, to be with a man like that, otherwise it could be the end of you two."

I blinked at her. Her tone had been gentle but firm, so I didn't take offense. I just didn't agree. "I don't have low self-esteem. I just know that I'm not in that league."

She shook her head stubbornly, her silky black hair moving across her shoulders with the movement, her rosebud mouth pursing. "That's ludicrous. Answer one question for me. Have you ever been approached by a modeling scout before?"

I flushed. "Not by anyone serious. A few people have said something, but I knew they were just trying to scam me."

She gave me a sympathetic look. "Seriously, as someone who has a real hetero-girl-crush on you, you need to work on your self-esteem. You're stunning, and you need to just acknowledge the fact and then get over it."

The whole conversation made me uncomfortable. "Um, thanks. So did we have any other details to go over for the showing?"

She sighed and shook her head. "No. Let's go grab Frankie and get something to eat. I can't come to town and not see her. She'd kill me."

We had an impromptu girls' lunch. I wasn't sure if it was a late lunch or an early dinner.

Frankie greeted me with a hug, a kiss on the cheek, and a huge grin. She wore her usual half-shirt with daisy dukes, showing off her myriad tattoos.

"I just spoke to James," she told us. "He needs to work for a few hours, and he told me to keep you entertained. Sucker." She rubbed her hands together like an evil cartoon character. "I have plans."

Danika laughed richly. "Oh boy. He's in trouble, huh?"

Frankie nodded. I tried to follow the strange conversation.

"First we eat," she told us.

We went to the casino's Mexican restaurant. We ordered and started snacking on chips and salsa.

"Do you mind if I bring Tristan to Bianca's gallery showing?" Frankie asked Danika, studying her closely.

Danika didn't hesitate. "Why would I mind? Bring whoever you want."

"Well, I know you aren't speaking to him…"

"That's not true. He and I have absolutely nothing to talk about, but I'm not avoiding him."

Frankie nodded. "Good. Because I have a red carpet thing for my show coming up. It's in town next week, and I want you to come. I was worried you wouldn't come, since Tristan will be there, but now you can't use that as an excuse."

Danika just shrugged. "If you want me there, I'll be there. Tristan and I will just stay out of each other's way."

Frankie sighed. "You used to be best friends. I wish you guys would at least start talking again."

Danika gave her a hard look. "Don't meddle, Frankie. Trust me when I say that you don't want to press this issue. I can be civil, but he and I will *never* be close again. We are bad for each other, even as friends. Bad things happen when we get together."

"You'd feel better if you forgave him—"

"I did forgive him. We went through all of that when he was doing the rehab thing. I'm over it, but forgiving doesn't mean that I'm willing to make all of the same stupid mistakes again."

"You know he's in love with you, right?"

Danika laughed, and it was a bitter sound. "Please. Don't make me laugh. That man isn't capable of it. Now drop it, Frankie, before I leave."

Frankie threw up her hands in defeat, her mouth twisting. "Okay, okay, I'm sorry. Consider it dropped."

Food arrived, and the two women pretended like the whole

awkward interaction had never happened.

I followed suit, though I was beyond curious about whatever had happened between Danika and Tristan.

CHAPTER TWENTY-EIGHT

Mr. Incensed

We gorged ourselves on cheese enchiladas and chiles rellenos. I was over-stuffed when I finished, but I'd found my new favorite restaurant for comfort food.

The meal went smoothly after their little confrontation, and the women laughed and joked like old friends. We were finishing our meal when Frankie looked at me with a wicked smile, rubbing her hands together.

"How do you feel about branding James onto your body? Just something little. *He* did it for *you*. Don't you want to return the favor?"

I should've known that was what she'd been plotting. She was a tattoo artist, after all. I considered her idea, not dismissing it out of hand. I was finding new ways to surprise myself daily. "What did you have in mind?" I asked her warily.

She waved Danika out of her seat. "May I borrow your back for a moment, Danika?" she asked cheerfully.

Danika just stood up and turned around as though they did this every day.

Frankie circled a small spot on the other woman's shoulder blade. "James. Right here. Identical size, color and style as the Bianca on his chest. What do you think?"

I was shocked to find myself warming to the idea. I knew that James had done something so extreme to prove something to me, the same thing that he seemed to need me to prove to him. I took a deep breath. "The same size as his?" I asked.

Frankie whooped, sensing victory. "Yes, but on your back. I know James well enough to know that he wouldn't like a boob tat. Let's do this!"

Frankie had to have a brief but firm conversation with the camera crew and producer that taped her reality show. They were *not* going to tape this tattoo.

Blake insisted on searching the place, but I was surprised when she didn't try to butt in when she saw what we were obviously doing. She just stood outside of the curtained area and waited for me.

In a shockingly short time I found myself lying on my stomach on Frankie's table, my silk blouse pulled up over my shoulder, my bra unclasped. The position pushed hard on my newly pierced nipples, but I didn't complain. I imagined that I wouldn't even feel that pain when she started in with the needle.

"James is going to *kill* me," Frankie muttered as she traced the pattern onto my back. "He'll be mad at me for a while just for seeing and touching this much of your skin."

Danika was giggling as she watched, a clear accessory to the crime.

"Really?" I asked Frankie, not sure if she was serious.

"Oh yeah."

"Why?"

"He's got you collared, Bianca. That's some real serious shit for him. He's possessive as all hell about every inch of you."

"But it's for a tattoo. I know he'll get testy about that at first, but to get possessive about you touching my shoulder blade just seems so unreasonable."

She laughed. "If you think that there's anything reasonable about a Dom, you've been misinformed, my friend. He's going to be *incensed* about this, but he'll get over it, and I know that eventually he'll love having his name on you."

I sighed, thinking that she was probably right.

The tattoo was a shorter process than I thought it would be, though it *was* a small tattoo.

It stung, but the pain wasn't at all as bad as I'd heard. After she'd worked on the area for just a few minutes, it all became one sort of throbbing sting, and by the end, I even liked the feeling. I understood a bit why some of my friends thought that tattoos were addictive.

Frankie showed me when she'd finished, and I felt a little thrill when I saw his name on my skin. *I could get used to this*, I thought. Which was good, because it was permanent.

She spread gel on the area and covered it with a small plastic film.

"Go shirtless as much as you can, at home. Let it air out. A consolation prize for James, I guess. You do have a fabulous rack."

I sent her a look. She'd never seen my rack, *but oh well*, I'd take it as a compliment.

She grabbed her tiny purse, grinning at us. "I'm getting the hell outta Dodge. He won't want to see me for a few days, so I'm going to make myself scarce. I'll see you at the red carpet event for my show."

"Coward!" Danika yelled at her as she took off in a hurry.

Danika walked me through the casino and to the executive offices, Blake and Henry trailing us silently. I had to stop and stare when we passed by one of the hotel's auditoriums. It had a giant poster displayed of what the theatre featured, which was a long line of showgirls, kicking their legs high in the air, showing off all of their assets, and right smack in the middle of the picture, his arm around two of the showgirls, was a grinning James.

Danika shook her head when she saw it. "If it makes you feel any better, that was taken years ago."

I shrugged, but I couldn't help but wonder how many of the women in that chorus line he'd slept with.

"There seem to be a lot of things that he did years ago that just keep popping up," I said, my tone neutral. I didn't feel neutral, though.

She grimaced. "That sex tape... I heard about that. And just when he's cleaned up his act. Life is funny like that, making us pay for the same stupid mistakes even after we've learned from them thoroughly."

Now that sounded like a heartfelt statement. I studied her, still dying to know what had happened between her and the sexy as hell Tristan. I wouldn't pry, though. Perhaps we'd get more chances to hang out, and someday she'd just tell me about it.

Danika walked me to the office reception before saying her goodbyes. We set up another meeting for the following week. She was coming all the way back to Vegas just to meet me again, but she didn't seem to mind.

Reception led me immediately into James's office, but I saw that he was busy on the phone as I walked in. Blake only followed me to the door. She didn't seem to need to search the office, with James already there.

I sat in the chair directly in front of his desk, crossing my legs and watching him. I was torn on when to tell him about the tattoo. Should I just let him find it on his own? Chances were, if I did it that way, we'd be on the verge of having sex, and he was bound to be in a better mood about it...

James looked up, a phone to his ear. His eyes changed when he saw me, going from business-like and serious to smoldering between one blink and the next. I adored that I could put that look in his eye just by being there.

He held up a finger to me to show that he would only be another minute. I just nodded, watching him. The view never got old.

He hung up the phone and smiled at me. "We'll go to my house from here. Stephan is out but he says he'll crash there with us tonight. He doesn't mind staying with us until the danger's past."

I was relieved, though I hadn't really thought that Stephan would give him a hard time.

The tattoo just didn't come up, or rather, I didn't work up the nerve to bring it up, until he found it himself that night.

Frankie had predicted his reaction well. He was completely incensed.

He was at my back, peeling off my shirt when he spotted it.

I knew what was coming, and so I stiffened just before he did.

His eyes bored into my back for long moments before he began to curse, succinctly and fluently. He finished his tirade with an impassioned, "I'll kill her."

"She said you'd say that," I told him.

That just made him curse even more. "I can't believe I didn't see it coming, when she called me up saying that you were all doing a girls' day, and that I should keep on working. I *knew* she wanted to get her hands on you."

I shot him an exasperated look. "You really think that she did all of this just so that she could very briefly touch me? She was completely professional, James."

"I should have known she would try this, but I can't believe that you agreed to it. What were you *thinking*?"

"You did the same thing for me—to prove something to me. You wanted me to see that you really were devoted to me, and that you wanted a long-term commitment. I was trying to do the same thing for you. I wanted you to see that I'm just as committed. It's not something that should make you jealous. I *branded* your name on my shoulder, and all you can do is get jealous that someone else was holding the needle. I didn't do this because Frankie wanted me to. I did it for you. We belong to each other, James, and now we *both* have the ink to prove it. I thought that you would love seeing your name on me."

In terms of defusing his anger, it worked like a charm. He pressed hard against my back, murmuring into my ear. "I do love seeing that on you. How could I ever stay mad, when you say such wonderful things to me? So tell me, Bianca, just how committed are you? Committed enough to take my name and wear my ring? Devoted enough to like the sound of Bianca Cavendish?"

My heart tried to pound right out of my chest. Because I knew he wasn't really joking, even though his tone was light. And because it didn't only make me want to panic anymore to hear him say a thing like that. Now a picture was beginning to form in my mind of something real and sustaining for us. Perhaps what had happened to my mother hadn't forever ruined any possibility of my own happily ever after. The thought was both encouraging and terrifying.

James didn't wait for me to answer. He knew me too well.

He kissed my neck. "Start growing accustomed to the idea, Love, and try not to tie yourself in knots second-guessing yourself. And try to remember that I'm head over heels in love with you, and that I've never even come close to saying those words to another person."

"I love you, too," I whispered back, loving him more at that moment than I'd even thought possible. How could I ever have imagined that Mr. Beautiful could be so incredibly sensitive to my needs? It was as though he'd known me forever.

If I was surprised at how quickly he dropped the subject of the tattoo with me, I was equally *unsurprised* at how he didn't drop the subject with Frankie. Even a full week later, at her show's Vegas Strip red carpet event, James was giving her the cold shoulder.

James wore a black tux with a black shirt and white bow tie. It was very fitted, very fashion forward, very supermodel James.

I wore a little white dress with silver accents. It was short enough to be Vegas appropriate, with a halter neck that I thought was flattering, though the back came up high enough to cover my new tattoo. Unlike James, I wasn't trying to show it off to the world right off the bat.

Shiny red heels took all of the innocence out of the color of the dress, and James seemed a little dumbstruck when I walked out of the closet in the sexy getup. The look on his face told me I'd chosen just right.

The mood of this red carpet was actually a fun vibe, as opposed to the tenser one I'd attended before. People dressed up, but it was more sexy Las Vegas dress-up than stuffy ballroom. Even Frankie decided to forgo her usual half-shirt, cutoff shorts look and wore a tiny red dress that looked sinful.

It was Frankie's night, and she'd been thoughtful enough to extend an invitation to Stephan and Javier. James had bought them their own custom tailored tuxes, and the two men were grinning from ear to ear as we all walked the red carpet together.

Frankie rushed to hug a stiff James as soon as she spotted us at the event.

"Will you at least talk to me about it? You can't freeze me out forever, James," she said into his cheek.

"Oh, we'll talk," he told her ominously.

She just smiled, seeming to take that as a good sign.

She greeted Stephan and Javier like they were all old friends, before moving to me. She pointedly didn't try to hug me, just bending at the waist to give me a jaunty little bow. "Bianca, the lion tamer," she said, grinning at James.

I put a hand on his arm, wishing he would just let it go. But James was James, and he would get there in his own time.

Frankie seemed to know him well enough to see that, and gave him space.

We ran into Tristan next. He was looking debonair in a black tux as he posed for one of the photo ops. The photographers seemed to be in a frenzy to get shots of him. I shot James a puzzled look.

"Is he famous or something?" I asked.

James grinned and then laughed. "Or something. He stars in the magic show at the Cavendish property, and he's the lead singer in a band that had two hit singles last year. It doesn't make me even a little bit sad that you aren't a fan of his."

Tristan turned to us the instant he finished with the shots. He grinned that wicked grin of his from ear to ear when he saw me.

He moved as though to hug me the second he got within our reach, but James was expecting that. James moved in between us, catching the other man in a bear hug and saying something that I couldn't make out into his ear.

Tristan just threw his head back and laughed.

The two men were of the same height, but Tristan had James beat in bulk. Where James was ripped but elegant, Tristan looked like a linebacker in a suit.

James pulled away from the other man, and moved me very obviously into his body, shielding me. I thought it was ridiculous, but it still made me smile.

I gave Tristan a little wave.

He bent forward in a solicitous bow, but his wicked eyes never left my face, and his smile didn't falter. He flashed one of his dangerous dimples my way.

"So no touching," he said in his deep, rich voice. "Can I at least see her tattoo? I heard all about it. I heard her back was lovely, just like the rest of her."

He was clearly baiting James, but he still got an unexpected giggle out of me. The man was outrageous.

James agreed with me, and he was not nearly as upset with the other man's comments as I'd thought he'd be. "Outrageous bastard," he muttered, but with little heat. Perhaps being deliberately baited had made him see how over the top possessive he was being. Or perhaps the two men were better friends than I'd realized. *Who knew with Mr. Beautiful?*

We introduced Tristan to Stephan and Javier. Of course, Stephan knew who he was. He was the media savvy of the two of us. I didn't know how I'd been so clueless as to his identity. If he had a headlining show in Vegas, there must have been billboards for him everywhere. I made a note to keep an eye out for his ads.

My suspicion that James and Tristan were actually close friends was reaffirmed at the way the two men joked and generally gave each other shit for a solid twenty minutes amidst the red carpet chaos. Only good friends could give each other that much grief without any real low blows. Tristan had to know about the sex tape, everyone seemed to, but he never mentioned it. Most of his jabs involved talking about how pretty James was, which didn't bother James at all.

And James never mentioned Danika, who I had discerned right away was Tristan's own sore spot. Most of the jabs aimed Tristan's way were comments about 'singing magicians', which only seemed to make Tristan smile.

At one point Tristan ran his hand through his hair, then pointedly checked his watch, which looked familiar. "Are you about done harassing me, pretty boy?" he asked.

James cursed, then held out his hand. "Give me my watch back," he said.

Tristan waved the watch at him. "It's almost my birthday. Can't we just call it even?"

James shook his head, grinning. "I don't like you that much."

Tristan was handing it back to him when his expression became arrested, his eyes moving to look at something behind us. Something raw moved behind those golden depths that seemed impossibly sad for the charismatic man.

I glanced behind us.

Danika approached. She was looking at us, not at Tristan,

but she seemed different than I'd ever seen her, more stiff, her limp more pronounced. If I hadn't known these two had a history, I would have quickly caught on by the way they changed when in each other's vicinity.

She wore a long silver gown that hugged her perfect figure like a glove. Her straight, blue-black hair was parted down the middle and hanging down her back. The severe and simple style brought out the elegance of her face, the rosebud lips, the high-cheekbones, and those stunning, pale-gray eyes.

Danika strode directly to me, bestowing a kiss on my cheek. She was unsmiling but polite down to her toes. "So lovely to see you again, Bianca."

She nodded to James, who introduced her to Stephan and Javier.

"Hello, Danika," Tristan said softly, after all of the introductions had been made.

She nodded in his general direction, but didn't look at him. "Hello, Tristan."

"It's great to see you," he told her. "You look exquisite, as always."

She smiled tightly. "Sure," she said.

A man approached her from behind, wrapping a hand around her waist and smiling warmly. He was about my height, with medium brown hair and a light build. He was handsome, in a nondescript kind of way, but I thought that he complimented Danika well. They made an elegant couple.

She touched his shoulder lightly. "Everyone, this is Andrew."

"Her boyfriend," Andrew added.

She gave us another tight smile, then introduced the group to him.

I snuck one glance at Tristan, but the way he was looking at Danika was so blatant and raw that I quickly looked away. Being around the two of them felt like overhearing a couple's worst fight. It felt like we should all excuse ourselves and leave them alone to sort things out, Andrew included.

Danika and Andrew quickly made their excuses and moved on.

Tristan quickly followed suit. "If you'll excuse me, I need to go punch something now, so that I don't give in to the urge to punch some*one*." With that telling remark, he strode away.

"I take it there's beef between Tristan and Andrew?" I made it a question.

James shrugged. "I don't know that they've ever met before. I think it's just the beef that Tristan would have with any man that Danika might date. He's been in love with her since I met him. For five years, at least. Poor bastard."

CHAPTER TWENTY-NINE

Mr. Distraught

James stayed glued to my side almost constantly for an entire week. If I wasn't working a flight, he was there, and I couldn't say I minded it a bit, though I began to suspect the reason.

He was terrified that I would watch the video of him and Jolene. He hadn't asked me not to watch the thing, but he knew me well enough to suspect that I would want to view what was out there for the world to see.

And so I didn't find myself alone for nearly a week after the sex tape's release. James had worked plenty in that week, but only when I was working, or when I had someone keeping me company. Lana took me shopping; Stephan sat with me while I painted. Marnie and Judith flew to New York to spend the afternoon with me. Danika dropped in for an afternoon to observe my current projects. I had a constant barrage of friends to keep me company if James had to work and I didn't, and I didn't think for a second that any of it was a coincidence.

I was in the New York apartment, painting, when it dawned on me that I was actually alone.

I glanced at the computer in my studio but just continued to paint. But once the thought occurred, I found it difficult to focus on anything else. I knew I'd have to watch it eventually, and it seemed for the best to just get it over with. It seemed like the whole world must have watched that video by now, and he was *my* devoted lover, so why shouldn't *I* get to see it?

I was sitting at the computer and searching for it online before I could give it much more thought. I typed 'James Cavendish sex tape' into the search engine. It was that easy.

My gut knotted painfully from the moment I dragged the mouse over the play button. Every instinct I had told me to just turn it off. Some things you couldn't take back, and watching James have sex with another woman, a woman I'd met, one who I openly disliked, couldn't be a healthy thing for our relationship. Still, I watched.

It hadn't been taped in any place that I recognized. I'd expected that. It was a small room with a big bed, and the camera must have been hidden somewhere high in the room, aimed down, and in the corner.

The small room was empty for long moments before Jolene walked in and knelt on the floor in front of the bed.

She was wearing a tiny black see-through slip that hung at her hips and didn't cover a thing. I recognized that slip, or at least the style of it. It felt like a slap in the face to see that he'd had me wear something so similar to what *she* had worn for him. It wasn't a good start, not that there was any way the horrid video *could* have had a good start.

She knelt there, all of her glorious assets displayed, her pierced nipples jutting out for drawn-out moments before James joined her in the room. Someone, either the person who had released the video or the person whose site I was watching it on, had added snarky little comments to the video. Directly beneath Jolene, '***HOTTEST FUCKING BITCH EVER!***' was scrawled in hot pink.

James was shirtless, wearing just unbuttoned slacks. His body was ripped up and spectacular, though he was slightly thinner back then, his hair a little longer, the dirty blond strands tied back from his face.

His face was a mask of cold indifference, only his dominant persona present that I could see. He said something to her and she bowed lower. There was no audio, aside from a particularly graphic rap song about being a pimp playing in the background, courtesy of the video's editor.

He pulled her up by the hair and led her the short distance to the bed. She kept her eyes downcast the entire time.

The bed was designed vaguely like a smaller version of the beds that James had in his homes, with a sturdy frame and a top designed for bondage. This bed had bars lining the top. James tied her arms above her head with swift motions. I couldn't make out his words, and he didn't speak much, but when he did, Jolene shuddered in pleasure. She reminded me of a cat in heat, with her back arched and her wiggling body responding to his every movement. I hated to watch it, but I didn't stop. I felt compelled to finish it, some part of me having to see if he showed her even a glimmer of the tenderness he showed me in our passionate moments.

He stood behind her once she was secured. He pressed against her, and had to bend down far to say something into her ear. I thought pettily to myself that she was too short for him. The height difference looked ridiculous. She barely came to his chest.

She shuddered and he moved away. He walked out of the room without looking back, returning after a brief time with an object clutched in one hand.

It was a cat o' nine, with long tails that were tipped with small silver balls. It looked brutal, and it wasn't anything he'd ever used on me. He said something to her just before he began to work her over.

From the first strike, the music in the video changed to '*Smack My Bitch Up*'. Whoever had edited the video seemed to have enjoyed themselves.

He worked her over thoroughly, showing no mercy. She kept her head bent forward, her eyes downcast the entire time. She seemed like a different person than the Jolene that I'd been subjected to.

Her body writhed, her big breasts quivering with every hard strike. The flesh of her butt and thighs was crisscrossed with pink welts by the time he let up.

I felt like I was watching in slow motion as he dropped the whip and began to unbutton his pants. My hands fisted, my nails digging hard into my palms. This was going to hurt me to watch. Still, I couldn't look away.

He pulled his thick erection free.

'HOLY HUGE DICK!' scrolled along the bottom of the screen.

I despised with a passion whoever had edited the thing.

I thought I might be ill as he stroked himself, standing just behind her.

He pulled a condom out of his pocket, ripping it open and rolling it on with smooth, practiced motions.

He poised himself behind her, his huge arousal looking even bigger against her petite form. I knew it was totally irrational, but God, I hated her.

My hand covered my mouth as he drove into her. I'd known before I turned it on that it would be bad for my heart to watch it, but I had the thought again.

He fucked her so hard that it must have hurt, though I supposed that was the point. She shuddered as she came, and he pulled out of her, still hard, while those waves of pleasure still wracked her body.

He turned her, and I realized that as hard as that had been to watch, it was about to get worse.

She started to raise her eyes to him as he entered her then, but he said something and her eyes lowered again. I felt the fist around my heart loosen just a bit. There was no eye contact as he pounded into her from that angle. He fucked her hard until he had her shuttering again, and then again.

New words scrolled along the bottom of the screen. ***'RICH, GORGEOUS, AND HE FUCKS LIKE A MACHINE. WHAT'S NOT TO LOVE?'***

Again, I had some nasty thoughts about the editor.

He pulled out of her roughly, and I saw his cock twitching inside of that tight rubber with his own release. Unfortunately, the video was good enough that I could make out every detail, even the tip of the condom filling with cum.

At least he hadn't come inside of her. And at least he'd worn that rubber. I knew it was ridiculous to feel possessive of a body that I hadn't even known at the time of the video, but knowing didn't change the feeling.

He left her tied to the bed and strode from the room. When he came back in, he was fully dressed in a suit.

It didn't look like they said another word to each other, and she never once raised her eyes to him as he untied her and she lay down on the bed. She was curling her body around a pillow as he strode from the room. He never looked back.

My heart was pounding as the video ended. It had hurt to watch it, but I felt like I'd learned something important. It was a fact that James had been a slut before he'd met me. As much as the images in the video had bothered me, there wasn't an instant of their interaction where he'd shared anything but his body and his cold domination with her. There had been nothing that I would have called intimacy between the two of them.

He'd told me once that sex had just been a bodily function for him before he'd met me, and I'd just seen the proof of it. I knew it was perverse, but I felt both sick and relieved at the same time.

A movement out of the corner of my eye caught my attention. I turned to look.

James stood in the doorway.

His face was stricken—his eyes bleak, as he looked at the

computer screen. I wondered how long he'd been there, but obviously it had been long enough to see what I was watching.

Too late, I closed out the window of that horrid video.

I looked back at him, but he wasn't looking at me. His eyes were glazed and unseeing, still glued to the computer. He took a step back and closed the door behind him, leaving me alone in the room.

I just sat there for a few minutes, my mind still processing what I'd seen. I needed a minute to compose myself before we spoke about it, if there was even anything to say.

So he'd had sex with that horrible woman, probably too many times to count. Watching it had at least given me some clarity. James at his angriest, at his coldest, at his most furious, had never been to me what he was to Jolene. They had been a Dom and a sub letting off steam, nothing else.

Although I hadn't realized it at the time, James had always been different with me. Looking back on it now, James had shown me a profound tenderness and love that belonged only to me, from our very first time together. I realized that I needed to value that more, because it was more precious of a gift than I'd allowed myself to see. He was my Dom, and I was his sub, but our love had turned it into so much more than what I'd seen on that video. Yes, James had been a hedonist and a slut before I'd met him, but I saw now that I'd been his first lover. He'd changed his rules for me. He bended for me constantly. Because he loved me.

I sat and brooded for maybe ten minutes before I got up and followed him.

I thought I'd find him in our bedroom. It was empty. I found my phone and called him. He didn't answer. I searched the huge apartment for him, even venturing tentatively onto the fourth floor in my efforts.

I finally resorted to calling Blake.

"Ms. Karlsson," she answered promptly.

"Blake, do you know where James is? Did he leave the apartment?"

"Yes, Ma'am. He left just a few minutes after he'd arrived."

"Do you know where he went?"

"No..."

"Can you find out?" I asked, starting to panic a little.

I wanted to see him. I didn't want him thinking the worst about my reaction to watching that video, as I knew he would.

"I'll make some calls, Ms. Karlsson."

"Thank you," I said.

She hung up.

She called back about ten minutes later. "I couldn't locate him, Ms. Karlsson. Clark isn't picking up, and he's the only one with Mr. Cavendish. The only answer I could get from the others is that he went out."

CHAPTER THIRTY

Mr. Kinky

I tried to just wait after that, but I was restless and worried. I had no clue where he could have gone. I didn't know where he'd go if he was going out and upset. It was only two in the afternoon. *Had he just gone back to work?* I hadn't a clue.

I tried hard just to wait patiently for him to return. I tried to paint, but it was no good. I tried to watch TV, but I was hopelessly distracted. I called Stephan, who was in Vegas with Javier, but he hadn't heard from James. I told him what had happened.

"Are you okay?" he asked. "Do you want to talk about it?"

Of course my feelings would be his first concern, I thought.

"I'm fine," I told him. "It sucked, but it's not as though James has ever made a secret of his past. If anything, it made me see that what he did with those other women is *not* the same thing that we do. I'm worried about *him*, not me. The look in his eyes, Stephan... I feel like I broke his heart again. I need to find him."

He had no idea where James had gone either, but Stephan did what he did best. We talked for hours, about everything, but mostly about James, and I felt better when we said goodbye.

That good feeling lasted only an hour when there was still no sign of James. It was almost seven p.m. when I got desperate.

I was wearing a small slip of a dress, sans bra. It was an 'around the house in the hottest part of the summer' kind of outfit. I took the time to put on a bra, and found some comfortable shoes that matched the sleeveless, off-white dress. I called Blake as I grabbed my bag. I was at the top of the stairs when she answered.

"I'm going out," I told her before she could say a word.

"I'll meet you at the elevator."

And she was there, quick as a flash.

The rest of the security was waiting in the lobby for us. They hadn't replaced Johnny, and I was fine with that. I figured if this many people couldn't protect me, it was a lost cause, anyway.

No one asked me where we were going until we were all in the large black SUV that had been designated for my use.

"The Cavendish Hotel," I said. It was only a guess on my part, but I could see him going to his office if he was upset.

Security escorted me to the office suites, and I thought I must have been right as I saw that his receptionist was still on duty. She nodded for me to enter his office, as though she'd been instructed just to let me in.

No one followed me as I opened his door tentatively.

James was there, sitting at his desk, staring blankly at his computer, his hand unmoving on his mouse.

I stepped inside and shut the door softly behind me. I walked to him, but he didn't look at me.

Still, I saw something wounded and vulnerable move behind those tarnished eyes of his as I approached.

"James," I said softly.

"I'm sorry," he said brokenly, his voice no more than a whisper. "I only seem to disappoint you. If it makes you feel better, I'm beginning to hate the man I was before I met you."

I stroked a hand over his hair. "Of course that doesn't make me feel better. As far as I can tell, you've always been wonderful, even during your slutty days."

"I feel like life was easy before I met you, because it didn't matter," he said in a rough voice, leaning into my hand. "*Nothing* mattered before I knew you. I was a pretender, playing at life with monopoly money. I didn't *feel* anything. Nothing ever really changed because *I just I didn't care.* And now that it does matter—now that everything matters, it's so much harder, because things have weight now, and my life has substance. You can hurt a thing with substance. I've become vulnerable, where nothing could have hurt me before. My mistakes, even my past ones, will have consequences now."

I moved into him, pulling his head into my chest. He nuzzled there, making me sway with the force of his affection. I kissed the top of his head comfortingly. "I understand completely, James. I fought my feelings for you for so long for just that reason. Letting you in meant opening myself up to a pain I thought I was immune to, because I had become frozen to all of it. I was unfair to you, and even to some of my friends. You were right when you told me that I have room in my heart for more than Stephan. You read me so well without me ever having to say the words. It astounds me. Perhaps we *were* made for each other. You're making me a believer, my love."

He wrapped his arms around me. "I'm sorry you had to see that video, Bianca. I tried so hard to keep it from getting out."

I rubbed my cheek against that silky hair. "You didn't make me watch it. I take responsibility for that. And I learned something important from it. It did hurt to watch you with her, but I think it was worth it, in a way."

He pulled away far enough to give me a genuinely baffled look. "Why?! How?"

I gave him a small smile and some very solid eye contact. "Because I learned that you may have fucked a lot of women, James, but I'm your first lover."

"Yes," he rasped, kissing me like he owned me. I loved that

kiss, and yes, that ownership.

"You're so different with me," I told him as he pulled away long enough to pull me on top of him. I straddled him in his chair. "You always were, from the very beginning."

"Yes," he murmured, undoing his slacks to pull out that delicious cock. It was hard as a poker and ready to go, as ever. "I've told you this. It's unfortunate that you had to see me at my worst to believe it." He ripped off my panties as he spoke, making the words come out harsh and raw.

He impaled me on his arousal forcefully, not checking if I was ready—not letting me respond. It didn't matter. I shuddered with the pleasure, and the pain, of his possession.

He didn't move once he'd seated me to the hilt, but held me there, looking up at me with his heart in his eyes. I loved those eyes so much.

I cupped his cheek. "You're so different with me," I repeated. "You never made me look down; you never let me look away from you. You never walked away from me."

He shook his head. "Never."

"I loved your eyes first," I told him, repeating his words from a few weeks ago back to him, because it was true, and because we were two halves of a whole—we had been all along, and he'd been so clever to know it right away. I used to think it was insanity, but now I was beginning to think that it was pure brilliance. "I see it, too, James. I see the other half of my soul in you."

He jerked against me suddenly, grinding me against him. He never broke eye contact as he came inside of me.

He pulled my forehead to his, giving me a self-deprecating grin. "Well, that was embarrassing. I feel like a teenager. I'll have to make it up to you."

I smiled back, far from upset about it. I loved affecting him so powerfully that he lost control like that.

"I have no doubt that you will," I said, meaning it. If we were keeping score on orgasms, I was in the lead by four to one, at least. The man always could play my body like a drum.

He slid a hand between our bodies, moving his thumb in soft circles over my clit, circling his hips to move his thick length inside of me in an intoxicating grind.

"Touch me," he said roughly. I relished the chance. It seemed like more often than not only he did the touching.

I ran my hands over his chest and up to his shoulders. I cupped his face in my hands before running my hungry fingers to the buttons of his shirt. I loosened it clumsily, popping a few unfortunate buttons as I went. I moaned when I got his chest bared enough to stroke that perfect golden skin.

He brought me like that, with those little circles of his hips and that clever thumb, his skin under my hands. It was a gentle wave of sensations.

He grabbed my hips firmly and thrust harder as I still quivered around him. Big hard thrusts turned into rough bucks. He bucked me nearly off his length before yanking me back onto him. What had started gentle turned into a deliciously rough ride as I was still recovering from the first orgasm.

His eyes turned from tender between one hard thrust and the next, taking on a possessive gleam. He didn't even have to say the words. I knew what he wanted. "I'm yours, James. Yours."

Those tarnished depths glittered at me as he made me fall over that fine edge again. He didn't let up, pounding me until I knew I'd be deliciously sore, topping me from the bottom, controlling my body's movements without having to utter a word. I loved that the most, that I could put myself into his control and, at least here, like this, he always knew just what I needed.

He brought me again and watched my eyes as I fell apart before he let himself pour into me with that rough little moan that I loved best.

He was pulling himself out of me when he froze. His eyes

shot to mine, his concerned. "You're bleeding," he told me.

I grimaced. "Ich. I'm starting my period. Sorry. I think maybe we jumpstarted it."

He laughed, looking relieved. "As long as I didn't do it. And don't be sorry. I don't mind."

He pushed my hips back against the edge of his desk, pushing my dress up high. I tried to bat his hands away.

He laughed again. "This is where you draw the line? I'll never understand why some things are more taboo than others."

"And that's what makes you so kinky, the fact that you don't see the difference."

He just shrugged. He was at peace with the kinky part. "Lift up your leg. Let me look at you."

I batted his hands away again, cringing when I saw the blood on his suit. "I don't even want to know the price of the suit we just destroyed."

He looked down at himself and shrugged. "I don't give a fuck about the suit. I do give a fuck about that scandalized look on your face. You have to realize that's just like blood in the water for me."

"Literally," I muttered, still batting his hands away.

"Get your ass on the desk," he said with a grin. "I want to go down on you while you blush like that."

I glared at him, painfully embarrassed. Just the thought had me frozen to the spot in mortification.

"I'm going down on you," he told me in a stern voice, though the smile still playing around his mouth kind of ruined it. "On the desk or in the shower. I'll let you pick that much."

"Shower," I said quickly. It seemed far preferable. At least there wouldn't be a mess in the shower.

He pulled me into the bathroom, stripping us both and leaving our clothes in messy heaps on the floor.

He didn't draw it out, pushing me against the tiled wall and going to his knees in the steamy spray. He buried his face against my core, throwing my thigh over his shoulder. I gripped his hair, letting him take most of my weight as he worked his clever tongue against me. And if his tongue was clever, his fingers were *brilliant*. Both worked me, playing on different nerves, drawing moans out of me, and pushing me over that fine edge in swift moments. I lost all recollection of my own embarrassment under his perfect touch.

He stood, driving hard into me even as he straightened. I whimpered, waves of pleasure still rocking through me deliciously. I was a little sore, but conditioned as I was, that sore only added to the pleasure.

He kissed me hard, driving his tongue into my mouth as he drove his rampant cock into my core. I tasted myself on him—and him, all mixed with the taste of copper. It was different, but not unpleasant.

"See," he said, driving into me, pounding me into the wall, my thigh slung over his arm and pushed high. "You can still come when you're bleeding. It doesn't magically turn off your orgasm button."

I tried to give him an exasperated look, but it was hard to manage when he was fucking the sense right out of me. "I-I didn't...mmm...think...that's..."

"Your body belongs to me, Bianca, no matter the fucking time of the month," he growled against me. Only he could find a way to use my period as a way to show his possession. It was my last thought before he pounded them all right out of me, and I came again, gasping into his mouth. He kept thrusting, finally arching up high, pushing me up with the motion as he bottomed out hard. He grunted and shuddered against me, his hand sliding up into my hair as he let me see what his pleasure did to him through those turquoise depths. I loved every second of it.

We were dried off and getting dressed before he spoke again, his back to me.

"I guess I earned my red wings." There was a smile in his voice.

I blushed down to my toes.

CHAPTER THIRTY-ONE

Mr. Domesticated

The issue of the sex tape still ran rampant through the headlines, but as far as James and I were concerned, it was old news. We had moved on. I took that as an encouraging sign. We were good together. We hashed things out and they were settled, instead of coming up again and again, like they seemed to in so many toxic relationships that I'd observed.

That Friday marked our last New York layover. The crew wanted to go out, of course, but James wanted to have a late lunch with his friends Parker and Sophia. I didn't see why we couldn't do both.

Sophia met us at the door to their luxury apartment, a wriggling child in her arms. I thought it was a boy, though his hair was kind of long, and his face was so pretty that it was hard to tell at a glance.

James swung the child from her arms and up onto his shoulders without a word. "This is Elliot," he told me with his most charming smile. "Elliot, this is Bianca. Say nice to meet you, Bianca."

I smiled up at the pretty boy. He had raven black hair like his father, but with his mother's adorable curls, and slate gray eyes that studied me intently. "Nishe to meet you, Banca," he said with a nod. He hugged the top of James's head, rubbing his cheek against that dark golden hair. "I mish'd you, Jamesh."

James reached up and tickled the little boy's knee. Elliot curled tighter against him, dissolving into helpless giggles.

Parker cooked for us all, which I found charming. I knew he was important in the business world, the heir to his family's lucrative business empire, but you wouldn't know it by the way he cooked for and served us all.

He and Sophia were clearly madly in love. It was something you could tell just from the way that they looked at each other. They acted like newlyweds, though they'd been married for years.

We stayed for hours, talking and playing with Elliot. James was wonderful with him, rolling around with him on the carpet like he was a child himself.

It wasn't that I didn't like kids. I thought little Elliot was to die for cute. I just didn't think that I was suited to have them myself. I had too many dark thoughts and fears about life that I didn't think normal people dealt with, and I didn't want to pass my own twisted baggage onto another generation.

I really liked Parker and Sophia. They seemed genuinely nice, and they really seemed to care about James. I also found it particularly encouraging that the decent people in his life were now outnumbering the crazy bitches.

I was troubled as we left, though. Seeing James interact with Elliot had only made it clearer that he wanted his own children.

"James, I'm not sure that being a mother is something I'm suited fo—"

He pulled me against him, covering my mouth with his hand. He softened the gesture by kissing the top of my head. He murmured into my ear just before the elevator door opened. "It doesn't matter, Love. We have all the time in the world to decide, and I'll let the decision be yours alone. I can't live without you. That's all there is to say about it."

I wished it was so simple, but he obviously wanted children. The thought of being the only thing that kept him from being a father filled me with guilt. I didn't know if I could be that selfish.

The crazy celebration at Red later that night was just what I needed to snap me out of that kind of thinking. Everyone was in good spirits. Our crew, sans Melissa, was there to see Stephan and I off, since we were the only ones taking the furlough right away, and they all toasted us and wished us well, and made us feel good in general, but sad to be leaving such a fun group of people. Still, none of it gave me second thoughts. I knew that what I was doing just made the most sense for me, all things considered.

The end of my career as a flight attendant was strangely anti-climactic. I worked my last turn on Sunday, and then on Monday, I went from being a full-time flight attendant to being a full-time aspiring painter. It was daunting, but exhilarating.

Stephan and Javier ended up taking the furlough as well, thanks to the rare opportunity they were getting to open their own bar in one of the strip's hottest casinos. They had plenty of work ahead of them, but not many people got the funding they did, no questions asked. We were all grateful to James for doing something so life-changing for them.

We went to L.A. the night before the gallery showing, staying at the Cavendish Resort property there, which was conveniently located next door to the Cavendish Gallery.

I got a preview of the gallery that night, and I was floored by the wonders Danika had worked. My paintings were shown at their best, the frames exquisite, the lighting in every room just perfect, the paintings grouped together by color, displayed to complement each other in the best way possible.

Danika gave us a tour of the gallery, every room displaying my paintings. I felt the need to hug the woman when we finished, grateful and in awe of what she'd done with my work.

I felt nervous anxiety course through me at even the thought of the event, but it turned out to be a pleasant evening. I had already determined that I wouldn't read any of the negative reviews about my work. No one was more critical of my work than I was, and I knew it would just wreak havoc on my creativity to obsess about the negative, so I enjoyed the event for what it was; an evening of meeting new people, and a chance to see some friendly faces.

I wore a dark gray halter dress that I felt flattered my figure, and James wore a matching tux with a light blue tie.

James stayed on my arm for the entire evening, the perfect, attentive escort. And of course, the most expensive arm candy on the face of the earth.

I even sold some paintings, which I'd thought was highly unlikely when I saw how they'd been priced. Some of the larger ones had gone for over fifty thousand dollars. It surprised me so much that I was a little in shock when Danika gave me the news. She catalogued every single painting sold for me, telling me who had purchased what and for how much.

She hugged me, beaming. She had become the biggest cheerleader for my work, and I was so grateful for that. She was a steady kind of woman, and so obviously one of substance, with clout in the art world. Having someone like that back my work with such sincerity was a confidence booster that I needed in a very fundamental way at this stage in my career. James and Stephan were fans of my work, but having a professional supporting my work, someone who wasn't my best friend or my boyfriend, was a boon that I wouldn't soon forget.

Some of the much smaller paintings sold for around the ten thousand dollar mark. Danika informed us of this with a disclaimer, "This is only because this is your first show. At the next one your work will earn bigger price tags; I guarantee it. You'll see numbers at least double or triple what we're seeing tonight." This floored me. I had thought that the prices were over the top for *this one*...

Frankie was there. She had Tristan, and her girlfriend, Estella, in tow, as threatened. I recalled Tristan's description of Estella as a little Latin fireball, and I knew within moments of meeting Estella that it was apt. She had thick, wavy black hair that fell nearly to her waist, an hourglass body that wouldn't quit, and a sassy attitude that was fun, flirtatious, and over the top. She and Frankie had visible chemistry, sharing telling looks and comments that could have made even James blush.

Tristan, Frankie, and Estella hit it off with Stephan and Javier, and the five of them spent a lot of the evening talking and laughing, making the entire event more fun.

We observed one of those volatile moments when Danika and Tristan shared the same air, just in passing, and it was as intense as the first time we'd seen it. James and I shared a look when Danika took her stiff, polite leave of him. As much as Danika may have wanted it to be different, there were still strong feelings between those two. But baggage could be a powerful thing, and feelings weren't always enough.

I had invited my half-brother, Sven and his girlfriend, Adele, and I was flattered and pleased that they were able to make it.

Adele looked like a model, with the right height and build, but not the over the top beautiful kind. She was no Lana. She had the sort of nondescript good looks that probably got her a lot of work, since it made her more versatile. Her hair was light brown, hanging straight to her shoulders, her eyes a nice, soft brown.

She had a sweet smile, and she was very present, like she was happy to be just where she was. I liked her. When Sven had said he was dating a model, I had pictured the vacant-eyed, narcissistic type, and Adele far exceeded my expectations, unfair as they may have been.

Blake and company weren't shadowing my every step, since the guest list was very exclusive, and they were guarding the entrances and exits doggedly. I thought it was nice to be able to go to the bathroom without having a shadow, although James did close to the same thing, walking me down the hallway to the gallery's restroom, and waiting for me diligently in the nearest showing room.

I was finishing when the bathroom door opened and closed, then opened again.

"Now you're following me?" an agitated female voice asked.

I recognized it instantly as Danika.

"If that's the only way you'll talk to me, then yes," a man answered.

I recognized that deep, gravelly voice, as well. It was Tristan.

"We have nothing to talk abo—" Danika began.

"I still think about you *every single day,*" Tristan interrupted harshly. "Let's talk about *that.*"

I held perfectly still, now officially eavesdropping from inside of a bathroom stall.

"Oh, please. Take your guilt and get the fuck away from me, Tristan. I want *nothing* to do with it."

"The guilt isn't what I was talking about," he said, his voice low and raw. "It's you I think about. *Always* you."

She snorted inelegantly. It was very un-Danika-like. "Please! You stopped trying to call me years ago. I haven't heard a word from you since right after rehab, when you went on your repentance tour."

"I didn't trust myself, Danika. I needed my sobriety. I'm nothing without it, and you were a lovely trigger for me. That look in your eyes, after all that I'd done... The way you looked at me like I was scum, and knowing that I deserved all of your antipathy. I knew that if you looked at me like that again, I'd hit rock bottom, and this time I wouldn't come back from it."

"I'm with someone, Tristan," she said brusquely.

"And if you weren't? Would you be willing to talk to me—to spend time with me, if you *weren't* with someone?"

"*No!* Bad things happen when we get together, Tristan. You and I are nothing but trouble. Time hasn't changed that. Please, just stay away from me."

I heard movement and then Tristan's agonized whisper, "Danika, I'm so sorry. I'll never stop missing you. You were my best friend. Can you ever forgive me for what I did?"

Danika's answer was quick, sure and final. "I forgave you a long time ago, Tristan, but I will *never* forget. Please keep your distance."

The door opened and closed. Twice. I waited a few more minutes before coming out, feeling guilty for being so nosy. I should have said something the second I heard them talking, but instead, to spare us all an awkward moment, and yes, because I was curious, I'd overheard that painful and personal exchange.

I compounded my sins by immediately telling James what I'd heard. I wanted to hear his take on it.

His brow furrowed and he shook his head. "I really don't know what happened between them. Frankie is close friends with both of them, but even she won't talk about it. I assume they used to date, because Tristan is so obviously in love with her, but even that is speculation on my part. And I know that he had something to do with the injury that gave her that limp, but that's all. I don't know what caused that injury, or what his part was in it. He just mentioned to me once that Danika used to be an amazing dancer, and that he'd ruined it for her."

"That's awful," I said.

He nodded. "Yes. There's a lot of bad baggage there, but what he said to you at lunch the other day was actually the most I've heard him talk about it in one sitting. Neither of them are forthcoming about it. We'll probably never know all of the ugly details."

I knew that he was probably right.

"Do you mind if I go and check to see if he's okay?" James

asked.

"Not at all," I reassured him, thinking that he was the sweetest, most thoughtful man in the world.

Danika approached me, looking more serious than she had for most of the night. Every time she had sought me out before, she had been beaming, ecstatic to give me the news of another sale.

"I'm sorry you had to hear that little exchange in the bathroom," she said, meeting my eyes steadily.

I thought I must have blushed down to my toes. "I am *so* sorry about that."

She waved me off. "It was hardly your fault. You were just using the restroom. But I saw your shoes under the stall, and I wanted to explain myself. I probably sounded like a cold bitch."

I stopped her, holding my hand up. "You didn't. I understand completely. Sometimes protecting your heart is the only way to keep your sanity."

She nodded, her mouth firm. "Yes, exactly. I won't get mixed up with him again, and I refuse to lead him on. When I was younger, and stupid, I thought that he was the most wonderful and exciting thing in the world. I fell crazy, stupid, jump off a cliff in love with him. It was like being in love with a tornado. And when he was done with me, I felt like I'd *been* in a tornado. It took me years to pick up all of the pieces he'd left me in, but I did it, and I *won't* go back. These days I want stability in my life. I need it."

I nodded. I could well understand that. When you'd been through hell, stability was heaven.

She seemed to see that she'd made her point. She patted me on the shoulder and walked away.

Blake had come to hover near me when James had gone to find Tristan. As on top of things as ever, she was able to direct me to him, as well.

He was outside, speaking to Frankie and Tristan in a private patio area. James had his back to the door, his hands in his pockets.

I approached the three of them tentatively, not wanting to intrude.

Tristan was sucking on a cigarette like his life depended on it, his eyes wide on Frankie as she threw her arms in the air and spoke to him in a low voice, obviously giving him a piece of her mind. He'd taken off his tuxedo jacket and loosened his tie. The crisp white sleeves of his tux were rolled up to reveal tatted up forearms. He'd played well at being clean cut for a few hours, but his bad boy had obviously broken back out.

Tristan saw me first. He exhaled. "Bianca, help me! Frankie is a little termagant. Please tell her that one cigarette is not going to kill me."

James turned to look at me, his eyes warm as they ran over me. He snagged my arm as I came into reach, pulling my back to his front and kissing the top of my head.

One of Frankie's tiny fingers poked into Tristan's massive chest. "This is not about one cigarette. This is about having one short conversation with her, and picking up a habit you quit five years ago. You need to call your sponsor right this second!"

Tristan rolled his eyes, taking another long drag of the cigarette. "You know, nagging can be a trigger."

"This isn't a joke," she fumed, sounding as much worried as mad. "I'm worried about you. You're acting strange, and the first thing you tried to do was slip away by yourself. The last thing you need to do is be alone right now."

"I'm not on suicide watch, Frankie. I'm smoking one fucking cigarette and then I'll go back in, k? If you're that worried about me, maybe you and your girl should sleep with me tonight. I shouldn't be alone in my big, huge, lonely bed."

She threw her hands in the air. "Like you have any trouble finding bodies to warm that bed."

"You said it yourself. I'm in a vulnerable place right now, and

I should be surrounded by people I love. So come sleep with me, Frankie."

She smacked him hard on the arm. "When is the 'trying to get the lesbian to sleep with me' bit going to get old? I would *really* love to know."

He grinned, flashing deep dimples at her. He was putting on a good tough guy show, but he still looked like he was hurting. "You aren't 'the lesbian', you're my *favorite* lesbian. And I was only talking about cuddling. Your dirty mind did the rest."

She sighed, looking defeated. "Fine. I'll come cuddle with you tonight if it means you won't be alone. No hitting on my girlfriend, though."

They made a funny pair. The top of her head barely reached his chest, and she was clearly unimpressed that he towered over her and weighed at least twice as much as she did.

Tristan finished his cigarette like it was the last one on earth, enjoying it to the last drag. He and Frankie headed back inside together, but James held me back from following them.

He cupped my face, smiling down at me. "Since I have you alone, I wanted to tell you something; I'm really proud of you. You already know that I'm your biggest fan, but I just wanted you to know that tonight was a huge accomplishment. I know you have yourself convinced that I did all of this for you, but it's just not true. I set up the meeting. That was all. The second Danika saw your work she was smitten, and you would have had this showing with or without a connection to me. Those paintings sold because people wanted them, and found value in them. You have a talent that brings me to my knees. Thank you for sharing it with the world."

"Thank you," I told him simply, feeling my eyes get just a touch moist. The damned man made me so emotional. And he had a way with words that got me every time. "I love you to distraction, James."

His eyes smiled into mine. "Yes. I love you like that. The

world went from black and white and into color when I laid eyes on you, my love. There'll be no going back."

It was such a perfect moment that I had to beat back those evil doubts in my mind that told me something this perfect just had to come to a short, bad end. *Life can just be good*, I told myself. *This bad feeling is not a premonition. Nothing bad will happen to us.* I'd had to tell this to myself a lot lately.

Towards the end of the evening, Tristan bought my largest landscape and a smaller still-life. Frankie bought a painting as well. It was a watercolor of the fat cat from my yard. She said she was going to put it up in her tattoo shop for the world to see. She even harassed James that he should give her the portrait of me that had inspired the tattoo on his back. He took it well, which told me he'd forgiven her for the tattoo on *my* back.

Sven bought one of my small acrylic paintings of a desert flower.

I insisted repeatedly that he didn't have to buy anything.

"I want to," he told me firmly. "It would mean a lot to me to have something that you made hanging in my home, and I love this picture."

"I'll paint you something for free! You shouldn't have to pay thirteen grand just for a reminder. It's not too late to change your mind."

He shook his head. "No. This is perfect. Though, if you ever want to paint me something, I certainly won't dissuade you!"

It warmed me and embarrassed me a little that everyone was being so supportive.

As the night grew to a close, I felt giddy with the realization that I'd actually enjoyed myself. The evening had far exceeded my expectations. My nerves hadn't allowed me to look forward to the launch of my new career, but I loved that I could look back on my debut with relief and pleasure. It was over, and it had actually been a success.

There was a small blemish on the evening, as we took our leave of the gallery.

The gallery was a large three-story building, set up in a trendy area and situated adjacent to the Cavendish L.A. hotel and sharing a back parking lot with that property. We exited out of the front, where we had entered. A small red carpet had been set up outside for photo ops prior to the event. A fairly polite crowd of photographers had snapped shots of us going in. A larger crowd had gathered by the time we left, very late into the evening. I was surprised they'd waited so long. And even stranger to me was the crowd of bystanders gathered behind them, just watching for our departure.

James maneuvered himself closer to the crowd, though there was a barricade that separated them. He threw an arm around my shoulders, his opposite hand moving to the diamond hoop attached to my choker.

We had made it maybe six steps when there was a collective gasp from the crowd, and I turned just in time to see Blake jump a few inches into the air and catch a large plastic cup in her hand mid-air. The lid of the thing flew off, and dark soda and ice went flying in every direction, but it was still an impressive catch. It had been aimed at either James, myself, or both, but not even a drop of it reached us. Blake was drenched. She looked unperturbed about her own wet shirt and face. She threw the cup on the ground and scanned the crowd, a very hostile look on her face.

It was as though the drink throwing had opened a floodgate. People began to shout lewd comments in our direction. I couldn't make them all out, but the loudest comments seemed to be coming from women, and aimed at James.

"You are so fucking hot!" a woman shrieked.

"With a dick that huge, you can spank me anytime!" another one shouted.

It was all so silly that a giggle escaped me as Clark ushered us into the limo. Blake followed us in.

"Good catch, Blake," James said. "I'm giving you a raise for not letting a drop of that reach Bianca."

She nodded solemnly. "Just doing my job, sir."

Her response sobered me up a little, because I began to think about just what her job was. If it had been a bullet instead of a drink, she probably would have done the same thing. I hated that. I didn't want to get hurt, but the thought of someone being harmed in my place seemed even worse to me.

CHAPTER THIRTY-TWO

Mr. Matchmaker

I barely took a breath after my last flight before it was time for our trip to Japan. I was more excited than I'd ever been about a trip as we got ready. I'd traveled a lot for work, but always for short trips with short layovers, more work than play, and something as frivolous as two solid weeks of being a tourist was such a treat. James would have to work a little, he'd told me, since we were visiting his Tokyo property, but even he would be off work for the majority of the trip.

I knew it was a very long flight—we could be on the plane for up to fourteen hours, and that those hours would feel like days, but my mind was already in Tokyo as we boarded the jet.

James was doing his usual control freak buckling me in thing when he informed me of a minor detour. "We're going to go have lunch in Maui first," he said, his tone idle.

My brow furrowed. It seemed a little out of the way... "Maui?" I asked him.

He shrugged and gave me his most charming smile. "I want you to guess why."

There was only one thing that made me think of Maui. "Something to do with Lana?" I guessed.

He shrugged again. "I can't help myself. It's the first time she's opened up about it. I set up a lunch with this Akira guy. I know I'm meddling, but somebody needs to do it."

I studied him, and felt myself fall a little deeper. He had such a romantic soul. Just knowing him had made *me* more romantic. It was a contagious state of mind. "What do you plan to say to him?"

He kissed the tip of my nose as the plane began to move. "Not much. First, I just wanted to take his measure, to see if he was worthy of someone as stalwart as Lana. And if he is, I'm only going to tell him that he needs to man up. A man in love has to make the first move. It's the least he can do."

I smiled at him. I could feel how soft that smile was. "So you're the matchmaking type?" It reminded me so much of Stephan. "Are you going to be setting up all of our friends?"

He returned my soft smile in spades. "Love is like that. It's like a wildfire in my blood, and now that I know what it feels like, it's made me generous. I feel like the world should get the privilege. And if I can help someone I care about find it, then certainly I'll try."

"That's so sweet," I told him sincerely.

He smiled into my eyes, and his smile wasn't sweet at all. "You won't think I'm sweet in about ten minutes, when I tie you to my bed and fuck the sense out of you."

I felt parts low in my body clench. "You're in such a romantic mood. Aren't you going to call it making love today?"

"How about we call it lovingly fucking your brains out?"

I laughed. That did sound more apt, I thought.

James wore me out for hours before he let up enough for me to catch a little nap. The man redefined the word insatiable. It felt like I'd barely caught a moment's sleep when he was waking me up again.

We stopped by the Middleton Resort to freshen up before our lunch with Akira. James changed into his version of vacation casual, which consisted of a soft white V-neck that set off both his muscles and his golden skin to perfection. He wore low-slung, pale-gray cargo shorts, and loafers with no socks. I studied his ankles with singular fascination.

"If anyone had told me that ankles could be sexy before I met you, I would have said they'd lost it."

He grinned. "I've always thought yours were sexy. The first milestone on my way up from the ground and up to paradise, Love."

I laughed. Of course he took it there.

I changed into a silky pink tank and dark gray shorts that were borderline too skimpy. I wore white flip-flops entirely for comfort.

James eyed up my legs. He traced my collar absently. "Even without heels, you have the sexiest legs on the planet."

He had worked me over hard, but I still felt that drugging feeling of wanting that only he could inspire move through my system.

We met Akira at the Middleton Resort's cantina. The instant I saw Akira, I understood the appeal. He was a huge man. I'd never seen James standing side by side with anyone taller than himself before Akira, I realized, as he shook hands with the other man, who stood a good two inches taller than James. He was an intimidating man, but God, was he a sight.

He had classic Hawaiian features, with thick dark brows over handsome brown eyes, and a generous mouth with a mean twist. He had wavy black hair, and everything about him was big, but it was all muscle. The man took good care of himself, going by the bulky muscles moving restlessly under his suit.

He treated me with marked deference right from the start. James, not so much. He had no qualms about going after the other man right from the get go.

"You went out with Lana. I saw you with her in the papers once." Akira's tone could not be mistaken for friendly or indifferent.

James grinned. Perversely, I thought that James saw Akira's hostility as a good sign. And perversely, I thought he might be right. "We've been friends for years. We've accompanied each other to a few social events."

"What does that mean, exactly? I read a piece that said you had dated."

James studied the other man. "Why do you ask? Is it idle curiosity, or are you jealous?"

Akira didn't answer, just stared at James like he wanted to strangle him.

James was far from intimidated. "I want to know because of Lana. I'd like to know how you feel about her."

Akira silently fumed. It was easy to see that he was a volatile man, but I could also see that he was one that had spent time working on controlling his temper.

James sighed. "You're difficult. Leave it to Lana. She has such a soothing way about her, so of course she would be in love with a walking powder keg of a man. Life is funny that way."

I would have sworn that Akira's dark skin was turning red.

"I'll level with you, Akira. Lana doesn't date; she never has, so she certainly never dated me. She's been hung up on you for so long, and so badly, that she's never even wanted to date. She's been pining for you for years. I've checked up on you. You're single, you're straight, so what the fuck is your problem? Don't you care about her?"

Akira flushed. Very carefully, he set clenched fists on top of the table. "Why the fuck is it your business?" he growled.

James leaned forward, undeterred. "Because I care about Lana, and because I know she'll never come to you herself. It's time to man up, Akira. If you love her, it is *your* job to show her."

Akira tapped a giant fist to the table. The table bounced a little, because a tap from a man his size was like a full on punch from another man. "How do you propose I do that? I doubt she'd take my calls, and she hasn't been back to the island even once since she left."

"Call her dad. She's a workaholic. Get him to send her here on business. If you can't get her to stay, that's your own fault."

Akira took this better than I would have expected, just setting his mouth into a hard line and nodding thoughtfully. "You swear you never touched her?"

James threw his hands up. "I never even tried. I swear it! It's probably the reason we've stayed such close friends."

We had lunch and took our leave of Akira. He was severe but polite as we parted. He was an unreadable sort of guy, but I thought that he had warmed to James at least a little by the time we left. With me, he was perfectly polite, though of course I'd never been romantically connected to Lana in the media, as James had.

The next leg of the flight was longer, though sharing a spacious private jet with James for eight more hours was no hardship.

The private jet wasn't designed with a normal galley, or a normal anything, really. The flight attendant and our security had their own enclosed space between us and the flight deck, where they could both have privacy, and give us some. James took advantage of this to the fullest.

The plane had barely reached ten thousand feet when he was kneeling in front of my seat, bending down to kiss my thighs, nuzzling his way between, spreading them wider as buried his face against my sex. I was still wearing my shorts as he teased my clit with his nose.

He had gone from buckled up and innocently sitting next to me to making me pant for him in seconds flat. He stripped my shorts and panties off and I gripped his hair into my fists as he set to work on me bare.

"You're insatiable," I gasped as he licked at me like he would never stop.

"Yes," he murmured against my skin. "I'll never have my fill of you, and I'll never let you forget it, but you're hardly one to talk, Love."

CHAPTER THIRTY-THREE

Mr. Indulgent

The Cavendish property was located in the Ginza district in Tokyo. I had gotten every tourist booklet that I could get my hands on about the city, but James had a wealth of information, as well, since he had apparently spent plenty of time in Tokyo himself. According to my tourist booklet, and James, Ginza was one of the main shopping districts in the city.

We were given the royal treatment from the moment we walked in the door. I was growing accustomed to it, though the Japanese took the royal treatment to a whole new level. I was still growing accustomed to the Japanese way of bowing in deference to one another. I found their manners charming, and tried to emulate them quickly, wanting to blend into the culture as much as possible, though of course it was impossible for me to blend in there. Still, I badly wanted to avoid standing out as a rude foreigner.

James had his manners down perfectly, as though he visited often. For all I knew, he did. He even spoke a convenient amount of the language. I had studied it, but I was hopelessly outclassed. One sentence of Japanese out of his mouth and I was lost, just watching him in awe and not understanding a word of it. The locals seemed to have no trouble, though.

We'd been discussing for weeks just what kind of a trip I had envisioned when I thought about visiting Tokyo. James seemed to find it charming that I'd only been thinking of a tourist type tour of the city. I wanted to use the subway, visit every temple, shrine and park, and all of the popular attractions. Basically, I wanted to see as much of the quirky city as humanly possible. The plan was for nine days around the city, then another four in the areas surrounding Mount Fuji, and then one day on top of the mountain itself. I had even talked James into camping out on top for a night. He had been easy to convince, considering that he'd never actually been camping before. I wasn't an expert on camping myself, but I was an expert on roughing it, and a night in a tent on top of a famous mountain just sounded like fun to me. I got the idea in my head, and James didn't even try to dissuade me.

"Of course, I'll arrange for supplies," was all he'd said, giving me his indulgent smile.

We started our first sightseeing day in Tokyo at the crack of dawn. We wore shorts, T-shirts, and comfortable shoes like the tourists we were, and set off on foot for our first destination. Kyokyo, the Imperial Palace, was only twenty minutes from our hotel, so we went there first. Our security trailed us at a somewhat discreet distance, and I almost forgot they were there for most of the day. The palace grounds alone took up most of our morning.

We encountered the scenic jogging trail that surrounded the palace grounds first. I had been reading aloud about the trail from a tour guidebook the night before, so James grinned as he pointed it out to me. "Wanna go for a jog?" he asked me.

I nodded and smiled. I wasn't a big jogger. Even when I did work out, it was usually lower impact cardio than an actual run, but it sounded perfect just then.

We jogged for maybe ten minutes, James keeping pace beside me, before I slowed to a brisk walk.

I grimaced at him. "I know this won't be a shocker, but you're in much better shape than I am."

He gave me a rather lascivious once-over. "I disagree. I like *your shape* much better, Love."

I laughed. The man could turn anything suggestive.

We spent hours walking the trail around the grounds and covering every inch of the scenic gardens inside. It was a romantic setting and James, being a romantic soul, used every bit of it to his advantage, clasping my hand and smiling into my eyes. If I wasn't already hopelessly in love with him, just one morning like this one and I swore he would have changed that.

We took our time exploring the palace, and when we were done, we found another charming park just a few blocks away. Children played some version of soccer in a shaded dirt field. The people we had encountered had been the epitome of polite so far, not even staring at us, though we must have seemed out of place to everyone there. The only difference were kids under fifteen. They stared unabashedly at us, their game coming to a halt as we strolled by. As we drew even with them, all of the young teenage boys raised their hands in the air, as though they had planned it, and began to cheer. I giggled at the strange reaction, looking at James. "What was that?" I asked him.

He was grinning. "I think we just found some new members of your fan club."

I rolled my eyes, still laughing. Boys were weird.

We strolled the large circular park, pausing when we caught sight of an impromptu concert in the park. A crowd had gathered to watch a small orchestra play.

James pulled me into his arms, handling me with mastery and gallantry, surely a rare combination. He moved into a light-stepping waltz, smiling down into my eyes.

"What a charming city," I told him, smiling back, enjoying the novelty of a morning dance in the park.

He nodded. "I'm finding a new love for this city. For everything. You've made the world a new and exciting place for me."

I flushed in pleasure, believing every intoxicating word he said to me.

We leisurely walked from the Imperial Palace district and back to the Ginza district, shopping a little, but mostly just exploring the fascinating city. We walked through a mall, and used a tour guidebook to try to find one of the large city gardens in the Tokyo Bay that I'd marked.

We were trying to decipher the map for maybe five minutes, laughing at our confusion, when Clark approached. He'd been hovering with Blake, following at a discreet distance all day.

"The Hamarikyu Gardens, right?" he asked, peeking at our map.

I nodded.

He pointed down a street. "That way," he said. He had apparently been here before. "We'll pass the fish market, which is closed for the day, but it's just a few blocks past that."

We thanked him and began to wander that way. James had an arm wrapped around my waist, holding me close, uncaring of the heat and humidity.

"We'll have to do the fish market tomorrow morning," James said. "It's worth it. Best sushi in the world."

I wasn't sure if it was the time of the day, or the day of the week, but the lovely gardens were nearly deserted, only the occasional painter capturing one of the park's landmarks visible. The beauty of the well-maintained gardens stood in stark contrast to the skyscrapers of the adjacent Shiodome district. We circled the large park leisurely, stopping often to enjoy views of the scenic garden, and the waters of the bay beside it.

"Let me know if you see something that you just have to paint," James told me, as we passed another artist. "I can have supplies brought right away, if you're so inclined. This place seems to inspire artists."

I smiled at him, loving that he tried so hard to understand me. I had just been thinking that I'd like to spend a morning painting here.

"You're so sweet," I told him.

He smiled, and it was as un-sweet as it could be. "I was just plotting where I would fuck you here. You have strange ideas about sweet."

I laughed. I had a feeling that seeing the world with James would give me strange ideas about a lot of things. "How do you propose we do that?"

His eyes smoldered at me. "You let me worry about that. There's a teahouse set on a tiny island in the center of the gardens. How would you like to attend a traditional Japanese tea ceremony?"

I was delighted by the idea. "I'd love nothing more. Except perhaps your other plans."

He winked at me, giving me a roguish smile. "There's no reason we can't do both."

The teahouse was quaint but I found it incredibly beautiful, the open windows with a view of the gardens like a frame for a perfect picture. We sat cross-legged on a tan bamboo mat while an ageless looking Japanese woman went through the painstaking and elegant ritual. I watched with rapt attention, fascinated with every detail, because every detail was so perfectly orchestrated. The simplest motions became art as the practiced woman moved fluidly through the ritual, the arms of her light pink kimono barely rippling as her arms moved.

James bowed low to her when she presented him with his tea, spouting off a fluent stream of Japanese that I couldn't begin to follow, but he was obviously praising her.

I felt a completely unreasonable wave of jealousy. I tamped it down, knowing that it was insane. But his praise directed at anyone but myself made me feel covetous of it.

The woman flushed at his praise, making her pale beauty even more pronounced.

I bowed low to her as she presented the tea to me, stumbling over my Japanese thank you. The woman was the epitome of grace, which made me feel a little clumsy just looking at her.

The woman left us alone after the drawn-out ritual was over, giving us the teahouse to ourselves. I knew that deferential privacy was the James Cavendish effect.

I gave James a sidelong look, still sipping my tea. He was watching me, and the look on his face made me squirm. He wore a slight smile, but his eyes had gone full on Dom.

"It made you jealous, just having me watch her do the tea ceremony, didn't it? You're that possessive of my affections now."

I wrinkled my nose, wishing that he couldn't read me quite so well. It was embarrassing to me that he knew just how unreasonably jealous I could be. I nodded. There was no point in hiding it, since he'd seen it clearly.

"She's beautiful, and you were fascinated by her," I said, as though I couldn't hold the words in. "Did you want her?" I asked, knowing it was a stupid question. I didn't want to know if he did, and I didn't want him to lie, so it was just masochistic to ask.

His eyes softened just a tad. "No, Love. The thought didn't even cross my mind. It did occur to me, though, that I would love for you to learn to do that. The thought of you serving me with such restraint is intoxicating..."

"I could never do it like her. She's perfect."

He ran his tongue over his teeth just so. "I wouldn't want you to do it like her. I'd want you to do it like yourself. What do you say? Would you like a kimono and some tea ceremony lessons?"

I nodded with no hesitation. "I'd love that."

He smiled, reaching a hand up to cup the back of my head.

He moved into me. "We'll devote a morning to it, then."

He kissed me, then pushed me to the floor, moving roughly on top of me. He ground his hard erection into me, still fully clothed, while he ravished my mouth. He showed none of his finesse as he gripped my hips and moved against me, biting hard on my lower lip. It was as though he wanted to be as savage as possible, a perfect contrast to our refined surroundings.

He pulled away, sitting up to watch me. His pretty mouth was a little mean as he smiled at me, running a hand through his hair.

"Stand up and take off your clothes. Every scrap," Mr. Cavendish told me.

I glanced around, a little shocked at the prospect, when I should be far beyond the point of shocking. Perhaps it was the perfect manners of everyone we'd run into, but it seemed a little wrong to do something so crass in the serene teahouse. Plus, there were open windows everywhere, and a good chance that we would be seen or heard.

"Can we?" I asked breathlessly.

That made him laugh, and as his Dom eyes played over my face I knew that he loved with a passion the scandalized look I now wore. "I'll do anything I please," he told me. "That was one of the *first* things you should have learned about me. Now take off your clothes, or I'll do something that really embarrasses you.

I obeyed, hurrying because I felt so awkward.

He tilted his head, leaning back on his hands. "Slowly. Draw it out. And touch your body for me as you show it to me."

I pulled my top over my head slowly, unclasping the front of my bra to let my breasts spill free.

"Fondle yourself. Show me how rough you like me to handle them."

I palmed the large globes firmly, pushing them together,

avoiding my still-tender nipples, but kneading at the flesh around them. I did like them handled roughly, but his hands were so much better suited to it than mine.

"Take off your shorts and panties now, but don't touch yourself."

I toed off my shoes, sliding my shorts and panties off in one smooth motion.

"Come here. I want you to put your foot on my shoulder. I need to see how wet you are before I've even touched you."

I obeyed carefully, leaning forward a little to keep my balance. The teahouse was lit only with natural light, but I still didn't think I'd ever felt more naked as I stared out of the open windows, scanning to make sure that no one was watching us.

He hummed in approval. "So wet already. Let me see how you touch yourself. Rub your clit for me."

I obeyed, but a little sound of disappointment escaped my throat. I wanted *him* to touch me.

"Don't complain. Say yes Mr. Cavendish, or I'll make you get yourself off."

"Yes, Mr. Cavendish," I murmured, trying not to sound resentful. He had me spoiled, after all. His touch was a drug that I could never go back from.

I circled my clit with a light touch, circling my hips as I did so. He watched closely, his eyelids getting heavy. He leaned close, holding my foot on his shoulder to keep me steady. I shuddered as I felt his breath on me.

"Get on your hands and knees," he told me when I'd worked myself into a fever pitch.

I obeyed, and he just watched me for a while. I heard the rustle of his clothing, the movement of his zipper, and then the sound of him shifting slightly on the bamboo mat.

"Arch your back," he told me. "Spread your legs a little wider. I'm going to ride you so hard that you're going to have sore knees and a tender cunt when I'm done."

I moaned and arched. He gripped my hair roughly, pulling my head back as he rammed into me hard. He set a jarring, brutal pace, such a stark contrast to our genteel surroundings, and I loved it just as much as he knew I would.

He had all of the smooth moves in the world but he used none of them, rutting into me with a harsh, single-minded purpose. I'd thought he'd taken me every way there was, but the way he took me then was so savagely violent, feeding both my need for pleasure and pain, that I came around him with a ragged sob, feeling punished and pleasured in equal parts.

My knees were sore by the time he found his own release, pulling hard on my hair as he reached the end of me with a rough grind of his hips. "Oh, Bianca," he moaned, and there was a world of praise in his voice, as though only I could undo him like that, and I closed my eyes with pure pleasure at the thought.

He folded himself against my back, giving his name on my back, and then my neck, a hard kiss. "So fucking perfect," he told me, still twitching inside of me. "Every inch of you was sent to me from heaven."

I smiled at the thought. It still caught me off guard sometimes, how whimsical and romantic he could be, especially after what we'd just done. "Only you could make rutting on the floor like animals into something romantic," I told him with a laugh.

He pulled out me with the most delicious little noise. "And why shouldn't it be? What isn't romantic about finding a few perfect moments of bliss with the woman I love?"

I couldn't come up with one thing.

We walked through the rest of the gardens leisurely, holding hands and sharing lingering touches and tender looks. His gaze was particularly warm when he looked at my pink knees. He loved to leave his mark on me.

We checked out the Tsukiji Fish Market in the morning, and we sampled some of the best sushi in the world there with an early lunch. We spent the entire afternoon at the famous Ueno Park and Zoo, enjoying people-watching and sightseeing.

Over the next few days, we visited every shrine, temple, museum, and worthwhile sight in the city. Clark or Blake would snap pictures of us in front of all of the famous landmarks. I thought we must have taken at least a thousand pictures within the first five days of the trip.

We shopped for hours in the huge discount mall set up around the Senso-ji Temple, and ate various forms of street food. I tried it all gamely, but I would sometimes catch James clenching his fists when he saw me trying something.

"What?" I asked with a laugh. He'd been scowling while I'd tried a bite of a fried octopus ball.

"If you get ill from eating that, I'm going to go wring that street vendor's neck."

I wasn't surprised. The man was never able to completely rein in his protective streak.

James seduced me in the Koishikawa Korakuen Gardens one morning, in a small shrine, in a private little glade. I was sure that Clark or Blake must have been standing by to guard against intruders, because he took his time on me there, bits of the sun bathing us through the leafy trees guarding our little slice of paradise.

We devoted an entire Sunday to Harajuku Street and the Meiji Shrine, since they were vast, but within walking distance of each other.

I tried not to be rude, but I couldn't help but watch as one of the intricate wedding processions moved through the Meiji Shrine.

James wrapped himself around my back. I watched for a long time, fascinated by the lovely spectacle of it. I glanced at James when we moved on. I'd been expecting him to make a few cracks about weddings, but he'd been unusually silent through it all.

"That was beautiful," I told him.

He just nodded, pursing his lips and looking down at our joined hands.

Harajuku Street was everything I'd imagined and more. I stopped and watched every time one of the Harajuku girls passed by, sometimes in packs, dressed like lollis, and gothic lollis, and some in full-on cosplay. I always got excited when I recognized the anime that they were imitating. James found this adorable, telling me so with his most indulgent smile.

I found us some matching T-shirts in an anime-themed shop. They were mock versions of school uniforms from an anime I liked. One was black, one white. I held them up and was startled when James shrugged out of his own shirt. I was as good as ogling his smooth golden chest as he pulled the white anime shirt on. It was tight as a glove.

I used a dressing room to change into my black version of the same shirt. The shop girl was giving James very wide eyes as he paid, and I couldn't blame her. He had just given her quite the show. James baring that much skin was a mouthwatering display, no matter the reason.

I thought it was so sweet that he was willing to indulge me by wearing the shirt for the rest of the day. The material was soft and thin, and I couldn't seem to keep my hands off his chest in it as we walked the crowded street. He didn't mind.

We spent an evening in Akihabara, the Electric City, even wandering into one of the famous maid cafés. There were cute Japanese girls that looked too young to be working serving us food, and kittens wandering the café, one even jumping onto our table to be petted. It was charming, but would have been more so if not for the older men that seemed to be there to ogle the way too young girls.

James was a big hit with the girls, of course. The maid that served us couldn't even look at him without blushing, and several asked to take pictures with him before we left, though there was a sign in English clearly stating that it cost forty-seven hundred yen to get pictures with *them*.

By the time we departed the city for the Mount Fuji portion of the trip, I felt I had seen and done every imaginable tourist attraction we could come up with.

CHAPTER THIRTY-FOUR

Mr. Forever

We took a train to Hakone to enjoy a day and night of hot springs before we climbed the majestic Mount Fuji. James had rented out an entire property for us to spend the day. It wasn't a Cavendish property, but it was impressive nonetheless. It was so huge that I honestly couldn't tell if it was supposed to be rented out as a hotel or a house.

The property boasted traditional Japanese structures, the back half of the property lining up with the lake and dotted with countless natural hot springs.

It was the most relaxing day we'd had since we'd gotten to Japan. We stayed in and made love for what felt like the entire day.

We weren't in the house for thirty minutes before James had dragged me to the hot springs, stripping us both as we walked.

The hot water felt delicious, the weather near the mountain marked degrees colder than in Tokyo. He shadowed me as I moved into the water, gliding to the very edge of the pool to gaze at the spectacular view.

He made love to me there, pressing me hard against the side of the pool as I gazed at a perfect view of the mountain while he fucked me senseless.

We got a late start on the climb up Mount Fuji the next day. James reassured me that we didn't need an early start if we were camping out, and that the views were even more beautiful in the summer's afternoon sun. So we had another lovely soak in the springs and then a leisurely lunch before finally heading out.

"Summer is best for Mount Fuji," James told me as we began our climb. "But we need to come back to Japan in the spring for the cherry blossoms."

We hiked side by side up the pronounced stone trail. I carried only the tiniest hydration pack. James wouldn't hear of me carrying anything else, but he and Clark had weighed themselves down heavily with camping supplies.

"Is there anything in the world that you haven't seen?" I asked him. "I'd love to go someplace that's actually new to you."

He stopped to give me one of his most intense, heart-stopping looks. "Everything feels new, now that I have you. The world's gone into color now, and I want to see it all again with you."

We made good time up the mountain, since we were all in good shape, and the ones' weighed down with heavy packs were in great shape. We stopped often to enjoy the views, but we made up for that by setting a brisk pace otherwise.

James handed me a lychee rice energy drink in a silver bag. It was a strange little on-the-run meal that we'd picked up a few times. It hardly fit in with his usual dieting standards, being mostly sugar and simple carbs, but he'd been pretty lax about that on vacation.

I drank the strange drink, which was basically a packet of calories on the go, and enjoyed the view.

I felt such a sense of wonder about where I was as I watched the great shadow of the mountain move across the land. The world felt so big here, and I so small, and I felt that was a good thing. So often in my life the world had felt too small, as though no matter where I went, all of my problems could still follow and devour me. I felt the opposite of that here—my problems becoming too small to even worry me.

I caught James watching me, a bemused look on his face.

I smiled at him. "I love it here," I told him.

One corner of his pretty mouth hitched up wryly. "I hope so. It seems we're spending the night. I must say I was surprised to find you were the camping type."

I shrugged. "I'm not, really. I've only been a few times with friends, but it was easy enough, and the thought of doing it here was just too tempting."

"When was the last time you went camping, then?"

I had to think about it. "Last summer, up at Mount Charleston, with our crew."

A brow rose. "Anyone I know?"

I sighed. "Murphy and Damien, and some people you don't know."

His jaw clenched.

I gave him an exasperated look. "Really, James. You just need to get over being jealous of him."

"I assume you didn't share a sleeping bag?"

I rolled my eyes, the beginnings of anger stirring. "No. I shared a small tent with Stephan."

He nodded. "I'm not jealous of him anymore. Or at least, I'm taking care of it."

I studied him, baffled. "What on earth does that mean?"

He grinned, the tightness in his expression just disappearing. "I've decided to set him up. If he's blissfully in love, perhaps he won't think about you so much."

That surprised a laugh out of me. "Are you really matchmaking again? You take the word controlling to a whole new level. Your control freak tendencies and that Cavendish charm are a dangerous combination to our friends' love lives."

He just shrugged. "I know he's your friend, and I actually

even like the guy, but just knowing the thoughts he must be having about you, considering the way that he feels, was driving me mad. To cope, I had to come up with a strategy on how to deal with him. Seeing him with Jessa was like a light switching on. He's into her, more than I think he realizes, but he was just so hung up on you for so long that he was blind to it. Don't get me wrong, I sympathize with that. Being unreasonably obsessed with you has become one of my favorite hobbies, but I'll be damned if anyone else gets the honor."

I thought about Damien and Jessa. "It's a match that makes sense to me."

"An old friend of mine is in need of a new flight crew for his private jet. I've recommended Murphy and Damien as his pilots, and Jessa as his flight attendant. It will put the two of them in close proximity often. All we can do is hope that will be enough."

"That's so sweet of you. I was just worrying about how Damien and Murphy might not get to work together anymore, and how sad that would be."

He winked at me. It made my stomach do little flips. "I know you were. I have my eye out for jobs for your friends, since so many will be unemployed within the year."

God, I love him, I thought, for the millionth time. "Thank you for that," I told him.

He stroked my cheek. "I love your soft heart. I'll make it my life's mission to accommodate it."

We continued to briskly climb the trail. Even stopping frequently to enjoy the incredible views, we made the climb in just over four hours.

We had a spectacular view of the sunset as we reached the crater at the top of the mountain.

"We couldn't have timed it more perfectly," I said, in awe of the view. It was unquestionably the most beautiful sunset I'd ever seen.

"Yes, I know," he said succinctly.

I shot him a look. "You did time it?"

"Yes. I wanted today to be special. I wanted it to be perfect."

I still studied the view as he spoke, but I felt him studying me. I shot him another quick glance. "What's so special about today?" I asked, a serious note in his tone alerting me to his mood.

My heart stopped and then did one slow turn in my chest as he got down on one knee in front of me.

"I wanted you to have a perfect view of the world that I want to lay at your feet, my love," he began. His eyes were clear and impossibly beautiful with what could only be a plea.

My eyes filled with tears as I saw what he was doing, and how painstaking of an effort he'd made for it to be perfect.

He pulled a small ring box out of his pocket and I gasped on a sob. He opened it, showing me a ring with a large, princess cut diamond, surrounded by sapphires. I realized immediately that it must have been his mother's engagement ring. It matched the earrings that he'd already given me.

"I'll love you 'til I die, Bianca. Marry me." There was no question in his voice. It was all in his eyes, a vulnerability that was as hard for me to resist as his sure domination.

I had been both dreading and anticipating this moment. He had given me clear warning, because he understood me so well. Marriage represented so many scary things for me, it always had, and it was hard to change the way I thought about it. It was hard, but not impossible, not since James had entered my life, turned everything upside down, and changed my mind about so many things.

I was shocked at how quickly I held my trembling left hand out to him. "Yes," I whispered. I spoke again, making my voice more firm, more sure. "Yes, James, I'll marry you."

I traced a tear down his cheek with my other hand while he slid the ring onto my finger. It was a perfect fit.

He stood and pulled me against his chest in one fluid movement, kissing me with rough tenderness. I kissed him back with a hunger that would never be slaked. There was no doubt in my mind that I would love him until my own death. *How not?*

We made love in the dirt, next to the great mountain's crater, and with the glorious sunset still bathing us in its light.

I gave no thought to being seen as he tore at my clothes. The temperature had cooled as we climbed higher, and we had briskly layered up as we went. He got me out of those layers even faster. He tore off my pants, just opening my top. He did even less for himself, just pulling his stiff length out of his pants and impaling me with one rough stroke. He moved inside of me, a world of raw need in his eyes, need and gratitude. He must have been uncertain of my answer, and still he'd asked.

He moved inside of me with harsh precision, hitting every sensitive spot perfectly and repeatedly, and with merciless force. He had me on the brink before he spoke. "Say it, Bianca."

"I'm yours, James."

"Forever," he added.

"Forever. Oh yes, I'm yours forever, James."

He came inside of me, arching high. His little movements inside of me as he finished, and a clever thumb on my clit, had me following soon enough.

We got dressed, smiling at each other like fools.

We found Clark and Blake pitching our tents a little ways down the trail, setting up the tents next to one of the small structures that dotted the surface of the top of the mountain.

Clark smiled the biggest smile I'd ever seen on him when he saw how we were smiling. "Congratulations," he told us with a nod.

"Thank you."

"Thanks."

"Oh," I said suddenly, only loud enough for James to hear. "I need to tell Stephan immediately. He'd be crushed if he wasn't one of the first to know."

"We'll let him know as soon as possible," he responded just as quietly, tugging my hand to lead me over to catch the last glorious minutes of the sunset.

"He'll be so happy," I told James quietly, feeling a little sad. I didn't want to see less of Stephan, but our lives were changing so quickly and in such strange ways that I couldn't help but be afraid that things wouldn't stay the same for us. He had been the most important thing in my life for so long...

"Bianca, my love, let me make you a promise," James said quietly, studying my face carefully. "No matter where we live, no matter what we do, we'll keep him close to us."

"You don't think that he and I are hopelessly co-dependent?" I asked him. I knew the answer. We were, but no part of me was prepared to change that.

He just smiled fondly. "I know that you are, but I think that, just sometimes, like in a marriage, or with just the right people, that can be okay. You two aren't toxic together. It's not that kind of co-dependence. You two survive together; you *thrive* together. I wouldn't dream of making you change that. I'm trying to join your family, not tear it apart, Love."

I didn't think he'd ever said anything that made me realize more profoundly just how much I loved him. Fear of what had happened to my mother hadn't been the only thing that had scared me about commitment. Losing Stephan in even small amounts had been a fear there, as well. I was so grateful and relieved that I could just put that fear away forever.

CHAPTER THIRTY-FIVE

Mr. Besotted

We went to a gala for charity the night news broke of our engagement, which was perhaps a mistake. The red carpet was pure chaos.

By sheer coincidence, the men's health magazine had released their cover and spread of James that same day. It had all turned out beautifully, but they had used several of the pictures with the both of us. The cover picture they'd used had actually been from one of the shots where James had his back to the camera, and I was clearly giggling into his shoulder. My laughing eyes were visible over his shoulder, his face was bent down to nuzzle into my ear, catching the edge of his besotted smile.

Needless to say, the release of the romantic pictures, combined with the first appearance of his bat-shit crazy tattoos, and the announcement of our engagement, had gotten the attention of the media, and we were bombarded the second we stepped out of the car. We couldn't even hear what the paparazzi were asking us, they were shouting so loudly over each other. Two overzealous male photographers even exchanged blows.

As soon as fists started swinging, our security ushered us

straight into the party.

Jackie had picked out a long gown for me that I had to lift high in order to move swiftly as we were ushered inside. It had a fitted champagne silk bodice that hung artfully off my shoulders, but just below my breasts it bled into a long, flowing crimson skirt. She'd paired it with shiny red patent leather shoes and I thought it might be my favorite dress to date. I felt feminine and sexy, and pretty enough to have the most gorgeous man in the world on my arm.

James wore a classic black tux, with a champagne colored shirt and a crisp black bow tie. He had a crimson handkerchief folded into his breast pocket. I wasn't sure if Jackie or James had set us up to match for the evening. It was anyone's guess at this point.

Inside was a bit of a crush, so much so that I hoped right away that we wouldn't be staying long. Especially since the first person we sighted was an irate Scott. We saw him coming from across the antechamber into the gala, and I noted again that he looked uncannily familiar.

"Why does he look so familiar to me?" I asked James, who was studying the other man with sharp intensity.

James laughed. "He's a very famous tennis player. I just assumed that you knew who he was. He's highly recognizable. I'll never stop loving the fact that you're completely unimpressed with celebrities."

I shrugged, thinking that it wasn't so much about not being impressed as it was about not keeping up with current affairs.

"I hope you're happy, James. Jolene and I have split up because of your *porno*," Scott began loudly the second he was within earshot. It was a bad start to the conversation, and I couldn't miss the fact that the entire room got quiet as they tried to overhear the two famous men having it out.

James stepped a little in front of me in an instinctive protective gesture. I didn't imagine that I was in any danger from anything but words, though, with our security out in force for the event.

"That doesn't make me happy, Scott, though I do think you can do better than a woman who's only interested in your money, and likely isn't even capable of fidelity. There's no reason why that video should have ended your relationship. That was taken at least three years ago, before you were even seeing each other."

Scott chewed on his lip, studying James intently. "You knew about that thing for three years, and never bothered to tell me?"

"No. I didn't know about it until a few weeks ago. That was taped without my knowledge. I never would have consented to it. No one in my position ever would."

"Well, it doesn't matter. I couldn't stay married to a woman that the world has seen having sex with you. A woman who released a sex tape of herself with another man while married to me."

"If it's any help, I don't believe that she had anything to do with the tape being released. She had nothing to gain from it, and everything to lose. All that video did was burn all of her bridges. Jolene is much too pragmatic to do something so emotional, and with nothing to gain."

Scott eyed him with suspicion. "Who else could it have been?"

"I don't know yet, but I am determined to find out. Would you like me to let you know when I have answers? Would that help?"

Scott nodded. "It's tearing me up, and I know you don't understand it, but I'm finding it impossible to just let her go. Knowing that she isn't still so hung up on you that she would do something like that just for spite *would* help. I think that the idea that she would release it, not caring if it ended us, is what bothers me the most."

"There's no accounting for taste, but I can well understand

being obsessed with a woman and not being able to let it go, Scott. I wish you the best. Perhaps she's changed."

"I know she's no angel, but I *like* what she is. If I could only get her to care for me, as I do for her, I think that we could have a good marriage."

I couldn't see his face, but I clearly saw James shrug from behind.

"I'm not sure it works that way, but I do know that people are capable of changing, and I hope for your sake that she'll change for you. I wish you nothing but the best, Scott. I always have."

Scott hesitated for another moment, looking unsure, before finally nodding. "I think I know that. I guess I have all along. It was just easier to blame you, yanno? Let me know if you find out anything." He was walking away before he'd even finished talking, his words trailing to us as he moved away.

It seemed to me that Scott could have apologized, being that he'd admitted that he'd been wrong about James, but I didn't say anything. Friendships could be complicated things, and I wouldn't dream of stepping in when I didn't understand theirs.

I did think that Scott and Jolene might just deserve each other, but I kept that thought to myself, as well.

I was happy when the next familiar faces we saw were friendly ones. Both Sophia and Parker embraced me warmly, gushing about the engagement. I flushed in pleasure, and if I was honest, a touch of trepidation. Some part of me screamed that this was all too much too fast every time I was reminded of what I'd agreed to.

"Have you hired a wedding planner? Do you know the venue?" Sophia asked, beaming at me.

I thought she was adorable, with her blonde curls and her enthusiasm, but her question intimidated the hell out of me.

"No," I said finally. "I haven't even thought about it."

Sophia seemed to sense my discomfiture. She touched my shoulder lightly. "There's no rush. And you can have any size wedding you want. Just be sure to invite *us*."

I nodded, my mind going a little blank at the thought of planning a wedding. "Of course. Small or large, you'll certainly be on the guest list. I can't say the same thing for your sister-in-law."

She laughed. "I would hope not. She'd try to burn the place down, the crazy twit."

That made me laugh. Crazy twit seemed like a perfect way to describe Jules, and I was sure that Sophia must have been even more fed up with her than I was, since she'd married into her family.

We mingled for a time, but I cut loose from James when I saw a restroom. Blake followed me in, even hovering outside the stall, but I was growing accustomed to it. Her relentless stoicism was even starting to grow on me.

I didn't take long in the restroom, but I heard some sort of commotion outside of my stall right before I re-emerged.

Blake was standing so close to another woman that I didn't even recognize her at first. I noticed that the bathroom attendant was absent before I caught enough of a glimpse of the woman to make out who it was.

"Jules," I said coldly when I saw her. "Blake, you can let her loose. I'm prepared this time, and she didn't bring her partner in crime."

Jules was decked out in a black, one-shoulder sheath. She looked polished and beautiful, but looks meant nothing if your insides were spoiled rotten.

Jules was smiling, a sharp malice in her eyes, when I saw her fully. Knowing her, that meant trouble. "I just wanted a word, Bianca. It's really kind of pathetic that you're so scared of me that you need a bodyguard now."

Blake had stepped out of the way, but she was braced to pounce on the other woman.

I smiled at Jules. It was an unpleasant smile. It felt

unpleasant. But I was done putting up with her crazy little scenes.

"Congratulations on the engagement. You must realize that it'll never last with James. He'll tire of you before the ink is dry, but good luck with that."

"That's what you wanted to say? What a waste of both of our time."

"No. That was a side note, actually," Jules replied, looking noticeably more agitated at my response. "What I came here to say to you is that I was the one that released that sex tape. I stole it from Jolene years ago, afraid she would do something crazy with it. She told me about it one night when she was hopped up on opiates, and so I knew she had a loose tongue. At the time, I wanted to save his reputation, as I couldn't let my future husband be seen in such a light. I just wanted you to know that it was me that put that out there. If he's going to go out of his way to be seen slumming it with you, then his reputation is already shit, so I wanted to *make it* shit."

I was so disgusted with her that I felt my mouth moving into a sneer. I hadn't even known I had it in me. "You're pathetic, you know that? He was never even your boyfriend, let alone your future husband." I held up my left hand, showing her my engagement ring. "James isn't subtle. He would have made himself plain either way, if he had any intention of marrying you. What did you even have to gain with any of this?"

She shrugged. "I wasted a lot of my prime years—"

"On a *delusion*," I interrupted her, unable to stop myself.

She looked ready to spit. "Revenge. I did it for revenge. It was that simple. And it felt good."

She was so smug when she said it, as though she'd accomplished something great, that I just snapped. "Well, it didn't work. He's still standing. Now get a fucking life." I was moving to her as I spoke. She and Jolene had caught me off guard when they'd cornered me before, and gotten the better of me in a physical altercation, but I'd been through hell and back, and I had no doubt in my mind that I could take the spoiled bitch.

I grabbed her by the hair before she saw my intent, and she barely even struggled as I dragged her across the room and into a stall. I dunked her head into the toilet while she pulled at my wrist, being very careful not to get my own hand wet. I held her there for one, two, three, four, five seconds before pulling her up and yanking her back out of the stall. I pushed her away from me, still only touching her hair.

She turned to me, looking shocked and scared and furious. "What the fuck is wrong with you?"

I smiled at her, showing a lot of teeth. "Revenge. I did it for revenge. It was that simple, and it felt good," I said, quoting her own ridiculous words back to her.

"I'll have you arrested! I'll-I'll sue you!" she sputtered.

I laughed. The bitch was an amateur. "You got rid of your only witness so that you could have it out with me. There's not a mark on you, and do you really think that my bodyguard is going to act as an eyewitness against me? I'd suggest you leave as quickly and quietly as you can, so that I'm not tempted to do it again. This was a waste of your time and mine. So go, and get yourself a fucking life."

She gave me one more hate-filled glare before she ran out of there like the place was on fire.

I glanced at Blake. She was smirking. It made me laugh again. "You think she'll leave me alone now?" I asked her, wanting her professional opinion.

She nodded. "Walking through that ball looking like that is probably the most humiliating thing that princess has ever had to go through, so I'm going to say yeah, she's most likely out of your hair now."

I nodded. "Good deal. That was the point. Enjoying myself was just a bonus."

Blake stifled a laugh.

I was still washing my hands, wanting to get all of the Jules off, when Lana and a frantic James burst through the door. I just raised a brow at them.

"Are you okay? What happened?" James asked, so obviously worried.

"We saw Jules tearing through the hallway, her hair wet, and her makeup a mess," Lana added, studying me carefully.

I shrugged. "She stole that video from Jolene, and put it on the internet. She came here to tell me that. I didn't take it well."

James shot Blake a questioning glance, approaching me. "What happened?"

"I dunked her face in the toilet. She left. I don't think she'll bother me again."

He reached me, running a hand over my hair with a soft touch. His brow furrowed for a moment as he processed that. He blinked a few times, then threw his head back and laughed.

CHAPTER THIRTY-SIX

Mr. Wretched

James hadn't wanted me to, but just a few days after I'd returned to Vegas, I went back to my old house to collect some things. Most of it would be packed away and moved to the bigger house, but I'd wanted to go through things myself before I let strangers tackle the project.

I shared a car with Stephan and Javier, who were giving Stephan's house similar treatment. Having Stephan nearby for the excursion had gone a long way towards easing Control Freak Cavendish's mind about the whole thing. Not that he could have stopped me, though he didn't have to leave work to escort me once he realized that Stephan was going. I didn't know what he thought that Stephan could do that my escort of armed guards couldn't, but that was just the way it was. The two men had bonded on a fundamental level that even I didn't fully understand. I could only be grateful for it.

I had tags to mark where I wanted my things to be moved to, since much of the household goods would be going into storage, and some to charity. James obviously had all of his properties stocked to the nines.

I only had a few small boxes for packing right away, and they filled slowly with small keepsakes and photographs.

Blake hovered in the house near me, Paterson patrolling directly outside, with Henry patrolling the neighborhood. Williams had a family emergency in California, and so was taking some personal leave. They hadn't been able to find him a replacement with just one day's notice, which was one of the reasons James had been so nervous about letting me come back to the house without him, even in the middle of the day.

Their boss's nervous reaction to this mundane outing seemed to have Blake on edge. I got nervous just looking at her. She kept pacing the house, looking out windows for no reason that I could see.

"Is everything okay?" I finally asked her.

She nodded, but her mouth was tight. "Yeah, just antsy today, I guess. I don't see Paterson out there, but that's normal. It's not even time for him to check in yet. I don't know what my problem is."

This was the chattiest I'd ever seen her, and it only seemed to make me *more* nervous, because it was a tell of her own nerves. Whatever strange mood had such an unflappable woman so anxious wasn't good for my peace of mind.

I went back to packing up some old pictures, smiling when I saw some old shots of Stephan and me. There were several shots from my twenty-first birthday party, when we'd run around like fools on the strip. Someone had taken about a dozen shots of Stephan giving me a piggy-back ride through the fountains at Caesar's Palace. We'd been dressed up, and we looked like crazy people, with the bottom of his pants wet, and my heels dragging in the water. I smiled at the picture. It was a fond memory, right around the time when things had really started to look up for us. The smile on Stephan's face warmed my heart, both now and then. He was grinning at the camera, and I was smiling at him, the fact that he was the dearest thing in the world to me clear in every line of my face.

I took the stack of photos to my purse, thinking to myself that

I had to give some of the photos to Stephan, and find a place of honor in my new house to put at least one of them.

I was just digging into my purse, still smiling at the memories, when my phone started to ring. I checked the screen.

It was James.

"Hey," I said into the phone, still smiling. "How's work going?"

"It could be going better, but at least it's almost done. My lawyers and Tristan's agent are making some revisions, but that shouldn't take more than thirty minutes or so, and then we'll be done, thank God. Tristan is trying to bankrupt the casino for some two-bit magic tricks." James had gone into work to hash out some details in Tristan's new contract, and I could tell by his tone that the other man must be close by and that he was trying to harass him.

"Tell Tristan I said hi," I told him.

"Bianca says hello," he relayed on the other end.

"I'll be heading over there when I finish," James explained to me. "Are you about done?"

I glanced around the room. I was pretty sure that I'd gotten everything that I'd wanted to pack myself, but I wanted to give the place another once-over, to be sure. "Yeah. That should be perfect."

"Tristan is coming over for dinner tonight. As if I'm not paying him enough to make rabbits disappear, now I have to make him dinner."

"I have a new trick where I can make pretty boy CEOs disappear," Tristan said loudly on the other end.

I laughed.

"Will you let the guys know that they're invited, as well?" James said.

I could hear the smile in his voice.

"That sounds fun," I said, meaning it. There was just something so playful and mischievous about Tristan. There was never a dull moment when that man was around. "I take it he got a favorable contract for next year's shows," I added.

"He signed on for another year, but we had to double the bastard's pay," he said without rancor.

He said something else but a noise outside distracted me at just that moment. *What had it been?* It hadn't been particularly loud, just something slamming against the concrete, but it sidetracked me enough that I completely tuned James out as he continued to talk on the other end of the line for several pregnant moments.

"Bianca?" he asked, snapping me out of my momentary distraction.

"Hmm? Oh, sorry," I said, trying to focus.

It could have been anything. A neighbor had been working on building something on his back patio earlier, and that had been much louder than that single slam had been. *What about that noise was troubling me so much?*

I kept my phone to my ear as I moved through the house, looking for Blake. The noise was probably nothing, but I figured that we would both feel better if she checked it out.

I heard it again as I moved into the kitchen. This time it was louder, and I could have sworn that it was accompanied by a low grunt of pain.

"Blake," I called out, sure now that something was wrong.

She burst into the kitchen right as James began to sound a little frantic on the other end of the phone.

"Bianca, what is it?" he was saying. "Is something wrong? Talk to me, Love."

I opened my mouth to answer, my eyes meeting Blake's, when I heard a noise that made my blood run cold and my heart stop in my chest. It was a loud echoing boom that I knew all too well, and it made me freeze in terror. A gasp escaped my throat, my free hand flying to my chest.

Blake was moving instantly, pushing me to the ground, her gun already in her hand. "Stay down, Bianca," she said. "Don't move, and whatever you do, don't leave this house. I'll be right back."

She disappeared towards the front of the house, though I thought that sound had come from the back.

I was listening so hard for what was going on in the back that it took me awhile to remember that James was still on the phone, which was surprising, since he'd been keeping up a steady, desperate dialogue the entire time.

"Tell me what's going on, Bianca? What was that noise? Why did Blake tell you to stay down? Where did she go? I need to know what's going on!"

I blinked, my mind going very shocky in reaction to that noise and the memories it dredged up. How did he not know what that noise had been? Could it sound so very different across the line?

That dreaded noise sounded again, and my body jerked as though I'd been hit, even though I was safe inside.

"We're on our way to you, Love, and we've put in a call to the police, but I need you to tell me what's going on. What was that noise?"

I swallowed hard, trying to focus on that beloved voice. I closed my eyes tight. "I love you, James," I told him softly.

I heard him take an unsteady breath. "What's happening over there?" he asked roughly. His voice broke on the words.

I shook my head, but of course he couldn't see it.

That noise sounded again, and I whimpered.

"I love you, James," I said again, my cheek on the cool linoleum of my kitchen floor. I was so happy, so unutterably relieved that he wasn't close enough to be hurt by whatever was happening in my backyard.

"Talk to me. I have to know what's going on. We're in the car now. We'll be there in less than twenty minutes, but you need to *talk to me*. What's all that noise?"

I didn't want to say it. It was completely ludicrous, but saying it would make it more real. The noise sounded again and I shuddered helplessly on the floor.

"Are those gunshots?" James asked in the most wretched voice. I could tell just by his tone that he was already certain of the answer, had likely guessed it with the first shot.

"Yes," I breathed. "In my backyard, I think. I'm scared, James. I need you to tell me that you love me back. Please. Just in case."

"No," he whispered. "I'll be right there. Are all of your doors locked up? Just stay hidden, and stay down. You're going to be fine, and I will be there so soon..."

I closed my eyes, just wanting to listen to his voice until the danger had passed. As though it would just magically pass after that many gunshots...

I was doing so well, just planning to stay right where I was, when I heard another sound that changed everything.

A rough shout sounded in the back. It was the shortest noise, and it should have been indistinguishable from all of the other sounds, but somehow I knew with absolute certainty just who it had been. I fought to breathe, because I suddenly felt like I was drowning. That shout had changed everything. I went in an instant from being a scared little cowering mouse to being so desperately terrified for someone other than myself that I began to stand on trembling limbs.

Another gunshot sounded, and then another. A rough shout that tore my heart into jagged little pieces was stopped short somewhere amidst those two loud bangs.

I began to move resolutely through the house. I didn't forget that I still held the phone. I'd gone from being in shock and into a desperate kind of clarity.

"I love you, James," I told him again. "So much. I'm so sorry." I hung up the phone, feeling it drop from my hand before I'd reached my back door. I took one deep breath before unlocking the door and sliding it open. Resolutely, I stepped outside.

CHAPTER THIRTY-SEVEN

Mr. Tragic

STEPHAN - MINUTES EARLIER

I was getting a lot done in a short amount of time when it came to packing up my house, right until the time that I ran into a box of photos. Javier and I studied the first stack of pictures and laughed. It was a large stack of snapshots from a company Christmas party from maybe three years ago. They'd been taken on a super cheap camera, so they were grainy with a lot of red eye, but they brought back good memories, and we sat down on my bed and went through them all carefully.

Javier giggled, flipping a picture to me. I laughed so hard that I had to sit down. Murphy had his shirt off in the photo, and was trying to do splits, with absolutely no success. That was funny, but the highlight in the photo was by far the look on Damien's face in the background. It was a mixture of admiration/horror/confusion. I must have been taking the picture, because Bianca was off to the side, doubled over laughing, and I wasn't next to her.

Javier flicked me another picturing, still smiling widely.

This one was a close-up of a still laughing Bianca. Her eyes were twinkling as she looked directly into the camera. It was a great picture of her, though she wouldn't notice or care how beautiful she'd looked in a bright green dress that night, her pale hair hanging smooth around her shoulders. I made a note to get a copy of it for James, who would love a picture of her laughing like that as much as I did. I sometimes thought that our fast friendship had been kind of like joining a club, one made up of men that thought that Bianca Karlsson was the most perfect woman on the planet.

Javier flipped me another picture, giggling harder than ever. I joined him with one glance at the image.

This one was of Murphy lying on his back on the ground. He held his arms up straight in front of him. His suit jacket and tie were crumpled all over the floor around him. I remembered that they'd gotten that way during his impromptu strip tease.

Marnie stood next to him in the photo, caught mid-curtsy motion. Javier flicked me another picture.

Murphy was making a valiant effort at bench-pressing the tiny woman.

Javier flicked me another picture.

The same tiny woman had collapsed onto him, and they were both laughing at his failure. We laughed even harder at the memory.

"I'm going to miss that job," I said wistfully.

"Well, we don't have to miss the people, which were what made it great. What do you want to bet that Damien and Murphy will be regulars at our bar?"

I smiled at him. "You're so right. We'll probably have to kick them out at closing time every night." The thought filled me with warmth. Our lives were changing, yes, but they were only getting better.

Javier was playing more than helping me pack, and I couldn't have cared less. I didn't mind doing it myself, and would have preferred his company, help or no.

I reached up to pull a box down from the top of my closet and felt his arms wrap around me from behind. He nuzzled into the middle of my back, purposely tickling me with his nose, and I turned into him with a laugh, pushing him until the back of his knees touched the bed. He fell back with a laugh, and I followed him down.

He tried to get up, but he'd started it, and I intended to finish it. I tickled him mercilessly, wrestling with him on the bed, pictures and clothes falling off with our exuberance.

"Uncle," he cried, still giggling. "Uncle!"

I let up, kissing him. He practically melted underneath me. I loved it. I could feel how I affected him, and I treasured that. I pulled back, stroking his cheek as I gazed into his eyes.

He opened his mouth to say something, but a loud bang made his breath catch.

I tensed for one long moment, still staring at him, before I sprang into action.

I stood up, pointing at him. "Stay here, and stay down, ok?"

He swallowed. "Was that a gunshot?" he asked in a very small noise.

"I'm not sure what that was," I lied. "But I just need to go check on Bianca."

I was already striding to the bedroom door before he spoke again.

"Don't go, Stephan. Please. I love you. Don't put yourself in danger."

I looked at him, my heart in my eyes. "I love you, too. Stay down. I have to make sure she's safe, Javier. I couldn't bear it if she were hurt."

I tried to appear calm as I closed the bedroom behind me, but I was tearing through the house like a madman the second it closed. A second and third gunshot had sounded by the time I reached my back door. My heart was trying to pound right out of my chest with the fear. I couldn't lose her. I was a survivor by nature, but I knew that I wouldn't survive *that*.

I unlocked, opened, and tore through that door in an instant, fueled by blind terror. If that monster had hurt her, if he had so much as bruised her, I swore that I would tear him apart with my bare hands.

A fourth shot sounded just before I vaulted over the tall barrier desperately, scraping my hands with the effort. I landed on the other side, taking in the bloody scene before me with shock and horror.

Bianca's father straightened over the fallen form of Blake. His chest was bloody, bloody circles blooming on his chest, but he was still standing. He held a small pistol in his beefy hand. It was so small against those huge hands that it almost looked like a toy.

Another body lay in the yard. Patterson, I thought, but I couldn't even spare him a glance as Sven Sr. pointed the gun at Blake, aiming to take another shot.

"No," I shouted, rushing at him.

He turned impossibly fast for such a big man. He smiled at me through bloody teeth as he aimed into my chest and fired.

My last thought was one of relief. Bianca wasn't amidst the casualties.

BIANCA

I stepped outside, into a bloody nightmare, my eyes going unerringly to the crumpled figure of Stephan. I didn't make a sound, but my face was wet with tears.

He has to be okay, I told myself. I could survive a lot of things, but I knew that losing Stephan wasn't one of them.

I was so intent on this thought that I didn't even look at the monster amidst the carnage for long moments. I had made my way closer to Stephan before I raised my eyes to those pale blue ones that looked so much like my own.

It was like staring into the eyes of a rabid animal, his

malevolence written in every tense line of his face. It was hard to imagine that he had ever been a sane person, looking at him now. But *had* he ever been sane? I couldn't have said. Perhaps sanity had never been the question. He wasn't even a human to me, but a monstrous demon that destroyed and terrified. And the only one who had ever been able to act as protection between him and me now lay crumpled at my feet, red circles on his chest. He had finally done it. The monster had broken me.

My instinct was to freeze, and so I watched without moving as he approached, some awful expression that was shaped like a smile overtaking his face.

I didn't have that violent thing inside of me like my father did. I didn't have an urge to hurt anyone, not for any reason. It wasn't even an urge that I understood. Or at least I hadn't—not until Stephan lay crumpled at my feet.

My eyes moved from that horrible face and to the tiny pistol at my father's side. I watched it like a lifeline, letting him see what I was looking at—what I'd fixated on.

He laughed, a dry cackle, and the madness of the laugh made me note, in an absentminded kind of way, that he was on something. Some kind of drug was racing through him, making him crazier, making him stronger, anesthetized to both pain and fear. The man had been a beast *without* some drug jacking up his system, so it was hardly a reassuring realization.

"*I warned you, sotnos.* I warned you that if you went to the police, no one could keep you safe from me, but you didn't believe me. And now your friend is dead. Was it worth it?"

I whimpered, a wholly involuntary sound. *He can't be dead*, I told myself. I had to believe it, or I would just crumple into a heap on the ground myself, and never get back up.

My eyes were still glued to that little pistol in his hand.

He laughed again, waving it at me. "You can't take your eyes off this. You think this will help you? You don't have the nerve, just like your mother. You couldn't hurt a fly. Worthless, mewling women."

He held it right in front of my face, smiling grimly, his bloodshot, crazy eyes glued to mine, their maniacal gleam piercing me. "Take it, if you dare. See what happens, sotnos."

I never looked away from his eyes. I couldn't remember a time when I hadn't hated him, but I felt it now like a fresh wound. I could kill him without remorse, I realized. He had done that to me, finally broken that part of me. I would not regret if he were dead, even if it was at my hand. I would be putting down a wild beast on a killing rampage. The only regret could be what he'd managed to do before he was stopped.

I wasn't my mother, though I could wish that I had only taken after her. As much as I wanted to run from the notion, I had enough of my father in me at least for *this*. It wasn't even a question, not even a split second of indecision, not with Stephan lying motionless at my feet. I had erred grievously, I saw clearly, in keeping his secret, in living in fear. Far better if he had killed me back then for turning him in than to let him wreak all of this destruction now. That was my regret, and I felt it keenly as I looked at him, surrounded by his victims.

If only I had looked beyond my own fear of what he had done, and thought about all that he was still capable of doing.

Yes, holding my silence for all those years was my regret, but it was my *only* regret. This thing I was about to do I would *not* regret, not for a moment.

I had no words for him. Nothing would do my hatred justice, and he wouldn't hear them besides. He had never valued me, and you didn't hear someone you didn't value. My words couldn't touch him. So I didn't bother to tell him how I felt. I *showed* him.

He handed that gun to me with no hesitation, no fear, and I took it, turning it into him with the same motion. I shoved it hard into his chest, aiming for his heart. I squeezed the trigger, barely even feeling the gun's recoil in my hand as it fired into him.

Foolishly, I thought that would be the end of it.

The monster laughed, wrenching the gun out of my hand. I'd shot him in his chest, a chest already red with his own blood, and he only laughed. I got this sudden crazy notion that he really wasn't human. *How was he still standing?*

He opened his mouth, and blood sprayed my face as he spoke. "My turn, sotnos."

He gripped my hair, pulling my head back, holding it immobile. I began to struggle, but it was no good.

He put the gun inside of my mouth with no effort at all, pushing my own hand over the handle, that maniac's smile still fixed on his face.

I jerked my face from side to side, caught between his hand in my hair and the gun in my mouth. I was still shaking my head desperately when two simultaneous gunshots sounded. The world went black.

STEPHAN

My chest was on fire. Every breath was agony but I managed to open my eyes just a crack when I heard her voice. Of course she had come for me.

No, no, no, I thought in despair, as I saw her father approach her.

It took me an excruciatingly long time to turn my head to the side. Blake lay unmoving, less than four feet away.

I felt a huge wave of relief as I realized that there was a gun near her side. I knew I couldn't make a sound as I dragged myself to it. It was a race, and I couldn't let the pain so much as slow me.

Another shot fired before I'd made it halfway, and I had to keep from crying out in distress, or from looking to see what had happened. There was no time to look. I needed to get that gun and fire.

I grabbed the gun with a trembling hand as soon as I got within reach. I rolled onto my back, the agony of the movement making my vision go fuzzy for precious moments.

I sighted on her father's head and fired.

No, I thought in agony when I saw that I was just a split second too late. Watching her fall at the same time as her father was a sight I'd never forget. *No. Please, no.*

I blacked out.

CHAPTER THIRTY-EIGHT

James

JAMES - MINUTES EARLIER

Normally I thoroughly enjoyed a good negotiation. Even knowing the likely results, I'd been known to draw them out. Not today, though. I felt a strange tension eating away at me. I enjoyed giving Tristan shit, as I always did, but it was a little lackluster today.

"These had better be some extra fancy card tricks," I told him as the lawyers were making yet another revision to the contract. It was pure cussed orneriness that drove me to say it to him. The man was a genius at his craft. In just a few short years, he had made his name in the world of big time Vegas magic shows. He had brought a stunning and gritty new flare to an industry that had desperately needed a makeover, and that was just with his sleight of hand alone. The best part was, I knew that he hadn't even begun to show us all of his tricks. He was constantly coming up with something new to show us. And as expected, the man knew just how much he was worth, and we would be paying him accordingly.

Tristan grinned, flashing white teeth at me. He checked his watch with a raised brow, very obviously flashing my own Rolex at me. I looked down at my bare wrist and cursed. He was an entire table's length away from me.

"How did you do that from over there?" I asked him.

He pointed at the lawyers that were currently haggling with his agent. "I believe it's your contract that stipulates that I'm not allowed to talk about things like that. Trade secrets and all. Your lawyers would probably have to make a revision if I told you. Do you really have that kind of time?" He tapped my watch for emphasis.

I laughed. It was hard not to. He was an obnoxious son of a bitch, but an endlessly entertaining one. "We'll have to revise it anyway, if you're planning to give yourself a fifty thousand dollar watch as a bonus."

He reached his hand across the table, the watch appearing in his palm in a blur. I reached to take it from him, and he had it on my wrist with the same blurring speed. I shook my head at him. Crafty bastard.

"Congratulations on the engagement. The news is everywhere. How did you get her to agree? I would have sworn Bianca had more sense."

I glared at him, but it was half-hearted at best. Just the mention of my upcoming nuptials only made me want to grin like a fool. "I begged her so pathetically that she finally just took pity on me," I told him.

"That was nice of her. She could do way better. No offense."

I just laughed, because he said no offense while so blatantly trying to offend. "None taken. Eventually she just found that she'd rather be able to keep track of the man who was stalking her so relentlessly. I promised her that she could put a bell on me."

Tristan shook his head. "Poor girl. She never had a chance. You probably courted her with your hostile takeover approach."

I rolled my eyes. "I don't even do hostile takeovers. Stick to magic tricks, Tristan. Your knowledge of the business world is embarrassing." I had found him to be uncannily proficient on the business end of his work, but this was just how we were. It was nice to be able to take shots at someone who was as insensitive as I was when it came to being insulted.

Tristan grinned. "Sure thing, Boss. Are you inviting me to dinner? If I'm gonna sign this paper for you, I expect you to at least cook me dinner. And I want to see your fiancée again."

"Why the hell not? Sure, come to dinner, if you can restrain yourself from stealing the silverware." I pulled out my phone. "Let me call Bianca. We'll invite the guys."

Bianca answered promptly. "Hey," she said, a smile in her voice. "How's work going?" That smile in her voice made me smile, and that voice made me hard between one breath and the next. Just one word from her, uttered in that steady timbre of hers, affected me more than any other woman had in my life. Images of all of the ways that I'd had her, all of the ways that I planned to fuck her mindless, flashed through my mind, distracting me like nothing else could. God, I wanted her. Just the thought of her was more erotic to me than actual sex had ever been with other women. I'd felt it from the start with her, and I was only falling deeper with time.

"It could be going better, but at least it's almost done," I told her, having to concentrate to do so. I made myself stop thinking about being inside of her for one innocent phone conversation, but it was a struggle. My cock twitched restlessly, and I was thankful that it was hidden under the conference table just then. "My lawyers and Tristan's agent are making some revisions, but that shouldn't take more than thirty minutes or so, and then we'll be done, thank God. Tristan is trying to bankrupt the casino for some two-bit magic tricks." I looked at Tristan, smiling as I said it.

He flipped me off.

"Tell Tristan I said hi," she said.

"Bianca says hello," I told Tristan, not liking his name on her lips, but tamping my outrageous jealousy down. That jealousy would become a problem for us if I didn't control it. I understood that. My need for us to work helped me to try to keep it to myself when I knew that it was unreasonable.

"I'll be heading over there when I finish," I told her. "Are you about done?" It didn't really matter to me if she was. I was impatient to see her, and I'd go and wait for her if necessary. I hoped that she wasn't getting tired of my company, because we'd only been apart for a few hours and already I was ravenous for the sight of her.

I was picturing how I would take her in that little house when she answered. "Yeah. That should be perfect."

I thought it would be perfect to fuck her one last time in that house, even if she was done packing. I would bury myself inside of her wherever I happened to find her. Maybe I would bend her over the kitchen counter, or take her on the dining room table. I shook myself. She'd put a spell on me, and I wouldn't be free of it any time soon. *Or ever,* I thought with a grin. Mrs. Cavendish had such a lovely ring to it.

"Tristan is coming over for dinner tonight. As if I'm not paying him enough to make rabbits disappear, now I have to make him dinner."

"I have a new trick where I can make pretty boy CEOs disappear," Tristan told me.

Bianca laughed into my ear. I loved that laugh.

"Will you let the guys know that they're invited, as well?" I asked, smiling.

"That sounds fun," she said. "I take it he got a favorable contract for next year's shows."

"He signed on for another year," I said, looking at Tristan with a raised brow, "but we had to double the bastard's pay. Funny how soon he forgets just who discovered his sorry ass."

Bianca had gone very quiet on the other end. My whole body tensed, as if bracing for a blow and not knowing where that blow could come from. I absently scratched at the scars on my wrists, my most nervous tell. I thought I had trained myself out of the habit. *What was wrong with me today?*

"Bianca?" I questioned. I would be fine if I just heard her voice again.

"Hmm? Oh, sorry," she said, the new distance in her voice just making me more agitated.

"Love, is something the matter?" I asked.

I stood and began to pace, unable to stand still. "You sound upset."

She didn't respond for endless moments. I was getting desperate when her voice sounded again.

"Blake!" she said, a clear thread of panic in her voice.

No, I thought, my heart trying to pound out of my chest.

I swung around, my gaze finding Clark. He was so good at reading me that he already had his phone out.

"Police?" he asked.

I nodded. It could be nothing, but I didn't give a fuck. If it was something, the sooner they were on their way, the better.

"Bianca, what is it?" I tried. "Is something wrong? Talk to me, Love."

An echoing bang on the other end of the line made my blood run cold. Bianca gasped into my ear.

No, I thought, and began to move.

"Stay down, Bianca," I heard Blake say on the other end. "Don't move, and whatever you do, don't leave this house. I'll be right back."

No. A mean fist gripped my heart.

I could hear her breathing, but as I spoke and cajoled and pleaded with her to tell me what was going on, she refrained from speaking for long moments on the other end. I recalled that terrible afternoon just months ago, watching the ambulance take her away, my heart in pieces as I waited in agony to see if she was okay.

Clark fell into step behind me without a word as I strode through the offices and to the elevator. I saw what floor it was on and took the stairs, not willing to wait, the phone still held to my ear. I took the stairs down at a sprint.

"Tell me what's going on, Bianca!" I tried again, tearing through the casino now. "What was that noise? Why did Blake tell you to stay down? Where did she go? I need to know what's going on!"

Another loud shot sounded on her end of the line, and I died a little inside just hearing it.

I tried my damnedest to sound calm, but it was a struggle. "We're on our way to you, Love, and we've put in a call to the police, but I need you to tell me what's going on. What was that noise?" I was grasping at straws, I knew, hoping I had somehow heard an engine backfiring in the distance. Twice...

"I love you, James," she said very softly.

It broke me, a feeling of helplessness and dread filling me.

"What's happening over there?" I asked roughly. I barely noticed that my voice broke on the words.

Another gunshot sounded on her end, and she whimpered. It wrecked me. I wanted to clutch my chest and howl with the fear, but instead I ran, determined to get to her.

"I love you, James," she said again. The resignation in her voice wasn't reassuring in the least.

Clark kept pace with me, and broke ahead as we reached the doors, talking frantically to the valet manager, procuring us a car with remarkable speed. He got behind the wheel as I took the passenger's seat. He was peeling out before I could finish buckling in.

"Talk to me," I told her desperately. "I have to know what's going on. We're in the car now. We'll be there in less than twenty minutes, but you need to *talk* to me. What's all that noise?"

Another shot sounded and I closed my eyes in dread. "Are

those gunshots?" I asked wretchedly. I had never felt so helpless and worthless in my life.

"Yes," she breathed. "In my backyard, I think. I'm scared, James. I need you to tell me that you love me back. Please. Just in case."

The starkest terror that I'd ever known gripped my chest. I wasn't a superstitious man, but I felt suddenly as though if I told her that now, it would be the last time, and I just couldn't do it. It was illogical, but I couldn't make myself say the words again until I held her in my arms.

"No," I whispered, that brutal refusal making my chest ache. "I'll be right there. Are all of your doors locked up? Just stay hidden, and stay down. You're going to be fine, and I will be there so soon to tell you those words."

She gasped suddenly, her breathing changing, as though she was moving. Panic had me firmly in its grasp and I had to just listen futilely as two more shots sounded in the background. Two ragged sobs escaped her throat as though torn from her.

No, no, no, I thought.

"I love you, James," she told me, her voice so steady now. Somehow, that terrified me more than anything else had. "So much. I'm so sorry."

I was yelling at her in a broken shout as she hung up on me.

CHAPTER THIRTY-NINE

Mr. Desolate

JAMES

I could have wished that the twenty minute drive was just a blur for me, but of course it wasn't. It was the longest drive of my life. I died a million little deaths on that drive, my mind going to the darkest places.

I even found myself cursing God, when I'd always been the most agnostic soul. *Why did he hate me so much?* I wondered angrily. First he took my parents, who I'd adored, and now I'd found a home and a family again, one that I coveted and worshipped with a single-minded purpose. I couldn't bear the thought that I would lose her just when I'd found her. I rejected the thought. This couldn't be happening. If her father had attacked her, surely the security had subdued him before he could have touched her. There was no acceptable alternative.

I watched the clock on the dash for the entire drive. Clark ran red lights, weaved through traffic, and drove like his life depended on it. He made good time, and we were pulling into her neighborhood less than fifteen minutes after we'd gotten into the car.

I was jumping out of the car before it had stopped, rushing to the front door. It was locked, and I cursed as I dug out my keys.

Absently I noted that Clark took another route, jumping the fence into the backyard while I entered the house. It was where she'd been when I'd been talking to her, so I looked inside first.

The first few rooms were empty, and I heard sirens drawing close as I scanned the kitchen.

Clark was standing in front of the back door that led into the yard from the bedroom when I stepped inside. My gut clenched, nearly doubling me over. The back door had been open...

I rushed forward, but Clark moved to stop me. He caught me before I reached the door.

I fought him in earnest. There were no seconds to waste.

"Please, James," he said in a soft voice I barely recognized as coming out of him. "You don't want to see what's back there. No one should have to see that. The paramedics are here. Let's let them in to do their jobs."

I heard a horrible whimper of a noise as though from a distance, barely noting that it had escaped from my own throat.

He would only say a thing like that if there was nothing to be done, and clearly Bianca was not in the house.

"Is she back there?" I asked him, my voice breaking on the words. It felt like every part of me was breaking.

He nodded, and a tear ran down his cheek. "You can't do anything for her, James, but you can save yourself the pain of seeing her like that."

Of course, I couldn't stay away. I refused to accept what his words implied, even as I felt my own face growing wet with tears.

"Let me by," I told him, a quaver in my voice. "I have to be with her."

He bowed his head and let me pass, seeing my resolve.

The sight that greeted me literally brought me to my knees.

There hadn't been a second since I'd met her that I felt as though I'd taken her for granted. I'd loved her, I'd treasured her,

I'd coveted her, and adored every inch of her, but it still didn't feel like it had been enough. I'd misstepped with her, I'd screwed up plenty, but we'd been working through it all. Life could have been perfect. All we'd needed was more time...

I crawled to her, only distantly noting that hers was not the only body lying in the small backyard.

She was on her back, her head turned sharply to the side, obscuring one side of her face. What was showing of her face was strangely intact, almost peaceful. Her hair was spread around her, the pale blonde strands now wet and dyed red with blood. I tried to tell myself that she might be fine, that she *could* survive this, but I could see clearly from where the blood pooled that it must be a head wound.

Raw sounds of anguish tore out of me with every movement as I made my way to her.

Lightly, carefully, as though she were made of glass, I held her hand and sobbed. I wouldn't survive this. I didn't *want* to survive this. There was nothing in the world that I wanted to live for after enduring this.

For the first time in my life, I began to pray. For her life or my death, I didn't know. I would have taken either just then.

I didn't even look up as the paramedics arrived in force. I only noticed the body that had been lying beside hers as it was shifted away. Apparently, the paramedics weren't going to try to help that one, since it was missing a head. Its massive torso was riddled with holes, and I perceived that it had been her father. His death gave me no satisfaction. It wasn't enough, and certainly, he hadn't died in time to spare her.

How had it come to this? I wondered wretchedly.

My vision was blurred and I just couldn't bring myself to focus on anything but that hand. It was limp in mine, but unscathed, and if I looked up, I knew there was a good chance I'd find answers that I wasn't willing to accept. Somehow, uncertainty was something to cling to when the worst-case scenario was so much more likely than the alternative.

A paramedic was crouched on the other side of her, but I couldn't look directly at him, couldn't let myself see what he found as he swiftly checked her vitals.

The paramedic called out loudly. I didn't catch what he said. My mind wasn't processing words just then. I was still focused with a single-minded purpose on that lovely hand. There was no telling how long I crouched there, motionless with dread, trying to prolong the moments, telling myself she would be fine, but filled with a stark desolation that made it hard to even breathe.

The paramedic said something else, and I didn't realize that he was speaking to me until someone nudged me rather impatiently from behind. I blinked at the man, not really seeing him as I tried to hear what he was saying.

"Please move, sir. We need to get her on a stretcher. You're in the way."

I moved automatically, so unused to being told what to do that I obeyed instinctively, knowing that no one would dare give me an order if it wasn't important.

I only shifted back the slightest amount, but a stretcher was being pushed persistently against me until I backed away far enough to give them room to work.

I pushed back with desperation when I realized that they were going to put her on the stretcher.

I won't let them take her away from me, I thought. *I'll die before I let them put her in a bag.*

Big arms circled me from behind, pulling me back. "Let them work, James," Tristan said gently into my ear. I hadn't even realized that he'd followed us here.

"Sir, every second you delay us could be crucial to her survival," the other paramedic said, clear impatience in his tone.

I let Tristan pull me back as I tried to process those words.

Survival, he'd said, as though she had a chance. They

weren't putting her in a bag; they were staunching the flow of blood from the side of her head and moving her.

He'd said survival, I thought again. They weren't taking her away because she was dead. *They thought they could help her.*

I hovered close, my thoughts becoming slowly more coherent as I began to realize that she wasn't dead, and *God willing*, she might survive. With desperation, I began to let myself hope, every inch of me trembling.

I gave them room to work, but I hovered as close as possible, desperate to see what they would do, fearing that if I so much as glanced away from her I might lose her.

I was moving around her, trying to get closer to her without getting in the way, and so I saw when the first paramedic shifted her head enough to apply pressure to her wound. I whimpered when I saw the bloody hole in the side of her face. It was up near the spot where her jaw met her ear, or at least I thought that it was. It was hard to tell with all of that blood.

I never took my eyes off her, and what they were doing to help her, but I began to hear the other sounds in the yard as still more paramedics arrived. I heard another man sobbing. It had been going on for a while, but I hadn't really noticed it—I was making so much noise myself.

Javier, I thought, dawning horror making me search him out. He hovered over the fallen form of Stephan. A paramedic was busy staunching the flow of blood from Stephan's chest, prepping him to get on a stretcher, another man helping him. *No*, I thought, *please no.* They both had to live.

I followed the stretcher closely as they moved her, and no one dared tell me not to. I watched her chest as she breathed faintly on the long drive to the hospital. *It's a miracle*, I thought. *He put that gun in her mouth and pulled the trigger, and if she survives it, I have witnessed a miracle.* I made crazy promises to God on that long drive, promises to give him my soul in exchange for that miracle.

I wasn't myself as I followed her unconscious form inside the hospital. I felt disconnected from reality as they worked on her. I began to fight when they wouldn't let me follow her into surgery. Clark and Tristan had to snap me out of it. It wasn't until the world came back into focus that I realized that I had been in shock.

"James, you need to be *present* for this," Tristan was telling me, his voice firm, his eyes steady. "Your influence can help them. I guarantee it. You can't follow her into surgery, but you can call in some favors."

"Buy the fucking hospital if you want them to give Bianca, Stephan, and Blake their best chances," Clark added.

The nurse was putting a blanket over my shoulders, saying soothing things, and shooting Tristan and Clark perplexed looks. Tristan understood me well, though, and his tactic couldn't have been more brilliant. I didn't have time to wallow in this, and certainly none to agonize about it. What I needed was action. The more the better. There were things I could do to help.

"Get the board of directors and the head of the hospital on the phone," I told Clark. "If they ask what it concerns, tell them that someone is willing to donate an obscene amount of money for some special treatment."

He nodded, and moved away, a small, satisfied smile gracing his mouth. I remembered that he'd said Blake, as well. I was relieved that she at least had a chance. I also knew that the names he hadn't mentioned were surely dead. Paterson and Henry had fallen in their duty of protecting Bianca. I made a note to pay out the families of both men. It was the smallest consolation, but at least neither of them had left behind children, or wives.

My first call was to my offices in Vegas, and then New York—to my second-in-command. I enlisted all of the help at my disposal to get the ball rolling faster.

CHAPTER FORTY

Mr. Helpless

BIANCA

I woke with a violent jerk, my thoughts going immediately to Stephan. It was as though the sight of him lying there, lifeless, with bloody holes in his chest, had just been circling around in my head while I was out. I remembered everything as though it had happened just instants before, though I knew very well that I was in a hospital by the familiar sounds and smells.

I turned my head sharply, seeking out James. The short motion made my head ache and the side of my face burned sharply.

I felt my hand in his and knew that he'd stayed at my side for the ordeal. I saw in his weary, grief-stricken face how it had cost him, what he'd been put through.

"Stephan?" was the first word out of my mouth. It was agony to try to talk. I had to speak through my teeth, since I could barely open my mouth. I ignored the pain, focusing on James, desperate for an answer.

James raised his bloodshot, agonized eyes to mine. Those turquoise depths had never looked so relieved. He gasped in a breath, as though coming up for air. He blinked at me several times before he found his voice. "He's recovering from surgery."

I only heard his voice in one ear, and wondered vaguely if I'd lost the hearing in the other. But that didn't matter. Nothing mattered to me but finding out about Stephan just then.

"How badly was he hurt? Will he be okay? I need to see him now," I said, trying to sit up.

He paused for a long time to choose his words, and that scared me more than anything. "He's in the ICU. He was badly hurt. No one can see him—"

I pulled the IV from my arm, sitting up. The pain in my head and ear temporarily darkened my vision and a dull roar started up in the ear that was working. "I need to see him *now*."

I didn't realize what a commotion I'd caused until I'd been wrestled back into the bed, and saw the amount of people that had gathered to restrain me.

My eyes sought out James while a nurse shoved needles into my arm. I felt terrible as I saw the tears running down his cheeks and the helpless look on his face. "Please, James. I have to see him."

Finally he nodded. "Please don't do that again. I'll arrange for you to see him, but you must stay in your bed."

I nodded, closing my eyes in relief. He would do as he said. He always had.

I didn't sleep, but I didn't open my eyes again until I felt my bed begin to move. A team of nurses surrounded me, James at my right, clutching my hand as he followed beside the wheeled hospital bed. "Who else made it?" I asked James, bracing myself for the answer.

"Blake was wounded badly, but they're telling me now that she'll make it."

"So that means that..." I swallowed hard, finding it hard to finish the sentence.

"Paterson and Henry died before the paramedics could arrive.

Your…father did as well."

I processed that, blinking away tears. "You wouldn't believe how many holes he had in his chest, and still he kept coming…"

"It was a bullet to the brain that ended him," James told me. "Stephan came to just long enough to take him out. I owe him yet another debt that I can never repay."

My chest burned and I shut my eyes, letting awful tears run down my cheeks. Of course Stephan had survived long enough to save me. *My hero*. I couldn't lose him. My eyes shot back open as a thought occurred. "Did he see my father shoot me?"

"He must have. They deduced that your father must have gotten off the shot just before Stephan fired. They tell me your struggle is all that saved you. He shot into your cheek. There was damage, but he missed his target."

I tried to touch the bandaged side of my face. "How on earth?"

"You've lost significant hearing in that ear, and they had to do surgery on your jaw. There will be scarring along your jaw and cheek, but we will make sure it's minimized as much as possible. You will have the best plastic surgeons in the world at your disposal."

He continued to talk, but I barely even heard him, my mind still on Stephan. I couldn't care less about the scarring, my jaw, or even the loss of hearing. I was alive. The rest were details.

But Stephan… Stephan had to live. "How long was I out?"

"Four days."

"Tell me about Stephan's wounds."

"Both bullets missed his heart, if only barely, but one punctured a lung, and he's had some internal bleeding that has persisted. The doctor who performed the surgery believes that it was a success, but he says that Stephan won't be out of danger until his vitals stabilize. It's been very touch and go. They tell me he's improved, followed by a decline, but he's getting the best care available, and he's a healthy young man, so they say we can be hopeful, even though he's not yet stabilized."

"If I see him, if I speak to him, it will help," I said, more hopeful than certain. "If he knows I made it, he'll pull through. He would have been devastated if he watched my father shoot me. This will help."

My vision was completely blurred with tears as they rolled my bed beside Stephan's. They wheeled me as close as possible, my feet pointed in the direction of his headrest. They were considerate enough to bring our unencumbered hands close. Javier was on the other side of him, his head bent over his other IV covered hand.

I gripped his fingers in mine, squeezing. "I made it, Stephan. I'm fine. You saved me again, but you need to wake up now. You were hurt, but it's nothing that you can't survive. *Please,* wake up." I got louder as I spoke, my voice rough with emotion.

He didn't so much as twitch. I glanced at his heart rate monitor, but could make no sense of it. I glanced at the closest nurse. "Have his vitals improved?" I asked her.

She pursed her lips. "They haven't altered."

They let me linger for a few more minutes, and I murmured soothingly to Stephan. He never responded, never moved. I hadn't really thought he would, but I felt a crushing disappointment as they wheeled me away from him. Some part of me had been arrogantly hoping that the sound of my voice, and the knowledge that I had survived, would be enough to rouse him. He had been my last thought as I'd blacked out, and my first thought on waking. Knowing him as I did, I had just assumed that seeing me fall had been like that for him. *Perhaps it really was beyond his control.* That thought defeated me more than anything.

I drifted off as they carted me back to my own room, and I knew by the floaty feeling that it was a drug induced sleep.

When I woke again, James was watching for it. He was

speaking to me the instant my eyes blinked open groggily.

"He's improved. Less than two hours after you spoke to him, he opened his eyes for the first time, and they tell me his vitals have finally begun to improve. The doctor went so far as to say that there is a good chance that he will pull through."

"How long was I asleep for?"

"Only four hours. Stephan's first word was your name. He was just as frantic to see you, though he was in no condition to pull his own IV out."

There was a reprimand in his voice, and I could hardly blame him. I studied him, trying to see just how much he'd been damaged by it all, because I knew for a certainty that he had.

"You were right," I told him, "I shouldn't have gone back to the house." I'd been so sure he was just overreacting, but somehow his instincts had been dead on. I'd never dreamed that my father could still get to me with so many people protecting me, but he had managed to beat all reasonable odds. "Are you furious with me?"

His face went a little slack, as though the question had caught him completely off guard. "The thought never even occurred. There's no room left in me for fury. After thinking you were dead, then realizing that you would live, I'm only capable of relief. We may have to start going to church now."

"Church?" I asked, perplexed.

"Yes. I prayed for a miracle, and you survived."

I supposed that it was all rather miraculous, and I was more grateful for my life than I'd ever been after the ordeal, but I had more questions. "Was my father on something? He took so much damage, and still he kept coming." I spoke slowly and carefully. Speaking would be rough for a while, and I knew that my words were hard to understand.

James nodded. "Yes. He was on several somethings. Some mix of crystal meth and bath salts. Your father ambushed Henry, then beat him to death with a large rock a few blocks from your house. He took his gun, and walked to your house. He jumped the fence in back and landed on Paterson, who shot him. He shot him back, a point blank shot to the chest. They said it killed Paterson almost instantly, partially because of the type of bullets in the gun, and the range of the shot."

"Blake confronted him, and shot him again in the chest. They deduced that this made him drop his gun. He then picked up Paterson's gun. This was a smaller gun, with lighter ammo, and what he shot all three of you with, which is most likely why you survived. Henry's gun is the one that Stephan found and used to shoot your father in the head. Let's just say that gun had more effect on a giant, drug-crazed man, especially since Stephan had such unerring aim. The bodyguards were trained to shoot for the heart, but Stephan went for a headshot."

I nodded, thankful that he'd given me a full explanation, but devastated by all of the senseless loss. "Those poor men."

James nodded gravely. "Yes, I know. So much went wrong. It's hard to imagine that one man wreaked so much havoc when he was outnumbered like that, but they say the mix of drugs gave him a superhuman burst of strength. None of us considered that possibility, much to my everlasting regret."

I squeezed his hand, which enveloped mine warmly. I searched his beautiful eyes, knowing that he felt a crushing guilt like I did. "I'm so sorry, James. If I'd had any ide—"

"Don't," he interrupted. He gentled his voice, and his eyes. "Please don't. We can't take anything back, just as we couldn't have seen the future. All we can do is be thankful that it wasn't worse. When I first set foot into that backyard, I was convinced that my worst nightmare had come to fruition. I'll never stop being grateful that you survived that. We are unspeakably lucky that there weren't more lives lost. All three of you were critical just days ago, and are now on the road to recovery."

It was several days before Stephan was moved from the ICU, and we were both awake to see each other. We had a teary-eyed reunion, clutching hands and sobbing like babies.

"I was so afraid that you wouldn't recover," I gasped.

He gave a strangled half-laugh, half-sob. "*You* were afraid? I watched him shoot you in the head. I don't think I'll ever fully recover from the sight."

I winced at the visual. "But you saved me."

"Always, Buttercup," he said, squeezing my hand hard. "Always."

He continued, quickly switching to a lighter topic. "Would it be tacky for me to get engaged just over a week after you did?"

I looked around for Javier, taken aback at the question. We were completely alone, even James giving us a moment of privacy.

"You're engaged?" I questioned.

He shook his head, wearing his most boyish grin. "No, but I want to propose. I wanted to get your blessing first."

I gave him an exasperated look, then laughed. "Yes. If you want to be silly and ask for my blessing, then you have it. Always. Nothing would make me happier."

"It's going to be smooth sailing from here on out, Bee. We've earned it."

I returned his carefree smile, hoping that he might be right.

CHAPTER FORTY-ONE

Epilogue

NEARLY ONE YEAR LATER

I took deep breaths. I counted. I made my whole body relax. I was nervous—very nervous, and skittish, but much less so, than I'd thought I would be for this day.

"Deep breaths, Buttercup," Stephan said gently. I couldn't look at him today. He, more than anyone, made me emotional today. There was just so much joy in his eyes, so much barely suppressed excitement. It made me want to bawl like a baby and I had just sat through a painstakingly elaborate makeup process. Not to mention that my goal for the day was *not* to lose it in front of four hundred wedding guests.

"If you make her mess up her make-up right now, I will kick you," Lana told him, but her tone was pure affection. Stephan and Lana had taken to each other like, well-like Stephan and I. She threatened to steal him from me nearly every time the three of us got together.

Lana looked stunning, of course, in a lavender dress that made those astonishing purple eyes stand out even more. She'd picked the color. As was her custom, she'd taken over that entire part of the process. I hadn't balked. On the contrary,

I'd only been relieved. This sort of event was well out of my area of expertise. I had never been the girl who dreamed of this, let alone ever thought of planning one of the things. I had gratefully taken all of the help I could get.

"Bianca, you should know that I've been put on guard duty by your determined bridegroom. He said that if you tried to run, I would get to tackle you."

That made me laugh, and relieved some of the tension, as it was meant to.

"I don't know if anyone's told you this," she continued. "But I have quite the reputation as a kick-ass fighter in Maui, so I wouldn't test me if I were you."

Not only had someone told me that story, *everyone* had. Lana's Tutu, and her auntie, and even Akira loved to tell that story in great detail, and often. One girl fight and they thought she was the lightweight champ…

Lana wasn't finished, but she'd moved on from Stephan and me. She had an elegant finger pointed at the two mischievous pixies who wore gowns that matched her own. "And *you*. The Debauched Duo. You had better stay away from my brother at the reception. I saw the way you were eyeing him. Don't even think about it. I have plans for him that involves him finally settling down, and the two of you wouldn't know settled if it invited you to a threesome!"

They just giggled, completely unfazed.

"We already bagged that one," Marnie gasped.

"Double teamed him after the rehearsal dinner!" Judith said.

"He was awesome," Marnie added.

Lana rubbed her temples. "Oh, God! I don't know who's more hopeless. Him or you two?"

"Them," Jessa added from where she was getting her hair finished up. "I've known them for years. Definitely them."

"They told me a story about seducing a priest one time," Danika told Lana, giving her a sympathetic look. "Your brother is easy, but these two are *nymphos*. So if we're talking hopeless, I vote them."

"I swear I saw them eyeing up the minister that's performing the nuptials," Sophia added helpfully, adjusting the sleeve of her own lavender gown.

"I'm almost positive they were trying to hit on my dad last night, before they disappeared with Lana's brother," Jackie added from where she was working on my hem. I glanced down at her as she continued. "My poor father's been a widower for five years, and he's approaching sixty. They could have given him a heart attack."

Marnie and Judith just giggled, enjoying the banter.

It all helped. I needed distraction. It wasn't that I had doubts about James. I was sure of him, sure that I needed him, and that he was good for me. It was just the actual marriage part that got me scared. And the over the top wedding, which had started out so small, wasn't helping. It had just sort of built into this thing that I couldn't control anymore, though I wasn't sure I ever could have. *We should have eloped...*

I never thought I'd be that person with more bridesmaids than I could keep track of, but there it was. I had opened my heart to more than Stephan, and it had opened like a dam breaking. There were so many people that I valued in my life now. My heart was no longer a block of ice with one thawed part just for Stephan. It was warm in my chest now. I was alive as I never could have been if I hadn't met James. He had been right from the start. We were made for each other, and he had made me a better woman, a more complete one, when I'd let him into my heart.

I had calmed considerably by the time Javier peeked his head into the room.

We had decided on an outdoor wedding in the late spring, because we both loved the idea of a wedding amidst blooming flowers. James had chosen Wyoming, insisting that there was no other place we could have our vows, since this was where he swore I'd fallen in love with him. He claimed that I'd fallen for his mind-boggling equestrian skills first... I hadn't been able to change his mind on that idea—I'd even admitted to him just how quickly I really had fallen for him, but he heard none of it. I didn't really mind. I couldn't think of a place I'd have preferred for such a beautiful day.

The ranch had been transformed for the big event, a huge clearing at the front of the house painstakingly perfected for the ceremony. It was a vision of tall grass and wildflowers, well-groomed where the guests were seated, with flowers planted all along the perimeter, but the rest left running wild with riotous white and violet wildflowers.

Large tents had been set up on the side of the property for the reception that would follow.

One of the living areas near the front of the house had been turned into my bridal party's prep station. The groomsmen waited just outside, in the light-filled foyer, for the bridesmaids.

"Showtime," Javier told us, grinning.

Stephan and Javier had been more impulsive than we had, and had already gotten married over Christmas. They'd had a gorgeous commitment ceremony in Bali, with a reception afterwards that had turned into a four-day long party with all of their closest friends. The entire trip had been magical, and I'd never seen two happier newlyweds. Even several months later, they were both still glowing with it.

Stephan was happier than I'd ever seen him. Two months ago, he'd even been contacted by one of his sisters. She had just turned eighteen, and moved away for college. She'd found him on Facebook, sending him an earnest message about wanting to meet him. She had apologized for the way he'd been treated by their family, though of course she'd been too young at the time to have anything to do with the way things had happened. Stephan had told me that they were getting to know each other slowly, but that they were chatting nearly every day now.

Javier blew us a kiss before letting the door swing back closed on him. He'd ended up as part of the groom's party. Dividing our friends had turned into quite the debate. We'd had a row over who would get Stephan. The very idea had made me furious.

In the end, we'd decided on gender-bending wedding parties, with Frankie as James's best woman, and Stephan as my best man. It only made sense. James had argued that he should get Lana, and I'd made a case for myself getting Javier, but in the end we'd let *them* choose, so Javier was a groomsmen, and Lana was mine. I knew it was a sign of how blessed we were, that our friends were so intertwined that they belonged to us both.

One of the biggest wedding party upheavals was kneeling at my feet, fretting about some minor detail on the hem of my gown. Jackie had taken some getting used to, but I'd more than gotten used to her. Our friendship had grown over countless thoughtful little notes that she'd left in my closet. Lana had been so right about her—that she needed to be challenged. Something in her nature held a constant need for it, and I didn't mind obliging. First, I'd insisted on only wearing up and coming designers' clothes for months, which had made her want to pull her hair out, but I saw that she grew to love the idea, the discovery of new designers presenting that challenge that she craved.

She'd learned to respect me, and as that respect had budded, so had our friendship. And when we'd begun to hunt for my wedding gown, it had grown into a bonafide bond. I'd realized that I had room in my heart for another sister.

Jackie and I hadn't taken to each other right away, but you wouldn't know it now. As she'd obsessed over finding the perfect dress, I'd begun to tell her little details that I might like for a gown, and she had added her own persistent suggestions. When she'd begun to make elaborate sketches for the elusive dress, I'd been impressed with her vision, and made the offhanded suggestion that she should design it herself. She'd taken that suggestion to heart, and designed the perfect gown for me. I knew by her talent, and the way the task seemed to fulfill her, that it wouldn't be her last.

The women began to file from the room, giving me encouraging looks before they left. The looks made me feel a bit like a crazy woman, since they told me clearly that everyone was still a little afraid that I would turn into a runaway bride.

Stephan and I peeked our heads around the corner to catch a glimpse of the altar.

James already stood there, looking too perfect to be real in a sharply tailored tuxedo. He wore the classic black jacket and trouser, with an off-white silk shirt, vest, and tie. His hair was styled artfully out of his face. Frankie stood next to him, decked out in her own sexy version of a tux.

He saw us looking and grinned. He knew I'd be nervous for this, just as I knew that he wouldn't. We shared one of those complex looks that said we understood each other. His look took the form of an indulgent smile, and mine was a bit of a pained grimace. I ducked back into the room.

In addition to being my best man, Stephan was walking me down the aisle. That one hadn't even been a question. He wore a tux that was nearly identical to James's, but with a lavender silk tie. He kept an eye out for our cue to go, naming off the bridal party as they walked, and keeping me up to date on every detail, Stephan style.

"First is Elliot. He's got the ring on top of his head, and he's hopping."

I giggled.

"Now it's Parker and Sophia. They're right on his tail, in case he runs off. Oops, he made a dash... No, he's okay now. I think he was just faking them out."

We shared a grin. Elliot was too adorable.

"Next up are Lana and Akira. He looks mean as ever, and she is the picture of elegance. Seeing them side by side, they just make sense, but you'd have to see it to believe it, since they're so dissimilar."

I had to agree with that observation.

"Now it's Murphy and Judith. They actually look like they're trying to behave themselves. I was expecting a little dance down the aisle, YouTube style."

"Murphy asked me if he could dance, and I said I didn't mind, as long as no one expected me to," I said.

"Oh, well, there he goes. They're doing that shuffle dance. It definitely looks like they practiced." We shared a laughed.

"And now Javier and Marnie," Stephan continued. "He looks sexy as hell, and he just winked at me as he passed the door. Now it's Jessa and Damien. They have huge smiles on their faces."

He paused watching, his smile fading just a touch. "Next up are Tristan and Danika. It hurts my heart to see those two around each other."

I knew just what he meant. There was still such a feeling of unresolved issues when the two of them got together. Danika hadn't been thrilled with the pairing, but she'd been a good sport about it. Always, though, she treated Tristan with cool civility.

"Sven Jr. and Adele are up. They look very model-y."

"Is that a real word?" I asked playfully.

"Sure. Last up are Jackie and Camden," he continued. "He just gave her a roguish smile, and she took his arm without sparing him a glance. They make a strange pairing."

I had to agree. Lana's brother, Camden, was the opposite of Jackie in just about every way I could think of. He was tall and muscular, with wavy golden hair like his sister, and those same startling violet eyes. He dwarfed the tiny figure of Jackie, and was as playful as she was serious.

Stephan stepped back from the open doorway when the last couple had departed, moving quickly to adjust my skirt, smoothing out my short lace train.

The dress had turned out exquisitely. It was pale cream, with intricate gold-threaded lace, lush detailing along every inch. It was sleeveless, with a high-collared neckline of sheerest lace, so sheer that my locked-on choker was clearly visible underneath. Jackie'd had the enterprising idea of cutting a hole out for the hoop in the collar, and it had worked perfectly. My choker looked like part of the dress. Underneath I wore a plain white, strapless sheath that came to just above my knees. The lace gown overlaying that was longer, the hem touching the floor, the train trailing lightly behind me. I'd had to be talked into a train, and we'd finally compromised on one that no one would have to carry for me.

He handed me my large bouquet. It was a lovely mix of violet lilies, purple roses, and tidy little white calla lilies. The same flowers had been interwoven into a wreath on my head, showcasing my long hair, which had been painstakingly curled into ringlets that hung down my back.

He touched my cheek lightly, a world of joy in his twinkling blue eyes, before offering me his arm. We began our slow-paced walk down the flower-lined aisle, the sun at our backs, our movements synched from years of perfect accord.

James was a jealous man, the most possessive man I'd ever met. I doubted that there was a thing about me that he didn't consider *his*. But he had never made me choose, never made me question or compromise one thing about my relationship with Stephan. He had only accepted, as much as that acceptance must have gone against all of his natural inclinations. I thought that was perhaps the surest sign of his love for me—that he would so obviously put my needs before his own. His love was such a beautiful thing, always so perfectly suited to my own needs, and so unselfish in its way.

He'd made me a believer. We'd been together for nearly a year now, and I was well and truly convinced that we really were made for each other. Life wasn't perfect, but it was pretty close.

I had thought that looking at Stephan would make me lose it today, but as we drew closer, I realized that the look in Mr. Beautiful's eyes would be my real undoing. He didn't bother to hide from our guests those tender eyes that he had just for me. No one there could doubt that he was crazy about me. I didn't know how I'd ever doubted it myself. Though I *had* seen the world with different eyes back then. *How could I have known that I was being swept into my very own fairytale?* I'd never believed in such things.

Stephan handed me to James when we got into reach. James gave me his softest smile, one hand rising to brush the one lone tear that had managed to make its way silently down my cheek.

Abruptly, he pulled me close and kissed me. It lasted long enough, and held enough passion, to draw loud cheers and guffaws from the crowd, and one loudly cleared throat from the minister. I was breathless as he pulled back with a wicked smile.

"It was that or drag you into the nearest room. I couldn't have you wearing that kissable look for the entire ceremony and not address it," he murmured to me, shameless as ever.

I was still recovering as the minister began to speak. I let the official words wash over me, my eyes steady, if a little moist, on my love's.

"We are gathered here today to take part in the most time-honored celebration of the human family, uniting this man and woman in marriage," the minister began.

I listened to each word of the ceremony carefully, trying to take it all in, but my eyes didn't waver from his.

We recited our vows, and my voice was as steady as I could make it for my own part. We had opted for short, traditional ones, because I had a strong aversion to public speaking.

Tears ran silently down my cheeks for a lot of it, but James held it together for the most part. That is, right until the end, when the minister was reciting a small part that James had wanted to add.

The minister read, quoting the Benediction of the Apaches.

"Now you will feel no rain,
For each of you will be shelter to the other.
Now you will feel no cold,
For each of you will be warmth to the other.
Now there is no more loneliness for you."

His gaze never wavered from mine, even as they filled with tears, the tears swiftly overflowing, running down his cheeks before the minister had finished the line.

I reached up and softly wiped them away with my hands. It was only fair. He had been quietly drying my tears through the entire ceremony.

"For each of you will be companion to the other.
Now you are two bodies,
But there is only one life before you."

There were a few more lines in that lovely addition to the vows, but I barely heard them as I watched my bridegroom's trembling lips form the words, "I love you," in a hushed whisper.

Vaguely, I heard the famous line about kissing the bride, but I hadn't even registered the words before James was pulling me against him in a soft, sweet kiss. It was a kiss full of finesse, and held a promise of forever. My own lips answered that promise eagerly.

I gasped and let out an embarrassed little screech as he suddenly lifted me high in the air. He laughed, spinning me.

My hands gripped his shoulders as his eyes laughed into mine.

"We did it, Love," he told me softly, his voice filled with quiet wonder. "You're mine, forever, Mrs. Cavendish."

I shook my head at him as he lowered me slowly back to the ground. His joy was infectious, and I was quickly laughing with him. "You're insane. I've been yours all along, Mr. Cavendish."

5 YEARS LATER

I awoke to the strangest sensation in my lower regions, which had grown almost numb over the past few weeks.

I patted the hand that was wrapped around my middle. "James," I gasped.

I felt him tense against me, instantly awake. "Is it time, Bianca?"

I bit my lip, mortified. "I don't know. Either my water just broke or I wet myself."

The bastard laughed, and I elbowed him hard. He was up and at my side of the bed, grinning like a loon, between one second and the next. He studied my wet legs and I squeezed my eyes shut tight, as embarrassed as I'd ever been in my life.

"Did my water break?" I asked him.

He continued to study me, his brow furrowed. "I don't know how to tell. You can't tell?"

I shrugged, miserable. "It's all just numb at the moment." I swallowed, hating to ask. "Will you smell it?"

He wasn't offended. He never was. He was the most dutiful

of husbands for a first time pregnant mess of a woman.

I couldn't look at him as he tentatively checked.

"No scent. I think we're having our baby, Love."

We both knew what to do, and James sprang into action, but I couldn't seem to move at first, overwhelmed at the thought that the next time we came back here, we would be bringing a baby home with us.

I heard James talking on his phone in the closet. "Stephan. It's time. You have five minutes to meet us at the car, or else you'll have to meet us at the hospital." He paused. "Very sure. Her water broke. We all get to meet our baby today."

He was back at my side a few moments later, already dressed. I wasn't much help as he pulled off my nightgown, and slipped a comfortable frock over my head.

"Can you stand?" he asked gently.

I nodded, and stood slowly, feeling ungainly. James helped me, his strong arms keeping me steady until I could stand on my own.

He knelt at my feet, using a wet cloth to clean me, and changing my underwear without a word. He wrapped an arm around my waist, the other firmly holding my arm, as he led me down the stairs, and to the garage.

Clark and Blake were waiting for us beside a large black SUV. We had packed for the hospital months ago, courtesy of Control Freak Cavendish, so I was relieved not to have to worry about it just then.

James made sure I was comfortably ensconced and securely buckled in before he got in himself. My huge belly had made everything difficult lately, and I'd never appreciated his unending solicitude more than I had during the trials of pregnancy.

Clark backed the car out, getting just outside of the colossal garage before stopping, a huge grin on his face as he glanced back at us. "The guys made it," he told us.

I glanced behind the car, seeing our two favorite neighbors

booking it across the property, Stephan leaving Javier in the dust on his way to our car.

James and I shared a happy smile.

Seconds later Stephan was getting into the car, breathless and shooting me concerned looks. He climbed into the row of seats behind us, moving directly behind me so he could kiss the top of my head before he sat.

"How are you? How's our baby?" he asked me, looking at James.

James couldn't stop grinning. "Our baby is ready to meet us today."

I rubbed my belly, trying not to stress out about the ordeal to come. James saw my action, and bent down to kiss my belly, as he had countless times over the last eight and a half months. I stroked a hand over his silky hair.

Javier climbed into the car as James was still paying homage to my big belly. He smiled at the sight. "We won't be seeing that quite so often after today," he said.

I patted James on the head. "I'll miss it," I said softly.

He shifted so he could meet my eyes, his cheek still pressed softly to my belly. "We can do this as many times as you want, Mrs. Cavendish."

We were ten minutes from the hospital, and it was a talkative car ride, so the drive went by in a flash, as did my admission into the hospital, expedited by my ungodly rich husband. They had me in a bed in what I figured had to be a record.

Dr. Lisa practically met us there, looking as though she hadn't been dragged out of bed, though I knew that she had. She smiled at me reassuringly. "You're going to be a mother today," she told me, after a short examination.

It was a daunting thought.

Several harrowing hours later, more so for James than for me, I thought, and a little bundle of joy was placed in my arms.

I had been so sure that a child would open up old wounds—

just rip apart the things inside of me that had never quite healed. Even after I'd been sure that I did want children, and even during the pregnancy, when I'd felt those first profound stirrings of the perfect love of a mother, I'd felt that doubt. There was no way that I could have known that seeing our son's perfect face would have the opposite effect. It hadn't ripped me open. It didn't aggravate those wounds. Like my love for James, it only healed me. As James always said he had done with me, I fell in love with Duncan Stephan Cavendish at first sight.

BOOKS BY R.K. LILLEY
IN FLIGHT(UP IN THE AIR #1)
MILE HIGH(UP IN THE AIR #2)
GROUNDED(UP IN THE AIR #3)
AND COMING SOON... LANA

UNDER THE PSEUDONYM REBECCA K. LILLEY
BREATHING FIRE

5804787R00203

Made in the USA
San Bernardino, CA
22 November 2013